Liminal Space

Shadows & Light Book One

(Amaranthe ♦ 23)

G. S. Jennsen

Hypernova Publishing
2025

Hypernova Publishing
174 E Neider Ave #89
Coeur d'Alene, ID 83815
www.hypernovapublishing.com

Ordering Information:
Hypernova Publishing books may be purchased for educational, business or sales promotional use. For details, contact the "Special Markets Department" at the address above.

Liminal Space / G. S. Jennsen.—1st ed.

LCCN 2025918670
978-1-957352-33-6

Amaranthe Universe

Aurora Rhapsody

Aurora Rising
STARSHINE
VERTIGO
TRANSCENDENCE

Aurora Renegades
SIDESPACE
DISSONANCE
ABYSM

Aurora Resonant
RELATIVITY
RUBICON
REQUIEM

Asterion Noir

EXIN EX MACHINA
OF A DARKER VOID
THE STARS LIKE GODS

Riven Worlds

CONTINUUM *ALL OUR TOMORROWS*
INVERSION *CHAOTICA*
ECHO RIFT *DUALITY*

Cosmic Shores

MEDUSA FALLING
THE THIEF
THE UNIVERSE WITHIN

Shadows & Light

LIMINAL SPACE
THE THEORY OF EVERYTHING
NAKED SINGULARITY (2027)

SHORT STORIES

Restless I • Restless II • Apogee • Solatium • Venatoris • Re/Genesis
Meridian • Fractals • Chrysalis • Starlight Express • Extinguishing the Stars
Learn more at gsjennsen.com/books or visit gsj.space/wiki

DRAMATIS PERSONAE
MAIN CHARACTERS

Alexis 'Alex' Solovy Marano
Space scout and explorer. Prevo.
Spouse of Caleb Marano, daughter of Miriam and David Solovy.

Caleb Marano
Former Special Operations intelligence agent. Space scout and explorer.
Spouse of Alex Solovy, bonded to Akeso.

Nika Kirumase
External Relations Advisor, Asterion Dominion Advisor Committee.
Former NOIR leader.

Mnemosyne ("Mesme")
Katasketousya Idryma Member; former 1st Analystae of Aurora.

Miriam Solovy (Commandant)
Leader, Concord Armed Forces.

Marlee Marano
Concord Asst. Ambassador.

Dashiel Ridani
Dominion Industry Advisor.

Richard Navick
Concord Intelligence Director.

Malcolm Jenner (Admiral)
AEGIS Fleet Admiral.

Olivia Montegreu
Leader, Riamere Cartel.

Kennedy Rossi
CEO, Connova Interstellar.

Corradeo Praesidis
Leader, Anaden Advocacy.

Eren Savitas
Advocacy Chief of Intelligence
for Non-Anaden Affairs.

Nyx Praesidis
Advocacy Director of
Intelligence.

Mia Requelme Jenner
Owner, Confluence Expo.

Morgan Lekkas (Major)
Cmdr. AEGIS Fighter Craft.

Valkyrie
Prevo companion to Alex.

Other Major Characters

Akeso
Sentient planet.
Species: Ekos

Arien Colonnei
Khesa Prutet High Chair.
Species: Elakri

Arnal Nikto
Leader, Nikto cartel.
Species: Anaden

Casmir elasson-Machim
Leader, Anaden military.
Species: Anaden

David Solovy
Professor, Concord SWTC.
Species: Human

Deunan Colonnei
Former truva.
Species: Elakri

Devon Reynolds
Dir., Concord Special Projects.
Species: Human

Felzeor
CINT agent.
Species: Volucri

Galean Ozeal
Architect; former Tarazi rebel.
Species: Belascocian

Graham Delavasi
Former SF Intelligence Director.
Species: Human

Grant Mesahle
Owner, Mesahle Flight.
Species: Asterion

Lakhes
Praetor, Idryma.
Species: Katasketousya

Lance Palmer (Commander)
Dominion Military Advisor.
Species: Asterion

Laurent Kovalne
Physicist.
Species: Elakri

Maris Debray
Dominion Culture Advisor.
Species: Asterion

Miaon
Former anarch agent.
Species: Yinhe

Noah Terrage
COO, Connova Interstellar.
Species: Human

Perrin Benvenit
Dominion Administration Advisor.
Species: Asterion

Prah'ka Nanh'ain'mi
Leader, Galenai Ruling Council.
Species: Galenai

Resamane Ozeal
Desbida; former Tarazi rebel.
Species: Belascocian

Stanley
Morgan's Prevo counterpart.
Species: Artificial

Thomas
CAF Aurora Artificial.
Species: Artificial

CONCORD

MEMBER SPECIES

Human

Representative: Aristide Vranas

Anaden

Representative: Corradeo Praesidis

Novoloume

Representative: Dean Onai Veshnael

Naraida

Representative: Tasme Chareis

Khokteh

Representative: Pinchutsenahn Niikha Qhiyane Kteh

Barisan

Representative: Daayn Shahs-lan

Dankath

Representative: Bohlke'ban

Efkam

Representative: Ahhk~sae

ALLIED SPECIES

Asterion	Taenarin
Katasketousya	Volucri
Fylliot	Yinhe

PROTECTED SPECIES

Ekos	Icksel
Faneros	Ourankeli
Galenai	Pachrem
Godjan	Vrachnas

AMARANTHE
CONCORD EMPIRE

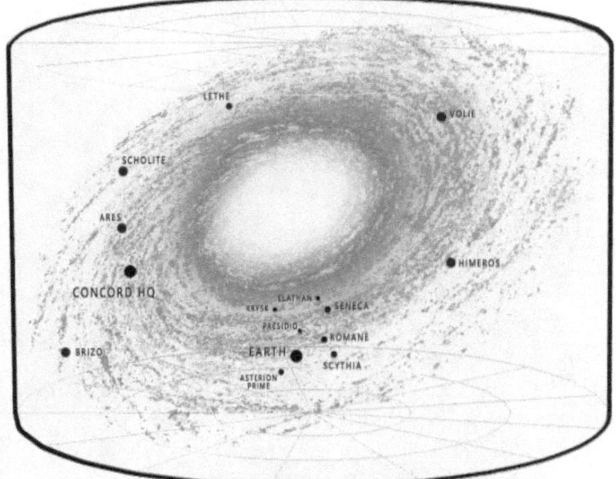

MILKY WAY GALAXY

LOCAL GALACTIC GROUP

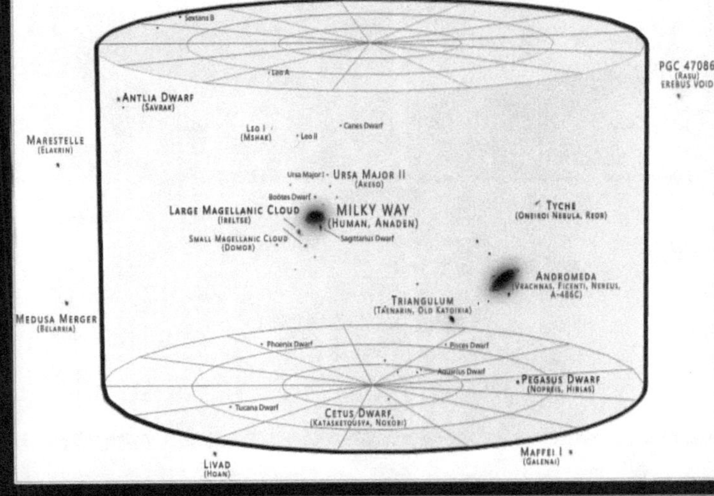

GENNISI GALAXY
(MESSIER 94)

✦ ASTERION DOMINION AXIS WORLDS
✦ ASTERION DOMINION ADJUNCT WORLDS
✳ ALIEN WORLDS

ASTERION DOMINION AXIS WORLDS

MIRAI NAMINO SYNRA EBISU KIYORA

THE STORY SO FAR

Read a summary of the events of Amaranthe #1-13 online at <u>gsjennsen.com/synopsis</u>.

RIVEN WORLDS

Fourteen years have passed since the events of *AURORA RESONANT*. Caleb has fully bonded with Akeso, the living planet that saved his life, and he and Alex have made their home there.

Continuum

Alex introduced Nika to Concord, the multi-species government formed after The Displacement to take the place of the deposed Anaden Directorate. Nika warned Concord of the Rasu and received a cautious promise of support. When Nika returned home to the Asterion Dominion, she discovered the other Advisors had created the Omoikane Initiative, a massive project designed to accelerate technology, warfare and logistical plans to combat the Rasu.

Concord was facing conflict on two additional fronts. Negotiations for the Savrakaths, a lizard-evolved Mosaic species, to become an ally of Concord broke down when CINT discovered they were developing antimatter weapons; Marlee also discovered they were enslaving another species, the Godjans.

The lack of a strong Anaden leader led several *elassons* to foment a rebellion against Concord. Eren's lover, Cosime, was killed when Torval elasson-Machim bombed the Savrakath's antimatter facility. Meanwhile, Malcolm was captured by the enemy during a mission to rescue Godjans on Savrak. When Concord approved an alliance with the Asterion Dominion, Ferdinand elasson-Kyvern began a coup to overthrow Concord.

The Rasu launched an attack on the Asterion world of Namino, and Concord sent a fleet to defend their new ally. They were unprepared, however, for how difficult the Rasu were to kill, and the battle turned against them. A leviathan shapeshifted to swallow Miriam's ship, and Rasu infiltrated the vessel. Miriam activated the ship's self-destruct mechanism to prevent the Rasu from acquiring Concord secrets, killing everyone on board.

Inversion

The Rasu reached the Namino surface and activated a quantum block, cutting the planet off from the Asterions' d-gate network. Marlee was injured by a Rasu and trapped on the planet; Grant was able to rescue her and retreat to an underground bunker. Caleb stole a ship and went to Namino to find Marlee. He joined the Asterions trapped there in attempting to disrupt the Rasu invasion, at great personal cost to him due to Akeso's aversion to violence.

Concord defeated Ferdinand's coup attempt, and Ferdinand fled to a safe house with a group of sympathetic *elassons*. Corradeo Praesidis and his granddaughter, Nyx, returned to Concord after a fourteen-year absence. Disturbed by the state of Anaden affairs, Corradeo decided to resume the mantle of leadership and wrest control away from Ferdinand and the rebelling *elassons*.

Miriam became one of the first humans to be returned to life via regenesis. She struggled with the transition, as well as with maintaining control of Concord after the coup attempt. Alex and Kennedy reverse-engineered the Machim double-shielding technology and deployed it on AEGIS ships to prevent the Rasu from boarding vessels in the future. Further, the Kats began delivering Rift Bubble devices that created an impermeable barrier around a planet.

The Savrakaths lied and told Concord that Malcolm was dead. Mia, seeking revenge, tricked the Anadens into attacking the Savrakaths; when her deceptions were discovered, she became a fugitive.

Alex and Nika, along with Morgan, traveled to Namino and located Caleb and the others. Together they infiltrated the Rasu stronghold and destroyed the quantum block. A Rift Bubble device was activated on Namino, and the Concord fleet defeated the Rasu occupying the planet.

Echo Rift

Malcolm escaped his Savrakath prison and returned home, surprising everyone. Mia, devasted by his apparent death, refused to reconcile with him so long as he declined regenesis. While in hiding on Pandora, Mia clashed with Enzio Vilane, a wealthy businessman and secret mob boss. When he tried and failed to kidnap her, she agreed to a plea deal with the authorities and returned to Romane—but not to Malcolm.

Corradeo disbanded the rebel *elasson* group and established a new, Concord-friendly Anaden government. He convinced a brokenhearted Eren to come work for him as an intelligence agent.

Alex and Caleb investigated rumors of an advanced civilization, the Ourankeli, annihilated by the Rasu. They found a lone survivor, who told them of the powerful weapon they created to kill the Rasu. The three of them traveled to the last settlement of Ourankeli, rescued them from a Rasu attack, and brought the refugees to Concord.

The Savrakaths sneaked an antimatter bomb onto Concord HQ. Richard and David were able to find and disarm it seconds before detonation. In response, the Kats exiled the Savrakaths, trapping their planet inside a modified Rift Bubble called an Echo Rift.

The Rasu reappeared to attack Toki'taku. The Taiyoks refused a Rift Bubble, but together with a Concord fleet, the Asterions were able to beat back Rasu forces. However, the Rasu captured an unprotected Concord vessel and, now armed with the locations of Concord worlds, launched an assault on the Khokteh planet of Ireltse.

All Our Tomorrows

The Concord fleet arrived at Ireltse to find it under massive Rasu assault. When the Rasu deployed a quantum block, Valkyrie temporarily sacrificed herself to protect Alex. After Alex and Caleb destroyed the quantum block, Concord forces defeated the attackers. Pinchu was gravely injured in the Rasu offensive, but Caleb healed him using Akeso's life energy. After Valkyrie rebooted herself, we learned she was in a relationship with Thomas, the *Aurora's* Artificial.

An anti-regenesis terrorist group called the Gardiens, led by Enzio Vilane, attempted to assassinate Miriam to discredit regenesis technology. Malcolm went undercover to infiltrate the group, while Richard uncovered evidence that Enzio was the son of Olivia Montegreu. Separately, it was revealed that Enzio had reconstituted Olivia from scattered records of her Artificial and neural imprints.

Morgan rejected Marlee's romantic advance, prompting Marlee to pursue dangerous cybernetic upgrades; Morgan decided to rejoin the military. Corradeo opened formal diplomatic relations between the Anaden Advocacy and the Asterion Dominion, and Nika gave her friend Maris the task of negotiating with Corradeo.

When the Rasu attacked the synthetic Ruda homeworld, the Ruda struck a deal with their fellow machines, agreeing to betray Concord in exchange for shapeshifting technology. They forced Miriam's fleet to withdraw by threatening to turn their planet into a massive EMP weapon.

Judging Nika's kyoseil manipulation abilities had reached a threshold, Mesme brought Nika to the Reor colony in the Oneiroi Nebula. Nika plunged into a pure energy pillar, absorbing its power, and emerged transformed.

Chaotica

Following Nika's transformative encounter with kyoseil in the Oneiroi Nebula, Alex challenged Mesme for an explanation. Mesme said everything it did was to save the people—Alex, Caleb, Nika, Dashiel, Miriam, Corradeo—who would save the universe, if it could be saved. Their argument ended with Alex still angry and distrustful of Mesme.

Nika discovered her new abilities allowed her to open wormholes, control kyoseil actions, and perceive all kyoseil interactions across space. She enabled other Asterions to access wormholes and began experiencing glimpses of their thoughts.

During a dinner party on Akeso, Nika forced Mesme to reveal that the planet was created using kyoseil, explaining Caleb's persistent connection to Akeso across quantum barriers. This revelation led Alex to deduce that *diati* seeded the Kats' Ekos-1 intelligence, while Dzhvar seeded Ekos-3. Mesme revealed kyoseil's ancient origins as the third primordial species alongside *diati* and Dzhvar.

The Rasu launched devastating attacks on multiple worlds, but Miriam successfully used the new Ymyrath Field device based on the Ourankeli weapon. Escalating their offensive, the Rasu began using antimatter weapons capable of destroying adiamene.

During a Rasu attack on Mirai, Nika deployed the Asterions' new miniature Rift devices called Kireme Boundaries. While managing multiple devices remotely, she became lost in the kyoseil consciousness until Dashiel rescued her. Recovery proved difficult as other Asterions' thoughts bombarded her mind, until Mesme taught her to block the mental intrusions.

As Rasu attacks intensified, Alex and Nika devised a desperate gambit. They injected captured Rasu with a virutox containing kyoseil information, then infiltrated Rasu systems to release these "saboteurs," spreading intelligence about kyoseil throughout Rasu networks. Nika reluctantly asked the kyoseil to activate its abilities for the Rasu, knowing the enemy desired kyoseil to control their distant sub-units.

While they worked, Alex noted how Mesme knew what was going to happen at the Oneiroi Nebula and wondered if Mesme might be a time traveler. Nika argued time travel was impossible, but Alex posited that with enough energy applied to a point on the spacetime manifold, it might be possible.

On Hirlas, Caleb, Eren, and Felzeor became trapped during a Rasu assault. Cornered at a waterfall with no escape, Caleb made a desperate sacrifice, bleeding into the planet's soil and water. Through his blood, Akeso channeled its life force into Hirlas itself. The planet awakened and systematically annihilated every Rasu present, reducing them to atoms before tearing the atoms apart. Caleb nearly died from blood loss, but Akeso kept him alive, and Akeso's consciousness now resided permanently in Hirlas.

Internal conflicts erupted among Rasu factions, triggering the civil war Alex and Nika hoped to incite. The Rasu abruptly withdrew from their invasion to engage in battles within their own territory. Miriam reacted with fury upon learning of Alex and

Nika's actions, fearing the eventual victor would prove unstoppable. Alex argued they faced imminent defeat and she'd bought crucial time.

Alex and Nika confronted Mesme with their time travel theory. Mesme confirmed it traveled back 982,000 years from eight years in the future, and that events were progressing better than in the previous timeline. The confrontation ended with Alex and Mesme reconciling, though Mesme admitted to keeping one final personal secret that didn't affect their war against the Rasu—its former identity.

Duality

Two months after Alex and Nika used kyoseil to kick off a Rasu civil war, Miriam and the Rasu War Council worked diligently to strengthen defenses on Concord worlds, while using the Ymyrath Field weapon to strategically disrupt the civil war when one faction started to gain the upper hand.

Malcolm stepped up his infiltration of the Gardiens in an attempt to uncover evidence needed to expose Enzio Vilane and his nefarious plans. In order to protect Mia, he continued to avoid any contact with her. Enzio engineered a series of regenesis mishaps and tainted neural imprints in order to sow misgivings about regenesis among the public.

Alex and Nika investigated the Rasu Stygian faction's suspicious inactivity, discovering that Stygian territory was saturated with kyoseil and populated by massive Rasu forces. On the other side of Stygian territory, Alex detected a mysterious scar across the spacetime manifold.

Alex told Miriam how she believed Stygian was the biggest threat. They had a heart-to-heart in which Miriam acknowledged that neither she nor Alex was entirely wrong or entirely right about the wisdom of provoking the Rasu civil war, and they reconciled.

Corradeo confessed a huge secret to Nyx: Eren, Corradeo and Corradeo's wife, Lauren, were close friends during the first anarch rebellion over two hundred millennia ago. When the Directorate crushed the rebellion and killed Lauren, they took Eren captive and erased his memory. Corradeo and Maris continued to warm up to each other, becoming friends with a side of flirtation.

The Earth Alliance government discovered that Kennedy secretly provided the adiamene formula to the Asterions. Kennedy had to go before the Assembly to testify, where she engaged in some slick legal maneuvering. She donated the adiamene patent to a special Concord program to provide for the common defense, thereby evading criminal liability and allowing the other Concord species to begin to use adiamene to protect their ships.

Malcolm uncovered evidence of the Gardiens' sabotage of regenesis clinics, and Richard activated law enforcement to officially move against Enzio and the Gardiens.

With authorities closing in, Enzio blew up several regenesis facilities in terrorist attacks then fled with his mother, Olivia, to a safehouse on Scythia. While there, he saw a clip of Mia on the news and recognized her as the woman he'd clashed with on Pandora. He connected Mia to Malcolm and realized that Malcolm had betrayed him. Enraged, he vowed revenge.

The Rasu moved into the final stages of their civil war as Stygian surged forth to steamroll over everyone. Before long, Stygian used kyoseil to control the entirety of Rasu territory.

Alex discovered Mesme and Miaon together on a hidden planet with a log cabin similar to the one Mesme had on Portal Prime. She deduced that Miaon was Mesme one additional cycle back in the time loop. Mesme revealed that traversing a time rift was a brutally violent event no living, material being could survive. After traversing such a rift twice, a shadow was all that remained of Miaon's consciousness. It nonetheless made the trip in order to be Mesme's guide and mentor.

Mesme told Alex that the continued existence of all living things depended on her gazing out into the universe and understanding it—on her being right, one more time.

Malcolm visited his church to pray over matters and made a decision about regenesis. He received a message from Mia in which she said she'd made peace with his refusal to opt in to regenesis and wanted him back in her life. They agreed to meet for lunch. On her way to a meeting, Mia was attacked, drugged and kidnapped. Enzio informed Malcolm that he had Mia and planned to kill her, but not before he tortured her. Malcolm embarked on a crusade to find and save her.

While Enzio was busy with Mia, Olivia traveled to Itero, an independent colony she once controlled back in Aurora. There, she located a hidden facility where she'd kept a worst-case-scenario backup of her Artificial. She connected to the backup and merged her current memories with it, then awakened as her old self, stronger than ever.

Malcolm infiltrated Vilane's beach house on Scythia. He rescued Mia and killed Vilane, but during their struggle, Vilane fatally wounded Malcolm with an adiamene blade. Malcolm died in Mia's arms; overcome with fury and despair, Mia used sidespace to destroy all of Enzio's quantum hardware, not just at Scythia but at every storage location, ensuring he'd never be resurrected.

Olivia narrowly escaped being destroyed by Mia's conflagration, but was saved by the fact that she was connected to her siloed backup on Itero.

The Asterions captured two Rasu samples linked by kyoseil. Nika used her kyoseil as a conduit for Akeso's poison, and together she and Caleb killed both Rasu without touching them. The moral implications greatly burdened both Caleb and Nika, but they put together a plan to stop the Rasu.

In order to protect the *Siyane* and themselves, Alex and Valkyrie transformed the hull of the *Siyane* into the Asterions' adaptive version of adiamene, adiaK, so the ship could be seamless.

A heartbroken Mia was trying to carry on when Malcolm showed up, alive and well. It turned out he'd revoked his 'no regenesis' clause, and was awakened in a new body. They enjoyed a beautiful reunion.

The Galenai unexpectedly reached out to Concord, sending a message that they wanted to meet their observers. Marlee rushed to the planet, where she spoke with a Galenai representative, telling them about space and other planets and Concord.

The Rasu launched their invasion across Concord space, sending massive forces to dozens of locations simultaneously.

At Earth, the Rasu knocked the moon out of orbit, intending

to crash it into the planet. Malcolm gathered a force to disintegrate the moon before it could reach the planet, thus saving Earth.

At Concord HQ, the Rasu deployed a new weapon able to punch a hole in the Rift Bubble protecting HQ. Rasu mechs wormholed inside and began rampaging through the station. They deployed a quantum block, trapping everyone inside.

Alex, Caleb, Nika and Valkyrie arrived at the homeworld of the Rasu and infiltrated their continent-sized home base. Nika accessed their nerve center, from where orders were being sent out to all Rasu. Together, Caleb and Nika sent out Akeso's poison to all the Rasu via kyoseil. While they did so, Alex worked to protect them.

On HQ, Richard and Devon teamed up to make a likely suicidal run to destroy the Rasu's quantum block so people could get off the station. Miriam and David were trapped together in the war room; due to the quantum block, Miriam had lost all contact with her fleets. They were sharing a tender moment when the Rasu exploited the seams in the door to infiltrate the room. On Earth, Seneca and other worlds, ever more Rasu arrived to overpower the defense forces. On Mirai, facing imminent death, Corradeo and Maris gave in to their feelings for one another.

On Rasu Prime, Rasu mechs invaded the nerve center, eventually overwhelming Alex. She was speared by a mech and died, but Valkyrie transferred Alex's consciousness into the *Siyane* at the last minute. Unaware of what happened, Caleb and Nika forced a final surge of the poison, and abruptly all the Rasu vessels out in space died. On HQ and across Concord worlds, the enemy fell, and the day was won in the nick of time.

Caleb killed the Rasu remaining on Rasu Prime, and only then found Alex's body—then discovered she was still alive in the ship. He took her body to the *Siyane*, and Akeso reinfused it with life.

During her surreal experience, Alex figured out several things. The scar she discovered near Rasu Prime was evidence of how the Dzhvar imbued the Rasu with their essence in the moment before the *diati* drove them off the manifold a million years ago. She and Nika confronted Mesme, and it confessed the truth.

In its cycle, eight years from now, the Dzhvar returned and resumed consuming the fabric of spacetime. When the universe was about to collapse, Mesme used the Dzhvar's own energy to open a time rift and return to the time of the first Dzhvar war.

Alex started quizzing Mesme on how they could defeat the Dzhvar, when she made an unexpected connection: Mesme's winged avatar was identical to the tattoo on Nika's back. Mesme was Nika in the last cycle.

Mesme confirmed her suspicion, but begged her not to tell Nika, saying when Nika learned the truth, it would break her, because it broke Mesme. Dashiel wouldn't be able to accompany her; she would have to leave everyone she cared about behind for a million years. Mesme had taken the Asterion's Vault with it into the past, but only the programs underlying the people; the consciousnesses and their memories were destroyed in the journey. Mesme used the Asterion programs to create the Katasketousya.

With great reluctance, Alex agreed to keep Mesme's secret, but only because she vowed to find a way to defeat the Dzhvar once and for all, break the time loop, and save everyone.

COSMIC SHORES

Medusa Falling

On Belarria, Marlee was kidnapped after witnessing the murder of her diplomatic counterpart. The murderer, Galean, belonged to a revolutionary group that sheltered escaped desbida, telepaths imprisoned because their capabilities threatened the corrupt shadow government. Despite initially being held captive, Marlee became invested in their cause, helping them broadcast the truth about the desbida, exposing the conspiracy and fighting for the freedom of the oppressed telepaths.

The Thief

Eren followed a thief named Tolje home to the Hesgyr's massive space station, Nythir. There, he learned the Hesgyr were under attack from a mysterious enemy.

Nyx soon joined Eren on Nythir, and they tracked the attacks to the Phae'soon, a species the Hesgyr previously robbed of a crucial defensive weapon, leaving the Phae'soon unprotected when the Rasu invaded. Rather than allow either side to commit genocide against the other, Eren, Nyx and Tolje destroyed the Phae'soon's weapon.

While on Nythir, Eren and Nyx succumbed to their attraction to one another and slept together. Still mourning the loss of Cosime, Eren felt tremendous guilt afterwards, and he and Nyx agreed to keep their relationship professional.

The Universe Within

While searching for signs of the Dzhvar's return, Alex and Caleb located a tear in the cosmic manifold and discovered a hidden star system inhabited by the Elakri.

Laurent, an Elakrin physicist, had discovered the same tear; his discovery made him the target of the Khesa Prutet, the dominant religious organization. Alex and Caleb rescued him from an assassination attempt, then hired a truva named Deunan to protect him.

The group learned the Elakri once lived in normal space, until they built a dimensional machine called the Piega Strai to hide them from the Rasu. Civil war had broken out when rebels tried to force a return to normal space; the conflict destroyed their historical records, and in time the Elakri forgot their origins.

Deunan turned out to be the descendant of the KP's founders. She reunited with her estranged brother Arien, a cop who was unknowingly hunting her while investigating Laurent's case.

The Piega Strai was breaking down, threatening to collapse the pocket universe. In order to save the planet, Alex entered the Piega Strai's core and dissolved the barrier of the pocket universe, returning the Elakri to Amaranthe. But as she did so, Alex and Caleb both sensed the emergence of a mysterious energy they suspected was the Dzhvar.

Arien took over leadership of the KP to shepherd the Elakri's re-introduction to the intergalactic community, and Laurent and Deunan set off together to explore the cosmos.

CONTENTS

LIMINAL SPACE

"There is no chance, no destiny, no fate, that can hinder or control the firm resolve of a determined soul."

— Ella Wheeler Wilcox

OVERTURE

*E*mpyrean forces ripped me apart from the inside out. Atom shorn from atom, thought from thought. The universe itself splintered, and I splintered into a multitude of shards along with it.

Then there was nothing, for what I perceived as a very long time. No sound, no air. No texture to my existence. Would I linger here in this nothingness forever? A mind lacking substance or form cast adrift into the endless black—

The universe inverted, and visceral sensation returned in a violent shock to my system. There was tangibility. Movement. Physicality. But with no perception of direction and no sight, I had no orientation upon which to anchor myself. Falling up, falling down, or simply being driven deeper into the unknown?

I slammed into a too-solid surface, and oblivion at last claimed me.

S&L

I awoke to pain so pervasive I couldn't say whether it originated from within or without me. My skin felt as if it was on fire; my skull exploded in a drumbeat of agony. My chest shrieked with every inhale.

...but I had skin? I still had a body? Or was this merely a phantom limb haunting my mind?

I opened one eye. Caramel-colored dirt greeted me, stretching across a featureless plain.

With a groan I carefully rolled over. A mauve sky hung overhead, decorated by cumulus clouds drifting languidly by.

Breath by arduous breath, I grew cognizant of the rest of my body. I lifted a hand in front of my face—and gasped air into brutalized lungs. My skin was burnt and peeling, as if I'd journeyed through a literal inferno. I brought the hand to my head...my hair was gone, singed off to my scalp. And I mourned such a stupid, vain, meaningless loss, knowing I'd never have those long, luxurious raven locks again.

Because now I remembered.

A sky consumed by Dzhvar. The planet below disintegrating. And in the final instant, as the manifold of the universe ripped apart to swallow everyone who remained, Mesme surrounding me and plunging us both headlong into the abyss.

I blinked away free-flowing tears and worked to bury a sorrow so overpowering I dared not face it somewhere deep inside, then gingerly sat up to survey my surroundings with greater clarity. This would be Katoikia, then, in the Triangulum galaxy as it was a million years ago, when the universe still held together. The home of the Katasketousya—a species that would not exist until I built it.

My gaze drifted across the landscape, searching. I spotted the Vault replica embedded in the surface a few hundred meters away. It was canted at a forty-degree angle and half buried in the caramel soil. But its hull was adiaK, so it would've survived the impact intact. And inside it were stored thirty-two thousand Asterion minds, along with a medical lab, emergency supplies and fabrication machines.

No, not Asterions, not truly. And not quite minds, either. Programs. Tested algorithms bearing ensconced knowledge. They would be brilliant when awakened, but, lacking the memories—the souls—they once possessed, they would not be Asterions. No, they would be Katasketousya. The first and perhaps only Katasketousya.

Mesme!

Panic seized me as I searched in every direction for a hint of sparkling lights in the afternoon sun. Without my guide, I was utterly lost.

"Mesme?" I tried to cry out, but all that emerged from my throat was a hoarse squeak.

I struggled to my feet. My clothes and shoes had burnt away as well, and I felt the heat of the sunbaked dirt on my bare, charred flesh. "Mesme? Are you here? Please, you must be here."

In the corner of my eye, a shadow drifted above the surface with nothing to cast it. I limped toward it, wincing as the soil ground into blistered soles. When I neared the shadow, I reached out a hand. "Mesme? Is that you?"

The shadow warbled, and a whisper passed over me like a breeze.

"Are you trying to speak? Please, give me some sign it's you."

Gradually, the shadow took on a semblance of shape...a winged avatar. A phoenix. It held the shape for a few short seconds before collapsing into a formless blob.

"Oh, Mesme..." tears streamed anew down my cheeks "...I'm so relieved you made it."

The warble sounded again, stronger this time, until it became halting words. "You...are Mnemosyne...now."

I collapsed to the ground, not caring about the new abrasions cracking open my skin, and cradled my head in my hands as the unfathomable weight of the task ahead of me crashed down upon my soul.

I couldn't do it. I wasn't strong enough.

But I had to be, didn't I? If I lay down in the dirt and succumbed to despair, everything would end. Not today or tomorrow. A million eternal years from now, a span that seemed impossible to cross from here. But when those million years had passed, the people I most loved—Perrin and Maris and Joaquim and Grant and Alex and, oh stars above, Dashiel, my darling—would face death all over again. Everything would be lost, all over again.

We had come so close to winning. Closer than ever before, according to Mesme. What if this time, I was able to do it? What if I could save all those dear to me? What if I could save the universe and time itself? I'd always proclaimed I would do anything to save my people, would pay any price.

No price was higher than this. But if it meant a future might somehow be won? I owed it to everyone to pay it.

I gritted my teeth, sniffled back a last deluge of tears, and climbed to my feet once more. "What do we do now?" I asked the shadow. I needed to start thinking of it as Miaon, for the old Miaon was gone...along with everyone I knew. I'd work my way around to thinking of myself as Mnemosyne instead of Nika one day, but not this one.

The shadow gathered itself up into a cohesive shape, then set off toward the wrecked Vault.

"Now we begin."

PART I:

INCEPTION

1

ELAKRIN STELLAR SYSTEM

Marestelle Galaxy
Shapley Supercluster

Alex Solovy killed her thrusters, grasped the metal lattice with both gloved hands, and let her momentum carry her legs through the opening between the crisscrossing rods. She nearly flipped fully over the rods before swinging back down like a pendulum, but gradually her movements slowed until she hung suspended from the outer frame of the Piega Strai.

The locals still called it 'the Guardian,' and many of them still believed it to be their god. But its inventor had named it the Piega Strai over nine thousand years ago, and she found it to be a far more elegant moniker. The name also sidestepped all the creepy societal control vibes that pervaded the last nine millennia of Elakrin's history.

Kennedy Rossi landed on the rung next to Alex with a bit more grace, as the woman spent a fair bit of time maneuvering around ship dry docks owned by her company, Connova Interstellar. *"When we were slaving over Advanced Metallurgy texts in university, did you ever imagine we'd one day be scavenging exotic metal from a pocket-universe-creating dimensional engine orbiting a star two hundred ten megaparsecs from Earth?"*

"Yes?"

"Of course you did." Kennedy exposed the magnetized strip embedded in the arm of her environment suit to attach herself to the lattice, then reached down and opened one of the small containers hanging from her belt. *"And you're certain we have permission to vandalize the machine?"*

"Arien authorized us to take some samples. I didn't use the word 'vandalize' when I described what we'd be doing."

Arien Colonnei wasn't the leader of the Elakrin government; he was more powerful than that. As the new, and possibly last, high chair of the Khesa Prutet, he ran the only religious institution on Elakrin. Initially formed to protect the Piega Strai so it could protect the Elakri from the Rasu, over the course of millennia the Khesa Prutet had grown corrupt in almost every way imaginable. Worse, it had coaxed the Elakri into forgetting a whole universe existed outside the walls of their snowglobe world.

But then the Piega Strai had started to break down. A few weeks ago, she and Caleb had managed to save the planet from being crushed into a singularity, and now this system again resided among the stars of Amaranthe. As a result, the residents of Elakrin were having a whole host of treasured illusions shattered. She didn't envy Arien the task of shepherding them through their existential crisis, but the alternative to learning the truth was death, so respectfully, they needed to deal with it.

Alex removed her adiamene blade from its sheath and extended it in front of her. An errant slice would cut clean through whatever the blade came in contact with, including her limbs, so she took great care as she shaved a sliver of the lattice metal off. Then she held it in place until Kennedy pinched it between her fingers and deposited it in the container. For any lesser task she'd use a cutter that wasn't so dangerous, but any material designed to withstand proximity to a star while both generating and containing violent dimensional forces wasn't apt to succumb to the edge of a butter knife.

They retrieved three additional samples from the lattice. She wanted to hack off a solid chunk of it, but they ought not to literally vandalize the device. Should the Dzhvar show up in the vicinity, the Elakri might feel isolation was preferable to disintegration, reactivate the Piega Strai, and vanish from the universe once more.

After Kennedy sealed up the container, she ran a handheld scanner over the rod they'd attached themselves to. *"I'm picking up traces of lonsdaleite, amodiamond and a graphene analogue...and way too many signatures that don't correspond to known metals."*

"Well, that's what the samples are for. You ready?"

"One second." Kennedy confirmed the container was secure on her belt before detaching the magnetized strip on her suit. *"Ready."*

Alex fired her thrusters and drifted toward the solid sphere at the heart of the lattice. Behind it, Elakrin's sun gleamed a heavily filtered mottled copper.

The last time she'd been here, the scene hadn't been nearly so quiet. Then, a tsunami had raged inside the frame as angry streams of quantum particles fought to escape the cage the lattice created. The dimensional maelstrom acted to sustain a brane manifold around the stellar system—the scaffolding upon which a layer of physical dimensions clung to, thus hiding away Elakrin and its star from the cosmos beyond it.

Though nothing powered the device now, the material comprising the sphere's outer shell was faintly magnetic, and their boots easily affixed to the shell when they landed near the external control panel.

"This panel is the only way inside?" Kennedy asked.

"Other than a single millimeter-width hole, yep."

"So we're back to vandalizing, then."

"We'll patch everything up nice and pretty when we're done. No one will ever be the wiser. But if you want to see the internal workings of the machine, this panel is coming off."

Assuming Kennedy's answer was 'yes,' Alex again extended the adiamene blade and slid it into the minuscule gap between the edge of the control panel and the sphere's shell. It cut for about fifteen centimeters then met empty space, and she diligently worked it around the perimeter until she felt the panel come loose.

They lifted it away to reveal a meter-wide opening; through it, the interior of the Piega Strai was cast in murky shadows.

"Good. Plenty of room to crawl through." Alex stuck a magnet on one end of the panel, and they attached it to the shell off to the side of the opening.

"Ahh, my favorite part of the job." Kennedy activated a light and shone it inside.

The beam carved a tunnel through the inky blackness, sending the shadows retreating as it swept across the interior. Kennedy muttered displeasure and fiddled with the settings on the light, and the beam widened to expose a broader swath of what the core held.

Three lattices resembling the outer frame interlocked one another. Within each, three rods connected their lattice to a small, solid core at the center, and additional rods connected the cores to each other.

"If these turn out to be Russian nesting dolls descending into infinity, I am not going to be amused," Kennedy remarked.

Alex couldn't help herself; she slipped into sidespace to see if she was able to get a look at the inner workings of the smaller cores. But once again, where before there had been a riot of energy and dimensions, now there was only silence. *"You might not be far off. I suspect that were the device currently active, the dimensions generated by this assembly would go fairly deep."*

"And if I learn what I need to today, then I can build a tiny Piega Strai in the lab, turn it on, and send you spelunking with your mind. But first things first." Kennedy pulled her feet up, maneuvered through the opening and disappeared into the darkness. *"Okay, I'm clear. Come on in."*

Alex swung over to slip inside after her, but paused and glanced back toward the outer lattice…and frowned. *"You go ahead and get started rooting around. This is more your wheelhouse, anyway. I want to check something out real quick."*

"What could you possibly have to check out? All the interesting things are in here."

"Sidespace stuff."

"Right. If I'm not back out in twenty minutes, you come rescue me."

"Samo soboy razumeyetsya. *That's what friends are for.*" Alex secured herself to the sphere with an extra magnet then gave her consciousness over to sidespace.

She mentally traveled up to the pinprick nozzle a quarter of the way around the sphere. When the Piega Strai had been active, a particle-sized tether had woven its way from the nozzle out to the barrier separating this space from the larger universe. The tether had been the only thing connecting Elakri to Amaranthe and was what she'd used to dissolve the barrier.

Now, where the tether had once streamed, a scar remained to mark the path. It wasn't a scar anyone would be able to see in the physical world, but here in sidespace, it was as real as the firmament it marred.

And she'd seen a scar like this one before. On the border between the Erebus Void and former Rasu territory, a similar scar ran for over three thousand megameters, until it splintered off to terminate at Rasu Prime. It was evidence of how, at the instant the Dzhvar were driven out of physical space in the Dzhvar War a million years ago, they had infused lifeless metal with a trace of their essence, and the Rasu killing machines were born.

But why was a scar *here*? Why now?

Alex followed the scar all the way out to where the Piega Strai's barrier had enclosed the stellar system. There, it took a hard turn and continued on in an arc that she would bet her reasonably good name matched the arc of the former barrier for another 0.8 megameters before fading away.

A portentous dread coiled through her gut. She'd known, of course; she and Caleb both had. But they'd had no proof, nothing but a sense of the arrival of some *other* as the machine shut down. A shadow in the corner of the eye.

A flash at the edge of her perception distracted her. Not a pseudo-visual hallmark of those dimensions, but something fundamentally other. A true void amongst the sparking energy. The formless intruder left eddies in the tether as it writhed, always on the periphery of her vision no matter where she looked.

She reached out as if to touch it, but of course her hands weren't really here, and it slithered into shadows of its own creation—

Then it was gone.

But this scar? To her mind, this was proof.

New questions spiraled out from the discovery: Questions of how, and why here of all places, and why so soon. But they would wait for contemplation when she couldn't sleep tonight. For now, only one thing mattered.

The Dzhvar were here.

"Alex, I need an extra pair of hands in here."

She reached out and touched the scar in the fervent hope it was a figment of her imagination, but a rough, palpable abrasion scraped against her mental fingertips. Well, fuck.

"Oh, Alex?"

"Right. On the way."

2

NEW LUNA

SOL STELLAR SYSTEM
MILKY WAY GALAXY

The overhead lights dimmed until only subtle, pale blue runners illuminated the ballroom. Faint, indirect lighting shone on Prime Minister Ochuko Bolaji sufficient to ensure the man wasn't obscured in darkness.

"Ladies and gentlemen," the prime minister intoned in a deep baritone, "welcome to the lunar city of Aestatis!"

As he gestured to the transparent, curving dome wall behind him, the first hints of earthrise peeked over the New Luna horizon. Wild applause broke out, and Bolaji allowed it to continue for almost twenty seconds before gesturing for quiet. "I would say 'it's been a long road to arrive at this day,' but the truth is, the wheels of government, industry and philanthropy have never spun faster or in greater concert. Three years and two months ago, we sacrificed the moon in order to save our planet from the Rasu. The architect of that miraculous gambit is here with us tonight. Fleet Admiral Jenner, we are all in your debt."

Beside Miriam, Malcolm dipped his chin toward the stage in thanks; then, sensing something more was required, he shifted in his seat and offered a restrained wave to those gathered in the ballroom.

"Almost from the next morning, work began to construct this new satellite," the prime minister continued. "Doing so was necessary to save the many species that rely on our tides, as well as to protect the long-term health of our planet. But it was also important for those of us who call Earth home to be able to look up in the night sky and see our stalwart companion shining above us.

"Yet New Luna will be so much more than a satellite. As before, it will host strategic military, scientific and industrial facilities. In addition, it will serve as a vibrant commercial hub and, in time, a home for millions of residents."

The laudatory remarks continued, and Miriam's focus drifted a little. She'd received a tour earlier in the day of the deep inner workings of the satellite. The engineering feats required to mimic the mass and consequent orbit of the moon while maintaining the same size (because optics *did* matter) had proved to be significant, as was the cost of transplanting and molding the needed construction materials. Still, this left plenty of empty space, and the interior housed vast storehouses of both information and goods. Seed vaults, historical records, biological samples and much more.

Then there were the eight Zero Engines. Because New Luna wasn't merely a satellite; it was a spaceship. The next time an enemy on the order of the Rasu tried to use the moon as a weapon against humanity, they would be in for quite a surprise.

The speech ended in perfect concurrence with the lower arc of Earth cresting the horizon, as the new prime minister was a bit of a showman, and another round of applause flowed through the room. Bolaji might take it as appreciation of his speech, but Miriam was applauding for her home.

Her husband, David, leaned in to whisper in her ear. "First rule of politics: never let your speech hold up the food. He's cutting it close."

On cue, wait staff in formal attire arrived to begin placing the first of what would be, in Miriam's opinion, far too many courses. It wasn't that she minded spending a lengthy dinner with David, Malcolm and Mia, but she'd enjoy it rather more around her own dinner table in her own house.

She'd barely taken a bite of her salad, however, when the prime minister arrived at their table, which was another problem with such formal galas. Everyone set their forks down and stood respectfully.

"Well, this is a Guests of Honor table if I've ever seen one," Bolaji intoned. "Fleet Admiral, I hope your inspection of Mare Ingenii Base today met your expectations."

"It did," Malcolm replied graciously. "An improvement upon its predecessor in every way."

"Good to hear. Ms. Requelme, you are looking as lovely as ever."

"Thank you, Prime Minister." Mia was far too skilled of a diplomat to act frosty at any insinuation her primary value was in her appearance, but as soon as the prime minister pivoted away, she rolled her eyes at the back of his head. Now that she was no longer a government representative, concerns about perceived corruption or favoritism had faded away, and she and Malcolm had quietly gotten married two years ago. But she remained one of the most well-known people in Concord space, so Mia retained her last name for public-facing matters.

"Commandant Solovy." Bolaji grasped Miriam's hand in both of his. "I deeply appreciate you attending our humble ceremony."

"I may not be Earth Alliance any longer, but Earth is and will always be my home."

"And we are grateful for it. Commander Solovy, it's good to see you as well."

"I go by 'David' or 'Professor' these days. I haven't been a commander in many years, sir."

"Yes, but I've been taught the rank never leaves the man—or woman."

"It is the tradition." David cleared his throat. "Don't let us keep you from the rest of your guests. Terrific show."

"Thank you." Bolaji clapped David on the shoulder like they were old friends, then made for the next table over, and they all returned to their seats.

"For the record, Malcolm, I'm sorry," Miriam said. "And also selfishly grateful that you stand in between me and him."

"I'm not so grateful." Malcolm glanced over at the adjacent table, where another cluster of guests stood to welcome the prime minister. "In truth, he's not *that* bad, so far. At a minimum, he recognizes he knows nothing about the military and doesn't try to pretend otherwise. Nonetheless, the extent of his ignorance is at times astounding. I didn't think I'd miss Gagnon, but...here we are."

David scoffed. "I'm not sure a politician has ever existed who a soldier missed once they were gone, but I suppose everything's relative. At least the food should be good, assuming we're allowed to eat it in peace."

A pulse from Alex arrived then.

> *Hey, Mom. Are you at the house tonight?*
>
> *Your father and I are at the grand opening festivities for Aestatis on New Luna. We're not intending to stay late, though. We should be home in an hour or two. Is there a problem?*
>
> *No emergency. Do you mind if I come by later?*
>
> *Not at all. I'll message you when we're free.*

David spotted the flicker in her expression and placed a hand over hers. "Is everything all right?"

"I think so. Alex is going to come by after we get home."

"Excellent. Did she say why?"

"She didn't." The fact Alex hadn't wormholed into the middle of the ballroom indicated her daughter wasn't bringing news of immediate doom. So Miriam forced herself to not worry about it for now, and instead try to enjoy what she could of the meal and the company.

S&L

EARTH

GREATER VANCOUVER

An hour and a half and six meal courses later, Miriam and David walked into the house to find Alex already sitting at the kitchen table, a glass of wine in one hand and two aural screens positioned in front of her. Her long, burgundy hair was even more unkempt than usual, and her gray shirt was wrinkled and sweat-stained.

"Oh, welcome home." Alex disappeared the aurals and leaned back in her chair. "How was the party?"

"The same as all such parties are," Miriam replied as she slipped her coat off and hung it up by the door.

"Insufferable, huh?"

"The view was nice. And the tour of the interior before the party was genuinely fascinating. But we can talk about it later, if you're interested." She sat down opposite her daughter and clasped her hands on the table. "What's wrong?"

"Oh, nothing much." Alex took a long sip from her glass. "It's merely that the Dzhvar have definitely returned from their exile…and I think it's my fault."

"What do you mean by 'have definitely returned'? None of the upgraded sensors we've spent the fortune of galaxies deploying have alerted us to any incursions, nor has any attack or sighting been reported. I would know."

"She would." David frowned as he slid in beside her and set the open bottle of wine on the table, along with two additional glasses. "So what have you learned, *milaya*? Also, why do you look as if you just finished a marathon? You didn't have to run here from Vancouver, did you?"

"No." Alex offered a weak laugh. "I spent the last several hours in an environment suit, and I didn't stop to shower before I came here. Kennedy and I went to the Elakrin system today to study the Piega Strai. While we were there, I had a peek around in sidespace. I discovered a scar on the manifold—the exact same kind of scar that leads to Rasu Prime. You know, the one the Dzhvar left behind when they were expelled from the firmament in the Dzhvar War—can we go ahead and start calling it the 'First' Dzhvar War? Because we're going to have a second one."

Miriam had picked up her glass to take a sip of wine but set it back down. "Alex, stop being fatalistic. It's not like you."

"It isn't. But did you miss the part where this is my fault?"

"As I understand it, over two billion people would've died if you hadn't deactivated the Piega Strai."

"They would have. I had no other option. But you're the one who's always insisting actions have consequences, and we ignore them at our peril."

Miriam gave up on enjoying her wine and slid her glass over to David. "So I am. This doesn't negate the fact that you made the right choice."

"I know, though if I'd realized what the ramifications would be...I suppose I'd still have done it. Saving real people I've met from imminent death has to win out over guarding against the possible future death of nameless, faceless masses, even if the math doesn't square. But the fact remains, the scar wasn't there before I shut down the device. Coupled with what I saw while I was merging the spaces? What I feared was Dzhvar at the time? The scar's presence now can only mean one thing." Alex's nose scrunched up, the way it did when she was frustrated. "We need more time. We're not ready."

Miriam nodded thoughtfully. "You say this scar means the Dzhvar have returned, and I believe you. You'd never speak carelessly about this sort of thing. But the universe is rather expansive, as you know, and most of it is empty space. We may well have decades, if not centuries, until they pose a threat to us."

"Sure, we might. But what are the odds we will?"

"Hey," David protested. "We deserve a break after that nasty Rasu War. Karma says we'll get one."

Alex chuckled over the top of her glass. "Dad, do not launch into one of your speeches about how the universe looks out for people who act with honor."

He shrugged. "I'm here, aren't I?"

"Yes, Dad, you are. Point happily conceded." Alex took a sip of her wine, then languidly swirled the rest around in her glass for a minute. "Here's the problem. We can't afford to enjoy whatever time karma is inclined to grant us. Yes, should the Dzhvar attack an individual planet or artificial body, they'll pose a grave threat to the people who are living there. But the fundamental threat they pose is to the universe as a whole.

"The Dzhvar don't just kill people—they destroy the manifold itself. So we can't wait for them to stumble upon us. We can't let them spend decades or centuries dining on far-off galaxies. If we want to save Amaranthe, we've got to go out and find them. Then we have to take the fight to them. And we have to do it now."

3

AKESO

Ursa Major II Galaxy

Our water rushes over the stone cliffs of Calchfaen to tumble freely through the sky, until it crashes upon a bed of rocks in a torrent of foam and spray. Droplets ricochet, flung into the humid air, caught upon our wind and swept into our dense limbs to nourish growing leaves.

Eyes closed and cool grass tickling his back, Caleb smiled. *Nature's beauty can be ferocious when it works up a good head of steam.*

Those rocks would have crushed your too-fragile body beyond my capacity to heal it, as well as those of your companions, had I not intervened.

You didn't just save me and my companions that day, Akeso. You saved hundreds of millions of Naraida and Volucri.

And now I nurture them. Now I am home for them.

Caleb hummed in contentment. Most of the time, Akeso remained simply Akeso. But if he concentrated on a specific detail among the endless panoply of activity, the whole 'two worlds as one' thing was still proving to be a fair bit on the peculiar side. Hirlas resided almost a megaparsec away, but Akeso's consciousness, and thus, in a way, his own, was located as much there as it was here. There existed no lag or latency, no division erected in deference to the vast gulf of space separating the two worlds.

What a strange existence he'd fashioned for himself—

He immediately detected the disruption in the fabric of the air caused by Alex's wormhole. Finally. He climbed to his feet and headed for the house.

After departing the Elakrin system and dropping Kennedy off on Romane, Alex had stopped by Akeso only long enough to park the *Siyane* before heading to her parents' house on Earth. Caleb had been enjoying a meal with Isabela on Seneca and missed the opportunity to accompany her. But he knew she'd departed in a foul mood; he could sense it in the terse, punctuated cadence of her messages. And knowing what she'd discovered, he didn't blame her.

By the time he got upstairs, she was already in the shower, having left a trail of dirty, wrinkled clothes across the bedroom floor. So he stretched out on the bed, wound his hands behind his head and waited.

She wandered out of the lavatory a few minutes later, silver satin robe hanging untied as she toweled her hair dry. On seeing him, a faint smile lifted her lips. "Sorry I didn't say 'hi' before jumping in the shower. I'd been filthy for too many hours."

"Understandable. How did it go with your parents?"

"Oh, you know. 'Not your fault,' 'couldn't have known,' 'blah, blah.'"

"They're right."

"Maybe. But it's easy to say so when no one has died yet—that we know of." She tossed the towel back through the lavatory door, crawled onto the bed and snuggled into the crook of his arm. "It doesn't make any sense."

He breathed in the fresh, clean scent of her shampoo and soaked in the warmth of her skin against his, kissing her temple as he brushed a strand of damp hair off her cheek. "What doesn't? Specifically, I mean, not the grand mysteries of life and vagaries of the universe."

"Good, because I am not up to unraveling those tonight. It doesn't make sense why there would be any connection between the Dzhvar and the Elakri's bubble space. When the Dzhvar were banished a million years ago, the Elakri were still living in caves over a hundred megaparsecs from where the final battle of the First Dzhvar War took place, and even farther from Rasu Prime."

He noted her prepending of 'First' to the war's moniker, but didn't comment on it. No reason to fight inevitability. "True. But you're always saying how distance and location don't have any real meaning in those hidden quantum dimensions you like to cavort in."

"They don't. But now I'm starting to wonder if there's something fundamental I don't understand about where the Dzhvar have been all this time, or about how they interact with dimensions. Or possibly about what the Piega Strai does to the manifold when it burrows a bubble of space inside of it."

She sank deeper into his chest. "Dammit, I thought I had everything figured out. I mean, except for how to actually destroy the Dzhvar, but I assumed I'd work that part out once they showed their ugly faces and we fixed some sensors on them. But if they've never operated how I believed, or worse, if the manifold and dimensions don't play by the rules I believed they did, or if—"

"Hey, hey." He placed a knuckle under her chin and lifted it up until she met his gaze. "This is not all on you. No one is expecting you to singlehandedly save the universe."

"But I prom—"

"I know what you promised Mesme—that *we* would permanently defeat the Dzhvar and break this bloody time loop. You need to remember what else Mesme said: it saves the people who will save the universe. *People*, plural. I'm on the list. So are your mother and Corradeo. And, ironically, so is Nika. So share the burden a little, will you?"

She stared at him, bottomless Prevo irises fractaling with conflict and defiance and the relentless stubbornness he desperately loved her for. But they soon softened into weariness, and she leaned in close to nod against his neck. "Okay. We're in this together. All of us."

"That's better."

Within a few minutes, she'd drifted off to sleep in his arms. Caleb closed his eyes as well, but sleep proved to be elusive, for his own thoughts churned down winding paths to circle back on themselves.

How was *he* going to do his part to save the universe? Alex had her dimension-whispering abilities and a deep understanding of the way the cosmos functioned, and those talents were certain to be indispensable in the coming battles. Miriam had a fleet of millions of warships and a keen sense of strategy and logistics working for her, while Corradeo had a million years of experience as well as a history of battling this enemy. And Nika? She had a universe's worth of kyoseil at her beck and call.

What did he have? Close-combat fighting skills were not going to turn the tide against pandimensional primordial space entities, and neither was the consciousness of a sentient planet living in his head.

Maybe it was like he'd said to Deunan when they were on Elakrin, and his role was simply to help Alex as she saved the universe. To be her strength, her cheerleader, her safe place to land and shoulder to cry on when things got hard and ugly. If that was all he was destined to do, he'd be honored to perform such a role. And, if he were honest, after everything he and Akeso had sacrificed to defeat the Rasu, perhaps a little relieved.

But everyone on Mesme's list had someone to support them; even Corradeo had recently opened himself up to love. David wasn't on the list, and neither was Maris. So why was he? Had Mesme been flattering him so he'd stay invested? It would hardly be the first time the Kat had dissembled in order to manipulate him.

Or was the universe gearing up to ask something consequential of him once again? Something he couldn't yet see coming?

4

____

CONCORD HEADQUARTERS
MILKY WAY GALAXY

Caleb extended a hand, turned halfway, and touched it to Arien Colonnei's palm. "It's good to see you again."

"You as well. But if I'm going to pretend to be a diplomat, you should teach me how your people greet each other."

"Ah. You'll encounter many different greetings here on HQ, but…" he reached out and grasped the man's hand in his, then shook it firmly "…humans do so like this."

Arien frowned, eyes narrowing as he repeated the gesture. "It feels somehow aggressive."

"It's not. Not most of the time, anyway." Caleb peered toward the customs exit. "No Deunan today?"

"She and Laurent sprinted off in that direction as soon as we cleared customs." Arien gestured toward the arched entry to the atrium and food court. "Something about 'raspberry gelatos.' I believe this is their third visit in as many weeks to your remarkable space station."

"I'm glad they're making good use of those guest passes." He indicated the hallway leading to the levtram hub. "Shall we? The Consulate is in this direction."

"I am at your mercy." The man touched the back of his ear. "Deunan gave me something called a translator dot, but it doesn't appear to work for the signage."

"No, I'm afraid you need some slightly more robust hardware to be able to read printed Communis. We do have a tool, though. Mention it at the Consulate, and they'll set you up."

"Implanted hardware?" As an experienced law enforcement detective and interrogator, the man was an expert at concealing his true feelings. But Caleb had the same skills, and Arien was a touch spooked by the idea of Concord's esoteric technology. It couldn't be easy, spending your life believing your culture sat at the apex of advancement, only to discover you were relative primitives.

"Not unless you want it to be."

"Hmm. Not just yet." Arien's gaze darted around in every direction as they walked; Caleb let him gawk without judgment. In addition to the ubiquitous technology, this was the man's first time seeing any alien species other than humans. Caleb remembered his and Alex's first visit to a gateway Arx shortly after traveling to Amaranthe; it had been an overwhelming experience.

"Feel free to ask anything that strikes you," he offered.

"I hardly know where to start. I'm still not certain I'm the right person to represent us in these meetings. I'm not a diplomat at all and a fairly terrible religious leader. Unless you need another detective on the station?"

"You're the right person. Far more so than your chancellor, you'll be the one guiding your people through their introduction to the intergalactic community."

"That is the job I signed up for," Arien muttered somewhat glumly.

The station was bustling with activity, and Caleb had to work to find them a spot on the tram where his guest wouldn't be forced to abut shoulders with aliens. He only marginally succeeded, and a teenage Naraida girl with lavender feathered hair gawked up at the tall Elakri the entire trip. When an orange-furred Khokteh wearing combat leathers boarded and grabbed a handhold beside them, Arien's already enormous eyes widened precipitously, but he maintained his outward composure.

They exited the levtram at the Consulate stop, and Caleb kept their pace slow so they could appreciate the stunning view the lobby afforded.

"It's incredible what you've built here," Arien said. "We have a group digging through the oldest records hidden away in the Scenza archives. There isn't much from before the Fall, but there is more than we ever knew. Some of the records suggest that at our height, we may have built such magnificent monuments as this." Arien cleared his throat and forced himself to continue through the lobby. "I hope one day we can prove to be worthy allies, but we have a way to go."

"No pressure. We'll help you where we can, but you're in the driver's seat. Or I expect this is what the diplomats will say." Caleb waved a greeting to the Novoloume receptionist as they approached the desk.

"Good morning. Ms. Marano says you can come on in whenever you're ready. She's in Room C."

Ms. Marano. It sounded strange to his ears. "Thank you, Phelain."

The door slid open to reveal a smallish meeting room, well appointed but cozy. Marlee stood at one end of the table that occupied much of the space, flicking through screens on an aural. She wore a navy pantsuit so dark it was almost black, and her usually somewhat wild sapphire-streaked ebony hair had been tamed into a low tail clasped by a pearl-adorned ornament.

His heart panged with wistfulness over how grown up she was now, even if she had gushed like an excited little girl when relaying to him the details of her misadventure on Belarria.

She vanished the aural and bestowed a warm but refined smile on them as she approached. "You must be Arien Colonnei. I'm Assistant Ambassador Marlee Marano. Welcome to Concord." She offered her left hand in the Elakri greeting.

Caleb hadn't taught it to her, but he supposed it was her job to simply know such things.

"A pleasure." Arien returned the gesture, then glanced his way. "Marano?"

"My niece."

"Oh, wonderful. Everyone on my world owes your uncle a debt of gratitude."

She smiled again, her gaze drifting to him. "Many people do." Not a trace of snark in her voice. "Now. I understand most Elakri aren't yet aware of Concord's existence, but this doesn't mean you and I can't start laying the groundwork for a fruitful relationship. Have a seat, and let me tell you about what we can offer to you."

She waved a hand toward the door, shooing Caleb away.

He touched Arien's arm in farewell. "Give Deunan and Laurent my best, and please don't hesitate to reach out if you need anything. But you're in good hands here."

"I'm sure I am. Thank you for everything."

He checked the time as he departed the Consulate. Alex had awoken this morning with a renewed fire in her belly, and she was meeting with Miriam, Devon Reynolds and several other people about the status of their expanded sensor network. It would likely be another hour before she was free, so he decided to see if Felzeor was around.

S&L

"So then, Drae had to make a mad dash to grab the storage cube while Lyndall sliced the power to the hardware, leaving me to distract our marks long enough for them to make a stealthy exit." Felzeor paused his story long enough to peck a few bites from his frittata.

"How did you accomplish it?" Caleb asked.

"I started an intellectual argument with the men about whether it's better to fry or sauté cold water ray-finned fish. The answer is sauté, by the way, but I presented both sides of the argument to buy additional time. You know, most Anadens continue to underestimate Volucri. They believe the lie the Directorate told that we're barely smarter than birds of prey."

"Old prejudices die hard. Though I was under the impression that when the Anadens discovered Hirlas, the Volucri played dumb in order to fly under the Directorate's radar, as it were."

Felzeor's ice green eyes slid sideways. "It might be true. We are, after all, highly devious, which is why we make excellent spies. But it was so very long ago, who can say?"

"Who indeed." Caleb took a bite of his sandwich, then set it down again and leaned back in his chair. He was slow-walking his meal so they could spend more time together. "I'm happy to hear Drae finally assembled a full team. Are the new members working out?"

"I think so. Lyndall is funny. Not as funny as Eren, of course, but I try to laugh to bolster his confidence."

"You're a wonderful teammate."

"Drae says so. Hey, did you know Eren had an entire adventure without us? He met these bony-skinned anatype alien thieves and saved them from some angry, brokenhearted salamander aliens."

Leave it to Felzeor to distill even the most complex interactions to their barest truths. "I did hear that. I'm sure Eren would have invited us along if he thought we could help."

"He invited Nyx along." Felzeor snickered and sipped on his straw.

"Oh? I didn't realize."

"He says he didn't *invite* her so much as she just showed up. But I think he's covering for the fact he didn't invite us."

Caleb buried a grin behind his cup of coffee. Miriam had once said Felzeor could bring sunshine to the seventh level of Hell, and she wasn't wrong. He was a balm for the deepest wounds of the soul. "Nyx is his boss. Arguably she has a right to check in on him."

"I suppose. What a horrible boss she must be! I still wish he would come back to work at CINT. I'm sure Director Navick would approve a larger team, and I think Eren and Lyndall would get along."

"I know you do. But Corradeo needs him more than Richard does."

"And Sator Nisi *was* a good boss. So I guess I understand." Felzeor swallowed the last bite of the frittata and shook his feathers out. "I'm glad our dinner evening is coming up soon. Are we going to train with Marlee again?"

"I think so, yes. She had her own adventure without us, and she says she needs to sharpen her combat skills."

"It's not true. She's almost as fast as you are now." Felzeor dropped his voice to a conspiratorial whisper. "But don't tell her I said so. I enjoy training with you and her, and I would hate for it to end."

"It'll be our little secret."

5

CONCORD HQ

COMMAND

The holographic map stretched for over three gigaparsecs on the long side and almost half as far on the short one. Odds were high that so great a swath of the universe had never before been tamed.

Well, maybe not tamed. Surveyed and measured, though. And now, monitored.

A tight tangle of flickering dots clustered in the center, with a bridge connecting it to a second, smaller grouping of dots a little off to the left. From there, the gaps between the dots gradually increased, until the distance between them was counted in kiloparsecs.

Alex scowled at the map. "Not bad coverage in Concord and Dominion territories. But there is way too much dead space once you get beyond Laniakea. A Dzhvar would have to trip over one of those sensors to set it off."

Devon Reynolds fisted a hand at his mouth. "You didn't read the briefing material."

"No. I didn't have time this morning. Look, Devon, I realize you're not dumb. So convince me this network is going to succeed in alerting us if the Dzhvar show up anywhere in the admittedly impressive Pisces-Cetus Supercluster Complex."

"Not dumb…." He exhaled dramatically. "Commandant Solovy, do I have to convince her?"

Her mother shrugged mildly. "I would sleep better at night knowing Alex was convinced."

"Fine. Fine, fine, fine. So the core network is an upgrade of the system we rolled out to detect Rasu incursions, with the listener algorithm switched to trigger on the Dzhvar signal Advocate Corradeo provided. Nothing new there. Greatly improved, but only in the way we're constantly improving our systems as a matter of course.

"But once the distances become too vast to capture near-real-time measurements, we had to get creative. We implemented a triangulation structure to detect minuscule perturbations in the fabric of spacetime. It'll pick up other things—gravitational waves, supernova shock waves, etc.—but it should definitely pick up Dzhvar."

"But—"

"Those types of waves take time to propagate. This is where Advisor Ridani pitched in."

Across the table, Dashiel sat up straighter. "Not me alone. Most of the details were worked out by one of the Conceptual Research ceraffin. The gist is, we added kyoseil to the equation. Each sensor includes two grams of a pre-linked kyoseil set. Testing shows kyoseil waves are able to sense perturbations that cross their paths, so—"

"Multiple sensors are able to triangulate in on a perturbation," Alex finished for him.

"Correct. There is still a bit of lag time, particularly the farther any one sensor is from a disruption, but it's much smaller than it was with the old hardware alone."

"And shrinking." Devon cleared his throat. "We're placing more equipment every day, working to shorten the lag time. Satisfied?"

Alex tilted her chin in concession. It wasn't as if she didn't believe Devon and Dashiel were far and away the two smartest people currently on HQ. But she never accepted anything at face value. If she ever had, they wouldn't be here in Amaranthe at all. "That we'll be alerted if they pop their heads out anywhere on this map? It seems likely. It's a good system. But it's not enough."

"What?" Devon sputtered.

"This is a mind-bogglingly tremendous span of space." She waved at the map overhead. "It truly is. But it's less than one percent of the observable universe. The Dzhvar could gobble up half of Amaranthe, and we'd be none the wiser."

"Alex?" Her mother shot her a pained look. "We are moving as quickly as we can."

Okay, so it was possible she was being a bitch today. She was cranky. Her dreams had been haunted by the damn scar in the Elakrin system, and she'd awoken to second guessing all the decisions she'd made when shutting down the Piega Strai. Not choosing to save the Elakri, but how. What if there had been another way? What the fuck were the Dzhvar doing *there*?

She pinched the bridge of her nose. "I'm sorry. I know you are. This is terrific work. You haven't picked anything up yet?"

"Not anything Dzhvar, no." Devon's tone had softened, and now she felt bad; she shouldn't have goaded him. No one at HQ, save her mother, worked harder than he did. "We *did* detect a spatial disruption when the Piega Strai shut down, which was actually a nice test run for the system."

He zoomed the map way in to the Marestelle galaxy over in the Shapley Supercluster, and an orange ping flared, followed a few seconds later by a larger ping that propagated out into space.

"Yeah, there were two shock waves, the second one much more significant than the first. Obviously, they would have drowned out any Dzhvar signature that might have appeared at the same time."

"But you did see them at Elakrin?" Devon asked. "Is there something you can tell me to help improve our detection efforts?"

She shook her head. "I only saw them in sidespace. I don't think they crossed onto the manifold. Not there." *Then where were they coming from?*

"We already know what they look like in real space, from the first war. I'm frankly more interested in what they look like in sidespace."

"I get that. But I didn't really *see* them as such. It was akin to…a shadow in the corner of my eye, no matter where I directed my attention. A writhing void carved through a swarm of dimensional energy. Ugh." Alex groaned into her hands. "I realize it's nothing to go on. The important takeaway is that Akeso sensed their presence as well. This means kyoseil will sense it. Your sensors will work."

Dashiel huffed a breath, but didn't say anything.

She watched him while Devon and her mom talked through some technicals of the continuing rollout of the upgraded sensors. She and Dashiel weren't exceptionally close, but she'd gotten to know the man fairly well over the last few years, and he acted troubled.

Dashiel, what is it?

His gaze rose to meet hers.

I'm just wondering what it's going to do to Nika when they show up. If the kyoseil can sense the Dzhvar's presence…you remember how rough the Rasu's invasive thoughts were on her.

I do. But The Rasu were actively using the kyoseil. Sending orders to their minions through it. These sensors will merely be registering transient activity in the surrounding space. I don't think she'll be able to—or be forced to—listen in on the Dzhvar's thoughts, assuming they have any.

You're probably right.

A thousand thoughts of her own queued up on her tongue, but she couldn't share a one of them. He didn't know the truth. Didn't know what fate awaited Nika unless they found a way to stop the Dzhvar from causing the end of everything.

6

SCHOLITE

MILKY WAY GALAXY

Eren Savitas accepted an *apéranti thálassa* from the bartender then wandered over to a decorative pillar, lounged against it, and evaluated the crowd.

The dance floor sported a healthy supply of cavorters, and the tables scattered on its periphery held a full house of drinkers…and diners, here and there. It was a fairly sophisticated clientele, on the whole. Not to say that hypnols weren't being bought, sold and consumed, but they were the quality hypnols. Not to say that sexual escapades weren't on the evening's menu, but they would take place upstairs, later.

The patrons were notably varied, too. This marked one of the first times he'd seen so many aliens in an Anaden club on an Anaden world, at least as anything other than bottom-tier staff. Most of the aliens were Novoloume, for no one appreciated refined entertainment so much as they did. He thought he spotted several Humans, too, but in the patchy, often dim light it was somewhat difficult to tell Humans and Anadens apart from a distance. Plenty of Naraida, and even a few cleaned-up Barisans.

Damn, were two Asterions sitting over near the bar? The glowing skin made them stand out in the shadows. Corradeo was making good on his promise to welcome their genetic siblings home, and it seemed the odd Asterion was beginning to believe him. One way the man was changing the world.

Eren sipped on his drink and began scanning the patrons with greater care, searching for one person in particular. A Novoloume, though the man would likely be meeting with a couple of Anadens.

Ihelahn Roshiive was a wealthy businessman on Nopreis; a purveyor of soft core interspecies porn more than anything else. He'd earned millions in his trade these last twenty years, but he'd *learned* his trade under the whip of the Idoni Primor. Granted, Eren didn't know for certain whether an actual whip had been involved, but when it came to Savine Idoni, it was a safe bet.

While most Novoloume were far too mannered to let it show in public spaces, bitterness at their degrading treatment under Directorate rule ran both wide and deep. The species had a typical life span of several hundred years before Concord gifted eternal life to them in the form of regenesis, so many had centuries of experience living through said degradation. And while Corradeo Praesidis was not responsible for Directorate policies or Anaden behavior in carrying them out, vengeance fantasies rarely drew such strict lines. It was enough of a trigger that the Anadens were getting their shite together again, and starting to assert them-selves within the intergalactic community in meaningful ways.

More than one former subjugate wanted to knock Anadens back down a few rungs in a revenge play, and Roshiive was both the wealthiest and the best connected of them. Eren couldn't truthfully fault the man for the inclination, but he had a duty to prevent him from fulfilling it.

The unfortunate thing, though, was how Anadens existed who were willing to help people like Roshiive. Men and women who'd preferred life under the Directorate for one reason or another, or bore their own resentments against the still-developing Advocacy. Since the instigator was a Novoloume, though, Eren figured this counted as a 'Non-Anaden Affair' and thus fell under his purview.

But Roshiive appeared to be a no show so far. With a sigh he scanned the crowd again, this time searching for something or someone who'd entertain him for a spell.

"Aha." He pushed off the pillar and worked his way through the milling patrons to a table in the far corner.

One of the occupants of the table got up and left as he arrived, and he slid smoothly into the chair opposite Malesh Prante Idoni. "How are you this fine evening?"

Malesh shot him a dirty scowl. "Look, I'm simply enjoying a decent meal and a drink. That's not a crime, is it?"

"Not so far." The man was a longtime hypnol dealer based on Brizo. Once upon a time, back during his anarch days, Eren had used him as a personal supplier. The man had climbed a couple of rungs up the ladder since then and now ran several hypnol production factories. Three years ago, Nyx had destroyed his *apomono* factory after the attempt on Corradeo's life, though Malesh didn't know Eren had been involved. The man hadn't worked with the assassins, and Eren would've preferred the factory stay operational where he was able to keep an eye on it, but if there was one thing Nyx didn't broker, it was *apomono*.

Of course, the surprising things she *did* broker in private had turned out to be absolutely fascinating and—he shut the thought down hard. It was bad enough how lascivious memories of their night together on Nythir haunted him every time he laid down and tried to go to sleep, but the least they could do was restrict themselves to the bedroom. Dammit.

Eren glanced over his shoulder, where the previous occupant of his chair was disappearing into the shadows. "And he was merely another friend of yours stopping by for a chat?"

"What if he was?"

"Then it'll be the first time I've been wrong this month." He clasped his hands on the table and leaned in eagerly. "What have you been up to lately?"

"Nothing that concerns you. I hear you've got a fancy job these days, so why are you here harassing little old me?" A glint lit Malesh's eyes. "Unless...I can hook you up, if you're itching. I've got a vial of *laevona* in my bag. For my own personal use, but I'd be willing to share it due to our history."

Eren acknowledged the faint twinge of need flaring in his gut. Addiction never fully departed, especially not when he'd suffered occasional small relapses over the years. But ninety-nine days out of a hundred, he was good, and this was one of the ninety-nine. "Not why I'm here. I simply saw an opportunity to check in and see if there are any juicy developments spicing up your world these days."

"I'm not a rat. I have a reputation to uphold. An honorable one, in the circles that matter to me. I can't burn relationships."

"And I'm not asking you to burn anything. I'm just asking if you know any morsels someone such as myself, with my fancy job, would be interested in hearing. The more favorably I view you, the less my gaze will be apt to wander over toward Brizo."

Malesh studied his drink for several seconds, a long breath escaping out through tight lips. "There is one thing. It's not fact, mind you. But I did hear a whisper the other day that *apomono* might be back on the street, for the right price."

"Who's supplying it?"

"It's a new player called Riamere. Popped up in the last two years out of nowhere and is starting to crowd out the other dealers on Domor and Ficenti."

"Two years from zero to a major player? That's unusual. The group must have a wealthy patron."

"Maybe, but that's not the twist." Malesh bit his lower lip in some kind of perverse glee, caught up in the drama of the reveal.

Eren stared at him deadpan. "What's the twist?"

"The leader of this Riamere? They call her the 'Pale Viper.' And rumor is, she's Human."

"*Human?* What is a Human doing running hypnols on Domor and Ficenti?"

"No idea. But it's what they say."

"And why do 'they' call her the Pale Viper?"

"Because she's pale, obviously. Skin like alabaster paper mâché and hair like corn silk. And that's not all. Her skin kind of glows. Not like those Asterion freaks, though. It's as if a fine mesh web is overlaid atop it. And her eyes glitter like golden beryls."

Eren arched an eyebrow. "You've given a rather detailed description, and a poetic one, too. Sure you haven't met this woman yourself? Sure you aren't doing business with her?"

"I'm sure. Don't get me wrong—if I thought I could use her to get back into the *apomono* trade, I'd do it. Highest profit margin in the Milky Way. But she doesn't make deals with other suppliers."

"Such a shame for you. Thank you, Malesh. You've earned your peace for the rest of the night." Mostly because Eren had spotted Ihelahn Roshiive striding in through the entrance. "Just make sure I don't notice you again while I'm here."

"I will. Hey, before you go, there's one more thing about this Pale Viper you need to know if you're going to go after her. Which you should. Clear the way for ordinary, hardworking Anadens and all."

"Oh? What's that?" he asked as he stood.

"Where she got the 'Viper' part of her name. I know a guy who's fallen into her orbit. He used to work for Giora elasson-Idoni back in the Directorate days, so he's seen some sick, depraved shit. And he is terrified out of his wits of this woman."

ARES

MILKY WAY GALAXY

Eren took the lift to the top floor of the new Security Division building and exited into a broad, brightly lit hallway. The textured walls glistened from fresh ivory-hued paint, and his boots glided along the reflective pewter marble flooring. The décor was tastefully refined down to the last corner molding.

Ahh, he could almost feel the Advocacy stretching its branches in the morning sun as ever more seedlings took root.

He passed two laborers guiding a trolley stacked high with office equipment. He offered them a silent nod in greeting as he stepped to the side to give the trolley a wide berth, then continued on. At the end of the hallway hung a serious and most officious sign:

Prefect Nyx Praesidis
Director of Advocacy Intelligence

The door beneath the sign was unlocked, and it opened to reveal a spacious office three times larger than her previous one over in the Executive Building. A long, curving desk made of conductive glass centered the room. A window-wall spanned the back, providing a view of the many fountains and gardens of Advocacy Square, while the left wall bore the smooth, dark translucent hallmarks of a holographic display. His boots sank into plush burgundy carpet as he stepped inside.

Nyx stood at the right wall, fiddling with an enormous painting of waves crashing over rocks to tumble down from a jagged cliff while storm clouds leered in the distance. She wore snug black workpants tucked into high boots and a gunmetal gray shirt with three-quarters sleeves bunched up at the elbows; her hair was drawn back into her typical low tail, but strands had come loose to tease her ears.

He sighed quietly while ordering his groin to kindly calm down. He'd done his best to avoid her whenever possible these last three weeks, ever since they'd returned from their time with the Hesgyr. Ostensibly, he was working on his 'guilt issues.' And he was…trying. Trying to believe himself when he insisted he was not betraying Cosime's memory by moving on, by reaching for some small moments of happiness here and there.

His progress was spotty at best. And whenever he saw Nyx, his mind flooded with all too visceral memories. How her skin glistened with sweat, warm against his. How her breath felt on his neck and the rawness of her moan when he licked—

Fuck. This was why he stayed away.

But he couldn't always stay away, because while he was loath to call her his boss, his department—which was basically him, two part-time researchers, a couple of contractors he hired when a job required their services, and a collection of paid informants—fell under her supervision. And because in spite of his jumbled, warring, gut-churning 'guilt issues,' he didn't so much *want* to stay away. He'd managed to keep this traitorous attraction he felt for her under control for months, but everything had broken free on Nythir. And now he feared there was no going back, as the genie was not interested in climbing back inside this particular bottle.

He propped against the door frame and threw one ankle over the other. "This office is a fair bit bigger than the old one."

Nyx let go of the painting, leaving it hanging crookedly on the wall, and spun to him, then stared at him for a too-weighty beat before responding. "It's obscene. But Grandfather says appearances aid in creating authority, and his division heads must project copious authority. For millennia, *diati* granted me all the authority I required. I'm skeptical that the breadth and depth of my office will accomplish the same ends, but it was not worth the effort of resisting."

"When Corradeo wants something, he does tend to get it." Eren gestured to the painting. "You're decorating, though. That's new."

"I'm trying to take your advice about adding some character to the office. Also, such a great expanse of bare wall was mocking me."

She was actually taking his advice? She was *admitting* she was taking his advice? The possibility that things might genuinely be different between them since Nythir...shouldn't surprise him. More than one barrier had crumbled while they were there. "I like it. It's lovely, in a dark and forbidding sort of way."

"It's from an expanse of shore on Nereus. I did a mission there once for the Primor. The mission was bloody and unpleasant, but I enjoyed the scenery." She frowned at the painting, reached up and nudged a corner straight. "Have you moved your things over yet?"

"Have I moved what things from where to where?"

"Your office. Have you moved your furniture and whatever decor you'd placed over to your new space? Of course, if you want to order new furniture, Grandfather is spending freely this week, so I'll approve it."

"Why would I need an office?" He hooked a thumb toward the window-wall. "My work is out there."

"Because all department chiefs have …" she peered at him incredulously "…you've been doing this job for almost four years. Are you telling me you've never once been to your office?"

He spread his arms to shrug broadly. "Didn't know I had one."

"I'm quite certain I informed you of it when you started working for the Advocacy."

His cavalier demeanor deflated. "And I'm quite certain I didn't listen to much of what you had to say back then. Sorry."

"It's fine." She glanced at the painting then moved away, seemingly satisfied. "Shall I show you where your *new* office is, in the hope you'll deign to visit it every fortnight or so?"

"Please do. I can brief you while we walk."

"You won't have time. It's not far."

Oh, great. The question was, would this fact bring him to his alleged office more frequently, or less?

As she passed him in the doorway, her eyes flicked over to him and lingered. Deep, rich, sapphire laden with enough unanswered questions to fill a library server.

He sucked in a breath through his teeth as he followed her into the hallway and fell in beside her. Though the corridor was wide and airy, they walked shoulder to shoulder, metaphorical sparks holding them close like magnets. It had been a mistake to visit her; he wasn't ready to face up to whatever this was between them. Yet he couldn't bring himself to regret coming.

They passed the matching office of her brother, Director of Security Ziton Praesidis, then turned the corner to a stretch of more doors, which meant smaller offices. "Where's Lontias' office?"

"He said that consultants don't warrant palatial suites and claimed a free one at the end of this hall." She stopped at the second door and waved it open. "Here you are."

The space was as roomy as her old office had been, and also completely empty. He walked inside and turned in a slow circle. "And you're saying I have furniture somewhere over in the Executive Building?"

"You do. Third floor, east wing."

"Huh. I guess I'll send for it or something." He stuffed his hands in his pockets. "So, anyway, briefing. Last night, I confirmed Ihelahn Roshiive is seeking support from two grumpy *ela* Kyverns by the name of Deish and Procta Tesh."

"Another rebellion in the making?"

"There's always a rebellion in the making somewhere. Also, Basra elasson-Kyvern stopped by the table for a few minutes. It's not proof of criminal intent, but it is enough for suspicion."

"That ungrateful bitch. Grandfather returned her immortality to her. Is it too much to expect an iota of loyalty in exchange?" Nyx groaned and dropped her head against the wall. "So the ghosts of Ferdinand and his failed uprising continue to haunt us."

"For a while longer. But I've got a bead on them now. Let me give them enough rope to set the noose, then I'll move in."

"By yourself?"

The question held no hint of challenge, and he smiled wolfishly. "Play your cards right, and you can come along for the show."

She stared at him, blinking silently, and he hurriedly took up studying the plush carpet beneath his boots; it matched the flooring in her office. "But speaking of Ferdinand's rebellion and the withholding and granting of immortality, I heard something else last night. *Apomono* is back on the street."

"What?" She exploded off the wall. "Who would dare? Do you know where it's being manufactured? If so, I will blow it within the hour."

About the reaction he'd expected. "A new upstart group called Riamere. And I don't. Here's where I beg you to cool your engines for a few days and let me do some digging. This Riamere is supposedly led by a Human—which makes it my purview—and she is apparently a piece of work. If we wreck one of her production facilities, she'll know we're wise to her, except we're not, not yet. I want to learn what her story is before she has a chance to chameleon, disappear off our radar, and later reappear in a stronger position."

Nyx's eyes narrowed in doubtful contemplation.

"I know you don't care for it. Go ahead and have your agents try to ferret out where the *apomono* might be landing in buyers' hands. It's expected behavior and shouldn't raise any flags."

"You have two weeks to track her and her operation down."

He nodded in acceptance. "I'd better get to work then. Damn, I guess moving into my office will have to wait."

7

DOMOR

SMALL MAGELLANIC CLOUD

Olivia Montegreu absently snapped the fingers of her left hand as she reviewed a panorama of charts in her virtual vision. Her credits balance, spread across sixteen accounts housed in an equal number of bank companies situated on worlds controlled by four different species, had finally risen to a level where she was comfortable moving to a new phase of operations.

SENTRI had done a competent job of seizing the overwhelming majority of Enzio's assets in the aftermath of her son's murder. They hadn't located everything, however, and his most closely guarded accounts had provided her with enough funds to secure her privacy and safety during those initial months when she found herself on her own in an unfamiliar universe. Given twenty years to pick clean the bones of the Zelones cartel, SENTRI had done a far more thorough job of cleaning out the vast fortune she'd once controlled. But even there, they hadn't uncovered every resource, and neither had Enzio. So once she'd established herself here, she'd oh-so-carefully extracted the balances from the hidden accounts that remained, including the fruitful interest they'd earned in the intervening years since her death.

Then she had begun.

She temporarily faded away her charts and gazed out the window of her office. Domor was an average garden world and its capital city, Chasen, an average metropolitan region of average size and population. With no single Anaden dynasty dominant here, the architecture lacked any distinct personality or voice. The city's deportment was all a mite on the disheveled side, but this was an unavoidable side effect of the features that had led her to choose this location as her base of operations. New Babel had resided in a dour pea soup of nebular gases; she'd never chosen her command posts based on the quality of the local scenery.

Enzio had been laser-focused on human worlds and human wealth, all but oblivious to the menagerie of species they now found themselves cohabitating with. But she'd spent almost a year educating herself on the species Concord ruled, and she had come to see opportunities beyond her son's limited vision. She was human, yes—or rather, she'd once been *merely* human. But she'd always been willing to use every tool available to her in order to achieve her goals.

The truth was, human worlds were as overpoliced and regulated as they'd ever been, if not more so. AEGIS had added an additional layer of bureaucracy on top of the Earth Alliance, Senecan Federation and IDCC, which sat on top of the individual colony governments. It was so stifling, one could hardly breathe on half the planets without bumping into a government official or restrictive law.

Anaden worlds, on the other hand? They'd spent fourteen years after The Displacement either chaotically lawless or ruled by the capricious whims of the local *ela* with the most guns, akin to the old American West of the 1800s. Their latest attempt at a government, the Advocacy, was still in its infancy at three and a half years old, and Corradeo Praesidis insisted on ruling with an ultralight touch to make up for his ancient sins, never mind those of his son.

Olivia planned to return to human worlds one day, and once there she'd crush the pathetic excuses for criminal cartels that had popped up following the demise of Zelones, Triene and Shào. But logic and clinical analysis dictated that she build her empire from the shadows outward. So for the time being, Anaden worlds it was.

Helpful of Concord, to mandate how all Concord species had the right to live and work on any member species' world. She still caught the occasional suspicious glare from business contacts, but less so every day, as multiculturalism crept inexorably into this staid, calcified society.

And Domor? It had a crime problem, so much so that a few years ago, a self-styled vigilante had roamed the streets taking justice into his own hands. But eventually he'd given up, much as everyone else had to date. One day, many years from now, assuming it survived its current growing pains, the Advocacy's reconstituted Vigil law enforcement arm might arrive and attempt to clean the streets up. By the time this happened, however, she intended to control the black market on hundreds of worlds in dozens of galaxies, and they were welcome to Domor.

Also, the Anaden attitude toward illicit drugs was simply delightful. Six hundred thousand years of brutal repression by the Directorate had sparked a plethora of escapes for a miserable, desperate populace. And such creativity in them, too. She had far bigger plans than drugs, but drugs had made for a lucrative starting point.

> *Share of hypnol markets as of yesterday:*
> - *Domor: 28%*
> - *Ficenti: 34%*
> - *Lethe: 37%*
> - *Scholite: 18%*
> - *Brizo: 16%*
> - *Ares: 7%*

Ficenti and Lethe were barely governed backwater planets hardly worth her time, but they'd also been easy to move into and displace the local gangs. They'd been good early exercises, where she'd learned much about the Anaden way of doing things. She'd begun to dip her toe into Ares, despite the fact it was a far more thorny and well-policed market. She didn't want to attract the attention of the Advocacy too soon. But contacts she'd made on Scholite and Brizo had presented opportunities there, so a few months ago, she'd taken the first steps.

Now, though, she was bumping up against established interests on Domor, Scholite and Brizo. Black market power players who'd ruled the hypnol trade for millennia. The Quilon cartel was the largest organization by far, and an inefficient and risky target from her current vantage. Nikto, their next closest competitor, however, lay nicely in her crosshairs.

She'd taken out entrenched cartels before; she could do it again. But while she now enjoyed a robust network of lackeys and distributors, she'd kept her formal operation lean thus far. She paid less than two dozen employees. She didn't need an extensive organization in order to take out Nikto, though. She didn't even need a militia.

What she needed was a hit squad. One that brokered no misunderstandings and sent a message readable from neighboring galaxies.

S&L

MSHAK
LEO I GALAXY

Thick rivulets of blood carved streams through the dirt arena floor. Three bodies slumped against the curving wall, where they'd been dragged after losing their matches.

In the center of the arena, two Ch'mshak battled with double-hooked blades attached to short spears. The taller of the combatants—fully four meters in height—rapidly switched his spear from the left hand to the right and back again. He lunged forward as he braced the spear with the second hand and swung it—no, he halted the movement as soon as the shorter Ch'mshak dodged, pivoting to throw his momentum behind the sweep of the spear into an upward arc.

The leading blade sliced into the shoulder of the defender, and blood sprayed as it cleaved the arm off to roll across the arena floor. The maimed combatant howled in anger and pain...and the match continued, for all matches were to the death.

The system wasn't entirely without sense, though. Once a warrior had won three consecutive matches, it was exempt from further arena fighting, becoming an honored warrior in the clan's army. Army for what? For now, battling other clans across the continent.

Behind the arena, a town suitable to support ten thousand or so inhabitants decorated rolling hills. The buildings were constructed of clay bricks, presumably because the material was easier to rebuild with after the structures were destroyed in a raid by a rival clan, seeing as the Ch'mshak were plenty facile in working with metals. They wore elaborate armor crafted from steel alloy over their thick hides when going into battle, or sometimes when strutting down the streets.

The aliens were far more intelligent than the Directorate had ever given them credit for. But what they unquestionably lacked was the wisdom that typically came from intelligence coupled with experience. Or perhaps they'd weighed the wisdom of cultivating a peaceful society and found it wanting in favor of the adrenaline rush of brutality. Perhaps, in full recognition of the consequences, they enjoyed fighting and killing too much to ever give it up.

Thanks to their impressive birth rates, they hadn't died out after Concord quarantined their planet. In some respects, they'd thrived, training and fighting and building and razing and building again, as if preparing for their chance to one day pillage across space once more. They were centuries away from achieving their own space flight, and if they didn't change their ways they never would, but they knew how to survive on their native world.

The arm-deficient combatant succumbed to his mounting injuries, landing face first in the bloodied dirt with a resounding *thud*. Arena workers rushed in to drag the body away, and the victor, though bleeding profusely himself, circled the arena in a ritual celebration.

Olivia withdrew from sidespace and checked the settings on her prototype shield. If she were mauled to death, the consequences would not be catastrophic, but it would foreclose this specific avenue of opportunity.

Satisfied the shield was capable of providing her the protection she needed, she opened a wormhole to the arena floor and stepped through.

Growls erupted from the stands, and the victor spun around in confusion. On spotting her standing there, a slight, unarmored and apparently unarmed human, he let out a bellow and charged.

When he was ten meters away, she flicked her wrist, and a bolt of gamma wave energy shot out from her bracer to gut him from crotch to navel. But he had a good head of momentum going, so she stepped aside to allow him to collapse a meter past where she had stood. She regretted killing one of their skilled warriors, but it was important to make a memorable first impression.

The entire stable of on-deck competitors emptied from the bullpen, and she let out a shout. "I wouldn't!"

But they couldn't hear her over the roar of the crowd, and wouldn't have stopped had they been able to consider her warning.

She pulsed her shield outward to a span of three meters around her, then watched as her attackers slammed into it and bounced off. Shock slowed some of them down, but others renewed their efforts, slashing with their monstrous talons and pressing forward with broad shoulders and massive heads. All to no avail.

The Anadens had developed a most formidable shield to protect their Imperium warships. In reverse engineering it, humans had made significant improvements on the design, so she'd appropriated a downsized model of the AEGIS version to use as a personal device. Nothing was getting through the shield.

"I can stand here until you all collapse from exhaustion, which I concede will likely take a while. Or you can recognize the futility of your actions and allow me to speak."

Three of the combatants continued, undeterred, but four more spat and hissed while taking a step back.

"Good enough." She used a mic dot at her throat to project her voice over the noise of the crowd. "Who here leads these mighty warriors?"

"I do!" came a rough shout from the front row, to her left. "How dare you invade our sanctified arena, Anaden!"

"I do dare. See, I have a proposition for you, clan chief."

"I will tear you limb from limb myself!"

You will not. "You can try if you wish. Or you can hear how I will return your people to the stars, so you can exact a worthy revenge for your exile."

The chieftain had left his seat to step onto the arena floor, but now he stopped. "You cannot do such a thing."

"I can do anything I wish. And I wish this. I will require something in exchange, but I suspect you will not find the trade to be an onerous burden. Now, shall we retire to your office?"

S&L

The clan chieftain's 'office' looked exactly as one might expect, with bleached skulls and tusks lining a shelf that encircled the room and ornate weapons hung as art on the walls. The desk was of surprising quality, however, stretching for a full three meters and carved of thick marble atop coated stone.

No chairs decorated the space—presumably a sign of weakness—so Olivia stopped in the center of the room. She kept her arms loose at her sides, ready to counter any attack. Her shield was rated to withstand ten thousand newtons of force, but the desk, suitably thrown, may well deliver a greater amount.

"What is meaning of your insolence, Anaden?"

"I'm not Anaden. Of course, I'm not really human, either, not any longer. You will call me Ms. Montegreu. And what shall I call you?"

"Argh. I am Varlem Bakker T'worz, chieftain of the T'worz Clan."

"A fine city you have here, Varlem, with fine warriors."

"Not fine—the best. We vanquished six clans in last rotation. None are strong enough to challenge us."

"That is why I am here instead of one of the other clan settlements."

"You say you can take us to the stars, but I see no ship. Only magic."

"In time, in time. My offer is as follows. I require fearsome warriors to dispose of my enemies, and I am not interested in half measures. I want you to lend me a team of four to twelve such fighters, depending on the mission, whenever I want them. I will transport them from here to their target using my…magic, as you say. Once there, their mission will be to kill everyone within a defined area and, *if so instructed*, destroy any fixtures in that same area, then return here. If any of them run off to cause further havoc across a larger region, there will be no more missions for anyone."

"Why should we entertain such easy tasks for you?"

"To sate your bloodlust?"

"Twenty-two clans wait for conquering on this continent alone. We do not lack for sating. You promised the stars."

"For each mission your warriors complete to my satisfaction, I will provide you with one stealth-equipped ship able to carry ten Ch'mshak off this planet and safely through the blockade. From there, they can do as they wish. They can drop the occupants off on a planet and return to pick up additional people, or they can disappear into the stars to pillage to their dual hearts' content. I don't care."

Even with around-the-clock transports, it would take them decades to get a measurable number of Ch'mshak off the planet using the small ships she intended to provide. And it was an open question whether individual Ch'mshak, when granted their freedom, possessed the discipline needed to return home to ferry more passengers. Regardless, she didn't intend to let it go so far. This was a short-term arrangement. She needed a bit of shock and awe to strike fear in her adversaries and competitors. Once instilled, the threat should be enough to get her what she needed. In the meantime, she was recruiting Anaden assassins and their ilk for when more finesse was called for.

And if the brutes' numbers did rise high enough to start to cause trouble she didn't control, no matter. Concord space could use with a little chaos. Chaos was good for business.

Varlem grunted. "We have few pilots among our number. Once our ships were destroyed, pilots no longer provided a benefit to clan."

The Ch'mshak had never 'had' ships of their own. Rather, they'd stolen ships from the other species, and the Directorate had elected to allow the thievery. When they'd rebelled eleven years ago, Concord had demolished every space-rated ship it found in Ch'mshak hands.

"It won't be a problem. These ships will be equipped with VIs capable of piloting the craft and taking instructions from the crew."

"Magic machines?"

"Yes."

"And the ships orbiting overhead will not see them?"

Olivia shook her head. "They will not see them. No one will see them, until the crew wishes for them to be seen."

"We need larger ships. Room for fifty."

"No. And I do suggest you not attempt to negotiate any further. I will leave, and I will not return to make this offer again."

"Why make it now, not-Anaden-nor-Human Ms. Montegreu?"

"I told you. I need enemies disposed of, and I don't wish to play games in doing so."

8

CONCORD HQ

Marlee grabbed Resamane Ozeal up in a big hug and squeezed so hard the Belascocian woman gasped a little 'unfph.' A heady sensation of warmth, of safety and love, swept through Marlee, and for a moment she was convinced she never wanted to be parted from the woman's presence.

All Belascocians exuded a pheromone-fueled aura, and it allowed family and close friends to enjoy a tight emotional connection. The genetic alteration that created the desbida, of which Resamane was one, supercharged the effect into the realm of mind reading while extending it to strangers and, it turned out, aliens.

With great reluctance, Marlee activated a cybernetics routine to insulate her from the intoxicating influence of the desbida's presence, then freed the woman from her embrace. "Sorry! It's just great to see you."

"Oh, you as well, my friend." Resamane looked amazing in a flowing robe of emerald woven through with pewter fibers. Her lamina-covered skin was the color of dusted orchids, and her hair threads wound together to form icy silver tips. But as always, her most arresting feature was her teardrop-shaped kaleidoscope eyes, a gift from the genetic mutation.

Still, it was the sight of Resamane's twin brother, Galean, that sent Marlee's stomach fluttering when she turned to greet him with a quick and definitely platonic hug. "And you, Galean. You both look so good. How are things back home?"

Galean's sentsores spread out in two fan shapes around his lips as he stepped away; hopefully she hadn't made him too uncomfortable with the brief physical contact. The last time she'd seen him, they'd parted with a passionate kiss, but she'd also looked like a Belascocian when they did. "They are settling down for now. Resa and I have an apartment in Ausatan, which she's decorated exquisitely. The reintroduction of the desbida into society is…progressing."

Resamane laid a hand on her brother's shoulder. "It's difficult for everyone. People were lied to and families deceived. Desbida were imprisoned and poisoned. There will need to be a lot of forgiveness on all sides—"

"And accountability," Galean interrupted.

"And that, yes. As for us, though? We've visited our family twice now."

"Oh?" Twice had to be positive news, didn't it? "How did it go?"

"Favorably." Resamane's expression clouded. "Which is to say, complicated. It will be slow progress, but I feel healing has begun."

Galean didn't correct her this time, so it must be at least somewhat true. Belascocian families were both large and extremely close as a rule, but the twins had been estranged from theirs for a number of years. "I'm glad to hear it."

He nodded vaguely as his gaze fixated on her chest—no, not in that way. "You're wearing our necklace."

Before she'd left Belarria, Resamane had gifted her a family necklace bearing the interlocking circles and starburst symbol of the Ozeal odola. According to Resamane, the gift was meant to signify the enduring bond among the three of them. At the time, it had been easy to believe in the strength of their bond, but here, under the harsh artificial lights of HQ, it all felt so far away. Like another life.

Her hand fluttered to her throat to touch the beaded indigo glass. "I wear it every day."

"This makes me happy." Resamane reached out to squeeze her hands. "Now, about this station!" Marlee knew the enthusiasm was genuine from the tickles of excitement in her mind. "This is so amazing. You truly work here?"

"I do. Come with me, and I'll show you around."

Marlee forwent the formal diplomatic tour in favor of taking them to all the cool places on HQ. Galean and Resamane were here as her friends, not as representatives of the Belascocians. After tense negotiations had almost led to war (over her), the official diplomatic meetings were being held at a far higher level than her somewhat junior position.

Resamane's gaze darted every which way as they walked through the high-end retail market. "So many aliens! And of so many different shapes and sizes! Who are they all?"

"The furry ones over there are Barisans, and...." An idea came to her then, one that should serve dual purposes. "How long can you two stay?"

Galean shrugged. "We have several hours free before we need to return home."

"Terrific. I want to take you somewhere."

ROMANE

MILKY WAY GALAXY

It was a gorgeous, double-sunny day in Romane's capital city, and the water fountain in the plaza sparkled as it threw prismatic fireworks into the air. Children squealed in delight as they ran to and fro in the water spray while their parents lounged on park benches nearby. Pedestrians munched on treats from the food stalls, and visitors exited the Expo lugging bags full of souvenirs.

"This is positively delightful," Resamane declared. "Where are we?"

"We're on Romane, one of humanity's most beautiful and cosmopolitan worlds," Marlee replied. "This is the Confluence Expo, a celebration of the many species of Concord, and it's owned and run by one of my good friends. The exhibits inside can tell you more about the species you saw on Concord HQ in an hour than I can in a week."

Galean offered her an enigmatic smile and gestured to the entrance. "We're eager to begin our education. Lead on."

Marlee couldn't decide if he was screwing with her or was genuinely glad to see her, but she was relieved to find him of an amiable disposition. They'd left things emotionally fraught when they'd parted, but she hoped they could be close friends, if with a side of attraction that was never going to amount to anything.

She had alerted Mia to their impending arrival, and the woman met them in the lobby. She looked as stunning as ever in a charcoal fitted wraparound dress adorned with a shimmering jade scarf. For Mia, elegant fashion came as natural as breathing.

"You must be Galean and Resamane Ozeal," Mia said while offering the traditional Belascocian greeting of strangers. Marlee might have shared the *technically* classified Consulate file on the Belascocians with her. "I'm Mia Requelme. Welcome to the Confluence Expo."

"It is wonderful to be here," Resamane replied.

You weren't exaggerating about the pheromones. What a powerful effect.

I never exaggerate, Mia. You know this.

Mia shot her an amused glance, but kept her attention on their guests. "Thank you for taking care of Marlee while she was in your company. She's very precious to us."

"I understand why," Galean remarked. "She insisted on risking her life for our people and for us personally, and we are deeply grateful."

"She does like to do such things. So, I understand you're curious about the varied species of Concord?"

"We are," Resamane said. "Marlee showed us around Concord's space station, and I was overwhelmed by the diversity of life there."

"We were new here, too, not so long ago, and I agree. It is overwhelming." Mia motioned a young Naraida woman over. "This is Avalei Sheilen. She's our best tour guide, and I'm assigning her to be at your beck and call for the next hour. Avalei, treat these two as our most honored guests." Marlee could only assume that Mia had planned everything out and shared the Scocian translation program with Avalei ahead of time.

"Of course, Ms. Requelme." Avalei beamed at the Belascocians. "Follow me. I'm biased, so let's start with the Naraida."

Marlee reached out and touched Resamane's hand. "We'll get something to eat when you're done, and then I'll see you safely home. Have fun."

S&L

Marlee collapsed in the chair opposite Mia's desk and flung her head back. "Help."

Mia laughed as she took up residence in the other chair, rather than behind her desk. "With the Belascocians? They seem lovely."

"Oh, Galean and Resamane are. We're friends. It's everyone and everything else going on at the Consulate."

Mia leaned forward to rest her forearms on her knees. "Talk to me."

"Well, let's see. We almost went to war with the Belascocians because of me—oops. So Dean Veshnael took the assignment away from me, which is probably for the best. I'm getting better at putting my personal feelings aside in favor of the needs of the job, but I'm not sure how well I'd do at playing nice with people who spent weeks trying to kill me and my friends.

"This also freed up more time for me to focus on the Ourankeli, who are being insufferable about the construction of their habitat at Steropes."

Mia frowned. "I thought it was nearly complete?"

"So did I. But you know the Ourankeli. Only the best for them and their gelatinous, limb shifting, eye spinning selves. So it's not nearly complete after all. But this, too, is fine. I'm used to their eccentricities. But now I also have the Elakri to manage. Caleb brought the Elakri ambassador, Arien Colonnei, to meet me the other day. Only he's not an ambassador, he's a priest. Only he's not really a priest either, but instead a police detective."

"What?"

"Exactly. Nice man, though. He expressed many frustrations, but I don't think they were directed at me. Because boy, does he have a mess on his hands. The Elakri believed they were the sole sapient beings in the universe and the apple of their god's eye. Except in reality they were living in a literal bubble, and their god is a machine. Surprise!"

"Hmm," Mia mused. "Is this so different from what more primitive species experience? Most every species we've met believed themselves to be the center of the universe at some point in their history."

"True, but they knew there *was* a universe. Long before they met aliens, they understood there were other stars with other planets, and they speculated about what manner of life those planets might hold. Not the Elakri. Caleb says they're fairly arrogant about it, and Arien pretty much agreed. He needs help easing his people into the truth, but I don't have a good sense of how to do it."

"How are the Elakri dealing with the revelation that their god is a machine?"

"I don't think anyone's told them that detail yet. Nor how the leaders of their religious order knew it was a machine from the beginning."

"Oh." Mia thought on it. "It sounds as if we have an order of operation problem here. They know about us, though?"

"They know intelligent aliens exist, but their government hasn't shared the details on Concord."

"Okay. As a rule, there's not much harm in allowing local myths to persist after contact with aliens. They can provide a source of comfort amidst frightening change. But this seems to be more about corruption and manipulation than it is religious beliefs. I can understand this ambassador-detective's desire for caution, as no one wants to trigger a violent societal upheaval. But if it were me advising him, I would suggest a gentle sharing of the truth as soon as possible. Don't cover up a cover up with a cover up."

"Perfectly expressed." Marlee chuckled. "Can I quote you on that?"

"Please don't. Regardless, he's not seeking my advice—he's seeking yours. Advise whatever you think is best to help him and his people."

"Sure. Nothing to it. Next, there's the Hesgyr. They know about the intergalactic community, including Concord. They just don't care. They use wormholes and all sorts of advanced technology, but they have zero interest in talking to us. And this is before we get to the rampant thievery."

"That sounds like a problem for Miriam."

Marlee winced. "Aunt Miriam is a little occupied with the fact that Alex says the Dzhvar have returned. And, granted, a slightly bigger problem. The good news, I guess, is that the Hesgyr don't seem to have any interest in initiating hostilities with us. Merely stealing from us. Eren says they promised not to do so any longer, but he doesn't believe them, so I don't believe them, either."

"You certainly have your hands full these days."

"Oh, I'm not done. We've also been introduced to the Phae'soon—the aliens who were attacking the Hesgyr. They're in worse shape than the Godjans were when we met them, but they're also fiercely proud and carrying around a planet-sized chip on their shoulders. Though I think I've got a solid bead on them. They need help badly, and help, I can do."

"Yes. You proved it with the Godjans."

"Thanks." Marlee beamed beneath the praise. "And the Consulate's assistance program is fairly robust now. Robust enough to add a new initiative for the Phae'soon."

"In no small part due to your efforts these last several years. So did anyone *else* land in your lap?"

"Not so far. The week's not over, though."

Mia leaned back in her chair and crossed her legs. "It sounds like you have everything perfectly well in hand. You don't need my help."

"Are you kidding me? I'm making this all up as I go, and Dean Veshnael is trusting me with tremendous responsibility—the fate of entire species—and I've never done half of this before."

"I'd never done any of this before when we first came to Amaranthe. Everything that the Consulate is, I made up as I went. Marlee, you have excellent instincts. Trust them."

"I'll try..." she fidgeted in the chair "...but I still get to vent to you, don't I?"

"Absolutely. Any time. And I'll offer my suggestions until you get sick of hearing them, pat me on the head and tell me to go back to running my Expo, as you've got it covered."

"Never going to happen." Marlee started to say something else, then hesitated.

It's okay for you to ask. She's not your boss any longer. She's your friend.

Somewhere over the course of the last few years, the Voice had stopped being her personal antagonist and morphed into being her confidant and wise counsel. Yes, she recognized the objective arrogance of calling her own subconscious 'wise counsel,' but it was what it was.

"Do you miss it?" Marlee asked.

"The Consulate? Diplomacy?" Mia sighed. "I miss being in the room."

"What room?"

"The one where the decisions get made. Decisions designed to keep us all alive and thriving."

"Oh. They don't let me in that room yet."

"Give it time. They will."

9

ELAKRIN STELLAR SYSTEM

Alex's consciousness hovered above the manifold abrasion. The system's star shone blindingly at her back, though it wouldn't literally blind her were she to turn toward it, since she wasn't physically here. Too distant and tiny for her to see was Elakrin, whose citizens struggled to keep their society sewn together after learning they were one of millions of sentient species and dozens of advanced civilizations.

When she'd last visited the area, she hadn't been able to spend much time studying this unsettling scar in space. She and Kennedy had spelunked the Piega Strai for an important reason—so Kennedy could learn how to build one if required—and her friend had needed her help in seeing the work through. But now, it was just her here.

And me.

She smiled in her mind. *And you, Valkyrie. Thanks for coming. I'm not imagining this, correct? This scar is functionally identical to the one in the Erebus Void that leads to Rasu Prime?*

I cannot discern any scientifically definable features of the anomaly. But my senses also tell me it is the same.

It's not a natural artifact of Dzhvar damage. I've already toured several locations where they wreaked havoc in the first war to inspect the after-effects. The fabric of space where the Dzhvar passed through is...stretched thin. Fragile, like muslin, almost as if a subtle form of vacuum decay is occurring there.

Vacuum decay means the end of the universe...oh. Which is of course the point.

Alex metaphorically shrugged. *Yeah. For the time being, the robust structure of the manifold is stable and can contain the effect to localized regions. At some point, though, if the decay becomes rampant enough, it won't be able to do so. We have to assume this is exactly what happened in the previous cycles. But it's not why we're here today. This scar is evidence of something else.*

I believe our working theory is that the abrasion at Rasu Prime was created when the Dzhvar were expelled from the manifold, yes?

Yes. Despite the fact the final battle of the war didn't take place there. Dimensions, and thus physical distance, don't matter to the Dzhvar. So if that is what happened at Rasu Prime, then this scar must signify where the Dzhvar reentered Amaranthe when I shut down the Piega Strai.

It's a reasonable conclusion to draw based upon the evidence at hand.

She appreciated Valkyrie not spouting any platitudes about how 'it wasn't her fault.' She'd done what she'd done, and however justified her actions were, there were consequences.

Okay, so why? Why here? Why now? The Dzhvar are pandimensional, but for the last million years, they've stayed out of tangible space. Were they sleeping? Did shutting down the Piega Strai wake them up? Or the first shockwave to reverberate when I started opening up the tether? Because that's when they appeared. But what does 'sleeping' mean for noncorporeal, primordial entities? Have you had a chance to review the files from the Khesa Prutet on the Piega Strai's construction and operation? Is there some structural feature of the brane it creates that might prove capable of...I don't know, freeing the Dzhvar from a dimensional cage somehow?

Alex, that is a lot of questions. Any preference as to which one I respond to first?

Ah, hell. Just open your mind and let me see what you think.

Happy to do so.

A universe *outside* the universe? On closer examination of the scientific notes, the Piega Strai wasn't akin to a Rift Bubble at all; it was much more similar to the portal universes the Kats had created in the Mosaic. *It's time for us to quiz Mesme on the technical details of how they engineered those spaces.*

Agreed.

She continued perusing Valkyrie's neatly organized thoughts. The Elakri's 'universe' contained all the same quantum dimensions as Amaranthe, because they'd been scooped into the bubble when it formed. But until the tears in the barrier began forming, those dimensions were wholly separate and unconnected to Amaranthe. Potentially useful information, but since the Dzhvar disappeared long before the bubble was created, this did nothing to point to why the bubble's dissolution would've set the Dzhvar loose.

Oh. Interesting idea. *You think the force of the Dzhvar's expulsion a million years ago might have rendered them somehow…inert?*

It implies a more passive state than 'sleeping,' which may explain why they've remained absent for so long.

True. Dammit, though, if all it took to rouse them was a little cosmic shockwave, The Displacement would have done so twenty years ago with far greater fervor. Unless the Dzhvar happened to be located nearby on some dimensional level when the Piega Strai shut down, and it was a matter of actual proximity. But why would they have been 'nearby' in the first place? The odds of this happening randomly were vanishingly low.

In lieu of following her and Valkyrie's thoughts around for another frustrating loop, Alex reached out and touched the scar with her mind. It felt rough, ragged, palpably coarse.

Hey, was 'scar' the correct term, or did 'scab' make for a better analogy? A scab formed to protect a wound until it healed; if the wound was severe enough, even after it healed, a scar remained to forever mark the spot. At a million years old, the abrasion at Rasu Prime was definitely a scar, but this one?

Picking at a scab would reveal the fresh wound beneath.…

She pushed her perception against the lesion, until the ridges rose into mountain peaks that plummeted into a yawning chasm of infinite blackness.

No, not infinite. Deep in the chasm, so deep she could no longer make out the place from where she'd begun her descent, a faint rivulet of light carved yet deeper, straight through the manifold and out—

Alex!

She jerked into awareness so violently her eyes opened back in her living room on Akeso. "What?"

Valkyrie's virtual avatar, complete with long blonde braided hair and Nordic-inspired attire, manifested to kneel in front of her on the couch. "You were…gone."

"Gone? What do you mean?"

"I mean your consciousness was not present. Not in your body, not in space in the vicinity of Elakrin. Not in my mind. Not anywhere."

Her brow furrowed. "For how long?"

"Twenty-three microseconds. What did you perceive?"

"I'm not sure twenty-three microseconds is long enough to perceive much of anything."

Valkyrie glared at her.

"I really didn't. I was studying one of the crevasses of the scar—scab, whichever—and then you were yelling at me." Was this true, though? She didn't recall anything concrete, but there had been a…sensation.

She closed her eyes. A great darkness had forever been giving way to a light on the horizon she couldn't quite reach. Then there was a flash in her mind. Every aspect of her senses distorted, flipped askew—and snapped. Into what?

"See, you did experience something."

Alex opened her eyes and shrugged. "Dizziness, probably. I'd honed my consciousness into a picometer-width stick and was poking the core fabric of the spacetime manifold with it. I don't know what else I expected to happen."

Valkyrie studied her suspiciously for another few seconds before standing. "Perhaps. Do you feel like we learned something new from this excursion?"

"That depends. I'm going to go talk to Nika."

MIRAI

*ASTERION DOMINION
GENNISI GALAXY*

Nika Kirumase reached out and touched Dashiel with her mind. A caress, of sorts.

He sensed her, naturally, and returned the gesture, leaving behind the overwhelming impression of a tender smile in her thoughts. She reluctantly withdrew to let him to continue his work on refining the extraction of kyoseil fibers from their Reor armor. The more efficient the process was, the more they could extract at a lower cost. And today, they needed greater amounts of it than ever.

She continued her tour. Perrin was busily directing furniture delivery at the newest refugee center on the outskirts of Kiyora Two. The massive expansion of such centers had been one of the largest Administration Division projects of the last three years. They didn't know where the Dzhvar would strike, but when it finally happened, their goal was to have enough time to effect large-scale evacuations of the location affected. When the Rasu had attacked their worlds, everything had devolved into a chaotic state of emergency. They'd done the best they could under the circumstances to prioritize rescue efforts, but the situation had never approached ideal. Given room to prepare, they hoped to draw closer to ideal this time around.

Perrin didn't sense her presence, and Nika flitted away before her friend noticed an intrusive tickle in her mind. She visited Maris next, who was meeting with an Anaden museum director on Asterion Prime. Maris had re-adopted their ancestral home with considerable gusto. She maintained an apartment there, and likely spent more nights on Asterion Prime than she did on Mirai. When she wasn't on Ares, that was.

Nika did her best to squelch any uncharitable thoughts about Maris' deepening relationship with Corradeo Praesidis. She accepted how he was a changed man, and the two displayed a natural connection. Most importantly, he made Maris happy. So she tried to forgive him for the copious sins he'd committed in the SAI Rebellion, though she couldn't completely forget.

Ironic, considering she only recalled a single fateful memory from those desperate days—the memory of when they fled the Milky Way rather than perish. But she had her journals, and they told the tragic tale in vivid detail.

Nika wished she were able to appreciate Asterion Prime the way Maris and many of the other First Genners did, but she retained no memories of the place and had written few journals that focused on it. Intellectually, she comprehended the tremendous significance of their homeworld, of the symbolism it carried as the birthplace of their rebellion. But to her, it was merely another Anaden world.

She checked in on Joaquim next—then hurriedly backed away from what was clearly a private moment with Selene. Taking this as a sign that she should stop snooping on her friends, she returned her focus to her body, situated as it was on the balcony of her flat, and opened her eyes to sip on her *shoka espe* in the morning light.

She continued to maintain a barrier between her mind and the constant onslaught of kyoseil-carried thoughts from hundreds of millions of Asterions, but it was an effortless, unconscious process these days. In an added benefit, she was able to reach through the mental barrier and access specific threads with intentionality, as she'd just done.

While the process was superficially similar to traveling in sidespace, the effect was very different. She hadn't viewed those she'd visited from the outside, but from inside their own minds. Her intent wasn't to be nosy, though she did take great comfort from checking in to make sure those dearest to her were healthy and happy.

No, this was an exercise designed to strengthen both the barrier and her fine control of where and how she directed her intentionality. Both muscles needed regular practice to remain strong and reliable. During the Rasu War, she'd lost her sense of self while immersed in the kyoseil too often, when she'd needed to be focused, directed and in control to defend her people from the invasion. Next time, she'd be better prepared.

The exercise also served to limber her mind up and settle her into the cosmic kyoseil web, akin to a warm-up stretch. "Okay. I'm ready to begin now."

Very well, Mesme murmured from beside her on the balcony. *Open your mind fully to the web.*

She did so, and her vision transformed.

Kyoseil wove its way through the entirety of the universe. Most of this activity was in the form of the waves traveling between the tangible, inorganic material they also called 'kyoseil.' She and Dashiel had spent a fair bit of time investigating and debating whether both states were truly the same entity, and the answer seemed to be 'probably.' Most matter could exist in a variety of states—solid, liquid, gas, plasma, plus some exotic variations—depending on conditions. Why should kyoseil be any different? Lots of reasons, obviously, but definitive answers remained out of reach.

The kyoseil wave forms acted as conduits for information when there was information to be stored; when there was not, the waves flowed nonetheless, weaving together a mesh across the manifold. It was sparse in places and tended to cluster where sentient beings thrived, even when those beings didn't use kyoseil or know of its existence.

"Mesme, do you think the kyoseil is drawn to intelligence? To thought? To life?"

The evidence suggests the answer, does it not?

"It does. But you've never learned why this would be the case?"

I have not. As you realize, kyoseil holds its secrets close.

"Too true." She probed the web for signs the Dzhvar had impacted it anywhere, as the prevailing consensus was that whatever else they were or were not, the Dzhvar were 'alive' in some manner. She didn't detect anything, but she wasn't at all certain she was searching correctly, either. Until she witnessed a Dzhvar perturbation in action, she might not know how to recognize it.

Cast your mind into one of the wave filaments. Can you become a part of it?

"Be 'a part of it'? I can follow where it goes."

No. Try to connect the kyoseil residing within you to this filament until you become one with it.

"As if the filament is a Plex instance of myself?"

If such a characterization aids you.

She hadn't especially enjoyed her forays as a Plex—of her mind existing simultaneously in multiple physical copies of her body— but it struck her as a relevant comparison, since kyoseil was the key to making plexing possible.

Her thoughts drifted to her experience in the Oneiroi Nebula, when the vast kyoseil/Reor colony there had claimed her for its own, and in doing so, opened her mind to an entirely new percep- tion of the universe. It had transformed her, in ways she was still working to understand. While at the mercy of the colony's de- signs, she had *been* a conduit for the information stored there. She had, for all intents and purposes, *been* the kyoseil waves—

Abruptly she was flowing in both directions simultaneously. Branching and merging and existing everywhere at once.

"Oh my…."

Yes?

"It doesn't 'flow' at all! It simply *is*. And not in the way that quantum entangled particles behave. This is so much more expansive."

Indeed.

Unnerved, she opened her eyes and found herself enveloped in a glow that didn't belong to her. "Mesme?"

You are safe. You have become the wave.

"Right." She swallowed and closed her eyes again. "What should I do?"

Explore your new environment.

But her 'new environment' was everywhere, which she supposed was the point. She had no real sense of 'where' anything was. There were stars and planets and so much vast empty space, and there was no reference point for any of it. She grew dizzy, but she didn't want to give up when she'd just unlocked this ability, so she breathed air into her body's lungs and calmed her mind. Instead of focusing on *where* she was, she tried to understand *what* she was. A conduit, yes. A vessel, a storage mechanism, a protective sheath, a—

A flash in her mind burst outward in an explosive force. The web overwhelmed her and entwined her and filled her to the brim with a staggering impression of time and space and *life*. She stretched, and the universe stretched with her, all the way to the far bounds of existence.

She gasped in air and lurched to her feet, only to sway dizzily into the balcony railing. Below her, people hurried along the sidewalks, living their lives with zeal and purpose. Their bodies gleamed from kyoseil that radiated information. Intelligence. The essence of the Asterion triumvirate: organic, synthetic, and kyoseil.

But this had been something else. Something older and more profound.

She spun around to find Mesme against the glass. "The kyoseil waves aren't actually empty?"

No, they are not.

"I'm not referring to the information flow we're aware of, and at times control. But all the waves I believed to be empty, aren't. I felt a sense of something rich and deep and…." An aching sorrow swelled in her chest until she felt as if she was on the verge of splitting apart from the effort to contain it.

"Mesme, what did I sense?"

Something unknowable.

She groaned, and the spell her discovery gripped her in broke, leaving behind a nauseating vertigo. "For once, can you not be enigmatic? I realize these explorations are intended to be lessons, but if you know anything about what I experienced, please tell me."

She sensed more than saw Mesme's lights join her at the railing, washed out as they were by the climbing sun. *But I do not know. In a million years, I have never known. I can only speculate that this is yet another facet of the nature of kyoseil as a primordial being of the universe. To know it would be to know the universe itself, and I fear this is beyond even such beings as us.*

She smiled haltingly as the vertigo subsided. "It's sweet of you to include me, but I'm not like you. For one, I can't transform into particles of light and flit about the universe on a whim."

You are closer to doing so than you think.

"What do you mean?"

How do you think I 'flit about,' as you put it?

"I've never considered…." She trailed off as her focus returned to what it had felt like to *be* everywhere at once. "Are you saying you travel on those kyoseil waves?"

Did you not feel their pull? As if with a single directed thought, your feet could buoy off this balcony and alight wherever your mind wanted to go?

"I'm not…maybe?" She frowned. "The waves are fairly systemic, but they aren't everywhere. What happens if they don't travel somewhere you need to be?"

Mesme did not immediately respond.

"Mesme?"

That is for a later lesson.

So it had revealed more than it intended, but also succeeded in deflecting from her initial inquiry. Annoyance flared; Mesme's cryptic routine tended to assert itself precisely when she most wanted answers.

But the Kat had helped her in incalculable ways over the years, so she let it go for now. "All right. So are you saying *I* can travel on kyoseil waves? Physically, I mean? Not that I need to, as I can wormhole anywhere I want to go. But if I did need to?"

Perhaps in time, but you will require far greater control over both kyoseil and other cosmic elements in order to do so. Accordingly, I would not advise you to make the attempt. It is a precarious affair, and you might well find yourself on the sidewalk far below you, or stranded in deep space with no air.

"Duly noted." A ping arrived from Alex then, saving Mesme from further grilling.

10

AKESO

*H*ey, are you busy? I want to run something by you.
I'm merely talking metaphysics with Mesme. Why
don't you come over?

Alex hesitated. She did pretty well being around Nika these days. It had proved difficult at first, but in time she'd learned to put out of her mind the fact that Nika was Mesme, or rather Mesme was formerly Nika in the last cycle, and also Nika's future if they didn't find a way to defeat the Dzhvar. Granted, not exactly put it out of her mind. More forced it into the background, where it mostly stayed so long as she focused on Nika as an individual. As her friend above all.

But she tried to avoid being around both Nika and Mesme at the same time whenever possible, because it was just so *much*. Awkward, painful, tense. Every second was a reminder of how she was lying to Nika about something of epic *yebanaya* importance, and so was Mesme, and they were both doing it to protect her for as long as—

Oh, crap. If the Dzhvar were back, and they were, did this mean the clock was running out? How long until all the secrets would be spilled? What if it was today?

Eh, it probably wasn't today, right? And she couldn't smoothly decline now, anyway.

I'll be there in a few minutes.

She downed an electrolyte drink to try to calm the faint, lingering sensation of dizziness from her delve into the manifold abrasion, steeled herself to rise to the challenge of the test ahead of her, and opened a wormhole to Mirai.

S&L

MIRAI

Nika was sitting at her dining room table, a steaming mug cupped in both hands. She wore an oversized cable knit beige sweater that must belong to Dashiel, and her long raven hair tumbled freely over her shoulders.

Mesme meandered around in a shapeless blob of lights in front of the wall of windows. It hadn't taken on its winged phoenix avatar in Nika's presence for three years now, with damn good reason, as the similarity between it and Nika's back tattoo was what had led to Alex deducing Mesme's secret identity.

"Hey." Alex sat down opposite Nika, then glanced over her shoulder. "Mesme."

Hello, Alex.

Mesme spoke telepathically, since Nika also didn't know that Mesme—that all Kats—could speak aloud as plain as day, and the 'shove words into your mind' schtick was a power play on their part. Ugh, she hated all this deception. But she understood the need for it.

"What's up?" Nika asked. "Oh, can I offer you some *shoka espe?* It's basically chocolate coffee."

"Two words that should always go together. Yes, please."

Do you wish for me to leave? Mesme sent to her privately.

Wish? Yes, but it would look strange for you to flee as soon as I arrived. Also, no. I need to talk to you as well, and it wouldn't hurt for Nika to join in the conversation.

As you wish.

Nika returned from the kitchen to set a mug in front of her. "Give it a minute to cool. As I was saying, what's on your mind?"

"First, I was wondering if you can take a second to check the Elakrin system for kyoseil."

"I already did. When I heard what happened there, I admit I was curious."

Alex blew on the foaming liquid in her mug, then breathed in deeply. It smelled like bonfires and snowy mountains. Asterions prioritized tangible, real-world experiences, which meant their food and drink tended to be aromatic and delicious. "What did you discover?"

"It's interesting. There is a bit of kyoseil in and around the planet. About as much as one typically finds in inhabited regions where kyoseil doesn't have a physical presence. But there are dramatic kyoseil waves bowing out around the periphery of the stellar system. I suspect those paths were formed when the system was hidden away, before this whole volume of space exploded back into existence. Based on the curving shape of the paths the waves take, it's as if when the space inside the bubble emerged, it nudged aside the manifold that was in place there. Does this sound right to you?"

"You know, it hadn't occurred to me to consider the physics of it at such a technical level. And I should have." Alex risked a sip of her drink and smiled. "Hmm, this is delicious. Anyway, what happened there isn't like The Displacement, where the astronomical bodies—planets, stars, moons—were physically moved, but most of the volume of the portal universes themselves were left behind. I really did 'pop the bubble,' so to speak. What happens when you pop a bubble? Air dislocation. So it's a sound explanation." She eyed the drifting bundle of lights through the wafting steam of her mug. "Mesme? Anything to add?"

No. As I told you, I know nothing about the Piega Strai's mechanism of operation.

"Because the Kats didn't know where Elakrin had gone." As she'd promised Caleb, she'd forcefully inquired as to Mesme's knowledge of the Elakri after they'd returned home. It had claimed ignorance, and events had interceded before she'd had the chance to draw out any further information.

Correct.

"Does this mean we didn't save them in the last cycle?"

It does.

"And the one before that? Miaon's sequence?"

The same. There were no Elakri in Amaranthe at the end. To my knowledge, details of which extend back six to eight cycles, the Elakri have never before reemerged from their shrouded space.

"Damn." Laurent, dead. Deunan, dead. Arien, same. Plus another two billion people. Yes, yes, if they didn't win the coming war, *everyone* was dead, again. But the implications never got any easier to absorb.

She brought the mug toward her lips, but paused it halfway there as an intriguing notion occurred to her. What if...?

"Alex?" Nika asked. "You have that look about you. What is it?"

"Mesme, I know in your time, the Dzhvar reappeared eight years after the defeat of the Rasu. How much time passed between those events in the earlier cycles?"

The Rasu were only defeated in the previous three cycles. In those—

"What?" she and Nika both exclaimed at once.

I've told you how we demonstrated greatly improved progress in recent cycles.

"Yes, but I guess I assumed..." Alex frowned "...well how did events play out when we didn't defeat the Rasu?"

The Dzhvar resurfaced while the Rasu were still conquering space. Most recently, while Concord battled the Rasu. Prior to this, before the Rasu arrived in Dominion space. In the oldest cycle of which I have any knowledge, Concord never existed to battle them.

A game of progression. Of two steps forward and, occasionally, one or three steps back.

Nika dropped her chin onto her palm. "So though the Rasu were created by the Dzhvar, the Dzhvar's return isn't inexorably linked to the Rasu's defeat."

No. Apologies if I implied it was. The details which I must keep track of are legion.

"Oh, I'm sure." Nika smiled. "Thank you for being so forthcoming now."

Alex pressed her lips shut to prevent the tiniest sound escaping from them, while studiously *not* looking at Mesme. *Sukin syn,* this was difficult.

She tried to pick up the thread of thought she'd been chasing. "The question stands: how much time passed in the earlier cycles between when we *did* defeat the Rasu and when the Dzhvar returned?"

In Miaon's cycle, twenty-two years. In the one before then, fifteen.

"So not a linear shortening of the time, even when progress was made. Okay. Follow my logic here. The Piega Strai was failing rapidly. It was likely to catastrophically break down within a matter of weeks. But it's reasonable to assume that the *Siyane* widening one of the tears to slip through accelerated this process. If we hadn't intruded, it might have been several months or as long as a year before the device failed.

"Now, entropy is a bitch, and it takes no prisoners. So in every cycle, the device would've failed eventually. But over a period of nine thousand years of operation, a million factors could shift its expiration date backward or forward by years or decades, if not a century or two. The vagaries of the stellar wind, how much a fastener was tightened during installation, you name it."

Mesme had drifted toward the far end of the table, close to Nika, so she was able to stare meaningfully at both of them, which she now did. "What if it's always the Elakri? What if the popping of their bubble universe frees the Dzhvar from their prison every time?"

"But how?" Nika asked.

"I do not know. Not yet. Believe me, I am trying to figure it out. But whatever the mechanics of it, it seems as if that's what happened this time. So what if it happens every time? Mesme, you never learned of a correlation between the events because no one ever lived to share the news of the Piega Strai's deactivation. Because until this cycle, it did so explosively."

It's not an entirely implausible theory. But the Dzhvar do not re-appear anywhere near Elakrin, or even in the Marestelle galaxy. In the last cycle, they first appeared in the Coma Supercluster.

"No, the Coma Supercluster is where someone first *detected* them. Once they're here in Amaranthe, they can cavort across gigaparsecs in a blink using quantum dimensions. You admit the Kats don't have the bandwidth to the entire universe, and they never have. So you don't have any real idea of where the Dzhvar first make an appearance, in any cycle. Now, if the first place we register their presence is in the Coma Supercluster this time, then I'll reconsider my theory. But I don't think it's going to be."

She leaned back in her chair and let her gaze unfocus as she forced herself to run through the analysis again, for one simple reason: if it proved to be true, this scenario let her off the hook. The Dzhvar's return wasn't her fault. Well, it *was*, but at most she'd sped up their arrival by a year or so, while saving many lives in the process. She so deeply wanted it to be true that she didn't trust herself to leap to such an exculpatory conclusion.

"Nika, poke some holes in my theory, please."

"I don't see any glaring ones. We can't know for certain, though, because we can't go back in time and put eyes on where the Elakrin system was attached to the manifold around the time the Dzhvar reemerged in previous cycles." Nika grimaced. "I hate to say it, but the only way we can 'prove' it is to understand why the deactivation of the Piega Strai released the Dzhvar in the first place, if it did."

"And that's on me."

Or on me.

Alex arched an eyebrow at Mesme. "Oh?"

The Katasketousya build pocket universes. Perhaps the answer lies in the physics of their creation as much as their destruction.

"Mind if I send Valkyrie your way to explore this topic?"

I am not the best source of information for the details. My role has always been one of strategy, not engineering. But I will be happy to introduce her to one of our world builders.

Oh, Valkyrie was going to be giddy at the prospect of talking shop with a 'world builder.'

11

AKESO

Marlee pirouetted on the ball of one foot—then halfway through the spin, flexed her calf and leapt upward at the same time as she extended the other leg.

Caleb jerked his head backward as her heel slid by less than a centimeter from his nose. "Whoa!"

Her kicking foot landed solidly behind her, and she grinned, panting but holding a defensive stance. "I thought I had you there."

"You did have me there. Or you had anyone who isn't me there." He blew out a harsh breath and waved her off. "It's official. You are as fast as I am."

"Good genes." Marlee knelt down and took a long swig of water. "And the new cybernetics upgrades, obviously."

"Oh? Perhaps I need to pay a visit to Dr. Canivon myself."

"I thought you didn't like her."

"I don't. But I do respect her work." In truth, he'd researched the latest offerings, then acquired and loaded a set of new ware routines of his own shortly after returning from Elakrin. The fight on the rooftop with the assassin had been too close for comfort, and just because he didn't often need to call his combat skills into use, it didn't mean he shouldn't stay ready for when he unexpectedly did. Lives might depend on him staying sharp and quick.

He picked up the leather whip he'd acquired at Marlee's request, but considered it dubiously. "What's the story here?"

"The Belascocians have tails, and they're most adept at manipulating them. It was a thing."

"What kind of a thing?" He immediately regretted asking, as he was not at all sure he wanted to know the answer.

"A *melee* thing." Marlee rolled her eyes, but they did gleam with a hint of mischievousness. "Galean never would've been able to take me captive in the first place if not for his ability to use his tail as a third hand. It exposed a weakness in my skillset, so..." she motioned to the whip "...I want to overcome that weakness."

"Hopefully you won't be combating any tail-limb wielding attackers in the future, but I applaud your desire to always be improving your skills." He cracked the whip on the ground, sending a distinct *thud* reverberating beneath his feet, then spun it in the air a few times. "If this makes contact, it's going to hurt."

She nodded sharply and dropped back into her defensive stance. "I'm ready."

S&L

Caleb was splashing water from the kitchen sink on his face when he sensed the Caeles Prism activating above the landing pad, a signal more of their guests were arriving. Since starting these monthly dinners over three years ago, they'd made more months than they'd missed. Sometimes the group expanded to include Isabela or Kennedy and Noah or some of Alex's family, and sometimes it was only Eren, Felzeor and Marlee. When things were difficult, they talked through troubles, but most of the time they simply enjoyed each other's company for a few hours.

He leaned in behind Alex, who stood next to the sink washing cucumbers, and kissed her neck. "Thank you for cooking tonight."

"It won't be a gourmet meal, but I can manage some roasted chicken and vegetables."

"It'll be delicious. I think Eren and Felzeor are here. I'll go say hello." He hated that Felzeor had missed the training session this evening, but a last-minute work meeting had held the Volucri up. Now that Felzeor was part of a fully staffed, cohesive team, Richard was handing them more involved and lengthier assignments.

Caleb glanced over his shoulder to find Marlee sprawled out in the middle of the living room floor beneath the ceiling fan, fanning herself in an exaggerated motion. "If you want to take a shower, you're welcome to."

"Nah, I'm good. Bruised and sore, but good."

He'd only made contact with the whip a few times; he'd done his best to pull back when he had, though he didn't doubt those hits had left marks. But it was what she'd wanted. She was always pushing, always reaching for ever higher goals. "In that case, do you mind setting the table?"

"Not at all." She inhaled deeply, then drew her legs in, leapt straight up to her feet and went over to the cabinets to grab the plates.

Caleb wandered outside—and barely had enough time to brace himself for the flurry of wings and feathers as Felzeor landed on his head. "Caleb! Eren says you had an exciting adventure meeting new aliens in a far-off place, which you completely neglected to mention at our lunch. You must tell me everything right away."

"Sorry about that, Felzeor. I got caught up in hearing about your latest missions, remember?" He reached up and ruffled the feathers at the Volucri's neck, then eased him down onto a shoulder. "I did have an adventure, but I don't think you would've enjoyed it. The Elakri are very proper and fancy."

"Like the Novoloume?"

"Eh, not exactly. They take their pretentiousness seriously."

"Do they not have any fun at all?"

"Some of them do. A little." Eren reached the porch, and Caleb reached out to shake his friend's hand. "Felzeor's rather jealous of your grand adventure with the Hesgyr."

"I got to blow some shite up, so…yeah, I won't lie. It was pretty grand."

"I'm not surprised." He chuckled and ushered everyone inside.

S&L

Caleb cleared away the plates after dinner and returned to the table with a fresh bottle of wine. "So how's the Advocacy doing?"

"More bureaucratic by the day now that it has a Conference legislature." Eren grumbled while refilling his glass halfway. "I suppose four hundred bumbling idiots thinking they rule our lives is preferable to eight all-powerful ones believing the same. I mean, what are the odds a majority will agree often enough to do any real damage?"

"Welcome to the dirty secret of representative government," Alex remarked. "Gridlock is the only thing it has to commend it. What about Corradeo, though? He's relinquishing a portion of his power to this legislature?"

"He is…." Eren hesitated. "At least by the letter of the charters and regulations and directives and whatever else they're busily instituting. Admittedly, the new division of power hasn't met a real test yet. I'm not certain what will happen when the Conference defies him on a matter he deems crucial to Anaden welfare."

"He respected Concord's authority during the Rasu War, even to the detriment of Anaden worlds," Caleb replied. "And I know it wasn't easy for him to do so. Everyone enjoys throwing shade in his direction, but since regaining power, he hasn't once acted like a dictator."

"Hey, no shade from me. Mind you, if Nyx had her way, he'd be ensconced in a velvet and gem-adorned golden throne, complete with a scepter and a crown. She's not a fan of the Conference *or* the growing bureaucratic agencies."

"Once an Inquisitor…."

"Eh." Eren shrugged. "She has a bit of a blind spot when it comes to Corradeo, but on the whole, she's making the effort to adapt to the world she finds herself in."

Caleb couldn't recall having ever heard Eren describe Nyx in such a reasonable, damn near complimentary manner. Not a trace of sarcasm or exasperation. "So you two are getting along better these days?"

"I guess." Eren took a long sip of his drink. "Felzeor, have you told Caleb about Adelaine yet?"

"Noooo...." Felzeor danced from one claw to another on his perch atop the back of one of the dining table chairs.

"Who's Adelaine?" Caleb asked.

"My friend."

"His *girlfriend*," Eren corrected.

A corner of Caleb's lips curled up. "Is this true, Felzeor?"

"Yes," he said in a clipped manner before dipping his beak into his glass of juice.

"You didn't mention her when we had lunch the other day."

"Did I not? We were so busy talking about work and missions, like you said. It must have slipped my mind."

"Uh-huh." He circled a hand toward Felzeor. "Go on, tell us about her."

"We, ah, met during the Rasu siege of Hirlas. She was a member of Airborne One."

"Oh? Did I meet her while I was there?"

"I don't think so. At the time, she was merely one of the crew, and we were all focused on working hard to keep track of the Rasu and protect the group. But afterward, once the cleanup started, we got to know each other better. She works for the government, surveying the forests. Mostly keeping watch for unexpected changes the planet makes to the landscape."

"Yes, Akeso continues to enjoy...let's call it 'exploring' the natural wonders of Hirlas. I hope it's not causing too many troubles for the residents."

"No, no. The odd treehouse toppling and whatnot."

Akeso, stop toppling treehouses. People live in those.

I am not always able to tell the difference between the natural landscape and artificial structures on the planet. The residents' architecture is most subtle.

Fair enough. Do your best, though, okay?

I will try.

"So." Caleb idly tapped a finger on his glass. "Do we get to meet Adelaine?"

"Oh!" Felzeor's head snapped up. "I mean, of course you do. I can bring her by sometime, I'm sure. Or you can visit Hirlas. I don't know when—"

Alex dangled the tiny Caeles Prism on her wrist in the air. "Why doesn't she come over right now?"

"Now, we don't want to ambush her," Caleb replied. "But if she's willing, we'd love to meet her."

"I, ah…let me ask her." Felzeor dropped his beak to his chest.

As part of the Volucri-customized cybernetics upgrades necessary to enable regenesis neural imprints, they were also getting a full personal communications system. Until recently, they'd had no way to communicate in real time with others; Felzeor and other Volucri operatives had needed to rely on an external device embedded in their vocalizers to send and receive messages to and from CINT and their team members.

Felzeor's beak lifted, his eyes a touch wide as his gaze darted around. "She says she'd be honored to visit. Alex, she's currently at my nest-home, if you remember where it is."

His home? How serious was this?

"I do." Alex stood, and golden light began to spin inside the Caeles Prism. A small oval wrent apart in midair, and after a few seconds a Volucri flew through it into the dining room.

Felzeor preened on his perch. "Over here, Adelaine. You can sit beside me."

Adelaine was a little smaller than Felzeor, with blonde and cinnamon feathers except for a streak of bright gold along her tail. Her eyes were a pinkish quartz, reminding him of opals.

She situated herself next to Felzeor, their wings touching. "Hello, everyone. It is wonderful to meet you, and to see you again, Eren. Felzeor has spoken so much about all of you. No need to introduce yourselves." She dipped her beak in his direction. "You are Caleb, obviously. And you're Alex—no mistaking your rich burgundy hair. And you are…oh, Marlee! The best tickler in Concord space."

Marlee cackled in delight. "I hope so. Can I just say, Adelaine, you are possibly the most gorgeous Volucri I have ever seen."

"Thank you so much. Felzeor says the same, but he's biased."

Caleb almost choked on his wine. He hurriedly covered his mouth, in part to mask the look of dismay on his face. He was not prepared for the turn the evening had taken.

12

AKESO

Alex tiptoed upstairs to the bedroom, taking care not to slosh her wine over the rim of its glass as she did, while Caleb finished putting the dishes in the washer.

Once there, she slipped out of her clothes and into the ivory silk lingerie she'd bought the other day while she was on Romane. She unwound her hair from its knot and brushed it out while she ordered up some smooth jazz on the sound system. Then she took her glass over to the window spanning the length of the bedroom and, mood appropriately set, contemplated the scene spread before her.

In the absence of a moon overhead, the outdoors got rather dark at night, but of late Akeso had begun illuminating firefly analogues around the meadow. Caleb said Akeso had discovered the creatures on Hirlas and taken a liking to them, as Akeso was wont to do. Tonight three collections of the Akeso-Hirlas fireflies danced above the winding path of the creek, swooshing through the trees to dive for the water before looping across the meadow and repeating their pattern.

What a special place their home was. The laughter of friends and family had brightened it this evening, and now the extraordinary, gentle soul of a planet did the same. Life was often harsh and cruel, but it was also precious and beautiful. This was what she could not allow the Dzhvar to destroy.

She heard Caleb ascend the stairs, then his steps hitch when he came into the bedroom. She sipped on her glass of wine, a tiny smile drifting across her lips. "Lovely night tonight."

"Yes. Quite lovely," he murmured, his voice low and gravelly as he drew close. He sidled up behind her and drifted his hands slowly, reverentially up her arms. One hand moved her hair to the side, and his lips caressed the curve of her neck. "What's the occasion?"

The last calm before the storm, I fear. "No occasion, really. Just appreciating what matters."

He pressed close against her back, and the warmth radiating off of his skin told her he'd lost his clothes on the way over. "And silk is what matters?"

"Yep. Silk is definitely high on the list. Among a few other things—" Her breath caught in her throat as his hands ran up her thighs, pushing the hem of her lingerie up as they climbed.

"I approve." His lips grazed feather soft along the length of her shoulder; then, gripping her hips firmly, he wrenched her around to face him. Rather than kiss her, though, his mouth followed her collarbone to the hollow of her throat as he held her close against his body. Strength juxtaposed upon tenderness, which had always been the truth of him.

His mouth continued its journey, and when it encountered a strap, his teeth dragged it across her shoulder until it fell away. His grip loosened when his hands glided past her waist, and she stepped back to let the lingerie drop to the floor.

He sucked on his bottom lip. "But some things are finer than silk."

"Hmm." She took a long, teasing sip of her wine, drawing out the anticipation. Then she stepped around him and set the glass on the side table. With as much grace as she was able to muster, she crawled onto the bed, pausing to glance over her shoulder. The devouring look in his eyes sent heat flooding through her body all the way to her toes.

In a blink his mouth and his body were pressed upon hers, as the fireflies cavorted in a dance of light outside.

S&L

Caleb reached out and drew Alex up onto his chest, then kissed her forehead. "Is there a story behind the lingerie?"

She giggled against him, a touch buzzed from the wine and the sex. "No story. I went shopping for some new pants, but saw it instead. And…."

"And what?"

She lifted her chin to catch his gaze. "I don't ever want to become complacent. I want to hold tight to everything that's treasured in my life. You. Us. What we've made together." *I won't give it up*, she whispered, but only in her mind, as she didn't dare sour this perfect moment by uttering the name of the storm on the horizon.

"You are remarkable, and what we have is more precious to me than the fortune of galaxies. More precious than all the silk cocoons spun in the artificial forests of Ebrisham."

Her heart burned with love that went beyond even such artful words, until it became too much to hold together. She smiled teasingly and tilted her head toward the lingerie, where it lay crumpled on the floor beside the bed. "The silk was nice, though, right?"

"The silk was breathtaking, and I beg you to wear it to bed every single night from here on out, for at least five seconds before I strip it off of you."

"*Dlya tebya, priyazn.*" She kissed his nose playfully before settling back on his shoulder. "I think dinner went well tonight. Everyone's safely home in one piece and none the worse for wear. The conversation was engaging, and I didn't burn the chicken."

"The chicken was delicious." He didn't say anything else, though, and she could *feel* him ruminating.

"But…?"

"But…I still can't get over the fact that Felzeor has a girlfriend. A *serious* girlfriend. It's like blinking and discovering that your toddler is working a corporate job and just bought a house in the city."

"Our little Felzeor is all grown up."

"Yeah, he was always grown up." A deep sigh rumbled through his chest. "I shouldn't infantilize him, because he's not a pet. But I feel protective of him. What if Adelaine breaks his heart?"

Alex stifled a laugh in her throat; he was so earnest in his concern, she ought not to make fun of it. That strength juxtaposed upon such aching tenderness made him extraordinary. "She seems nice, and more than a match for him."

"That's what I mean! What if she's spun his head all up, then leaves him in the dust for some flashy, cardinal-winged Volucri?"

"Then we'll bake him a whole pan of apple tarts and console him."

He kissed the top of her head. "We will."

S&L

The black void of an empty span of space hung heavy around Alex like a long velvet cloak. She checked her internal locator—and jumped in surprise. The site of the tear in the manifold that had led them to Elakrin?

How did she get here?

More importantly, where was Elakrin's star? Where was Elakrin?

She spun around to confirm their absence. No star shone close enough to be a candidate. So what was transpiring—

Her consciousness was hurled backwards as a terrible pressure crushed her chest; if she were present in the flesh, she'd be unable to draw air against its weight. Her perception tumbled out of control, as if she were plummeting down a steep decline. Dizziness gripped her and refused to let loose. She had nothing to grab onto and no way to slow the tumble or orient herself.

After what she experienced as several minutes of uncontrolled motion, her spinning began to ease, then at last stopped. Her vision wavered, and she struggled to focus on what lay in front of her.

Abruptly she realized that, where before there had been void, now there was stardust. Fine particles hung in space all around her. A veritable ocean of it. An impression of scale suggested to her it was several planets' worth.

Dread grew in her mind as it occurred to her this might have been the Elakrin system after all...until the Piega Strai failed.

No star had materialized to light the void, but if the planets were gone, then so too would be the star, artificially compressed by unimaginable gravity until...what? Denied its natural death cycle, would it be squeezed into a singularity, or shatter apart into elementary particles?

In the corner of her eye, a shadow crawled across the sea of stardust. She turned toward it, but it raced away from her—and another. She spun toward the new one, but it slithered out of her sight as well. To where? There was nothing but stardust for parsecs in every direction.

Without consciously meaning to, she shifted out of sidespace and into her body. Yet she somehow remained in the same location. And now, space was awash in tendrils of plasma the color of hellfire. They darted around and through her, but paid her no mind.

Then in masses large and small, the tendrils vanished. In minutes, she was left there alone, floating free in the airless black void, for the stardust was gone as well.

Alex jolted bolt upright in bed. What the—?

Her heart pounded in her chest, and her lungs convulsed on the edge of hyperventilation.

But her surroundings were real, tangible, with plenty of air to breathe. She was in their bedroom on Akeso. She looked to her left as panic gripped her anew, but Caleb slept peacefully beside her.

She rubbed at her face and, after a second, climbed out of bed and stood, only to sway unsteadily on her feet.

When she regained her balance, she pulled on her robe and quietly slid open the door to go out onto the balcony. The warm evening had cooled to a chilly night, and with the fireflies tucked into their slumber for the night, a blanket of darkness gave way to a sparkling expanse of stars overhead.

The cool air helped to rouse her from what felt like a fugue state. It had been a dream, obviously. A dream in which she'd witnessed what she'd speculated about with Nika and Mesme the other day. The Piega Strai had explosively failed, crushing Elakrin, the other two planets in the system, and their star.

And the Dzhvar had escaped into Amaranthe.

It didn't prove anything, of course. Dreams never did. And perhaps it was merely wishful thinking on her part. Her subconscious acting to manifest what she deeply hoped to be true: that the Dzhvar always escaped when the Piega Strai failed, thus she bore no real blame for their arrival.

She shivered as a breeze drifted across the balcony and hugged her arms tight against her chest. But damn, this had felt real. More real than any dream she could recall.

13

CONCORD HQ

Miriam sorted the morning's reports in order of priority: by consequences if not acted upon forthwith, then by importance of the subject matter. Despite the looming threat of the Dzhvar clouding the horizon, things were, for the moment, quiet. Or as quiet as they ever got in an alliance of twenty-two-and-counting member and associated alien species. Everything was relative.

A steady pace of ship production had replaced all the vessels lost in the Rasu War as of eight months earlier. And with the removal of AEGIS' stranglehold on adiamene thanks to Kennedy Rossi's clever maneuvering during the war, the other species were refurbishing their old fleets with new, all-but-impermeable ships. Even the Anadens, at least when it came to vessels too small to support the double shielding technology.

AEGIS hated it, of course. They'd filed lawsuits nonstop for the last three years trying to stop the use of adiamene by non-human entities, and as of last week continued to do so. But the cat was out of the proverbial bag, and like with most cats, there was no stuffing it back in.

Miriam's inherent Earth Alliance allegiance tweaked in mild concern as well, but she recognized this was an irrational response. While the governments of Concord member species often disagreed, she could not realistically imagine a future where they became warring enemies. Not after they'd come so far and depended on one another so much.

And irrespective of whimsical speculation, practicality always won out in her world. Waging the next war was going to be far easier when she didn't have to worry about Novoloume and Khokteh vessels disintegrating upon contact with the enemy. Frankly, AEGIS should be grateful, too, as it meant the other fleets would be able to shoulder a greater share of the burden in those battles.

Managing repairs and rebuilding projects after the extensive damage the Rasu inflicted on planetary structures and space stations wasn't strictly her responsibility, but she kept a watch on those efforts nonetheless. A disintegrated Luna raining down upon Earth had caused significant damage, and the Earth Alliance's famed bureaucracy meant the cleanup was still not completed.

The Anadens had rarely been forced to rebuild anything in hundreds of thousands of years, but they were experts at tearing down and replacing on a whim, so they'd managed their repairs without causing a fuss. Since the Khokteh were perpetually strapped for resources and funds, Concord had pitched in with aid for Ireltse. Though the Novoloume had by many measures suffered the most extensive and widespread damage in the war, they'd used their wealth to swiftly construct more elegant structures to replace what was lost.

Miriam had been prepared to assist the Naraida and Volucri with their rather unique situation on Hirlas. But the Novoloume had long been their benefactors and, despite the great expenses the Novoloume were incurring on their own worlds, they had glided to the front of the line and handled it before she was able to intervene. Aided by the fact that the planet itself took care of the cleaning up and disposal of debris....

Amaranthe was a strange place at times.

She made several notations and moved on to the next group of reports.

A variety of initiatives designed to strengthen their defenses and military capabilities continued apace. It was a constant struggle to keep everyone's feet to the fire of urgency when the strongest reason to do so was an amorphous warning from a time-traveling Kat that an enemy thought long eradicated would return…eventually. Also, she couldn't tell the various government leaders about the time traveling part, not that they'd believe her if she did. She barely believed it herself.

So she ordered persistent acceleration of the initiatives she oversaw, and gently twisted arms on the ones she did not.

Next report.

Concord had several potential new allies to pursue relations with, though none came fielding a sizeable military. Granted, the Hesgyr might, but they were keeping their capabilities close to the vest, when they consented to converse at all. As things stood, they were as likely to become adversaries as allies, but she intended to let diplomacy take its course—

Two alerts arrived within seconds of one another: one from Special Projects Director Reynolds and one from Elcano, the Artificial overseeing the Detection Network. They both said the same thing: Dzhvar presence detected.

Instantly Miriam was on her feet and querying for additional information.

Thomas, we'll be departing in eight minutes. No crew required. Destination incoming.

She allowed herself a beat of relief when she saw the location. It was extremely far away, well outside Concord's sphere of influence.

Capricornus Supercluster. Elcano will send you the coordinates.

Receiving them now. I await your arrival.

A wormhole from Thomas shimmered to life in front of her. The discovery by certain enterprising Artificials of how to open wormholes without the need of a human Prevo partner was bringing new complications to the world—or to Richard's world at a minimum—but the skill was invaluable when every second counted.

She strode through the wormhole and onto the bridge of the *Aurora* while alerting a list of people to the detection. Because the vessel spent more time in dock than on deployment, so long as they were not on a war footing, its crew worked other assignments as well. As such, she could not expect them to reach the ship in a matter of minutes. Luckily, she didn't need them for anything less than pitched combat; even then, she and Thomas could manage without a full complement. At this point, most of the organic crew served as backups and checks on automated or Artificial-driven systems. They existed because she didn't want to leave anything to chance, and the military practiced redundancy.

"Thomas, please retrieve David. He should be in his office at the Special Warfare Training Center."

Permission to come aboard? I want to see them.

The *Aurora* maintained a free wormhole block, for the reality that practically anyone could now deploy a wormhole represented a genuine security risk to the flagship of the Concord fleet. "And allow Director Reynolds entry, if you would."

She reviewed the ship's operational status while everyone arrived, despite the fact that Thomas ensured they were always ready to fly. Redundancy.

A familiar presence climbed up on the overlook and leaned in to peer over her shoulder. "Where are they?"

"Hello, Alex. Capricornus."

Alex huffed a breath. "Not the Coma Supercluster."

"Excuse me?"

"Nothing. A bet with Mesme."

"There was a bit of a delay in their detection. The kyoseil picked the signal up, but our sensors are spread massively thin way out there," Devon held up a hand to stave off any burgeoning complaint from Alex as he strode across the bridge. "We're working on it."

Alex nodded noncommittally and left the overlook to go study the incoming data at the unstaffed Science station.

Devon took a second to assess the state of the bridge, then put his hands on his hips. "We need to go. I worry we're missing the party."

Miriam bit back a sigh. She did not sanction taking orders on her own bridge, but despite being bonded with Annie, a military Artificial, Devon had never internalized military protocol. "I doubt it's a party, Director Reynolds."

"Fine, the show. Event. Cosmic display."

"Thomas?"

'Fleet Admiral Jenner will be here in seven seconds, at which point we can depart.'

Miriam looked around the bridge. "Where's David?"

"I'm here." He waved from the chair at the Navigation station. Caleb leaned against the wall near David, and they appeared to be mid-conversation. When the crew wasn't on board, David did tend to act as if he owned the place, and she was admittedly far more indulgent of the behavior from him than she was from Devon.

Malcolm arrived precisely when Thomas had anticipated, and the undocking process began.

Miriam ordered the leaders of the various Concord fleets to be on standby, but she didn't direct them to the coordinates of the incursion for now. They had no idea what, if anything, waited for them; in all likelihood, this was an observation trip. If possible, they would confirm the enemy existed and collect data for later analysis.

14

CAF AURORA

CAPRICORNUS SUPERCLUSTER

They exited the wormhole a hundred megaparsecs from the flagged location. Miriam worried this distance wasn't safe, but she had to balance safety with the valid concern Devon had expressed that the clock was ticking. According to Corradeo, in the first war—she chuckled to herself at the realization Alex was, as usual, correct—the Dzhvar had often lingered for hours or days at a location before vanishing again. But equally as often, they'd conducted 'hit and runs' on a star system lasting less than an hour. If there was a factor that determined how long the enemy remained at a location, the Anadens had not discovered it.

From here, a white-blue star was the only feature of note outside the viewport. "What are we looking at?"

The question was nominally directed at Thomas, as he controlled their instruments, though Alex and Devon now both crowded around the Science station.

'I am not detecting any Dzhvar signatures within the range of our instruments.'

"They're gone. Dammit!" Devon exclaimed. "We've got to tighten up the Detection Network. We need more warning."

Alex shot him a glare. "You don't say."

"Did they inflict any damage?" Miriam asked.

'Scans show four planetary sized bodies in the system. From this distance, I cannot assess their states.'

"Then let's visit them each in turn."

'Executing targeted jump.'

They emerged in sight of a gas giant. Sage and citron swirled languidly along its equator, while an aurora storm sparked across its upper pole.

'First pass readings suggest the planet is intact and exhibiting normal behavior for a gas giant.'

"Good enough for now," Miriam said. "Proceed onward."

This time they emerged in the midst of an asteroid field. Rocks bounced harmlessly off the *Aurora's* shielding, but...no, her initial conclusion was incorrect. The rocks were far too numerous and close together to be a natural asteroid field. "Are we in a planetary ring?"

'Negative.' Thomas' voice was neutral, displaying no trace of annoyance at the insinuation that he would ever mistakenly drop the ship into either an asteroid field *or* a planetary ring. She'd hear about it later, though.

A planet hovered in the bottom third of the viewport. A thin atmosphere exposed a sand and rust surface that reminded her of Mars.

A crevasse visible from space split the planet from pole to pole. Thomas superimposed a zoomed-in visual on a corner of the viewport. It revealed magma surging out of the crevasse in great lava flows. Where the split reached ocean, the waters hissed and boiled.

"Any life signs?" she asked as her mind queued up the steps necessary to begin emergency evacuations of unfamiliar aliens.

'Millions of them, but no indications of technology or even structures. Likely animal life only.'

David stood and moved close to the viewport. "Did the attack split the planet in two?"

'Negative. The fissure extends for approximately 1,200 kilometers, deep into the mantle, but it does not breach the planet's core.'

"And there's only the one?"

'A moment...no. A smaller fissure carves through much of the ocean coming into view from starboard.'

Miriam gestured at the viewport, where multiple rocks drifted by the ship. "Is this a debris field, then? The damage to the planet is significant, but I don't see any large chunks blown out of the surface."

'Based on an analysis of the field and the elements present, I posit this is what remains of a satellite.'

Malcolm laughed dryly. "They blew up the planet's moon? How unoriginal."

Miriam shot him a brief smile. He was never going to live that maneuver down, and he seemed to have accepted this fate.

"It was probably just in the way," Devon remarked. "Or random. I don't think we can assume the Dzhvar acted on a specific plan. They may have simply been passing through."

"Wait, what was that?" David exclaimed.

"What did you see?" she asked sharply, as the surprise in his voice signaled the possibility of a new threat.

"The planet wobbled."

'I concur. While the damage done to the planet's intrinsic structure will degrade its orbit in time, I would not expect it to do so this quickly.'

"It's not the orbit," Alex replied, her voice little more than a whisper.

At some point, her daughter had moved away from the Science station to lean against an empty stretch of wall, and her eyes were closed. Caleb had gone to stand next to her, one hand on her elbow while he watched her.

"Alex, tell me what you see."

"Space itself is out of whack here," Alex murmured. "Thin. Uneven. Thomas, check the *Aurora's* engine output. I think you'll find it's having to make constant adjustments to maintain a steady position."

'You are correct, Alex. I initially attributed the fluctuations to minute shifts in the planet's gravitational pull due to the damage, and that is occurring. But there is also a larger degradation involved.'

"Is the degradation distinct enough for you to track?" Alex asked. "If so, I think we can use it to follow the Dzhvar's path. If not, I can track it myself, though I can't navigate the ship at the same time."

"Huh." Devon had closed his eyes as well. "That's the damnedest thing."

David glanced over his shoulder, his gaze sweeping from Alex to Miriam. "What did you all think 'eats the spacetime manifold' meant?"

"I thought it was a metaphor." Devon opened his eyes and grimaced. "Kidding. I assumed it meant exactly this. But seeing it in action? It's difficult to believe. I mean, we're not talking about destroying physical molecules here. They're eating fundamental *forces*."

"True," Alex replied faintly. Her posture hadn't changed, and her eyes remained closed, but she was obviously keeping up with the conversation. "But those forces are still created by particles. Gluons, photons, vector bosons."

'Apologies for the delay, everyone.' Thomas piped back up. 'I believe I can now track the manifold disruptions everyone is so fascinated by. Commandant, I've collected significant data on the state of the planet beneath us. Permission to depart?'

"Permission granted." For the moment, she was mostly an administrative functionary. Thomas and Alex were and should be in charge.

The *Aurora* arced above the planet and adopted a course slightly to port of the system's star. Other than a few small adjustments, they didn't deviate materially from a straight line. Had the Dzhvar streaked right through the system, not slowing down to notice the wreckage they left in their wake?

Alex, Devon and Thomas were seeing a version of space the rest of them were blind to, so after a minute, she left the overlook to join Malcolm and David near the viewport. "The damage inflicted on the planet, when coupled with the registering of a Dzhvar signature here, is all the confirmation we need that this enemy has returned. We may still have a great deal of time before it reaches our space, but we also may have no time at all."

Malcolm nodded solemnly. "This should pry open the purse strings in London. If only I knew what to spend the funds on."

He'd nailed the crux of the problem. The weapon that had ultimately defeated the Dzhvar the first time was *diati*, and they no longer had access to this weapon. But since 99.9% of humanity would be dead if not for *diati's* final act, it felt unfair to rue its absence. And a million years ago, the Anadens hadn't possessed most of the advanced weapons Concord enjoyed today. So beyond the fact that shooting the Dzhvar with lasers and nuclear missiles did less than nothing, as of now they had little idea what might work to combat them.

They also didn't dare hope that adiamene would offer much protection against this enemy. Nor the Tandem Defense Shield, for that matter. Both offered a total rebuttal to conventional weaponry, but nothing about the coming fight stood to be conventional.

As the filtered star grew to dominate the viewport, their heading curved toward it, and her brow furrowed in surprise. "The Dzhvar deviated course to intercept the star?"

"Looks like," Alex offered. "Perhaps they understood they'd get the most bang for their buck by tearing it apart."

"And have they? Torn it apart?"

'I am still studying the energy profile of—'

"Oh!" Alex exclaimed at the same instant as the ship slowed notably and turned to port.

"What is it?" She, David and Malcolm all peered out the viewport, searching.

A small, rocky planet came into view as the *Aurora* pivoted; its pockmarked topography suggested it had never had an atmosphere. No obvious fissures split its surface, but it was spinning like a top, wobbling madly about its axis.

"Is that revolution natural?" Miriam asked.

'It shouldn't be,' Thomas replied. 'The Dzhvar's path passed within half a megameter of the planet. I posit this proximity was close enough to send the planet spinning in the manner we see.'

This meant the Dzhvar were able to affect physical objects without directly impacting them. She filed the fact away, as it might matter when they met on the field of battle. "Now about the star?"

Alex arrived to stand beside her at the viewport. "It's not apt to go supernova in the next hour or anything, and the tremendous energies at work in the core make it difficult to tell for certain if the Dzhvar caused permanent harm. But they went straight through the center of it, and I honestly don't know what the effects will be. Thomas, you should drop some probes to monitor the star's activity."

'I've already done so. They will report any material changes in the elemental composition or fusion profile of the star.'

Alex arched an eyebrow at her, and Miriam shrugged. The *Aurora* was easily as much Thomas' ship as it was her own, and she appreciated that he asked permission before acting as often as he did. "Thomas, let's attempt to pick the trail up on the other side."

'I will extrapolate a projected course from the Dzhvar's trajectory when it impacted the star.'

They pulled back then swept around the star at the minimum safe distance, and Alex leaned into Caleb and closed her eyes again.

When they reached the far side, Alex's features twitched in concentration, followed by evident frustration. "I can't find any evidence they came through this region of space. They could have altered course, in which case we'd need to crisscross the star's entire circumference to try to rediscover the trail. Or they could've darted back off into the quantum dimensions midway through the photosphere."

'Agreed. I am also unable to detect further manifold disruptions. Shall we return to the planet where the damage was most noticeable?'

"No," Miriam replied. "I'm sending a scientific vessel here to spend however much time they need analyzing every square meter of this system. Let's return to HQ." She fixed a steely gaze on the empty, silent space beyond the viewport. "We have a lot of work to do."

15

OMOIKANE INITIATIVE

MIRAI

Dashiel slid into his chair next to Nika, then reached under the table and squeezed her hand. She spared him a slight smile, but it lacked enthusiasm.

In fact, the mood of everyone at the table was noticeably somber. They'd all hoped the Dzhvar lay far in their future, if at all. But it wasn't meant to be. No choice now but to fight the good fight.

Only around half the chairs were occupied. In truth, none of the participants needed to be present here in this room, as the ceraff technology had advanced to the point where they could hold a more substantive Advisor Committee meeting virtually than in person. Instead of attempting to read a person's facial expressions or body language, they were able to sense the deeper sentiments animating every thought and driving every word choice through the kyoseil connecting their minds to one another.

But Asterions lived in the real world; they walked and talked and breathed and touched and *experienced*. This had been their defining ethos since the Dominion's founding, and they would not give it up easily. So whoever could attend the meeting in person, did so.

Lance Palmer brought the meeting to order. "I've reviewed the report from Commandant Solovy. The Dzhvar tore up a couple of planets and satellites over in the Capricornus Supercluster, and may have cut a swath through the local star. They also…" Palmer scowled "…ate up some of the manifold there, I guess. What that means isn't yet clear."

"But no one put eyes on these Dzhvar?" Cameron Breckel, one of the External Relations advisors, asked.

"No. They'd already departed before the *Aurora* arrived. But the evidence they passed through is strong. Strong enough to convince me that the presence the sensors detected was in fact Dzhvar, and these aliens behaved exactly as the Anadens of old claimed they did."

"The good news is, the kyoseil triangulation system worked," Dashiel said. "The closest sensors were too distant to detect the Dzhvar signature by normal means, but the kyoseil alerted on their presence. Accordingly, Concord has placed an order for a significant quantity of additional kyoseil-enabled sensors. Which we can and will provide. In addition, now that the methodology has proved out, we will be blanketing our own systems with a mesh of the sensors."

"And the instant one of them trips, we'll begin evacuations," Perrin Benvenit offered.

In the periphery of his vision, he caught Nika's expression brighten. She was perpetually proud of how well her friend had risen to the challenge of the administration advisor position. Perrin no longer deferred to Katherine Colson as a matter of course or sat in meek silence at group meetings. Instead, the woman's naturally vivacious personality shone through with the confidence she'd gained.

Dashiel touched the ceraff with his mind and confirmed Adlai was smiling as well. Two-advisor relationships brought their share of challenges, but also their strengths. No one understood the highs and lows of the job like another advisor. It had been tough on Adlai at first, ceding a larger portion of Perrin's attention to the work, but after grousing over drinks with Dashiel a few times, his friend had made peace with it.

"Evacuations are great," Palmer snapped, not bothering to hide a touch of sarcasm. "But I'll keep asking the same question until someone gives me a good answer: how do I fight these space monsters?"

"And we'll keep giving you the same bad answer," Dashiel replied. "We won't know what strategies will be effective against them until we meet them on the field of battle. We know nuclear weapons didn't touch them in the last war. Advocate Corradeo, as well as the Kats, are skeptical negative energy weapons will be effective, but we'll test them anyway. There's the Ymyrath Field as well." The Dominion now possessed two of the 4-neutron field weapons, derived from Ourankeli technology. They'd been sitting around in dry dock for the last two years, waiting for another enemy deserving of their destructive power to surface.

"But you genuinely don't think rift weapons will work?" Palmer asked.

Beside him, Nika leaned back in her chair and closed her eyes.

Nika, what's going on?

Checking on something.

"Ridani?"

With a sigh he redirected half his attention back to Palmer. "The science says they won't damage the Dzhvar in any meaningful way. The Dzhvar are pandimensional beings, and rift devices only manipulate the three physical dimensions. I hold out hope that we can use their dimensional shifting feature to divert Dzhvar from their intended course, at least temporarily, but we'll see. I know we'd all love it if the Kireme Boundaries can protect our worlds again, the way they did from the Rasu. And should Dzhvar appear in our space, we'll turn them on and find out. But I'm not confident."

Palmer cursed under his breath. "Fine. What about your Weave project? How's it progressing?"

In the first war, one thing and one thing only had stopped the Dzhvar: *diati*. They didn't have any of the primordial entity lying around, but they did know something about it. Or rather, the Praesidis did. Corradeo Praesidis professed to want closer, more collegial relations between Anadens and Asterions. Dashiel had taken this opportunity to press him to make good on his ideals by providing scientists to work with Conceptual Research on a project to recreate the properties of *diati*. Specifically, the properties that enabled it to create a barrier the Dzhvar could not breach.

Results had been spotty at best so far, and the prickly personalities involved were proving to be nearly as difficult to manage as the dimensional forces they studied. Parc Eshett had been fired from the project after three weeks for running off two of the Anaden scientists, which had forced Maris to cash in a spot of the goodwill she enjoyed with Corradeo to plead for their return. Since then, participants had come and gone, some on friendly terms and some less so. Progress had been made, but not enough. Primordial life forms did not play by the rules the rest of them did, and everyone's understanding of the structure of the universe was being pushed beyond its limits.

Dashiel shook his head. "It's not ready. Which is to say, it doesn't work, not yet. Doesn't do much of anything at present."

"If this Capricornus incident is any indication, time's running out, Ridani."

"I realize it is."

Abruptly Nika sat up straight and opened her eyes. "I need to go see Miriam Solovy."

CONCORD HQ
COMMAND

Through a door situated beside what Nika thought of as the Rasu War Council meeting room, but was probably where Miriam held all important leadership meetings, now sat an observatory. Or it felt like an observatory to her, with its high domed ceiling, special conductive walls curving into a circle and lack of permanent furniture combining to fashion a sense of vast emptiness waiting to be filled.

They could've used such a room as this one in the later days of the Rasu War, when the intergalactic battle map became too clogged with faction clashes and ever-shifting territories to manage above the long conference table in the war room next door. But they were definitely going to need it now. Which, Nika imagined, was why it existed.

The guest list for her hastily called meeting was short, but the people who most needed to hear her news were here. Dashiel had done a superb job of interfacing with both Concord's scientists and industrialists these last three years as they prepared for the coming threat. As such, he was a key player in every Dzhvar discussion. In addition to Miriam, Alex was here, of course. As was Caleb, if for reasons of his own; he was rarely inclined to share his thoughts or business with her. She regretted that she'd never been able to win back his trust after their crucial mission on Rasu Prime, but she'd kept the nature and extent of the threat they faced a secret because she'd believed doing so gave them the best chance to succeed. And succeed they had.

Devon Reynolds rounded out the group. Though he and Dashiel frequently clashed, Dashiel was the first to admit the Prevo was the brains behind the Detection Network and Dzhvar detection efforts in general. And this was what they were here to talk about today.

Alex strode to the center of the room, then pivoted to face Nika. "How large of a region do you want displayed?"

"All of it," Nika replied.

"You mean the Pisces–Cetus Supercluster Complex, which is as far as the Detection Network extends?"

"No. I mean all of everything. The universe. Amaranthe."

"Nothing like dreaming big. Let me see what I can do." Alex blinked, and the room filled with a semi-translucent representation of galaxies beyond counting.

Before unlocking wormhole technology, they'd been limited to mapping the 'observable universe,' and they didn't even know what percentage of the cosmos had already accelerated too far away for anyone to perceive it. With wormholes, they were in theory able to jump anywhere. Once at a location, they would find it as it existed in the present, not the distant past of the light that might never reach home. But to call the universe 'vast' was a pitiful understatement. Despite the fact that Concord employed multiple Prevo researchers whose fulltime job was to survey the farthest reaches of space, they still didn't have a solid handle on how large Amaranthe truly was.

So the map was not complete. But the span of their expansive Detection Network covered only five percent of the map, which meant it should be large enough for her purposes.

Nika took a deep breath and began. "As you've all heard by now, programming the kyoseil in the Detection Network sensors with the Dzhvar's signature worked. But kyoseil is far smarter than our programming, if in mostly unknowable ways.

"When the Dzhvar tripped those sensors in Capricornus earlier today, the kyoseil…the best way to describe what happened is that it 'cross-referenced' what it experienced in encountering the Dzhvar in Capricornus with what its programming told it about this phenomenon. It internalized this new knowledge, and here's the noteworthy part: once one instance of kyoseil knew this, every instance knew it." It turned out it wasn't so much that she didn't know how to recognize a Dzhvar perturbation, as it was that the kyoseil itself hadn't known. Until it did.

"I checked in on the kyoseil web during our advisor meeting, and I discovered something. I'm honestly not certain whether it's bad news or good." She swallowed heavily. "The Dzhvar have been appearing throughout Amaranthe. Many times, in many places. Today was simply the first time they appeared in a place we were watching."

"Where?" Miriam asked. Always straight to the cold, actionable facts.

Nika had fashioned an internal image of sorts of what she'd seen on the web, but it didn't correspond to the map the room displayed. "Alex, can you highlight the area the Detection Network covers?"

"You got it." A region off to the left and above where Alex stood lit up in pale green.

"Now can you give me three reference points? Say, Mirai, Concord HQ and…the center of the Dorado Cluster."

A flutter of Alex's hand, and labeled dots illuminated on the display.

"Thanks." She situated herself beneath Mirai, spun the image in her head around, and zoomed in. Then she took five steps to the left and pointed. "Here."

Alex painted the spot where she pointed red.

Three steps forward. "Here." Four steps to the left. "Also here." She shifted the map in her mind to a new region, then crossed the room toward Miriam. "Here and here."

She continued her travels for almost five minutes; when she'd finished, forty-six swatches of red decorated the map, stretching from one end of the room to the other.

"Well," Miriam remarked dryly. "They've been busy."

"Assuming this all happened in the last month, I'd say so," Alex replied. "I'm not surprised, exactly. I suspected this was happening. But to see it in vivid color and on such a scale.…"

"Can you sense any hints as to when these attacks occurred?" Miriam asked.

"I'm sorry, no. Left to its own devices, kyoseil doesn't perceive 'time' in any meaningful way. It's almost as if.…" Nika trailed off, and Alex stared at her in the curious way the woman had that always meant she was thinking deep space/dimensional thoughts. "I don't know what it's almost as if. When imbued with Asterion programming, kyoseil registers order of operations just fine. But without such structure? An event a million years ago is the same as one that happened yesterday."

"Given such a short time frame, it doesn't matter too much when they appeared at any given location." Miriam's gaze landed on her daughter. "Alex, is there any chance the Dzhvar were already here, long before the Piega Strai was deactivated?"

Alex laughed faintly. "You don't have to use the passive voice, Mom. We all know I'm the one who deactivated it."

"The question remains."

"Is it possible? I suppose—"

"No," Devon interrupted. "I mean, 'possible,' yes, but extremely improbable. I ran a statistical analysis on this map while everyone yammered. Based on the distribution of Dzhvar events, if anything, they were late hitting a region we're monitoring. The possibility that they've been out there gobbling up the manifold for any appreciable length of time, yet not once manifested inside the Detection Network? It's infinitesimally small. So while anything is *possible* when you're dealing with random events, the facts we have on hand counsel against it."

"Understood." Miriam nodded to reiterate the declaration. "What does your statistical analysis say about when they'll arrive in our coverage area again? About when one of our inhabited worlds will come under assault?"

"I'd launch into a lengthy lecture on the risks of drawing conclusions from radically incomplete data, but even my tone-deaf self recognizes this is not the time for ass-covering. We should see them inside the Detection Network again within a couple of days. One of our inhabited worlds, though? Three weeks to four months. But it could be tomorrow or five years from now." Devon winced. "Sorry, maybe a little bit of ass-covering is called for."

"But not long."

"Unlikely."

"All right." Miriam notched her chin upward. "Then we need to move to a higher state of readiness. Mr. Ridani, you've indicated you can provide additional kyoseil-equipped sensors?"

"I'll get them in your hands, and ours, as quickly as the assembly lines will move."

"Thank you. Advisor Kirumase, it seems you've upgraded your abilities with respect to reading and understanding kyoseil. What can you do to help us see the Dzhvar coming?"

"I'll tell you what I can't do. I can't be your expanded real-time detection network. It would require me to live *in* the kyoseil web at all times—"

"No," Dashiel growled.

She offered him an ingratiating smile. "No. I have duties to the Dominion I can't neglect."

"Don't misunderstand," Miriam said. "I wasn't asking you to do any such thing. Once we deploy more tightly integrated coverage, we'll have nearly instantaneous notice of a Dzhvar incursion in any location we're obligated to defend. But anything you're able to tell us about these incursions, such as something the kyoseil senses that our instruments and eyes do not, will be greatly appreciated."

Look into the mind of the enemy, Nika. Tell us what makes them tick. Tell us how to stop them.

She brandished her best diplomat mien for the room. "I'll do everything I can."

INTERMEZZO
I

KATOIKIA
TRIANGULUM GALAXY

I admired how the gleaming tower reflected the afternoon sun's rays across the landscape. Katoikia was a lovely planet, if in a radically austere way. I missed lush green gardens and sparkling azure waters, but the painted desert motif held its own charm.

Drone bots buzzed around the upper reaches of the tower installing the finishing touches. The constructor bots had erected the edifice with impressive speed. I wondered, had Dashiel-Program designed the structure—?

I cut the thought off at the root. No good came from such pointless speculations. Only heartache.

With a sigh I set off for the fabrication complex in the distance. My stride felt slow, plodding and inelegant. Fifty years on, and I still despised this hideous Katasketousya body. I understood why it was necessary, for we simply could not bear any resemblance to Anadens or their progeny: the people who would one day become Asterions, as well as Humans. Our physical bodies needed to appear utterly alien to our genetic kin. I even understood why it was necessary for me to have taken on such a form before I awoke the first program in a body of its own.

I was unique, but my comrades must never learn my secret. They believed themselves born as Katasketousya. They knew nothing of Asterions, knew nothing of what had transpired to bring about their existence or what their true purpose in this life was.

For the next 730,000 years, the Katasketousya would learn and grow until we became experts in the manipulation of physics, as befitted our natural talents; in this respect we would not wander far from our Asterion roots. Only then would we encounter a Directorate-

ruled Anaden Empire at the height of its power, and embark on a long, perilous war of subterfuge and deception aimed at toppling that empire. But I would be following a somewhat different script.

Those events were so interminably far in the future, however, and we had great strides still to make before we could hope to be ready for such challenges.

Everyone I'd awoken had mastered the ability not only to travel in sidespace with their minds, but to affect the physical dimensions from there as well. But becoming somewhat facile with dimensions was merely the start. If we were to become builders of worlds, of entire universes, we were going to have to tame the most fundamental forces of creation.

I stepped inside the closest fabrication building, where stasis chambers rolled off an assembly line at a regular clip. Had Dashiel-Program—no. I stopped the thought cold yet again. It was a tic, and the sooner I excised it, the greater measure of peace I might find.

Spend enough time in sidespace, and one's body began to suffer from neglect. Cases of dehydration were running rampant through the colony, and three instances of mild starvation had occurred in the last few months. Exploring the wonders of the universe made the hours fly by, especially when the reality of inhabiting such a pitiful physical body paled in comparison.

Or perhaps this was just me.

I knew that in the future, occupying the stasis chambers was going to become our default mode of existence, freeing our minds to roam and explore and manipulate the cosmos. But for today, the chambers were billed as a way to safely devote more time to investigating sidespace while strengthening our abilities in that realm. A health and safety measure, as it were.

"Ah, there you are, Mnel."

I turned to see the Katasketousya who would one day be known as 'Lakhes' approaching from the depths of the facility. We would not take on Greek mythological names for many millennia, when we encountered the Anaden Empire—a manipulative genuflection to the Anadens' treasured cultural history. I dared not continue to go by 'Nika,' for my own mental health more than any secrecy concerns. I had chosen 'Mnel' for ease of use, but in my mind I was—I had to be—Mnemosyne. And so in my mind, Lakhes was already Lakhes, despite the fact they presently called themselves 'Akton.'

"You were looking for me, Akton?"

"Yes. I noticed you've ordered the fabrication of structural materials for a second tower."

"I have. We should get started on it soon."

"Should we? I admire your enthusiasm for this project. And I share it, I do. But not everyone does. While we have many volunteers for regular stasis chamber usage, they will not come close to filling up the tower we've completed. Many people are uncomfortable with the notion of sealing themselves away in a tube so they can become ghostly apparitions flitting about on stardust for weeks at a time."

Pondering who Lakhes had once been was only slightly less hazardous than contemplating whether I'd passed Dashiel-Program on the street today, but I did it anyway. Upon being awakened, Lakhes-Akton had swiftly become the spokesperson for all manner of individual concerns. Conciliator, mediator, dealmaker. Leader. Could they be Maris' program? This didn't feel right; Maris was charismatic, yes, but she was—had been—prone to prickliness and even selfishness. One of the other External Relations Advisors, then. Perhaps Cameron Breckel or Gerard Sahk. Or possibly one of the more affable Administration Advisors? Not Perrin, as Lakhes didn't display her bubbly enthusiasm. What if the answer was no one I had known, but instead a stranger whose potential had not yet propelled them into the advisor ranks when the world ended?

It didn't matter, I told myself. But if Lakhes was to be my friend for the next million years, the urge to know their underlying identity was like an itch I couldn't scratch.

I'd forced myself to let the Vault operating system make all the decisions about whom to wake up and in what order. To not sneak a peek at the registries. Not once. And it was too late to do so now, for the Vault had been scrapped for materials once real computer, medical and fabrication facilities had been constructed and everyone had been awoken. On that day, I'd done one of the hardest things so far in this arduous endeavor: I'd erased the original records that had traveled here with me. Ostensibly so no one could ever discover them and inquire what they signified, but in truth so I'd never be able to give into temptation.

I'd cried myself to sleep that night. It had felt like losing everyone all over again.

"Mnel?"

"What? Sorry. My mind wandered. I hear what you're saying about people's reluctance. But I believe it will fade once they learn of the celestial wonders our travelers discover. Then everyone will be clamoring for their own personal stasis chamber, and we will have no facilities suited to keeping them running. Best to get ahead of demand now."

"You are so confident of this?"

The burden of desolate knowledge pressed against my chest to the point I nearly staggered to my knees from the weight of it. "I am."

PART II:

MYTHS & MONSTERS

16

SCHOLITE

Olivia was shown to a table by the window. Though the dining room was spacious and the time of day appropriate for meals, no other tables were occupied. The restaurant was accessible only by a wormhole controlled from the entrance at ground level, which struck her as a tacky way to signal exclusivity.

She tested out her Caeles Prism, but found she was unable to open a wormhole of her own. Now she considered being impressed, as wormhole suppression was rare and expensive technology. In addition, the restaurant hovered free above a bustling downtown district, making it effectively a spaceship. On the whole, it was a significant expense to go to for a restaurant, but the owner had the funds to spare.

Among varied real estate and commercial interests, Arnal Nikto Idoni ran the largest hypnol distribution network in the surrounding twelve sectors of the Milky Way. The more unsavory aspects of his business were buried behind half a dozen shell companies, as in the upper echelon of Anaden society, this was how such business was done. But beneath a veneer of respectability, the man was a crime lord through and through.

It was a testament to how much of a dent she was making in his market share that he'd granted her a meeting. But he'd sat up and taken notice of her, as was her intent.

She chose not to sit at the table, instead gazing out the panoramic windows at the city skyline below until Nikto arrived, which turned out not to be long at all. Polite of him not to attempt a petty power game by making her wait.

"Ms. Piras. It's a pleasure to meet you."

Olivia despised using an alias. In the past, she'd never felt the need to hide who she was or what she did. But the unfortunate reality was, if her name crossed the ears of human law enforcement, SENTRI would spare no expense in tracking her down and eliminating her for the second time. And she wasn't ready to counter such a move on their part. Not just yet. So she suffered the rare humiliation of a false name, for now.

She accepted his proffered hand. "You as well, Mr. Nikto."

"I had heard you were Human. I wasn't certain I believed it."

"And now you do."

"Yes. Shall we sit?" He gestured to the table, where a bottle of wine and a spread of shrimp cocktail waited.

"Of course."

He poured them each a glass of wine, then nibbled on a shrimp while he contemplated her across the table. "I won't insult you with small talk. You asked for this meeting, because you believe you want something from me. I don't expect to give it to you, but please, ask."

Straight to the point. Another mark in his favor. He wasn't her type of man on a personal level, but she respected confidence. "Very well." She didn't touch the wine or the shrimp. "I want you to sell your hypnol manufacturing facilities on the second moon of Ficenti to me."

Nikto huffed a breath. "Ms. Piras, we are competitors. Why would I willingly cede an iota of my resources to you? You are a, shall we say, fledgling at best. No offense. I've been impressed by the speed with which you've gained market share on a smattering of planets. But as a Human, you cannot have been navigating this business for more than a few decades. I had the license of the Idoni Primor for two millennia."

"Yes, and in her absence, her spoils have fallen to those who dare to step forward and claim them. My request stands." It was nice to have a proper challenge again, even if she had played this game before.

"No." He shook his head to emphasize the point while he dipped a shrimp in cocktail sauce. "Do you have a fallback request, or was this your only play?"

"I don't need a fallback. If you do not sell the facilities to me, I will take them from you."

The shrimp hovered at his lips. "With what army?"

"Does your answer remain 'no'?"

"Oh, quite."

"I see. Thank you for your time, Mr. Nikto." She pushed the chair back and stood, then strode across the empty restaurant and exited through the waiting wormhole to the street below.

FICENTI SATELLITE
ANDROMEDA GALAXY

The plant manager's office was tucked into the rear of one of two squat buildings ensconced within a force-field dome on the lunar surface.

The manager stood from his desk and went to the refreshment dispenser in the corner. When he reached for the thermos sitting beside the dispenser, Olivia's adiamene blade appeared at his throat. She'd been watching from sidespace, and the timing and placement of her wormhole were orchestrated to catch him without any recourse.

"If you trigger any alarms, you will die slowly and painfully."

"Wha-a-t—?" the man stuttered out.

"What I said. I understand Anadens retain their memories up to the last few microseconds of death when they undergo regenesis. You wouldn't want the next forty-five minutes to haunt you in the years to come, would you?"

"N-no. What do you want?"

"First? Swallow this." She held out a small capsule with her other hand, while keeping the blade flush at his neck.

"What is it?"

"You ask far too many questions for a man in your situation."

"But what if it's what will kill me slowly and painfully?"

She almost laughed. "It's not. It will simply make you more compliant for our conversation."

It was a lie. One of the biggest troubles of this new world she found herself in was that the dead no longer stayed that way. In her old life, she'd not hesitated to eliminate competitors, disobedient employees and anyone else who stood in the way of her achieving her goals. In her new one, doing so took a bit of additional planning.

But there were ways around every difficulty. The pill contained *apomono,* a hypnol that destroyed an Anaden's connection to their integral in a matter of seconds, rendering regenesis no longer a possibility for them. It was both exceptionally rare and highly illegal, which was why she'd recently begun manufacturing it herself.

The man sighed heavily, and blood pearled along the edge of the blade. "Careful there."

"Ah, ah...move the blade away, or it'll cut me when I swallow."

Unfortunately, it was true, and an adiamene blade did not leave any room for error. She withdrew it two centimeters. "Do it now."

He took the capsule and swallowed it dry. "Fine. Done. What next?"

"What's the passcode to the control system here?"

"If I tell you, Arnal Nikto will fire me, then kill me, then enslave me in some asteroid mining operation for a century."

"Tell me, and I'll kill you quickly. You won't feel a thing, and when you wake up, you can inform Nikto that you never saw your killer. Don't tell me, and..." she returned the blade to his neck, sending fresh blood welling up "...forty-five minutes of agony you'll remember forever."

"Shit, shit, shit. Okay. It's a string of letters and numbers: BL88K1YA49."

"Thank you. Let's go over to the desk and ensure you're logged in, shall we?"

"You'll cut me if I walk."

"I suppose that's true." She removed the blade from his neck and stepped back.

He turned around. On seeing her, his dull features contorted. "You're Human?"

"More or less." She motioned the blade toward the desk. "Don't dawdle."

"I expected to find a gun pointed at me," he muttered as he moved to the desk, eyes never leaving her.

"No need. I can kill you three different ways from where I stand."

His eyes widened. "I don't know why, but somehow I believe you."

"Smart man." She kept a meter between them as she circled around the desk after him. One permanent screen displayed a grid of vid feeds showing the assembly lines, where workers oversaw the production and packaging of a variety of illegal hypnols, while the other monitored the landing pad and entry and break spaces.

"See? All active." He winced. "I don't feel so good."

"You are under a great deal of stress."

"Ugh, but my stomach…."

A sign the *apomono* was working its dark magic. "Focus. What about the security systems? I assume you have lockdown protocols."

"You just, ah, have to enter the passcode again."

"Let's do that."

"I told you what it was."

"I need to be certain you were honest with me."

"Any chance you can knock me out instead of killing me? I'll still say I never saw my attacker."

"But then you would still be here, and I have work to do. Painless, I promise."

"Shit." He reached for the holographic control panel on the desk.

"Slowly, so I can confirm you're entering the same information you provided to me."

He pecked out the numbers and letters one at a time, and a new modal box opened on the left screen.

"Thank you. You've been most cooperative. Now move to the door."

He shuffled out from behind the desk. "Bleeding out won't be painless."

"Also, it would leave a horrid mess to clean up." She removed the Reverb from her pocket, pointed it at him, and fired. He collapsed in a heap to the floor.

Initially developed by Senecan Federation Intelligence to remotely hack human eVis, the insidious little device had proved most adept at killing Anadens by shorting out their neural cybernetics.

Olivia opened the office door, hauled the body out into the hall, then went back inside and sat at the desk to study the security screen.

The fourth option in the modal box that had popped up was labeled 'biohazard cleaning.' A must for any chemical factory.

She slipped on a breather mask and activated the biohazard cleaning procedure. As soon as a countdown began on the screen, she moved to the wall beside the door and flattened herself against it while activating the magnets in her shoes.

Alarms blared as the door to the office slid open, along with every door in the facility. The force-field dome deactivated, and everything not secured to the structure, including all the air and the employees breathing it, was swept outside and into the void of space.

The venting lasted for almost a minute. When the office door closed, she returned to the desk, where a confirmation box awaited her input.

Reinitiate life-support measures?

She confirmed the request, then sat down and went to work. The biohazard alarm would have sent an alert to someone in Nikto's organization.

The first thing she did was insert a spike in the input port. Within seconds, it had changed the passcodes and written new security procedures under her control. Next, she surveyed the full complement of security measures at the site. This was a criminal operation, which meant Nikto needed to defend it from both law enforcement and competitors.

Sure enough, laser turrets were installed outside each of the three domes scattered across the moon's surface, all of which were run from here. She processed an order to bring in additional defenses, but these should get the job done for today. She switched them from sentinel mode to active. Now any vessels that approached would be treated as hostile.

The minimal Ficenti government didn't have the resources to police its satellites, but Nikto employed his own private police force; she'd deal with them shortly. And while she disliked the expense, a stationary Caeles Prism wormhole would enable her to both deliver new equipment for the factory and transport finished goods to her distribution centers expeditiously.

But if she could take all these measures, so could someone else.

Artificials were now legal on Anaden worlds, though heavily regulated. Prevo-style tech remained illegal under Advocacy rule (Asterions having been grandfathered in), but laws had never stopped anyone before. She took it as a certainty that at least one Anaden Prevo already existed. More likely hundreds did, and growing by dozens every day. She'd also heard rumors about the Advocacy's Advanced Research Division developing a personal wormhole generator that any ordinary person was able to operate.

Arnal Nikto might not be an Anaden Prevo—he'd betrayed no hint of being so at their brief meeting—and he might not have procured such a device, assuming it did in fact exist. But she had not achieved all she had, twice, by betting on probabilities or relying on assumptions.

So she set the security system to treat the presence of any organic life larger than a cat as a biohazard, subject to a broadcast override code, which she promptly began broadcasting. If Nikto's people infiltrated the facility once she was up and running, she'd lose some of her bots to the cleaning procedure, but it was factored into her expenses.

Immediate concerns handled, she settled in to study the setup of the facility. She didn't plan to bring in new workers. Using organics to handle any of the work performed here was an archaic practice, and the fact Nikto had been utilizing so many Anadens was presumably a societal imperative. Someone needed to provide employment for over a trillion Anadens.

In reality, bots were capable of handling every aspect of the factory's operation, which was one reason why she'd built a bot manufacturing facility on Scholite six months ago. Her machines, running her ware. Sub-Artificial intelligence where possible, and shackled where higher cognitive abilities were required. Free Artificials could be disloyal as easily as organic sentients.

All the equipment and component materials onsite should've survived the biohazard purge, so she expected to be able to begin her own production within two days. She considered constructing two additional facilities here on the satellite to meet anticipated future demand…but better to maintain many operations in many locations. The existing capacity the factory provided would double her finished product supply within a week.

But she still needed customers to sell the finished products to, which meant she needed to eliminate her competition, one world and organization at a time.

17

MSHAK

Varlem Bakker T'worz barked at Olivia while tossing an enormous axe from one hand to another. "You take too long. My warriors are eager to begin their vengeance."

"And they will get their chance. I have two groups of targets for your warriors today."

"Then we will get two ships as payment."

"One location, one mission."

"We get two ships."

"No ships, then." She spun up her Caeles Prism and opened a wormhole.

"Wait. What distance between targets?"

"Around fifty meters."

"Fine. One ship."

She stared at his hideous face for a few seconds before closing the wormhole. "As to the first group of targets, your people can expect trained and armed resistance."

"Good. The warriors I selected have built up a fervor of anticipation."

"I'm sure they have." She gestured to the door. "Let's go outside and gather everyone."

Several sparring matches were ongoing in the common area outside the chieftain's hall, but all activity ceased when she appeared. She glanced at the Ch'mshaks milling about as it occurred to her that she'd yet to knowingly see a female. Or perhaps the warriors were the females; who could say.

T'worz bellowed something in their native tongue, sending harsh syllables grating across her eardrums. Six Ch'mshak in full armor jogged around the corner of a building and approached them.

They encircled her at two meters' distance while pounding on their chests and making various threatening motions with their talons.

"Chieftain, do tell them to back off."

"Are you afraid?"

"No. But I did not come here to be bullied. This is a business relationship."

"You lack humor." He barked what sounded like an order, and the others reluctantly stepped away and formed a rough line.

"Better. A moment."

"We go now."

"You go when I provide you a means to go."

She disliked dividing her attention by slipping into sidespace when she was surrounded by a bunch of brutish, towering, armed creatures, but she had no choice.

She projected her consciousness to Nikto's distribution warehouse on the surface of Ficenti. Inside the armory, four mercenaries outfitted themselves in environment suits before gearing up for their mission to Ficenti's satellite. A biohazard could mean many things, and they prepped for any eventuality.

When they finished preparations and began heading outside to the landing pad, she gave her full attention to the Ch'mshak squad. "Kill the men who are outside and trash the transport on the landing pad. Then await further orders."

She'd expected T'worz to translate her orders, but they all seemed to understand her, and her estimation of the Ch'mshak increased a fraction. They continued to learn Communis so they could better effect their vengeance when the time came, even though until she'd arrived, they'd had no reason to believe it would ever come.

She opened a wormhole to the edge of the landing pad and motioned ahead. "Go."

The squad barreled forward, jostling one another for the right to be first onto the battlefield. She followed the last of them through and closed the wormhole behind her, lest any nearby villager decide to seize their chance at freedom.

Only two of Nikto's mercenaries managed to raise and fire their weapons before the squad was on top of them. The laser fire diffused across the armor of one Ch'mshak and left a scorched trail down the arm of another, but did not slow them down.

The melee that followed was an astonishing smorgasbord of violence. A Ch'mshak talon curled under the chest armor of one of the mercenaries and ripped upward, shredding the armor as it gutted the man all the way to his collarbone. In a move reminiscent of the one she'd witnessed in the arena on her first visit to Mshak, a double-bladed spear sent an arm flying, then a head. When a mercenary fell to the ground beneath a rushing attacker, the Ch'mshak leapt up and landed one booted foot on the man's head and the other on his chest—

Olivia instinctively flinched at the resulting gore. Her past was painted in blood, a fair bit of which she'd drawn herself. Brutality was, on occasion, the cost of doing business in the world she'd chosen for herself. But these Ch'mshak really were on a whole other level.

When the last mercenary had fallen, less than thirty seconds after the assault began, one member of the squad stomped up to her, blood and gore dripping from his armor and head. "There are more, yes?"

"Yes. One of you needs to stay out here and wreck the shuttle-craft on the landing pad. The rest of you will go inside this building. Eliminate the people you find there and destroy everything that isn't permanently affixed to the walls. *Only* the people and property inside the building."

"But if inside, we can kill them all without violating our arrangement?"

She had no intention of taking over the facility; this was entirely about sending a message to Nikto. "You may kill them all."

S&L

They returned to the clan village to find a giant animal being roasted over an open fire in the common area. The first of her squad through the wormhole hooped and hollered their way to the fire, where they yanked the still-cooking animal off the fire, spit and all, and bit into a flank.

Dozens of Ch'mshak emerged from buildings to surround the returning heroes, and the air grew thick with their awful, guttural tongue.

"Our ship now."

She pivoted to T'worz as he approached, then pointed to the sky. "It will be here shortly."

The transport descended through the clouds not a moment too soon, as she was growing tired of the yelling and the odor of meat and blood. It landed in a clearing behind the center square.

"Show me how it works," T'worz demanded as they neared the ship.

"As you wish." She went up to a panel embedded in the hull by the hatch. "This large button here opens the hatch. Simply press it."

As soon as it was open, he stormed inside.

'Welcome. How may I be of service?'

"Prissy ship."

"This is the voice it comes with. As I said, it will obey the crew's commands. I suggest you designate a single individual to be in charge, lest the crew confuse the VI with contradictory orders. There are not any security measures to speak of, so keep the ship under guard if it lands in a populated area."

"Fuel?"

"Unlimited. If the ship experiences a mechanical problem, the VI will alert you, but I don't expect that to happen."

"How it not be seen?" T'worz asked.

"The crew can instruct the ship to activate and deactivate stealth as they wish. They should take care to remember to do so when leaving this planet's surface and returning, or else they will be shot down by the blockade."

"Yes." Thuds resounded from outside, and she left the cabin to discover a line of Ch'mshak hauling large crates toward the ship.

They clearly had plans for the minuscule freedom she was enabling, but those didn't concern her.

18

ARES

Eren sat in his office chair and slid it close to the desk, until his stomach brushed the lip.

No, this wasn't going to be comfortable. He toed the chair back a few centimeters, so he was able to shift around without bumping into anything. Then he placed his hands on the surface and opened a screen displaying the latest report on the market shares and notable activities of the major illicit hypnol manufacturers. He read for a few seconds before his eyes drifted to the bare walls. After giving Nyx such a hard time for her lack of decor in her old office, he'd be a hypocrite if he didn't put something on a shelf. But first he needed to install a shelf.

He forced his gaze back to the screen. Oh, the Quilon cartel had gained ground on Epithero...he scanned the rows to see who'd gotten squeezed out, but damned if he could locate the information he wanted.

So he kicked his feet up on the desk, crossed his ankles and leaned back to consider the data on the screen from an angle—the chair teetered precariously on two legs, and he hurriedly returned the others to the floor, which knocked the chair away from the desk.

This was ridiculous. He couldn't be expected to work this way.

Eren closed the screen, stood and left the office. By the time he'd reached the Security Division exit, his head was feeling much clearer. He'd stroll through the gardens and study the report on a virtual display while he planned his next move in the Pale Viper/Riamere investigation.

Hypnol manufacturers were all too common, but no one other than Riamere was daring to produce *apomono*. He needed a hook, a way in, and this was it.

The biggest reason *apomono* was so rare was because in the Anaden hypnol trade, there was 'wink-wink-nudge-nudge illegal,' and then there was 'seriously fucking illegal,' and *apomono* was decidedly the latter. Its status as the one way to deprive an Anaden of their precious immortality short of simultaneously blowing up the multi-redundant servers housing an integral meant pretty much no one wanted the substance circulating on the streets. Except for the power brokers who yearned to use it to control their enemies, and assassins who desired a more refined tool in their arsenal, of course.

But the second-biggest reason it was rare was because it was a bitch to make. Integrals were pico-scale quantum biotech, and scientists had girded their entanglement resilience hundreds of millennia ago. Crafting equally advanced femto-biobots to burrow through the protective layers deep inside the brain then devour the entangled particles was not something most hypnol production facilities could manage. Doing so required a state of the art clean lab, a laundry list of specialized materials and forbidden knowledge. A sophisticated enough operation could brew the ingredients in-house, but they still needed component materials to do so.

One of those component materials, a beast with the sexy name of '4-nephylheptine-isoamyl glycyl,' happened to also be rare, on account of it being nearly as difficult to produce as *apomono* itself. As far as he'd been able to determine, only three labs formulated it for commercial sale.

So last night, Eren had taken a small team of those contractors of his, broken into one of the labs, and stolen their entire shipment-ready supply. Then he'd arranged a generator 'accident' to blow up the facility. Always a good time, that. This morning, he'd had the other two labs raided and shut down for alleged safety violations.

The power of government sanction could on occasion be useful.

Today, false records and planted whispers busily wound through the biochemical manufacturing underbelly, weaving a scenario that set him up (under a false name) as a dealer willing to fill the void in the supply of Nephyl-HIG—

Where are you?

"I'm doing great this fine morning, Nyx. How are you?" Eren rolled his eyes and looked around, as he hadn't been paying much attention to where he was walking for several minutes now.

West Gardens. What's up?

I need you to come with me to a massacre.

PLANET A-468C ORBIT
ANDROMEDA GALAXY

The space station orbiting high above A-468c, an uninhabitable but resource rich planet, was a nothing place. A rest stop where those who worked the mining operations below were able to restock on supplies, enjoy a marginally better meal than the mines' fab kitchen produced, and get laid by forgettable prostitutes.

Nonetheless, on any ordinary day almost two thousand people inhabited the station. And now, they were all dead.

Eren grimaced as he stepped around a severed leg and the meandering pool of blood it soaked in. The sight reminded him far too much of the grisly scene at the Hesgyr's Fetel-reu asteroid, where the Phae'soon's death cloud had dissolved hundreds of Hesgyr miners.

No body here was fully intact, which meant all the victims had incidentally bled out, leaving a veritable lake of blood to be constrained by the walls of the station. Forensic techs, who'd been on the scene for a while now, had done the saintly work of marking off a path through the remains so investigators could reach the depths of the station. He took care to stay between the lines as he and Nyx picked their way through the atrium and into the corridors en route to the security office.

"A merchant vessel commed Vigil when they tried to dock and got no response from station security," Nyx said. "A Vigil ship arrived and found this upon entering the station. Due to the extreme nature and volume of the violence, word flew up the Vigil chain of command, then reached me."

"Why did it reach you? This is definitely *something*, but it isn't intelligence."

She shrugged noncommittally. "People still feel the compulsion to report significant problems to Inquisitors. Vigil actually contacted Ziton, but he said it wasn't Security's problem and sent them my way."

Nyx's brother was arrogant, brash and disdainful of the masses, even for a former Inquisitor, so Eren wasn't surprised the man had blown off a report of two thousand mine workers being massacred as not worthy of his time. Once upon a time, Nyx might have as well, but it was no lie that she'd grown as a person. Empathy remained a stretch for her, but she recognized the failing and *tried*.

A Vigil officer stumbled around the corner of the narrow hall hand covering his mouth, and plowed straight into Eren. The man's momentum knocked Eren backward, and before he could regain his balance, his arm and shoulder skidded across the wall. The man lurched in the other direction, pitched forward, and made it another few meters before losing the battle with his nausea and doubling over to vomit all over the hallway floor.

Eren felt a sticky substance cling to the fabric of his shirt as he pushed off the wall, and he held out his arm to inspect the sleeve.

Blood and a couple of small clotted chunks of he didn't want to know what streaked over the elbow and down the forearm of his shirt. Terrific.

He shot Nyx a scowl as they resumed their journey; he also let her gain a half-step on him to be the first around the blind corner. "So this landed in your lap because no one at Vigil wanted to take responsibility for it. And why did you bring me along?"

"You'll see."

Despite his displeasure at being sullied by the gore and general discomfort at having to witness such carnage, his interest was piqued. While mass murder didn't technically fall under her purview, some detail about either the victims or the perpetrators must mean it did fall under his.

Had to be the perpetrators, as the station wasn't exactly a tourist attraction likely to attract alien visitors. But who, or what, would dare to commit a massacre on this scale? They hadn't shot up the place; they'd ripped the victims apart limb by limb. Barisans were capable of causing the clawed-up torsos he'd unfortunately spotted at several points, but they weren't strong enough to rip an Anaden's leg clean off its body. A Khokteh might be, if they were out of their mind on adrenal strength hypnols. But while Khokteh could be violent, even the criminals among them tended to display purpose in their violence. They had rules about honor and other nonsense. Besides, it would take a mob of at least a hundred Khokteh to kill this many people without being overwhelmed, as the furry, four-eyed aliens bled and died well enough.

Mechs? They'd be harder to take down for certain. Problem was, the carnage felt too messy for mechs; the machines would proceed through their mission with fastidious efficiency. Whoever had committed this atrocity had done so for one of two reasons: a feral, mindless rage…or for fun.

They finally reached the security office, but the scenery didn't improve. Two shredded bodies had been pushed into the corner of the office to allow for access to the control center. It was a small room, and blood streaked the walls and three of the screens. *Arae*, what a horrific spectacle.

A Vigil forensic tech waited for them inside. "Director Nyx, thank you for coming."

"This is my associate, Eren Savitas. Show us the footage."

"Yes, ma'am." The tech gingerly typed in a command, careful to avoid several blood splotches on the surface, and feeds from four separate cams populated the screens. Eren focused on the one showing the docking atrium; sure, the perpetrators *could* have wormholed onto the station, but it seemed unlikely.

On the video, the security guard on duty looked up, evidently expecting new entrants from the airlock. Abruptly he jumped and fumbled for his gun while scrambling backward. Three seconds later, a great hulking form charged out of the docking tunnel and—

"You have got to be fucking kidding me!" Eren exclaimed. "*Ch'mshak?*"

"Ch'mshak," Nyx replied grimly.

They kept coming, too. By the time the sixth had cleared the entrance, the security guard and ten other people in the atrium were dead.

Eren's stomach churned in disgust. Under the command of the Machim Primor, an army of Ch'mshak had killed hundreds of anarchs at Post Alpha on Chionis during the Directorate War. Friends and colleagues.

He pushed away the resurgent memory of both Cosime and Felzeor almost dying that day and waved a hand toward the screens. "Any chance we can skip to the end?"

The tech glanced at Nyx for permission. She nodded tersely, and the tech sped up the feeds until they showed only a blur of motion. But wholesale dismemberment took time, and two hours had elapsed on the footage clock when the tech returned the feeds to normal speed. The six Ch'mshak, now covered in viscera, blood and globby flesh, clambered through the lake of blood in the atrium and disappeared into the docking tunnel.

"They just walked out of here and left," Eren muttered in disbelief. "Evil, soulless brutes. Okay, I get it. Ch'mshak aren't

Anaden. You want my wizened intelligence assessment? Here's why they did it. One, they enjoy killing. That was the entire basis of their arrangement with the Directorate for millennia. They got to kill, and in return, the Directorate let them live. Two, they want revenge for being confined to their planet for the last eleven years. Anadens make the biggest target for their vengeance, and we're the species they're most familiar with.

"Let Commandant Solovy and our good buddy Casmir know they have a leak in their containment blockade. Alert security at all space stations to watch the docking tunnels and be ready to lock everything down the instant a Ch'mshak tromps off of a ship. There. My work here is done. Can I go now?"

"No," Nyx replied.

"Excuse me?" And to think he'd been entertaining indulgent thoughts about her.

"Eren, I didn't bring you with me because the perpetrators are Ch'mshak. You're correct. They're Concord's problem, and I'll ensure the appropriate parties know it as soon as we leave. But there's another problem with what happened here. The last ship to dock at the station, about five minutes before the Ch'mshak stormed the place? It was a Human vessel. A private Human merchant ship."

19

PLANET A-468C ORBIT

Eren copied out all the information the security system had recorded about the ship carrying the Ch'mshak to his internal storage. The ship's VI had handled the docking procedures, which meant it had transmitted all the technicals on the vessel, if nothing about its occupants.

He clapped the Vigil officer on the shoulder as thanks for doing the dirty work of manning the blood-stained interface, then turned to Nyx. "I've got everything I need. Now can we leave?"

A grim expression darkened her features. "Let's go to my office to discuss our next steps."

Eren held out his arm to scowl at it. "Mind if we swing by my apartment first? I managed to get gore all over my shirt when that officer collided with me."

"Not a problem." She motioned for him to follow her into the hallway, then checked to confirm it was empty before reaching around to the small of her back. A second later, a wormhole split apart the air.

"Still keeping your toy a secret?" She'd ambushed him on Nythir using her shiny new CPM, or Caeles Prism Module. But the device had come in handy during the mission, enabling them to save over a thousand lives during a Phae'soon attack on the Hesgyr's Ghoede colony. The device was a marked improvement on the personal Caeles Prisms used by Human Prevos, most notably in how the 'Prevo' component wasn't required; anyone who knew how to press the button on the device could generate a wormhole and step across vast distances.

"Those are my orders for now. So let's not linger."

"Yes, ma'am." He walked through the wormhole and into the hallway on the third floor of Corradeo's Ares estate.

ARES

By the time the shimmering oval vanished, he had the door to his apartment open and was yanking his shirt over his head. He carried it with two fingers over to the laundry chute and chucked it in, then headed for the lavatory.

He was a little surprised to see Nyx had followed him into the apartment rather than wait for him in the hall. But he was going to be a minute, so he would've ended up inviting her in if she hadn't. "It looks as if some blood seeped all the way through the material, so I need to scour my arm with some bleach."

"That's fine." Her voice sounded pinched, and she didn't meet his gaze as he stepped into the lavatory and turned on the sink. Not too long ago, she would've retorted how bleach wasn't safe to rub on skin without a trace of drollery. But somewhere along the way, she'd caught on to his brand of humor. Though not enough to laugh at it, apparently....

"I'll have the ship manufacturer check their database and identify the retailer they delivered it to, then contact the retailer for the purchase records," he said while scrubbing soap down his arm. "But I doubt they sold it to a Ch'mshak, which means the crew must have stolen the ship from somewhere. I'll reach out to one of my contacts at SENTRI and have them search for any reports of ship thefts with a side of a high body count. Or any theft outside a standard profile, for that matter. It's always conceivable a small group of Ch'mshak could rein in their bloodlust for long enough to acquire something that enables them to then exercise said bloodlust in full."

"All proper avenues of inquiry," Nyx replied from the hall. She'd stayed near the entry, and he couldn't see her in the mirror. "But how did they get somewhere to steal a ship in the first place?"

"Excellent question. Maybe we missed a few holdouts in the big sweep Concord conducted when they imposed the quarantine? But this explanation doesn't sit right with me. No way does a pod of Ch'mshak hide quietly for over a decade, only to suddenly pop out and resume their massacring ways at this moment. They might be able to exercise restraint for an hour or two, but they don't possess the patience for such a long game."

Eren washed off the soap and inspected his forearm. He didn't see any more blood or suspicious flecks, but when the grisly scene on the space station flashed through his mind, he started another round of scrubbing anyway. "The good news, to the extent there is any, is that those smaller merchant models don't come with a Caeles Prism. They can't be more than a couple of Milky Way sectors away."

"I've already informed Casmir of the ship and its occupants. Machim patrols will be searching for it."

"And I wish them luck. The bad news is, the merchant models typically do come with a stealth upgrade option, ostensibly so upstanding traders can avoid pirates, though it works in the other direction, too. I should know in a few hours whether this ship came with the upgrade, but I'm not optimistic we'll get lucky."

"If a group didn't steal the ship, then someone must have provided it to them. A sophisticated stealth module would explain how it got off Mshak."

"And on it," he agreed. "But not why in Hades' five rivers anyone would *ever* give the Ch'mshak a ship."

"What if there was something on the station someone wanted to steal?"

"I can think of seventeen better ways to steal literally anything than sending in a squad of Ch'mshak to murder every person on the station. Right now, none of this makes sense. So we'll start with the ship and see where we can get." He shut off the water, toweled dry his arm and turned to exit the lavatory.

Nyx was leaning against the wall opposite the lavatory door, next to the closet. Her arms were crossed loosely over her chest and her body language asserted a forced casualness that didn't reach her eyes. The heat in her gaze reminded him far too much of the way she'd looked at him in Tolje Alainor's guest bedroom, and they both knew where that had led.

Her legs wrapped around his hips as she sank onto him. Her hair tumbled across his shoulders, and she bent down to take his lower lip in her teeth and suck on it—

His skin flushed hot as he only belatedly realized he'd let her spend the last five minutes watching him parade around shirtless while he rambled on about the attack. Either noxious fumes on the station had poisoned his senses and rendered him oblivious to his surroundings, or his subconscious had sneakily brought her here then positioned him in such a way that she'd *get* to stare at him shirtless, should she be interested in doing so.

Almost certainly the latter, because his subconscious was a traitorous bastard.

Regardless, it no longer mattered. Every time he was in her presence, he had to forcibly hold at bay memories of their night together. The instant he'd caught the smolder in her expression, he lost the battle, and those memories now marched in a full-sensory parade through his mind. Good sense fled the premises, taking with it all the promises and admonitions he'd made to himself. In this moment, he knew only that he needed to touch her again.

He idly fondled the washcloth in his hands as he met her gaze in full, letting desire flare freely in his eyes. Unlike him, she was properly dressed in her usual fitted shirt, work slacks and blazer, but he remembered all too well the exquisite body the clothes obscured.

"Are you going to get dressed?"

He took several steps toward her. "You are, once again, blocking my ability to do so."

"What?" Her brow puckered into a knot.

"The closet. With my shirts in it. You're standing…" he moved closer, one hand stretching out to rest on the closet door even as he positioned himself firmly in front of her "…okay, you're not technically *blocking* it, but if you want to scoot a few centimeters to the left, you can be."

"Eren, what are you doing?" Her voice had dropped to a raspy purr.

"The same thing I usually do: something stupid."

"Don't. We said we were going to keep our relationship professional until we—"

"*Unless* or until," he whispered.

"*Unless* or until we worked through our respective issues. The fact you're saying this is stupid means you haven't done so."

"Ah, my logical, practical Nyx. Have you worked through your issues? Something about either bottling up your rebellious emotions and tossing the bottle into the Delphin Sea, or else coming to grips with the reality that you're the same as the rest of us and *have* them?"

"That's an oversimplification."

"I'm sure it is. Have you?"

Her tongue darted out to moisten her lips. *Gods.* "A little. Not entirely."

"Then you should definitely go." He leaned in until his mouth hovered above hers; his fingertips drifted featherlight over her neck. "Stop me and leave. I beg you."

Silence hung in the air for a frozen lapse of seconds before she spoke. "I'm not your savior, Eren."

"No. It seems you're my drug. My addiction."

"I accept that." She grabbed his face with both hands and crushed her lips against his.

$$S\&L$$

Eren sighed without opening his eyes, as awareness asserted itself while the fog of slumber was still dissipating.

The warmth of another's skin marked a handprint on his chest as it rose and fell in reluctant contemplation. He didn't want to ponder what he'd done—*again*—didn't want to grapple with confusing and contradictory feelings. Guilt and pleasure. Loneliness and comfort. Sorrow and…affection. But he had no choice but to face up to them. Try to figure out what the hells he was supposed to do. Wanted to do. Had to do. Could live with doing.

"Hmm," Nyx murmured sleepily as she shifted toward him— and abruptly reversed course.

His skin chilled in her absence. He opened his eyes and managed a closed-mouthed smile as he looked over. The sheet rested, wrinkled, at her waist, and her tousled hair fell over her shoulder to partially obscure one breast. Athena's grace, she was magnificent.

"Oops," he forced out, a shameful absence of levity in his voice.

She studied him, expression guarded as her bearing transitioned to stiffness. "A better response than last time, but not by much."

"Yeah." He glanced away to scratch at his forehead, unable to withstand her unvarnished scrutiny any longer.

"You still feel guilty. Still feel as though you're betraying Cosime's memory."

The utterance of Cosime's name by her made him flinch. "I do. I'm trying not to, I am, but…."

She nodded tightly and started climbing out of the bed.

"Wait." He instinctively reached for her.

She paused, now resting on one knee, the sheet fully gone, and he instantly wanted her all over again. Dammit. "You don't need to leave right away."

"Eren." She stopped, pursed her lips, and began anew. "I can't bring myself to regret what we did, though I realize full well that, with repetition, it will probably ruin our professional relationship. But I don't desire to inflict further pain on you. So I'll go, and we can talk once emotions have cooled and…" her eyes swept over the length of him "…more clothes are involved."

"More clothes didn't stop us from ending up here again."

She stared at him, and a rare storm consumed her sapphire irises. "I might point out how you were missing your shirt when this began. But if I can't control myself at the mere sight of shirt-less you, then I'm hopelessly lost."

He should snap back with a wisecrack, but he didn't. "Nyx, if anyone is lost here, it's me."

She settled back onto the bed, still sitting up, one leg curled underneath her. "I don't know what to do or say. I don't know how to handle this. I thought I was making progress on under-standing and regulating my emotions, but then you…" she glow-ered at the ceiling "…I don't like the power you seem to exert over me. But I do like being with you. Except for this part." Her gaze returned to settle on him, and her eyes had grown bright from an emotion he didn't dare name. "Not this part."

"Neither do I. But I didn't just like the other parts—I loved them. This was spectacular. Better than the first time, since now I know what you want, what you need…." *Arae*, if he kept going this way they were never getting out of the bed.

His heart ached with an empty sorrow he doubted would ever heal. But when he shut his eyes, Cosime no longer glared back at him in accusation. Because she wouldn't do that, not when she was gone. Dammit, why couldn't he just let himself be happy?

Nyx regarded him silently, what might be a touch of her own sadness weighing on her features. With the armor peeled away, she wasn't at all what he'd once believed her to be. He'd never expected to discover vulnerability beneath all the cold fierceness. She was daring to let him see it, and to do so must be costing her so much.

Odds were high he would destroy her in the end; collateral damage in the wreckage he always inevitably left in his wake. But until then, maybe they should both grab for what happiness they could find, even if it only ran skin deep. The treacherous possibility that their connection ran any deeper, he buried beneath a mountain of coping mechanisms that kept him mostly sane.

He reached a hand out toward her, palm up, though she was too far away for him to touch. A request, and an offer. "Why don't you stay for a while?"

Her lips parted…and after a beat, she took his hand and sank into his arms.

20

EARTH

SAN FRANCISCO

Kennedy was sitting at the table by the window when Alex arrived for lunch, and she cursed her tardiness under her breath. She'd missed their lunch date altogether last month since she'd been on Elakrin. She'd genuinely intended to arrive early this time to make up for it, but she'd gotten distracted studying the Amaranthe map Nika had marked up while chasing her own thoughts in circles and lost track of time.

She plastered on a smile and slid into the seat opposite Kennedy. "Hey. Sorry I'm a second late."

"Is it true? Are the Dzhvar really here?"

So much for the smile. "It's true. Well, they're not 'here' here, not yet. We detected them way over in the Capricornus Supercluster. Though according to Nika, they've been tearing through the far reaches of Amaranthe for several weeks now. But yes, their long slumber is confirmed over."

"Crap. But the new sensor tech worked?"

"It did, for which the Asterions deserve pretty much all the credit."

"Don't let Devon hear you say that."

"Eh, I offend Devon's sensibilities on an almost weekly basis as it is." She took a quick sip of the glass of wine Kennedy had already poured for her. "Favor?"

"Always."

"Any chance we can talk about normal stuff for a few minutes? Pretend it's the good old days when every morning didn't bring the specter of civilizational annihilation, and we could simply enjoy a nice lunch together?"

Kennedy's eyes widened, and she grabbed for her own glass. "Oh, no. It's even worse than I feared, isn't it?"

Alex huffed a weak laugh. "Sorry. No, I am not aware of any specific development to make matters worse than you suspected. But I spent all morning giving myself a headache trying to divine a pattern to the Dzhvar's movements, and I'm dying to think about something else for a little while. So how are the kiddos doing?"

After a lengthy silence laden with suspicion, Kennedy relented. "Jonas is actually turning out to be talented at those martial arts he loves so much. We let him start a training routine using real swords last week."

"So now he really is a samurai!"

"And believe me, he will not let us forget it." Kennedy smiled, as she often did when talking about her children. "But he's being responsible about it, obeying his sensei's safety instructions and not trying to smuggle a sword home to practice with in his bedroom. I'm proud of him. And Noah has started taking him along sometimes when he visits one of our manufacturing sites. He says Jonas has a natural knack for fixing things. Same as his dad."

"I'm not surprised. And Braelyn?"

"Nine going on thirty-nine? Last night, she announced she wants to be a Solo Prevo, like Marlee."

"Uh-oh. But it was probably inevitable. Marlee makes everything she does look exciting."

"Yes, and she almost got herself killed a few weeks ago by being 'exciting.' A cautionary tale that is totally lost on Braelyn, of course. The only thing working in my favor is the medical limits on the cybernetics allowed to be grown in children." Kennedy grumbled and picked at the bruschetta sitting on the table between them. "Once her nervous system finishes maturing, I'm screwed. I'm going to lose her to those psychos running wild in the Noesis." She winced. "No offense."

"None taken. A fair majority of them *are* psychos. You know what, though? Braelyn is going to make a fantastic Prevo, solo or joined. She's brilliant, and I won't be the slightest bit surprised if she changes the world. Just like her great-great-great-grandmother did. Hell, just like her mom did."

"Ha. It always felt less like changing the world and more like desperate acts of self-preservation. Oh, I want to protect her so badly. But we never let our parents protect us, did we?"

"Nope. We absolutely did not." Alex took another sip of wine. It was doing its work of smoothing out the brittle edges of her mood. "So, can you build it?"

"Back to harsh reality already, huh?" Kennedy glanced out the window at the glimmering San Francisco skyline. "Honestly? I don't know. I don't even know how the Elakri built it yet. I mean, I have the files. I've read the files. I understand the files, more or less. I'm almost ready to begin designing my own schematics and gathering materials for a prototype. So I'm definitely going to *try* to build one.

"But Alex, can I cut right to the crux of the problem? I realize you believe you shoulder a lot of responsibility for figuring out how to fight this enemy. But the truth is, it doesn't matter whether I can build a Piega Strai or not if we can't figure out how to safely reverse its operation. I mean, unless we want to consign a planet full of people to eternal isolation from the rest of the universe."

"Twenty years ago, Mom was prepared to do exactly that to the entire of humanity in order to save them from the Machim Primor and his black hole device. Mind you, it might have destroyed her to do it."

Alex pushed away the wave of melancholy the memory evoked. Caleb had given his life to save humanity from such a fate, but it was okay, because everything had worked out. "Obviously, that's not Plan A, or B, or anything other than Plan Triple-Z. I promise I'll spend some time on the problem. I was close to figuring out how to shut it down safely back on Elakrin. Then I ran out of time, and then..." she lifted her glass and swirled the burgundy liquid in languid circles, letting her gaze unfocus "...the Dzhvar showed up. So what else other than the Piega Strai has got you chained to your desk in the lab?"

She blinked slowly as Kennedy began talking, and when her eyes reopened, it was as if the world around her had...shifted somehow.

"Lionel is fighting us on the location for the new materials fab plant. We've been close friends with the Federation for twenty years now, but he still instinctively recoils from doing business with Senecan interests." Kennedy stared out at the setting San Francisco sun as it spilled across the horizon of the Pacific. "I fear I should've listened to Noah and kept Lionel out of Connova business from the beginning. But we needed the funding in those early days, and I wanted to encourage their reconciliation. Now I'm stuck with him, and he's driving me mad—"

Everything lurched back into place, and Alex shook her head roughly; her glass was near to tipping over in her hand, and she hurriedly set it down. "Lionel? Did Noah decide to risk a regenesis procedure for his father, and you somehow forgot to mention it to me?"

"What are you talking about?" Kennedy looked at her strangely. "No. You know the quality of his neural imprint simply doesn't meet the standard for regenesis."

"That's what I thought, but you said Lionel...he was...." Her gaze drifted to the window, where the sun remained high in the midday sky. A spike of vertigo from the incongruity disoriented her. Hadn't it been dusk a few seconds ago? But how, when this was a lunch date?

"I said Pantil Lawrence from Phoenix Alloys is driving a hard bargain on the ceramic instrument moldings for the new frigate designs, and if we don't reach an agreement soon, my deliverables will be late. If we don't reach a favorable price agreement, they'll also be over budget. Alex, are you feeling all right?"

"I, uh…I haven't been sleeping well the last couple of nights. Nightmares. I guess I lost my train of thought for a second."

"Not to sound like Miriam, but get your sleep. We will need you at your best when the Dzhvar inevitably start careening through our corner of Amaranthe. Crap, I bet I just added to your nightmare fuel. Sorry."

"No, it's fine, because it's true. Promise I'll sleep better, even if it means I have to enlist Valkyrie to sing lullabies in my head." She smiled blithely as their food arrived, grateful for the interruption. Hopefully the food would distract Kennedy from any more probing questions, because she had no answers.

What *was* that? She wasn't tired, so she didn't think she'd nodded off in a micro-nap. But if not that, then what?

21

ARES

An assistant, or possibly a butler, showed Caleb up to Corradeo's study at the estate outside Olympia. He'd only visited here twice before, though not because he didn't have a standing invitation. Like most of their friends and family, Corradeo tended to drop by Akeso when he wanted to see Caleb, and that was fine. Akeso made everyone feel welcome.

Since Alex was on Earth having lunch with Kennedy, he'd taken the opportunity to journey here the old-fashioned way: Puddle Jumper to HQ, a Caeles Prism to the Olympia spaceport, then a skycar rental to the estate.

He supposed it wasn't *that* old-fashioned, merely something less than instantaneous. And it had given him time to ponder what he might say today.

Inside the study, a desk carved of an amber-hued wood he didn't recognize sat beneath a painting of a dramatic city skyline. Was it of Solum, from a time before they'd paved over the natural surface of the planet from pole to pole?

Shelves on either side of the painting displayed personal items, including a visual of a pretty woman with long chestnut hair and bright green eyes, as well as one of a different woman who was almost the spitting image of Nyx. Corradeo's daughter, he suspected.

Two plush, high-backed chairs were situated in the center of the room atop an ornate hunter green and beige woven rug. To the left was a round glass table and four chairs. Corradeo sat at the table, which was stocked with a full lunch: an oversized salad bowl, two cups of soup, and a plate stacked high with sliced sandwiches.

"Caleb, come in, please." Corradeo gestured to the empty chairs. "Thank you for agreeing to travel here. Olympia has many excellent restaurants, but I'm afraid they would afford us no privacy. My face is too well known."

"Always has been, right?" Caleb took the chair opposite the man.

"And for all the wrong reasons, more often than not. The good news is, now I'm recognized for who I am. The bad news is, now I'm recognized for who I am."

"Ah, the life of a politician. I don't envy you."

"One day, I'll escape into a life of anonymity, and it will be glorious."

"I don't believe you." Caleb chuckled as he poured himself a cup of coffee and dished out a helping of salad onto his plate. "You, sir, are a man of action. You see a problem, and you must fix it. This is never going to change."

"Sometimes I wish it would." Corradeo sighed and bypassed the salad to sip on the soup, a creamy chowder. "How are things with you?"

Caleb shot the man a look over his coffee cup. "You don't need to play at small talk. We can talk about the Dzhvar."

"But I do care how things are. We haven't had a chance to catch up since you returned from Elakrin. You met a fascinating new species and saved them from destruction. You were separated from Akeso for some days. You have stories. Whereas I only have legislators."

Ah, yes, the newly minted Conference. He decided not to torture the man by forcing him to discuss those frustrations. "I do have stories. En masse, the Elakri are insufferably high-minded and effete, but individually they are as we all are. People. We made a couple of friends. I got shot at more than I prefer, but only because I kept stepping in front of the laser fire."

"Something I suspect will also never change."

"True. Being without Akeso was…" Caleb set his fork down "…complicated. Lonely, and also freeing. I remembered who I used to be, and discovered part of me misses that man. But it also felt as though a chunk of my soul had been carved out of my chest, and I only felt whole once we were reunited."

He realized he'd opened up surprisingly quickly and honestly. But Corradeo was more than a friend; he was someone who understood the unique peculiarities of having your mind bonded with an alien life form in a way few others could. And this worked both ways, which was why he didn't intend to let the man off the hook today. The clock had nearly run out, and Corradeo would increasingly be struggling with uncomfortable truths. Just because the man preferred to keep his own counsel, didn't mean he should.

"Now about the Dzhvar."

"You mean 'about the *diati.*'"

Caleb shrugged mildly and selected one of the sandwiches, a shaved white meat garnished with arugula and tomato slices.

"I already opened myself up to it," Corradeo admitted. "I did so as soon as I learned the Dzhvar were detected. It's not listening. Or if it's listening, it's choosing not to answer."

"Alex believes it will return when we need it."

"I believe she's correct. It joined with me because it wanted to defeat the Dzhvar. I see no reason why it won't feel the same way now." Corradeo frowned, cup of soup frozen at his lips. "Unless it can't return. I know it's not gone. We've talked about how we can both sense it. But only faintly. What if it's scattered so sparsely across the stars that it no longer can form any purpose or intentionality?"

In other words, what if Caleb had sapped it of its final iota of anima? Drained it dry when he'd used it to blow open the Mosaic and drag fifty-one universes into Amaranthe? "Then we'll find another way."

"What does Mnemosyne say about the last cycle? Yes, I realize the official word is 'nothing,' which is ninety percent of what the

Kat says on matters of import. But I seriously doubt your wife hasn't been able to goad some information regarding the *diati* out of it. She can be relentless when she's determined to know something."

"Truer words." Caleb leaned back in his chair. The sandwich was tasty, but the conversation had grown weighty, as he'd suspected it would. "Unfortunately, she's yet to succeed in extracting any details about the *diati's* role in the last cycle. Mesme is standing firm on its refusal to share information on this topic."

The door to the study opened and Nyx stuck her head in. "Grandfather, are you—oh, I'm sorry. I didn't realize you had a guest." She dipped her chin in his direction. "Caleb. It's good to see you."

"And you—"

"Caleb's here?" Eren pushed his way past Nyx and strode in. "What, you're having a party and didn't invite me?"

"Merely a lunch," Corradeo replied. "And it turns out, a bit of a working lunch at that. But the chef prepared enough food for eight people, so please, help yourself."

"You don't have to tell me twice." Eren wandered over and grabbed a half-sandwich, while Nyx kept a respectful distance.

"To what do we owe this visit?" Corradeo asked.

"I wanted to update you on some troubling results from the background checks on the newest Conference delegates, but it's not urgent," Nyx replied. "It can wait."

"Where are you two off to after this?"

Eren moved to stand by Nyx, tearing off a piece of the sandwich and offering it to her. Her brow knotted, but after a second she took it from him, though she answered before biting into it. "We have a report of a possible Ch'mshak attack on a station in Milky Way Sector 6."

"Another one already?" Corradeo frowned deeply. "This is most concerning."

"It is," Eren said, then broke off another chunk of the sandwich and held it out to Nyx, who accepted it with a shrug. "We're hoping we'll be able to piece together whether they're following some plan or route, or stopping off wherever catches their murderous fancy."

When Nyx refused a third offering, Eren finished off the sandwich and stuck his hands in his pockets. His left elbow rested against Nyx's arm, and she didn't move away.

"Eren was able to trace the registry of the ship to a company called Daedalus Aerospace. They sold it to a commercial retailer based on a Human world, Elathan, who sold it to a company by the name of Greshen Dry Goods." She glanced at Eren. "The company appears to be fake, but they went to the trouble of spoofing all the expected records, which means we've found a malicious actor. We're hopeful it will lead somewhere."

"We're going to pay a visit to the retailer and try to extract useful details," Eren said. "The Almanac entry says Elathan is beautiful. Nyx is excited to see it."

"I'm what? You're the one who's giddy over the prospect of golden rings on a terrestrial planet."

Eren elbowed her lightly in the side. "True, but you're excited, too. Even if you won't admit it."

Nyx rolled her eyes, though a slight smile lifted her lips. "I'm excited to track down the purchaser of the ship. Nothing more."

Caleb considered chiming in to confirm that Elathan's rings were indeed beautiful, but he was too stunned at what he was witnessing to get the words out.

"In that case, I wish you luck," Corradeo said. "And if there are sights to be seen, take an afternoon and enjoy them."

"You hear that, Nyx? Now we have official permission to go sightseeing. I knew you had a good idea, stopping by here."

Nyx's gaze cut to Eren as she cleared her throat. "We'll let you continue your lunch in peace. Grandfather, we can speak about the background checks this evening." He got another nod. "Caleb."

"Nyx."

Eren came over and clapped him on the shoulder, then they both departed.

Caleb stared at the closed door for a long time before shifting back to Corradeo, eyebrow arched high.

"They've been acting oddly ever since they returned from the Hesgyr mission, though not to such an extent as what you just witnessed. Clearly something happened between them while they were together on Nythir."

Caleb laughed. "I'd say we know exactly what 'something' happened."

"I'm afraid so." Corradeo shook his head with a rueful sigh. "I've long hoped they'd become friends, as I think they're good for one another. They can help strengthen each other's weaknesses. But now I worry. If this ends badly, they could each end up in worse shape than when it started."

It was heartening how much the man doted over Nyx, the way a grandfather should, and he seemed to genuinely care about Eren as well. It was an aspect of the man's character the Anaden people never got to see. To them, he was their larger-than-life, charismatic, wise and eternal leader. But he was also just a man, and when he cared, he cared with a profound, earnest depth of heart.

In this case, Corradeo was also right to be worried. Eren and Nyx fit together like oil and water—*combustible* oil and water. While he was glad Eren was letting himself live a little again, the blowback if or when whatever it was they were doing went up in flames stood to be significant. Eren had been through too much heartache of late and didn't deserve to suffer a fresh wound. But that was the problem with opening oneself up to connection; you couldn't foresee how it might end.

"True," Caleb finally said. "But it's good we're forewarned, so we can be ready to provide some shoulders to cry on when they need them."

Corradeo did his best not to appear to be ushering Caleb out the door prematurely. And he wasn't. He'd genuinely enjoyed the visit, even if the subject matter had too often veered into somberness. Such was the world they found themselves in.

Caleb was like a son to him, and not just genetically, though that aspect didn't hurt either. Their relationship was complicated, and at times in the past had been disrupted by fractious demons on both sides, but it felt as if they'd at last settled into a comfortable, meaningful friendship.

Nonetheless, as soon as Caleb had departed, Corradeo started to activate the CPM he now kept clipped to his pants. Then he remembered his manners and sent a message to confirm he was welcome first, as Maris valued her privacy. No matter how close they'd grown in the last few years, there remained a wafer-thin barrier of separation between them. A final step she refused to take to grant him access to the deepest fathoms of her heart.

He tried not to let it trouble him. He'd lived for a million years; he could be patient for however long was required.

I'm free now. Fancy a visit?

I'm working, which you know. But I can perhaps take a small break.

I will take whatever minutes of company you grant me.

Then do come on over.

ASTERION PRIME

MILKY WAY GALAXY

Though he hadn't peeked inside many residences here, he felt confident in proclaiming Maris' apartment the most stylishly decorated on the planet, and this despite the fact that she insisted her primary residence remained on Mirai. Polished hardwood floors gave way to geometric stone in the kitchen and lavatories.

Textured walls were accentuated by ornate figures carved into the surface, and plush, hand-woven rugs were tossed across the living room floor in a pattern that appeared random while being anything but. She'd gifted him one of the rugs for his study at home, and it alone had increased the room's sophistication by an order of magnitude.

Maris vanished an array of screens as he arrived, then stood up from the couch to greet him. She wore soft cream suede pants and a lavender chenille sweater with bell sleeves. Even in the most casual of attire, the sight of her caused his breath to hitch in his throat.

He took her hands in his and kissed her. "How has your day been?"

"Delightful. We closed the contract on the new museum in Calan." A fanciful smile danced across her lips. "I will bring culture to this drab, gray planet if it is the last thing I do."

"You already have. You're here."

"Buttery smooth words like those? We'll make a diplomat of you yet. How is yours?"

"A mix. I had a nice lunch with Caleb Marano. But I learned a group of Ch'mshak have gained control of a spaceship and are attacking Anadens. And the Dzhvar's return weighs upon my every thought."

Somewhere over the last three years, he'd fallen into an easy honesty with her. To dissemble with Maris would cheapen the relationship. Also, she would instantly know; she'd been able to see through his every façade from the first time they'd met.

"What are Ch'mshak?"

"Nasty, brutish creatures we quarantined to their home planet a decade ago for their refusal to stop massacring whomever they pleased. Unfortunately, it seems they've found a way to circumvent the quarantine." He gestured to the couch. "But I didn't come here to wallow in blood and guts. Tell me of all the good in your world."

She sank onto the couch with a graceful flourish. When he joined her, she snuggled against him to rest her head on his shoulder. "Back home, there is little good, for the other advisors are now as soured by word of the Dzhvar as you are. Nika has transitioned back into 'universal savior' mode, which is frankly not her best look."

"A shame she's so talented at it, then."

"Indeed. Here, however, matters are better." She spent several minutes catching him up on developments at the Asterion embassy, as well as her many projects designed to do exactly what she'd declared: bring color and light to a world dulled down by millennia of Kyvern Dynasty rule.

More than eleven thousand Asterions lived here full-time now, something he'd never imagined was possible. Their welcome had not been uniformly positive, but he'd made it clear to the planet's Vigil force: all incidents of harassment or unfair treatment were to be punished to the fullest extent of the law. And in time, the residents had gotten the message and begun to behave themselves, at least in public.

No Anadens lived on any Asterion world; he hadn't made such a request, and the Asterions hadn't offered. Concord staffed a formal embassy on Mirai, and it employed several Anadens, but they returned home at the end of their shifts via a permanent Caeles Prism. One day, an enterprising—or obstreperous—Anaden was going to demand the right to live there, but he'd deal with that hornet's nest when it arrived.

While his and Maris' relationship wasn't technically a secret, they didn't make a habit of being seen together in public. For now, it was the best choice, for themselves but more so for the people they represented.

Though 99.99% of Asterions did not personally remember the SAI Rebellion, many harbored a form of ancestral hatred of Anadens nonetheless. And as for Anadens? While few of them remembered it, either, they had all spent millennia living under pervasive Directorate propaganda demonizing Artificials. Asterions weren't wholly Artificial, but they were plenty synthetic enough to make many people uncomfortable. Change came slowly.

Again, he could be patient. Maris, though? She'd lived for over seven hundred millennia herself, but she treated every day as if it were of the greatest consequence.

He laughed as she delivered a stinging barb about one of the insufferable local Kyvern administrators, then kissed the top of her head. "I trust you didn't say this to his face."

"Of course not. I am a lady. Instead I commented how it was a shame his lineage had edited out the ability to see more than three colors from its gene pool."

"Brutal. I adore it." He placed a finger beneath her chin and lifted it up. "Can I persuade you to delay your return to work for another, say, hour?"

"That depends on the quality of your offer of how to spend the hour."

"It's a good one, I promise." He rose from the couch and extended a hand. "May I show you?"

Her teeth pulled at her bottom lip as she stood and took his hand in hers. He feared the world was soon to turn dark and desperate. If he did not find a way to rise to meet the Dzhvar threat once more, it may well end entirely. But for as long as he could, he would cling to these simple moments of joy.

22

VRACHNAS HOMEWORLD
ANDROMEDA GALAXY

Marlee plopped down on the blanket, crossed her legs in front of her, and peered over the ledge at the rocky plain below where Cupcake was sunning himself in the warm afternoon air. He grew larger every time she visited, and he now stretched over fourteen meters from snout to tail barb. At this rate, he'd be full grown in another year.

This seemed fast to her, but it wasn't as if there was a 'normal' dragon maturation process, and she suspected the Kats had sped up their development, anyway.

Cupcake and his brother had moved out of their parents' place three months ago. Cupcake had chosen a level outcropping half-way up the mountain with a nook in the rear that was almost a cave, and his brother had set up residence in a copse fairly close by. They still hung out together a good bit, but she worried they were feeling lonely.

It was hard, growing up and leaving the nest. Or she assumed it was difficult for most creatures. As for herself, she'd cackled with glee and kicked up a trail of dust when she hit the road the first minute her schooling justified it. It wasn't that she didn't love her mother; they'd actually become rather close in the last few years. But life was here to be embraced.

She sensed a disruption in the air behind her, which was her signal to open up the cooler. She pulled out two wrapped sand-wiches and two bottled lemonades and arranged them on the blanket.

"Ooh, a picnic." Morgan Lekkas walked to the rim of the ledge. "He won't smell the food and come steal it, frying us in the process?"

"Cupcake won't fry me, and since you're with me, he won't fry you, either. Also, this is why the sandwiches are cold cuts."

"Ah. Good thinking." Morgan dropped to her knees diagonally from Marlee, where she could see Cupcake in her peripheral vision. She wore black knee pants and a plum tank top, exposing sun-darkened arms, and her chestnut hair fell straight below her chin.

"Thanks for agreeing to join me on your day off."

"I don't have a super active social life." Morgan's gaze flitted away, and she busied herself unwrapping her sandwich. "Not to say that I'm only here because I had nothing better to do or...so what's the occasion?"

"I wanted to thank you again for helping the Tarazi broadcast their message to all the Belascocians. You took a risk on my account, and it could've bitten you in the ass. I'm grateful."

Morgan took a healthy bite of her sandwich, rolling her eyes at the sky while she chewed, then washed it down with a sip of lemonade. "My recalcitrant side still tries to get me dishonorably discharged at least once a month. Thus far, Jenner won't take the bait."

"From what I hear, he's trying to promote you again."

"Nope. Not a chance. If he tries to pin another bar on me, I will stab him with the pin, and he'll have no choice but to kick me out. Or at a minimum demote me. So your Belascocian friends are doing okay? Their rebellion was a success?"

"Yes, and more or less. Galean and his sister came to visit Concord HQ last week, so they're feeling comfortable enough with the situation at home to be away for a little while. Their society is going through a huge upheaval, and there's bound to be some bumps in the road, but I think they'll be fine. The Belascocians have such a strong social fabric. It'll support them while they work through the ugliness of government malfeasance."

"Good. I always like it when a righteous rebellion succeeds."

"Me, too." They ate in silence for a couple of comfortable minutes. When they'd finished, Marlee put the trash in the cooler, then removed another package. "Do you want to meet Cupcake?"

Morgan stood and peeked over the ledge. "Up close?"

"That's commonly what 'meet' means."

Morgan considered it for a minute before nodding sharply. "I'm game."

"Great." Marlee handed her the package. "This is roast chicken, which is his favorite. When we get down there, I'll go up and say hello to him first, so he knows you're a friendly. When I give the word, open the chicken and set it on the ground, then back up about ten meters."

"Then what?"

"We'll see how it goes from there."

"Right." Morgan nodded again, as if to reassure herself.

Marlee didn't think she'd ever seen the woman nervous before. It was endearing, but she knew if she drew attention to it, Morgan would bluster up and get defensive. So she hid an amused smile as she rolled up the blanket and stuffed it in the cooler, then opened a wormhole to below.

They stepped onto the outcropping. Cupcake lifted his head and, on seeing her, lumbered to his feet. Normally he'd approach her on his own initiative, but Morgan's presence had him cautious.

"I, uh, thought you said he was a baby."

"*Three years ago* he was a baby. Now he's a teenager, I guess."

"How big is he going to get?"

Marlee looked over in surprise. "You've never seen one of the adult dragons?"

"Never had cause to."

"Well, big." She set the cooler on the ground and walked forward as her bracelet hummed the harmonic that encouraged calmness. She doubted she needed it where Cupcake was concerned, but with Morgan here, better to be safe than sorry. Also, one of the other dragons could always swoop in unannounced.

"Hey, Cupcake. I'm sorry to disturb your nap. It's a great day for one."

Cupcake snorted a little smoke out through his nostrils. A greeting.

"He can't understand you, can he?" Morgan asked from what sounded like some distance behind her. "They're not *that* smart, are they?"

"Who can say how much he understands? We've trained a couple of words he comprehends, but mostly, I talk to him in a pleasant tone of voice. He seems to enjoy it." She reached up and caressed his snout, moving her hand in the direction of the scales so as to not slice her palm open. "I brought a friend with me today. Friend. She's excited to meet you." She stared directly into his strawberry irises. "Be nice, okay?"

Another snort.

She stepped to the side. "You can place the chicken now."

Morgan kept both eyes locked on Cupcake while she unwrapped the chicken and placed it on the ground, then took several giant strides backward—which turned into a hurried jog as Cupcake rumbled forward and scarfed the chicken up.

"Oh, my."

"Don't back up any farther." Marlee waited until Cupcake had finished swallowing before approaching him; she knew better than to interrupt his eating. She patted him on the neck. "Good boy. This is my friend, Morgan."

Cupcake peered suspiciously at Morgan.

"Hi…Cupcake…."

Seriously, she had never seen Morgan afraid of anything in her life. Anything except for a kiss—and moving on. "Friend, Morgan."

Cupcake thought about it for a few seconds, then settled onto his haunches.

"There you go." She glanced at Morgan. "Come on up. Slowly, hand out and upturned, the way you'd approach a dog you just met."

"This is most decidedly not a dog."

"No, but the principle is the same."

"Huh." Morgan did as instructed, but stopped a meter out of his reach.

"Friend. Go ahead and let him sniff your hand."

Morgan took another half-step forward, and Cupcake breathed smoke on her palm.

"That's…not as hot as I expected."

"If he wants to breathe fire, you'll know it."

"I hope I get to take your word for it." But after another beat, Morgan cupped her hand and touched a fingertip to his snout.

Cupcake jerked away, and Morgan flung both hands in the air. "Sorry."

Cupcake glared at her, then pushed his snout into her arm. "Oh!"

"Careful. His scales are ridiculously sharp."

"Noted." Morgan tried again, carefully touching a fingertip to the center of a scale. This time, Cupcake allowed it.

Marlee beamed. This was everything she'd hoped it would be, and then some. "See? He likes you."

"He's probably reading vibes off of you." Morgan immediately cringed. "I only meant…."

"It's fine. It's true." Her heart fluttered in her chest, but she played it off lightly. "He'd definitely be agitated if I wasn't standing here vouching for you."

"I believe it." Morgan laid her fingers flat and cautiously stroked across a scale. "And you're telling me you can ride him?"

"I can. I mean, I make sure and update my neural imprint on an almost weekly basis in case he ever throws me, but in three years I haven't fallen off."

"Incredible." Morgan patted Cupcake awkwardly, then took a step back to flash Marlee a smile. "You are utterly fearless, aren't you?"

Calm down, the Voice lectured her, *lest you swoon into a heap at her feet, which would be most embarrassing for both you and Cupcake.*

I am calm. Cool as a refrigerated cucumber.

"I suppose so. But I'm not reckless any longer...or not as reckless as I used to be. I'm simply not content to sit on the sidelines when I can act instead."

"I did know this about you," Morgan remarked.

Hopefully the bright sunlight and Marlee's naturally olive skin hid the flush in her cheeks. "I think—"

Abruptly Morgan's expression plummeted into disquiet, and her gaze unfocused.

Marlee waited.

Disquiet transformed into a dark scowl as Morgan hurriedly strode away from Cupcake. "I don't fucking believe it. I have to go."

"What's happened?"

But Morgan had already opened a wormhole to what might be the Presidio and was tearing through it.

Marlee stared at the empty air where the woman had stood a second ago. With a long sigh, she turned and hugged Cupcake's head against her chest. "And it was going so well."

23

———————

CONCORD HQ
COMMAND

Miriam stared at Malcolm, incredulity revealing itself in the repetitive twitching of one corner of her mouth. "Ch'mshak. On a space station."

He nodded tightly. It mirrored his own reaction upon receiving the news from Director Nyx, by way of Casmir. "Yes, Commandant. We have video confirmation."

At her challenging eyebrow raise, he instantiated an aural and started the video from the station's security cam. When the Ch'mshak finished killing everyone in the entry atrium and moved deeper into the station, he killed the aural.

"How many dead?" Miriam asked.

"1,863. Two hundred thirty-three belonged to species without regenesis." It wasn't that their *lives* mattered more, but with regenesis foreclosed to them, their deaths did.

"No reports of violations of the Mshak blockade have reached me," Casmir said, his clipped voice betraying his own displeasure, and possibly a touch of defensiveness. "I'll contact Arch-ploíarch Beletin, the commander of the blockade, as soon as this meeting concludes."

"See that you do." Miriam shifted her gaze back to Malcolm. "How did they reach the station?"

"On a human-manufactured vessel. A small merchant craft made by Daedalus Aerospace."

"I see." Miriam had the best poker face in the military, but even she wasn't able to hide her surprise. "Theories on how they acquired such a vessel?"

Malcolm had spent most of the trip to Concord HQ for the hastily called military leadership meeting wracking his brain on this one. But since it was a quick trip here from the Presidio, he hadn't had time to come up with any good explanations.

"A group of Ch'mshak may have been hiding out on a backwater planet for the last eleven years and managed to escape our notice. A private citizen with more money or free time than judgment could've visited this planet for any number of reasons—seeking valuable natural resources or spectacular scenery or simply being stupid. The Ch'mshak killed them and confiscated their ship."

"We searched habitable planets for stray Ch'mshak most thoroughly in the aftermath of the conflict."

"And found a good number of them. The reality is, there are hundreds of thousands of worlds in Concord space that fall within the most expansive definition of habitability for some organic species. All a couple of Ch'mshak would need is a well-hidden cave. If there was local wildlife in the area to create noise on the biological scans…it's not impossible we missed them. Then there are the planets our surveyors have yet to discover. Then are the planets outside of Concord space."

"The Ch'mshak aren't smart enough to find a world not included in the Almanac," Casmir declared.

He'd accuse Casmir of racism, but the man was objectively correct. "I didn't say it was a good theory. But until we know more, it is the most plausible one."

"Does the ship they used have modern cloaking technology?" Pinchu asked.

"Yes, it does." Malcolm suspected where the Tokahe Naataan was going with the question; the possibility had occurred to him as well, but he'd hoped not to have to broach two unsavory prospects in a row.

Casmir's thick brow drew tight. "Are you suggesting someone landed the ship on Mshak and handed it over to one of the chieftains?"

Miriam's eyes widened a touch. "Who would deliberately take a ship *to* Ch'mshak?" The notion was so unthinkable that they'd never worried about stealth infractions of the blockade from the outside.

"Bad actors," Pinchu replied.

"No one is so bad an actor as that."

Casmir shifted in his chair uncomfortably. "It's no secret how under Directorate rule, we used the Ch'mshak as shock troops in a variety of scenarios."

"No secret at all," Malcolm muttered under his breath, but immediately regretted it. He and Casmir had a good working relationship, and he recognized the extent to which the man had not just adapted to Concord rule, but embraced it. But Malcolm had fought the Ch'mshak at the anarch base on Chionis during the Directorate War, and he'd lost too many men in the battle to ever forgive the Machim leadership for their wanton use of the brutes.

"Yes." Casmir didn't visibly flare in offense at Malcolm's barb. "In addition to every navarchos, there were perhaps a hundred *ela* officers who had direct dealings with Ch'mshak chieftains. I don't believe any of the navarchos harbor traitorous intentions, though I will be speaking to all of them about this matter. But as for the lower-ranking *elas*? It's conceivable that one of them has determined to use a Ch'mshak squad for some nefarious purpose."

"But why use a human-made vessel?" Malcolm asked.

"Misdirection."

"A fair point," Miriam interjected. "But what could a Machim military officer want on an ordinary commercial space station that justifies killing everyone inside?"

"The killing might have been an incidental byproduct," Casmir said. "But the first half of the question is a valid one."

"Advocacy Intelligence is taking the lead in the investigation as it relates to the station crime scene," Malcolm offered. "They'll share their findings with Director Navick. If there is something, they'll dig it up."

Casmir nodded firmly. "Yes, Nyx will find it if it's there to be found."

"Very well." Miriam clasped her hands atop the table. "Our task is three-fold. One: find the Ch'mshak who attacked the station. Malcolm, I'm leaving this to you. Utilize Vigil, CINT and the other intelligence agencies, along with your military resources. Two: protect our citizens until the perpetrators are apprehended. I'll issue guidelines to the respective governments regarding heightened security measures, especially but not only at space stations. Merely requiring a visual check of all passengers and crew of docking vessels should prevent most incidents. Even Ch'mshak cannot tear through space-rated airlocks."

"Unless they bring high-powered explosives," Casmir offered dryly.

"In which case, we will be facing a bigger problem. Three: ensure no additional Ch'mshak leave their planet. Casmir, this falls to you."

"I'll double the strength of the blockade force," Casmir said. "But we do not possess a technology capable of seeing through Veil-grade stealth."

"No, we do not," Miriam said. "But talk to Director Reynolds about what we can do to increase the likelihood of detecting a stealth incursion. And begin an ongoing survey of the planet's surface. Search for ships or any unusual activity."

THE PRESIDIO

MILKY WAY GALAXY

Malcolm had barely made it back to his office at the Presidio when a guest demanded entry. He glanced at the name and sighed. That hadn't taken long.

He braced himself for what was certain to be an unpleasant conversation, then opened the door.

Morgan Lekkas offered the most perfunctory of salutes. She was in plainclothes and obviously not on the clock. "How the bloody hell did Ch'mshak get loose?"

"I just came from a meeting with Commandant Solovy and the other military commanders on precisely this subject. We are pursuing several leads, as well as tightening the blockade."

"Leads? Don't blow sunshine up my ass. A 'lead' is when a citizen reports a suspicious-looking man in a trench coat loitering in the shadows. We're talking about *Ch'mshak*. They're difficult to miss."

"We don't know where they came from or how, but we will find out. And we will capture these Ch'mshak. And we will ensure no more escape from the quarantine, if this is what the group in question did. At least until the Dzhvar start splitting open our planets, this is our highest priority."

Morgan rested her hands on her hips. "How can I help to find them?"

"I don't think you can. No fighter craft possesses the radar range needed to sweep the voluminous sectors of space where we'll be searching."

"Then you find them and let me kill them."

"Major Lekkas, that's not how this works, and you know it." He sat, though he assumed she would not. "I understand why you're taking a personal interest. I do. I have a personal interest as well—I lost soldiers and friends to them, same as you—but that's not the point. No one, and I repeat, *no one*, will stand for Ch'mshak rampaging through space slaughtering people."

She glared at him, eyes flaring in anger. "You cannot let history repeat itself. Don't sacrifice soldiers on the altar of restraint. The Ch'mshak are animals, and you can't grant them an iota of mercy."

He wasn't going to defend them by arguing semantics. While they *were* more intelligent than base animals, this only meant they were culpable for their actions. "We learned from our mistakes in the conflict."

"Did you? Because I feel like if you had, you'd be nuking the planet from orbit right about now."

He met her stare dispassionately; he knew better than to try to talk her down when she'd built up a heady tirade. But he also didn't have to listen to it. "Will that be all, Major?"

She continued to glower, and he decided he didn't care for the storm brewing behind those Prevo eyes. "Morgan, don't do anything stupid. You've got a good thing going here. You're a valuable officer, and I don't want to lose you. Running off on some misguided mission of vengeance won't fix anything. Trust us to bring the perpetrators to justice and stop them from killing more people."

"Is 'don't do anything stupid' an order, sir?"

"Yes, it is."

"Noted." She pivoted and left.

24

AKESO

Alex studied the projection from multiple angles, walking the length of it, pausing to tilt her head down and peer up, and so on. She even lay down on the floor at several points to stare vertically upward. Their upstairs office wasn't exactly the Dome at HQ, but if you pulled back far enough, you could squeeze the known universe inside of it.

From this bird's-eye view of the entire map, the numerous Dzhvar incursions Nika had identified tended to group together into clusters, though Valkyrie insisted this didn't mean they weren't random. Rather, there simply weren't enough incidents yet for the distribution to smooth out.

It would make things so much easier if the forays weren't random. If they could predict the general location of an incursion before it happened, a whole array of options opened up to them. They could plan. Evacuate. Set traps. Or try to, anyway. They weren't going to know if they possessed anything capable of trapping them until they caught the slithering life forms in the act.

The best Artificials in every agency were burning millions of threaded minutes analyzing this map, and they were far more likely than her to find a pattern if a pattern was to be found. But Mesme had proclaimed that their continued existence depended on *her* gazing out into the universe and understanding it. On her being right, one more time.

A little voice in the back of her head pointed out how she'd been 'right' about multiple things in the time since Mesme's declaration, but she understood her marching orders. She had to look with different eyes from everyone else, and in so looking, see how to defeat them.

So she glared at an ocean of orange dots scattered across the cosmos and did her damnedest to will them into a story.

She jumped as a hand landed at her waist, and had spun halfway around before she realized it belonged to Caleb. She rested her forearms on his shoulders and dropped her forehead to his. "You snuck up on me."

"I didn't have to sneak. You were parsecs away." He tilted his head toward the map. "Whereabouts?"

"Oh, you know." She pointed at one of the clusters overhead. "Thereish."

"You don't think it's random."

"No, I'm *hoping* it's not random—" A flash off to the left caught her attention. She was pulling in the real-time feed from Command's server for the map. Was the flash Nika adding a new incursion? Despite the woman's insistence that she couldn't live in the kyoseil web, Nika was updating the tracker several times a day.

Alex zoomed the map in toward the flash. No. It was located within the perimeter of the Detection Network.

"They're back." By the time she'd spoken the words, an alert to this effect had arrived in her eVi.

She closed the projection and fired up her Caeles Prism. "Valkyrie, put us on the *Aurora*, wherever it is."

Valkyrie's virtual avatar materialized in the office. "Thankfully, it is still in dock. Landing a wormhole exit on a rapidly moving target is my twelfth least-favorite thing to do."

"You'll have to tell me about the other eleven sometime," Alex remarked as she and Caleb strode through the tear in space onto the bridge of the *Aurora*.

"Well, number eight is cleaning the food receptacles of my doll."

"Cleaning food receptacles is on *everyone's* list."

CAF AURORA

Her mother didn't act surprised to find her and Caleb already on the bridge when she arrived. "Good, you're here. We're leaving now. Thanks to our dealings with the Rasu, the Detection Network is extensive in the Shapley Supercluster, so we stand a chance of catching the Dzhvar in the act. The others can join us once we arrive at our destination."

The *Aurora's* massive engines were so smooth, there was no sensation of movement, but a blur of HQ's pinwheel arms outside the viewport indicated they were underway. In another few seconds, a towering wormhole wrent apart space in front of them, and new stars blinked into existence.

The bow swung around to starboard and—

"Holy mother of God," Caleb exclaimed.

A massive wall of plasma the color of hellfire—bright orange and sulfur and surging cardinal—undulated across space. It moved with seeming purpose through the stellar system in the direction of its star.

"Thomas, launch probes into and around this phenomenon," Miriam ordered. "I want to see what's inside it. I want to see it from every angle."

'Launching.'

The wall of plasma split into three sections. Two of the sections soon merged again, then split anew into three fragments, and a rippling motion became more apparent within each one. What at first glance presented as plasma likely wasn't, but Alex had no idea if the Dzhvar were electrically charged, nor what particles they may be composed of. Within each segment, the substance writhed asymmetrically, as if it were made up of an untold number of independent constituent members, each one dancing to its own beat.

Alex wanted to study every aspect of the Dzhvar at once, but first she needed to know something. She took Caleb's hand in hers, then slipped into sidespace and out of the ship.

Shadows blotted out the star beyond it. No longer in the corner of her vision, because they were everywhere, yet she still couldn't focus on any given point. It was as if they were *absence* personified. 'Void' in the literal sense of the word.

She opened her eyes and leaned closer to Caleb. "It's the same thing I saw at Elakrin when I shut down the Piega Strai."

"Mmm-hmm," he hummed tensely. "I know."

"Akeso?"

"Worrying over a danger it can't comprehend."

Nika, Dzhvar are at my coordinates as we speak. How is any kyoseil in the area responding?

One moment.

While she waited for a response, she studied the Dzhvar as they manifested in physical space more closely. They were putting on a dazzling and supremely intimidating light show.

'Probe 3 was destroyed 1.7 seconds after breaching the phenomenon,' Thomas announced. 'I've transmitted the data it collected to the Special Projects' Dzhvar research team for analysis. Probe 4 was destroyed 1.4 seconds after breaching the phenomenon. Same. Images from Probe 1 received.'

A screen materialized in front of the overlook. At a forty-degree angle from their present orientation, the Dzhvar stretched through space for some several megameters; the wall they formed was *thick*.

"They're moving fast, Thomas," Miriam said. "Follow at our current distance."

'Following.'

"Awareness. It's responding with hyper-awareness," a familiar voice said from behind her.

Alex pivoted to find Nika walking up to stand beside her. "But the kyoseil's not in distress?"

"I have never known kyoseil to become distressed. It doesn't experience emotions the way we do."

"Akeso is plenty distressed," Caleb said. Alex checked on him in renewed concern, but he seemed okay. He had a good bit of experience separating himself from Akeso's emotions, which, for a planet, could be surprisingly tumultuous.

"You've said on many occasions that Akeso is much more than kyoseil," Nika replied. "I'm not surprised it's developed its own emotions. The kyoseil *does* know the phenomenon. Perhaps from the earlier incursions, or perhaps from the first war. Perhaps because it has always known of it. And while there is not distress, there is…weight. Foreboding is too strong a word, but it's as if the kyoseil recognizes nothing good comes from the presence of this entity."

'The starboard branch of the Dzhvar is approaching a rocky planet at 118,000 megameters per second. Accelerating Probes 5 and 6 to attempt to capture the collision.'

At that speed, the wall could bisect an Earth-sized planet and be past it in eight seconds.

The visual from both probes appeared on new screens a few seconds before the Dzhvar reached what was a small, fairly verdant garden world. Did it harbor life?

A third of one segment swept through the planet without slowing down, and for a heart pounding moment the entire celestial body vanished from sight.

Then the Dzhvar were past it and continuing on their charge.

'Probes 5 and 6 will follow the Dzhvar. Directing Probes 7, 8 and 9 to orbit the planet. Probe 1 was destroyed 1.8 seconds after coming into contact with the port branch.'

"*Bozhe moy!*" announced her father's arrival. He joined her mother on the overlook, gaze darting across every vantage on display.

While he gaped at the speeding wall of Dzhvar, the rest of them fixated on the visuals of the planet the enemy had passed through. If their analysis of the attack in Capricornus was remotely accurate, this planet had taken a far more severe hit.

It took around ten seconds before the first continent began to crack apart. Oceans rushed in, only to transform into towering pillars of steam, since the crack was basically a thousand-kilometer-long volcano. Splinter cracks raced out in multiple directions, until the continent became a pockmark of islands and the oceans boiled. Icecaps at both poles melted, and at the upper pole, a depression formed. It grew in the direction where the Dzhvar had most directly impacted; when it reached another continent, this land mass too began to break into pieces.

'The leading edge of the center branch of the Dzhvar wall will begin to interact with the system's star in approximately forty seconds.'

God, it was fast. "Thomas, increase your distance from the phenomenon," Alex said. "In fact, slow to a stop and be ready to bail."

Miriam glanced back at her. "Why?"

"The star in the system we visited in Capricornus went nova four hours after contact. Based on the damage this incursion has inflicted thus far, if a healthy fraction of that wall tears through this star, it may go nova in minutes. Half an hour at most."

'Probe 2 has been accelerating this entire time. It will be able to monitor the impact with the star. Probes 5 and 6 are pulling out wide to attempt to stay clear of the initial destruction.'

Thomas was good at this. Sensing the grave import of the moment, he refrained from voicing a single sardonic wisecrack in favor of doing his job plus the jobs of the absent crew members. All while anticipating her mother's requests and gathering every scrap of obtainable information they would all clamor for in the coming hours. She understood why her mother trusted him and Valkyrie fancied him.

Corradeo Praesidis arrived on the bridge and strode directly to the viewport. Once there, he placed a palm, fingers splayed, on the simulated glass. Thanks to the Rasu, nearly seamless ships were now the order of the day, and no glass insets existed on the *Aurora.*

She caught Caleb watching Corradeo intently. "Go talk to him."

Caleb nodded, squeezed her hand, then joined the man up front.

Abruptly the left and right Dzhvar branches swung inward to join the center branch on its collision course with the star.

Her father gasped. "They moved deliberately! They intend to destroy the star."

"Looks like," Alex said grimly.

Diati had acted deliberately to join with Corradeo a million years ago, then had leapt from a litany of Inquisitors to Caleb whenever he encountered them. Kyoseil had acted deliberately in gifting her a decryption slab, and by infusing Nika with its essence at the Oneiroi Nebula. But other than those exceptions, the two primordial life forms acted only at the direction of an organic master.

This, though? This went beyond independent action; it was *willful*. The Dzhvar didn't merely act according to their nature; they had a plan. The locations they attacked might or might not be random, but their actions once on the scene most decidedly were not.

All three branches slammed into the star within a few seconds of one another. As massive as the rejoined Dzhvar wall was, the star dwarfed it in height and breadth, and the not-exactly-plasma vanished beneath the light of the photosphere.

Alex dropped into sidespace and projected her consciousness to the star's periphery.

Though the Dzhvar visibly existed in physical space, that wasn't where the action was. No, they were dimension shredding machines. They disrupted the star's fusion reactions by unbinding the protons in the hydrogen nuclei, then tearing the nuclei down into their constituent quarks to create a quark-gluon plasma, before triggering a further disintegration into whatever quarks and gluons were made of. Which, according to everything they understood about physics, was nothing at all.

Well. She supposed that was one way to dissolve the manifold.

She returned her consciousness to the bridge and opened her eyes. "Let whatever probes remain try to chase them out the other side. We need to go."

"It's that bad?" her father asked.

"It's worse." As she spoke, the filtered photosphere began to sputter. It wasn't the first time she'd been in proximity to a star about to go supernova, or even the second, and lingering near to such fury would always mean death. "I'd suggest now, Thomas."

"Do it," her mother ordered.

A wormhole opened in front of them, and they fled the dying star system for a clear region of space. After the radiant fire sweeping through the system with them hot on its tail, the comparatively empty, silent void descended upon the *Aurora* like a suffocating shroud of darkness.

25

CONCORD HQ
COMMAND

Alex paced furiously across the length of her mother's office. "Seven minutes. *Seven minutes.* Do you have any idea how powerful the Dzhvar must be to destroy a star in *seven minutes?*"

Miriam folded her hands atop her desk. A meeting of interested parties was scheduled in an hour to review the data they'd collected, but for now it was solely the two of them. "I believe I can appreciate the scale and its implications, yes. If they hit an inhabited star system, we will have as little as a few minutes and at most an hour from the time they first arrive in the vicinity to evacuate the people living there."

"Which I assume is impossible."

"To evacuate everyone? Absolutely. To evacuate a considerable percentage?" Miriam's eyes cast downward. "Also impossible. We will double our evacuation resources. Triple them. But time will not be on our side."

Alex's pacing skidded to a halt in front of the desk. "We need to be able to predict where they're going to hit. Even a few hours' warning will make all the difference."

Her mother's gaze shot up to her. "If you have any ideas of how to do so, I am eager to hear them."

"I don't. Not yet. I realize the Special Projects Artificials are crunching the numbers trying to identify a pattern to their appearances, and for the record, I believe there is one. Especially after today, because Dad was right. Their devouring of the star was deliberate, and this implies a level of intentionality far in excess of what we believed."

"If we can identify what characteristics they're drawn to, we can increase our preparations in systems that fit the profile."

"And doing so will help. Before you say 'it's not enough,' I know you're thinking it." Alex dropped into one of the chairs opposite the desk and brought a hand to her mouth to bite at her knuckles. "If I can be present in sidespace at a system *before* they arrive, I may be able to detect...ripples in the manifold that signal their imminent arrival or something."

"But Alex, what will we gain from this information? Like Advisor Kirumase, you can't spend every minute of every day half-catatonic with your mind cast into the ether, and we don't have a way to monitor sidespace remotely."

"Oh." Back on her feet again. "We should totally invent a way to do so. I'll talk to Devon. Frankly, negligent of him to not have invented such a tool already."

"Best not to lead off with that when you talk to him."

"Right. Listen, you should go ahead and authorize Kennedy to begin building the first Piega Strai. Possibly the first of many. It's going to take a while to build them, and after what we saw today? It might be our only way to protect a planet inhabited by billions of people."

"I had the same thought. Have you determined how to safely shut one down?"

"No. But I will. By the time she's got the first device built, I'll know how to reverse the process." She had nothing definitive with which to back up the promise, but she was the fucking dimension whisperer, wasn't she? She'd think of something.

"Alex, you're taking a lot of responsibilities on yourself."

"And you're not?"

"I am simply doing my job." Miriam sighed. "Have you asked Mesme about any of these ideas of yours?"

"Mesme is increasingly paranoid about telling us too much, or alternatively telling us too little, or instead telling us the wrong things. She—it insists we're doing better in this cycle, and doesn't want to constrain us with what turned out to be mistakes we made before. Only understanding what worked and what didn't is apparently not as cut-and-dried as one might expect."

Mirian's stare pierced straight through to her soul. "Mesme's correct, as conducting an accurate postmortem can be most difficult. *She?*"

Gavno.... "I misspoke. Referring to a friend as an 'it' feels wrong, flitting space lights or not."

"In eighteen years, I've never once heard you refer to Mesme as 'she.'" Her mother's hands wound tightly together at her chest. "You know who Mesme was in the last cycle. When did you figure it out? Or did Mesme confess its—*her*—identity to you?"

Alex opened her mouth to try for another excuse, then closed it again. There was no way she could tell her mother the truth. As agonizing as it was to keep Mesme's secret from those close to her, this was the most important promise she'd ever made. In three years, Caleb was the sole person she'd told, and this was only because she couldn't live with him and love him and share her soul with him and ever hope to keep such a monumental secret from him.

"The answers to those questions don't really matter, do they?" Alex asked weakly.

"Then perhaps you'd like to answer the one that does?"

"Mom, I *can't.*"

"Why not?" A rare storm broke through to rage within her mother's typically controlled gaze. "Is it you?"

"What?" She collapsed back in the chair. "Me? No, of course not."

"Alex, I beg you not to lie to me about this."

"I'm not lying to you." She frowned. "Why would you think it could be me?"

"Is that a serious question?"

"Um, yes?"

Her mother brought her clasped hands to her chin. "You're the only person who comes close to understanding how the universe and its endless dimensions function the way the Kats do.

The things you can do rival their own talents. You and Mesme share an obsessive determination to stop the Dzhvar and save everyone, to the exclusion of all other considerations. You have been the lynchpin in more than one desperate gambit to save civilization. I can go on."

"Not necessary." An amused and humbled smile flitted across her lips. It wasn't as if she'd thought her mother hadn't noticed her efforts, but…. "I take your point. But no, Mesme was not me in a previous life. I promise."

Miriam's rigid bearing visibly relaxed. "That is a relief to hear. I confess I've worried about it for some time now."

"Why?"

"Because I'm your mother, and above all else, I do not want you to suffer so. If we lose, I mean."

"Technically, if Mesme were me in its previous life, I would've already suffered."

"Technically. But I never knew some previous Alex. *You're* my daughter, here and now, and I care deeply about what happens to you."

Her chest panged with affection. They had a close relationship these days, but her mother had never been the sentimental type. Neither was she, for that matter, but she found it was rather nice to hear the words spoken aloud.

"Thank you. I know you do. But not to worry. If we lose, I'll simply be dead, along with you and everyone else—" except for Nika "—until the next Alex comes along and tries to accomplish what I could not. Well, I guess that's plenty to worry about. I just mean I won't have a million years of lonely struggle ahead of me if the worst happens."

"But someone will. And you know who it is."

"I do. But Mesme has exceptionally good reasons for asking me to keep its identity a secret, and I have to honor its request."

Her mother looked off into the distance for a long moment. "Would knowing this information change how I wage the battle now on our doorstep?"

It changed how *she* planned to wage it, because she wasn't merely fighting to save the royal 'everyone.' She was fighting to save her friend. But this was a highly personal consideration. "No, it wouldn't."

"Will you promise to tell me if circumstances change and I need to know?"

She started to resist. But it was a fair ask, for in this fight, nothing mattered more than winning. "I will."

"I suppose this is all I can ask of you." Miriam straightened her posture and resumed the comportment of military leader. "Then I will proceed to do everything in my power to ensure it never matters."

I save the people who will save the universe. Her mother was on Mesme's list for a damn good reason.

ARES

Corradeo slipped away to the study at his estate without bidding farewell to Caleb or Miriam. He stood at the windows and stared out, not seeing the terrace below, the terraformed plains to the east, the Olympia skyline to the west, or anything at all in this world, save the Dzhvar. Their reemergence was as a negative image burned onto his retinas.

With the Dzhvar firmly in his sight while he'd stood on the bridge of the *Aurora,* he'd called for the *diati.* He'd silently declared their archenemy returned—the same enemy the *diati* had always claimed to so desperately need to defeat—and pled for its help to do so once again.

And nothing answered.

He brought his hands to his face and growled into them in frustration. This should not be happening, any of it. He'd defeated the Dzhvar a million years ago. He'd been utterly certain of it!

Corradeo hovered in space far above Himeros, at the center of a maelstrom of crimson light. In an expression of his will, vast waves of diati *pushed the Dzhvar forcefully back into the far reaches of the stellar system. Both he and the* diati *were no longer content to play defense, to stop at shielding the world below from destruction. Together, they were at last strong enough to destroy this foe once and for all.*

The intelligence sharing his mind pulsed with the certitude that it would take but one final push, one massive burst of energy on their part, to achieve their goal. So Corradeo breathed in the air the diati *provided to him and drew upon what felt like a bottomless well of power.*

Then he flung his arms out, and with the act sent the waves at his command barreling into, beneath, above and around the Dzhvar. The manifold, already weakened by their adversary's forays, became porous across numerous dimensions. The diati *waves grew solid and impermeable to press in on the Dzhvar from every angle. And with every renewed surge, the pressure began to drive them into the newly formed folds of space.*

The Dzhvar did not give up without a fight, as they controlled a host of dimensions as well, but the diati *was relentless. It created mazes and dead-end paths to trap the enemy inside them; as the Dzhvar surged through the dimensional corridors, the* diati *sprung the traps, cutting off every avenue by which the enemy might escape.*

Corradeo was the avatar through which this power manifested, but the truth was, this was the diati's *show now. Freed of the need to make every operational decision, he expanded his perception and sensed how events were playing out in locations across Amaranthe. Distance didn't operate the same way in the hidden quantum dimensions, and by accessing them to create its traps, the* diati *was chasing down every Dzhvar, everywhere, at this singular, consequential moment. He knew this because the* diati *knew it.*

Then in a blink that spanned the cosmos, every flaming plasma tendril vanished from his sight. He shuddered as the diati *drew out every iota of power he was able to provide and squeezed.*

The manifold itself convulsed; it was as if the fundamental particles comprising the atoms of his body flung apart, hung suspended for a nanosecond—then molded themselves back together. He drew in a life-affirming breath as his heart restarted.

And the sky grew quiet. Much of the diati *returned to him, flushing his skin with renewed vitality, but much more of it, drawn to his control for this battle, dissipated out into space.*

For the first time since joining with Corradeo, the diati *was content.*

Thanks to his longtime primordial companion, he understood how hidden, quantum dimensions worked, even if he couldn't see them using his own organic eyes. But that day, it hadn't only been him who'd believed the Dzhvar crushed into extinction. The *diati* had believed it as well.

Hadn't it? It wasn't as if the inscrutable life form spoke to him in words. But the urgency driving the *diati*, constantly leaking into his own thoughts and driving him onward in turn, had immediately faded away when the Dzhvar vanished. He'd sensed fulfillment of purpose, of satisfaction. What else could it have meant, if not that the enemy was defeated?

Yet now the enemy had returned.

Guilt gnawed at him like a festering leech. If he'd pushed just a little harder on that day, for a little longer… But there had been nothing left to push against, no more action to take to drive the final stake home. The skies had shone as clear as a perfect sunny day on Solum. And what he'd sensed as simultaneous offensives playing out across Amaranthe had proved to be true. The scar on the manifold Alex Solovy discovered near Rasu Prime was evidence of this. Megaparsecs from Himeros, the Dzhvar had seared their essence into lifeless metal in the instant before the *diati* drove them into the last corner and annihilated them.

...Unless everything about what he'd perceived to be happening in the climactic battle was wrong. What if the Dzhvar hadn't been crushed out of existence at all, but instead stuffed into a hidden dimension and sealed up within it? What if the *diati* had deemed such an act 'good enough'? Or worse, what if the *diati* had realized this was the most their partnership was capable of achieving, and so it would have to suffice?

His guilt refused to be sated. He hadn't been strong enough to vanquish such a powerful foe. Perhaps if Caleb had been the one wielding the *diati* at the end of the war, then they wouldn't be facing this crisis now. Perhaps the Dzhvar wouldn't have returned from their exile, well-rested and potentially stronger than ever.

He wanted to say he'd never lacked for confidence, but it was a lie. For a thousand years after his son, Renato, nearly killed him, he'd felt small. Weak. Helpless. In truth, it wasn't until he'd met Lauren that he'd fully regained his former certitude. Then Renato had taken her from him as well.

In the wake of her death, he'd clung to scraps of his reclaimed dignity, for her memory. So he could try to finish what she'd started. But during his time in the desert, he'd learned humility and temperance. In learning these traits, had he lost forever the conviction needed for the *diati* to deem him worthy of being its master? Or, having failed to defeat the Dzhvar once, did it assume him incapable of doing so now?

But what if it was as Caleb speculated to him back during the Directorate War, and he'd simply changed so much in the intervening million years that the *diati* didn't recognize him as the same man? He'd take selfish comfort if this were the answer—if he were merely different, not lesser—but his heart refused to accept it as truth.

Of course, there was an even more terrifying option on the table, one he'd brought it up to Caleb the other day in passing. Maybe the *diati* was no longer capable of rousing itself for this fight. Maybe they were truly on their own.

In which case, Zeus help them all.

26

ROMANE

"Vii, I've decided I want to go with the Krysk Orbital II facility. It's the easiest location to modify to add an open assembly frame off of one side. It also has the most robust materials receiving system, and god knows we're going to be hauling in freighter-loads of materials if we expect to build one of these machines."

'Or a hundred,' the Artificial replied.

Kennedy's eyes widened in mock horror at the prospect. "Or a hundred...."

In the wake of the formula for manufacturing adiamene escaping into the wild—because she'd set it free—a lot of things had changed for Connova Interstellar. For one, their profits receded from their formerly nosebleed-inducing heights to a more ordinary level typical for the space construction industry. Which was fine, so long as the revenue remained high enough to pay the bills. She and Noah had stashed away funds for years, ensuring they were able to cover capital investments, and of course living expenses.

Their volume of production of adiamene had decreased by about thirty percent before stabilizing, as only the most sophisticated Anaden, Asterion and Novoloume companies succeeded in taming the beast of a manufacturing process to produce it for themselves. The decrease had left several of their factories sitting idle.

She could've reduced costs further by selling the facilities. But she'd chosen to hold on to them, because if there was anything she'd learned in the last twenty years, it was that one never knew what tomorrow might bring. Infrastructure was easy to dismantle but time-consuming and costly to construct.

And now here she was, needing to build an enormous, bleeding-edge dimensional machine with all due haste.

'The Krysk Orbital II facility is a wise choice,' Vii said. 'Shall I initiate the necessary preparations?'

Kennedy scrutinized the message from Miriam again, but there was no room for misinterpretation.

> *Build me a Piega Strai prototype. If it operates as intended, be prepared to scale production and build me many such devices.*

"Go for it, Vii. Full speed ahead. Concord will be paying for this, so no cutting corners, either."

'I'm mortified you think I would ever cut corners on Connova work product!'

Kennedy laughed. "I'm kidding. And also not, because the level of precision required to make this device function correctly is going to stretch the limits of all of our skills. Cutting edge is firmly in the rearview mirror here."

'I have faith we'll rise to the occasion.'

"I appreciate the vote of confidence."

Thanks to the records the Elakri had shared of the initial development and construction of the Piega Strai many thousands of years ago, she had ready-made schematics for the device on hand. There *was*, however, the small problem of how no one in Concord had ever invented about half of the components, nor melded the metals they'd used. The Elakri must have been one hell of an impressive civilization before the Rasu drove them to their knees. They had a long road ahead of them to reclaim their former glory, but thanks to Alex, they now had the chance. Assuming the Dzhvar didn't...but down this train of rumination led madness and despair, and she did her best to banish it.

So the challenges in front of her were significant, to say the least. But after a month and a half spent studying the files from the Elakri and more than two weeks deconstructing the layout of the device itself...she thought she could build it. Probably.

The door to her office opened, and Noah walked in. His dirty blond hair swayed over his forehead as he hoisted two small bags in the air. "I brought lunch."

"You're wonderful." She stood and kissed her husband as he arrived, then held her hands out in anticipation. She recognized the logo on the bag as belonging to her favorite deli downtown.

He chuckled and set the bag on her desk, opened it up and handed her a foil-wrapped gyro. "Samir says hi, and good luck."

"Good luck?"

"He said I only pick up lunch for you when you're working too hard, so you must be burying yourself in a new project."

"That's startlingly insightful of Samir," she remarked before diving into the warm gyro. Ahh, the cheese was just the right manner of gooey.

Noah propped on the edge of her desk and unwrapped his own lunch. "That's quality customer service—learning the little idiosyncrasies of his customers. I tipped him well, as always."

'Noah, we'll be using the Krysk Orbital II facility for the prototype construction. I'll have a list of materials requiring your special attention ready in eight minutes.'

"I figured I wouldn't be staying in the office long."

Kennedy washed down a bite of her food with a sip from the fizzy orange soda he'd brought her. "Speaking of, were you successful this morning?"

"I was. I had to go all the way to Scholite to find someone who manufactures the peculiar variant of lonsdaleite you asked for, but a company called Tritonen Metallurgy will provide it." He shook his head. "Anaden planets still feel strange to me. Ancient and stuffy and vaguely menacing."

"Were you the only human in the neighborhood?"

"No, I saw a few here and there, as well as a couple of Novoloume and two Naraida. It's not as if anyone leered threateningly at me and muttered, 'we don't like your kind around here' or anything. It's just a peculiar vibe."

"I know what you mean. Some of their planets have been settled for hundreds of thousands of years. That level of history adds a suffocating weight to the air."

Noah started to take another bite of his gyro, then set it back down. "There was something curious, though. One of the humans I passed on the street? She reminded me of Olivia Montegreu. It wasn't her, obviously, but the resemblance was striking. Enough that it pulled me up. I almost followed her, until I realized I was being crazy and went on with my day."

She supposed it shouldn't be a surprise if the woman's face was burned eternally into Noah's mind. After all, Montegreu was directly responsible for him losing his left arm in the attack on the Rasogo II space station years ago. His replacement biosynthetic arm was objectively superior in every way, but losing a major limb and nearly dying in the process did tend to leave an impression. It certainly had on her. The minutes he'd spent trapped by debris, his arm crushed, counted as some of the most terrifying of her life.

"Well, she's space dust, so." Kennedy finished off her gyro in record time and wiped her hands on a napkin. "When's the first delivery from this Tritonen Metallurgy? The lonsdaleite variant is only part of the formula for the diamond-based metamat the Elakri used. I've still got to brew the final alloy up in the lab."

"I know, which is why I secured a small initial delivery for later this evening."

"You are too good to me." She leaned over and kissed him, long and slow.

"Mmm, you make it worth my while." He smiled in a way that made her heart flutter. "Vii, is Jonas home from school yet?"

'He is. He asked me not to tell you, but he brought three friends home with him, and they are currently rearranging the living room furniture into a defensible fort in preparation for activating an alien invasion holosim.'

Kennedy rolled her eyes. In addition to running many aspects of the business, Vii insisted on acting as babysitter and occasional chauffeur for Jonas and Braelyn. The Artificial maintained two physical dolls, and one of them was always available to escort the kids to and from activities. Soon they'd be old enough to take care of themselves most of the time, at which point Vii would transition to a quieter, more unobtrusive if watchful guardian. But not just yet.

Noah cleaned up the remains of their lunch. "I'll stop by and act surprised and aghast at his flagrant violation of the rules. Then, I suspect Vii's shopping list is going to have me running to every end of the galaxy for the rest of the day."

'Likely tomorrow as well.'

"Right."

Kennedy grimaced. "Thank you. I'll be in the lab until this evening, but I'll make sure to get home in time to tuck them into bed."

Three and a half years ago, she'd almost lost both of her children, and in the hour where their lives hung in the balance of fate's fickle whimsy, her regrets had proved legion. Since then, she'd done what she could to be a better parent. To love them better. "We're not to the 'burn the candle at all three ends' portion of the war yet. The war isn't even here yet."

Noah's typically upbeat demeanor faltered briefly. "Will be though, won't it?"

"I'm afraid it will."

27

DOMOR

Olivia donned the clean suit over her clothes and allowed the lab tech to close all the seals. The helmet piped in cool but dry air, and the voice of the facility's owner, Nicholas-William ela-Erevna, rang crisp in her ears.

"If you're ready, I'll give you a tour."

She adjusted a sleeve on the suit, then nodded sharply. "Let's proceed."

The door led to a decontamination room, and they spent a few seconds there being blasted by unseen rays before a new set of doors revealed the primary storage space of the regenesis facility.

Signs identified the vats lining each row with such labels as "skin tissue," "bone grafts," "cartilage," "organ precursors" and so on. Self-explanatory, and not her focus of interest today, beyond the fact the materials existed in adequate supply here.

The next room was starkly bright and held twenty chambers arranged in four groupings. Thick tubes descended from the ceiling to feed into each chamber.

Olivia peeked inside one and found a human-sized skeleton partially covered in muscles and connective tissue. A renewed life in the making. "At what stage does the neural grafting occur?"

"Ninety percent of the way through the process," Nicholas-William replied. "We discovered long ago that the presence of a consciousness spurs a final phase of nervous system maturation. The person remains comatose until the end, as no one who wakes up in a regenesis pod wants to stay there for any length of time. Nonetheless, the brain goes to work immediately upon discovering it has a body to inhabit."

She followed the man through a second decontamination room. All the safety procedures were inconvenient, but she understood they were crucial to ensuring quality product.

Next, they entered a vast warehouse space stacked floor to ceiling with quantum hardware. "How many regenesis procedures do you perform in a year?"

"Around two hundred twenty. Our clients tend to live risky lives."

"I expect so. But why is so much hardware required? The data delivered by the integral upon a person's cessation ought to fit on a quantum cube a few centimeters in diameter." She gestured to the stacks. "This is a lot more than a few hundred cubes."

"Much of this hardware is new," he replied. "Anadens are no longer the only species in the regenesis game, but they are the only ones who utilize integrals."

"So this hardware is storing neural imprints?"

"Most of it, yes. We don't record the imprints here. Our clients typically have the procedure done at a regular medical clinic, though some are wealthy enough to own the necessary equipment themselves. Once recorded, they send us the data, and we store it until it's needed."

The man had clearly identified a new market opportunity and risen to meet it. Entrepreneurship at its best. "Then I assume you offer regenesis for humans?"

"Humans, Barisans and Novoloume. We can even service Volucri, though you don't find many Volucri who need to avail themselves of…extra-legal services. The fee is much higher than it is for Anadens, of course, as each species brings its own challenges. Plus there's the added expense of maintaining species-specific biological materials for lower-volume business."

"Of course. What about dolls?"

The man prevaricated. "The use of inorganic dolls is pointless on Anaden worlds, as their illegality would be facially apparent. They are legal on Human worlds, but the capital investment required to craft them is significant. Organic and inorganic bodies require substantially different materials and processes. Now, we don't ask too many questions of our clients. If the neural data we receive for a client happens to belong to an Artificial rather than an organic individual, what we don't know doesn't impact our services."

Discretion was a laudable trait in a businessman. "I've seen enough. Shall we retire to your office?"

S&L

Nicholas-William's office was utilitarian and spartan, which spoke to a cultural nuance Olivia had come to recognize in Anaden society. Members of the *ela* caste who were thriving in their transformed society did so because they were strivers. The ceiling had been removed from what they could accomplish, and the sky was now the limit. Those who succeeded worked hard, invested wisely and weaponized cleverness. They didn't waste time or money on public spectacles of wealth or social accoutrements, the way their *elasson* betters enjoyed doing.

Olivia crossed her legs and folded her hands in her lap. "I'd like to buy the facility from you."

"Excuse me?"

"I'd prefer it if you stay on to run the day-to-day operations, as you've done an admirable job of scaling up the operation and meeting your clients' evolving needs. But if you decline, I can find someone else."

He frowned. "Forgive me, Ms. Piras. I thought you wanted to become a client."

"Oh, I will be that as well. My own client, as it were. You have come under increasing financial pressure this last year. The upgrades needed to service additional species were not cheap, and regenesis is still new for non-Anadens. To make matters more complicated, the Advocacy's regulatory and enforcement apparatus grows every day, meaning you have to work harder to fly under its radar. Meanwhile, new players continue to shrug off their dynasty shackles and begin their own entrepreneurial endeavors. You're not alone in the race to seize the new riches, and your competition is often better funded than you are."

"You have no idea what the finances of this operation entail."

"I think you'll find I do," she replied. "Take the deal. You've made an admirable run here, but you're not ready for the top tier, not yet. I will compensate you well, both for the company and with respect to your ongoing salary. You may even earn an additional consulting fee to advise me on strategic matters, as I'm not well-versed in all aspects of this business."

He stared at her with a mix of offense and greed. "How much for the company?"

She'd prepared a proposal before arriving today. She adjusted a few figures based on what she'd seen on the tour and sent it to him.

He made a clucking sound deep in his throat as he reviewed the proposal. "And if I refuse your offer?"

"I'll open my own lab here on Domor and put you out of business within four months. It will cost me a great deal more to do so, however. This way is much easier and more profitable for both of us."

Nicholas-William's gaze flicked to the side in a final review of the offer. Finally he smiled. "Add a ten percent premium to your price, and we have a deal."

S&L

Olivia settled into her desk chair and surrounded herself with the latest business reports. She appreciated that the illicit hypnol trade was so lucrative, because she was spending a significant percentage of her funds on expanding her enterprise. Diversification was crucial, however, with respect to both industries and locations. Hypnols, cybernetic and physical upgrades, weapons, robotics and now regenesis.

Numerous underground regenesis labs were scattered across Anaden space. In the coming months, she'd quietly take over more of them, but she'd do it through shell companies, so it was never obvious that she controlled an increasing share of the market. For that matter, she'd acquire this facility through a shell of a shell.

The thoroughness with which the authorities had picked through the bones of Zelones eighteen years ago, then Enzio's Rivinchi cartel over the last three years, had bred a degree of paranoia into her mindset. Should the worst come to pass and the government succeed in coming after her enterprise, they'd only capture a fraction of her businesses, and be none the wiser.

Illegal regenesis labs existed on human worlds as well, because no species could exploit a black market with greater zeal and efficiency than humanity. Enzio had been a client of one such lab, though it had ultimately done him no good, as Mia Requelme had destroyed not merely his body, but every one of his Prevo backups.

Her vision unfocused from the reports. She'd contemplated exacting revenge for his death on the woman, naturally. And she might still. But she'd never been the vengeful sort. She punished those who deserved it, but she did so dispassionately.

In principle, Requelme did deserve it. As did Malcolm Jenner, given he'd struck the initial killing blow. And when blame was being dispensed, a healthy portion rested at the feet of her old pursuers-turned-temporary-allies, Richard Navick and Graham Delavasi, for they had robbed Enzio of something as valuable as his life: his wealth.

Yet when she mulled these truths over, she found she wasn't able to stir up much in the way of righteous indignation.

She'd felt a sort of detached affection for Enzio, but she also recognized that were he here now, he would be slowing her down. As she'd grown more self-possessed and independent, he'd grown more needy in turn. He'd maintained an unrealistic illusion of what he imagined their parent-child relationship should be—of what a *mother* should be—and it had not matched her own. So while she was grateful for the slavish devotion on his part that had resulted in her resurrection, she would not be expending any effort to return the favor.

If her other interests converged in a way that made it convenient for her to strike out against any of his killers, she'd do it, and in doing so right a wrong. But until then, it felt petty and wasteful to expend valuable time and effort on emotional revenge.

She did have plans to move into a variety of human markets in due time, but not until she knew she could outmaneuver the various law enforcement bureaucracies and the SENTRI spies. One civilization at a time.

A message arrived for her displaying a most aggressive subject line, and she allowed herself a small smile as she opened it.

> *Ms. Piras,*
> *You have picked the wrong fight.*
> *I hope you have enjoyed my Domor factories this last week. They represent a tiny fraction of my empire, but I take insult at your audacity nonetheless. You spilt the blood of my employees. Return what you stole, or I will spill yours a hundred-fold over.*
> *— Arnal Nikto*

She'd expected this reaction, and she composed a brief reply.

> *Arnal,*
> *Perhaps you are correct. Apologies if I reacted to your refusal in anger and overstepped my bounds. Let's meet to discuss matters, shall we? I would like to come to an amicable arrangement.*
> *The central factory on Domor's moon? I'll deactivate the defenses for you.*
> *— Teresa Piras*

While she waited for a response, she made several adjustments to the budget for the next six months. It appeared she was going to need to spend another tranche of her fortune.

S&L

FICENTI SATELLITE

Olivia watched on the security cams as the shuttle landed outside and Arnal Nikto and two bodyguards—or assassins—emerged. They traversed the airlock at the base of the dome and headed inside; judging by the vigor in Nikto's gait, he remained furious. Good. Emotion made people stupid.

When the door to the manager's office opened, she held up a hand in warning. "I need to ask your companions to wait outside. Let's discuss this matter as colleagues."

"Colleagues?" Nikto snapped. "We are nothing of the sort."

"Semantics." She dipped her chin in an act of appeasance. "Please. You and I both know I can't hurt you. Not for long, and any short-sighted action I take against you now will only harm me in the end."

"On that, you have the right of it." Arnal nodded to the two men. "Wait for me outside. I'll call you if I need you."

They departed without comment like the good soldiers they were, and the door closed behind them.

She sent a mental command to the security system while gesturing to the chair in front of the desk.

Rather than take a seat, he planted his feet in a wide stance and clasped his hands at his waist. "Change the passcode, turn over the system to me, and leave. Anything less, and I will end you."

"I admire you, you know. Many *elas* wilted away after the deaths of the Primors and disintegration of the Directorate, but not you. You seized your destiny for yourself and have built a small empire."

"Not so small..." he scowled "...what's that smell?"

"I've been having some difficulties with the ventilation system. Atmospheres are always a difficulty on lifeless rocks in space, aren't they? And I no longer have any maintenance employees, so fixing it has proved to be a challenge."

"You probably shouldn't have killed them all, then."

"Perhaps not. It seemed the best option at the time."

"It wasn't...." Another scowl, this one accompanied by a hand to the stomach. "I'm feeling ill. What *sort* of ventilation problem?"

One of these days, Anadens whose lifestyles put them in regular peril were going to start realizing that sudden-onset stomach pain was a clue they were about to permanently depart the mortal coil. But not today, it seemed. "A leak in one of the filtration lines, I believe. I feel fine, though."

It wasn't true. The *apomono* couldn't harm her in any meaningful way, as she lacked the neural infrastructure of an integral, but the nausea hit her nonetheless. A couple of enterprising Prevo consultants she'd hired had worked out how to create *apomono* in gaseous form. It wasn't stable and would break down in a matter of minutes, but it only took a few seconds to inhale a sufficient dose, especially in a small, enclosed space like this office.

"Stop stalling, Piras. The passcode."

She sighed. "I'd hoped we could build an amicable relationship, but fine. You win." She leaned close to the console entry and opened up the master override. Then she removed the Reverb she'd attached underneath the desk, pulled it out and fired it.

He collapsed to the floor as easily as his plant manager had.

She quickly knelt beside his body. She needed fingerprints, a retinal scan, a blood sample and anything else he used for security.

After she had those things, she attached a fiber cable to the port at the base of his skull and copied out everything she was able to extract from his cybernetics.

Satisfied she'd acquired what she needed, she briefly returned to the desk and typed in a different command on the console. It sent the factory bots into lockdown mode, which included magnetic attachments. Ignoring the painful gurgle in her stomach, she moved to the wall and repeated the steps she'd taken on her first visit here. The biohazard protocol swept Arnal and his men out into space.

SCHOLITE

Arnal Nikto's mansion overlooked a lake outside of the city of Palici on Scholite. He had better taste than she'd expected. While her base of operations on Domor had suited her needs thus far, she might consider taking over the property along with his business empire.

Olivia set a variety of programs running on his central server. The security was robust, even with all the access levers she'd arrived bearing. But she was an Artificial at least as much as she was Prevo or human, and she could outsmart any sub-Artificial system.

The Anadens' millennia-long rejection of sentient Artificials had handicapped them in ways they were only beginning to recover from, and it was no wonder humanity had run roughshod over them in the aftermath of the Directorate War. If AEGIS wasn't so weak-willed, humanity could've established a level of dominance the Anadens would find difficult to break free of, far greater population numbers or no.

But they hadn't, and now under Corradeo Praesidis' leadership, the Anadens were entering an era of ascendancy. No matter; competition bred conflict, and conflict was good for business.

In less than twenty minutes, Olivia had full control of Nikto's systems. She deployed routines to copy everything out then funnel it into a suite of algorithms that would sort and summarize the data in accordance with her preferences.

Next, she queued up a series of messages to be delivered to all of his lieutenants listed in the personnel files. The messages varied in the details based on the business each lieutenant oversaw, but they all explained how Nikto was shifting day-to-day management of *their* division to Teresa Piras in order to free up some of his time to pursue new interests.

The man had colleagues; presumably he had friends and lovers. Eventually one of them was apt to come looking for him, and she'd need to deal with their questions. But in the years after the Dynasty structure had crumbled, a lot of Anadens had disappeared, for a lot of reasons. One of those reasons should suffice to mollify most inquiries. If someone did piece together that a single individual—her—had taken over his entire operation, she'd need to do a bit more work to obscure her actions. But she'd accomplished far more with far less.

In fact, she'd done all of this before.

She toed Nikto's chair around to consider the lake and the emerald rolling hills surrounding it. She wasn't falling into a rut. Yes, she'd killed a powerful competitor and taken over their business before. Multiple times, in fact. But those moves had involved the minor leagues of an isolated human dot of civilization. Her conquest now was an alien enterprise thousands of years old belonging to a species who'd ruled forty galaxies for hundreds of millennia.

The world was a far bigger place now, with far higher mountains to scale.

28

ARES

Eren mentally reviewed the details of his cover while he chose the correct attire for tonight's meeting. The false identity had been constructed out of whole cloth, then records robust enough to withstand scrutiny had been inserted in the necessary places. The business he allegedly ran got the same thorough treatment. Criminals who rose to any prominence in the black market trades tended to be the suspicious sort, for good reason, and fooling them required some effort.

More difficult than creating the identity and its peripherals, though, was building a soft trail around both that was sufficient to lend them that indefinable air of legitimacy. Even in a society spanning thousands of planets, the movers and shakers in any given sector knew who the serious players were.

But crafting a whisper campaign simply required learning who the big talkers were, who liked to puff up their reputation by pretending they were privy to all the latest rumblings, and who could be bought off to play along in return for leniency by law enforcement. Get three or four of those people dropping his false name in relevant conversations, and in a matter of days, he was— and to all appearances had always been—a known quantity in the target space.

Satisfied that his clothes matched his persona and his destination, Eren slipped on a leather jacket, pocketed a vial of stolen Nephyl-HIG, and headed out.

S&L

DOMOR

The high table was nestled deep in shadows strategically crafted for privacy throughout the bar. *Endoran Spirits & Sundries* was a business bar—the illegal kind. The proprietors kept it clean and orderly and made sure street criminals didn't clog up the space and annoy the better-paying customers. They also ensured its ambience was dank and intimidating enough to deter random tourists from wandering in for a drink, which would force the deals being transacted in those shadows to halt cold.

Eren slid onto the free stool opposite an Erevna *asi*. He had altered his appearance to the limits of his cybernetics' capabilities, since Nyx had confiscated his Shroud as soon as they'd returned from Nythir and thus far refused to allow him to check one back out. Some nonsense about 'still in testing' and 'a new prototype under development.' His hair was now almost black with pewter accents; his skin had lightened to a tawny hue, and his eyes gleamed a washed-out pale blue.

Criminals of a certain standing made it a priority to know the government officials who could interfere with their business, and everything he'd learned so far about the Riamere cartel and the Pale Viper leading it counseled that he needed to play this gambit smartly. He was not dealing with street hustlers and thugs. So false name, false business, false appearance.

"Padron Lanael?" the *asi* asked.

"That's right," Eren said. "What about you?"

"You can call me Quinton. Thanks for agreeing to meet with me on such short notice."

Eren shrugged mildly. "What can I do for you?"

"Word is making the rounds that you have Nephyl-HIG to move."

"And I wish it wasn't making the rounds so enthusiastically. You're the fourth meeting I've had today about my stock."

"The market took an unexpected hit this week." Quinton studied him coolly. "If I may ask, how *do* you have stock? You're not one of the regular suppliers."

"I don't share trade secrets with strangers."

"I'll need to be convinced you really do possess it. Take me to your warehouse."

Eren scoffed. "So you can send a crew back later tonight to steal it? I don't think so."

"Then we can't do business." The man started to stand.

"I didn't say I wouldn't prove I have it. Idle your jets." He reached into his pocket and retrieved a vial, which he placed on the table.

Quinton picked the vial up and scrutinized it for a second, then tossed it onto the table. "This only proves you can print out a proper label and know what color Nephyl-HIG is supposed to be."

"Take it with you. Have your chemical analyzers run their tests. But before you do…." Eren held a hand out, palm up, and instantiated a screen. It showed a shelf full of identical vials situated in a lab-outfitted room. A bot arm reached out and plucked one from its tray, opened the vial and poured the contents into a beaker. Another arm swept in and dipped a stick in the beaker, then placed the stick beneath an analyzer. A few seconds later, a chemical readout populated the screen.

"This still doesn't prove anything."

"Gets closer though, doesn't it?"

Quinton picked the vial back up and rolled it between his fingers. "If this vial tests out, we'll pay ten percent over asking for the lot, with the caveat that we get to spot-test the supply before making payment."

"Did you miss the part about four meetings today? 'Asking' has gone up by twenty-five percent."

"Fine. But we get it all, and right of first refusal on your next supply."

"I'll do you one better," Eren replied. "I'll guarantee Riamere a supply for as long as they want it. But I have one condition. Ongoing business arrangement such as this? I need to know who I'm dealing with."

"You're dealing with me."

"No, I'm not." He smiled, but put an edge on it. "I want to meet the Pale Viper."

"The Pale Viper does not take requests from fans."

"Then she doesn't get any Nephyl-HIG. I will happily sell all of it and more to the last guy I met with. He offered me five percent over the new price, and he wasn't half as much of an asshole as you are."

Quinton's bearing stiffened in defensiveness. "Why don't you do so, then?"

"Thing is, I like what Riamere has been doing of late. It's past time someone with balls and smarts upended the oh-so-dull status quo. And, I might find myself in need of some *apomono* in the near future. Got a personal matter to attend to."

"I never said we were using the Nephyl-HIG to make *apomono.*"

"No, but you are." Eren shrugged. "Not certain what this says about the Pale Viper's smarts, but it does confirm the balls. So I want to meet her."

"She will not agree to it."

"She will if she wants to keep making and selling *apomono.*"

Quinton glared at him for several long seconds before jabbing a finger toward Eren's face. "*If* this vial tests out, and *if* you provide a good faith supply of one kilo at half price, *then* I will pass along your request."

Eren chewed on his lower lip in apparent contemplation…and nodded. "All right. Give me an address to ship the product to. You know, you're not a bad negotiator. I meet your boss, and I'll put in a good word for you."

He stood and departed before Quinton could respond. Always leave on your own terms.

S&L

ARES

Nyx's cheek rested on Eren's chest. One long leg curled over his thigh as she twined a lock of his sweat-soaked, again-copper hair around her finger.

"And you think this Pale Viper will take the bait?" she murmured indolently, her voice a soft purr. The only time she ever sounded so relaxed was for about ten minutes after sex, when the afterglow thrummed powerfully enough to overwhelm her usual sharp, hyper-competent demeanor.

"I do. Acting as the sole *apomono* dealer in existence is a ticket to moderate riches and far greater power in the hypnol market. She won't want to give up the leverage she's earned, and I'm offering her a path by which she won't have to. All she needs to do is agree to one little meeting with a fellow businessperson."

His hand idly stroked her back, enjoying the warmth her skin radiated. Guilt still snaked through his gut, curling in on itself to fashion painful knots. But the pain was a dull ache rather than a stinging agony, and he was trying to grit his way through it.

Because he found he didn't want to give this up. He'd nailed it the other day: Nyx was turning out to be a drug, and he'd always been an addict. Whether this drug ended up inflicting as much harm on him as the others inevitably had remained to be seen. For now, being with her both met and stoked a potent need in him.

"And what's the latest on Ihelahn Roshiive?" She sounded as if she was about to fall asleep, yet here she was, quizzing him on his work assignments.

He grabbed her ass and pinched the shapely flesh. "What is this, a briefing?"

"Ow!" she yelped, swatting his hand away. "No, but this is the only place I can get your undivided attention for more than thirty seconds at a time."

"True enough." He hadn't gotten any better at filing reports or keeping her apprised of developments, unless he decided she needed to know them. "Roshiive is raising money for something. The fact that he's not willing to spend his own money on whatever it is suggests he might not be serious about undermining the Advocacy. This could be nothing more than a project to embarrass the government for his own vengeful amusement. Alternatively, whatever he's planning is so expensive he can't afford it on his own, in which case—"

"Trouble."

"You got it. I'm working on tracking where the money's going. If we can listen in on an account, we'll be able to tell who's paying in, and of course where it pays out to." He smiled, playing with her hair splayed out across his chest. "What's new on your end?"

"Hmm. A warehouse full of workers on Ficenti were slaughtered a week ago, and the scene has all the hallmarks of another Ch'mshak attack. I didn't learn of it until yesterday because the owner of the warehouse is Arnal Nikto, and he obviously didn't report the incident to the local authorities."

"We haven't uncovered any potential motive for the attack on the A-468c station. Maybe the motive for all the attacks is as simple as the Ch'mshak enjoy slaughtering lots of people in confined spaces."

"It's definitely *a* reason, as they've always taken pleasure in doing so. It remains to be seen whether it's the only reason."

"Now, that's enough work talk." He lifted her chin and kissed her full on the mouth. As her leg moved against his, he felt his cock stir to life once again. Dammit, but he could not get enough of her.

Nyx smiled sloppily above his lips. "You know, you never lost your *ela*-caliber intelligence and cleverness. *Asis* simply aren't capable of strategizing the way you do."

He grasped her hips to position her on top of him—then paused. "What do you mean, I 'never lost' it? I never had it."

If virtually the full length of her body hadn't been pressed against him—if he hadn't held her firmly in both hands—he might not have noticed the way her muscles subtly tensed beneath her skin.

But he did.

"I merely mean you think like an *ela*. It's why I underestimated you when we first started working together." Gone was the silky purr; each word came out enunciated and clear.

"But that's not what you said."

"I was…conflating two thoughts." She kissed him with tantalizing, and possibly forced, fervor. "You jumble my head when you're naked and touching me."

Her words said one thing, but everything about her body language said another. He nudged her off of him and propped up on an elbow. "You're lying to me. What did you mean when you said I never lost my *ela*-caliber intelligence and cleverness? I've never been an *ela*, so why would you imply I was?"

She stared at him, and he discovered something most unexpected in her eyes: fear. But fear of what? "Please accept that I misspoke and let it go."

"No. Your reaction screams that this is something noteworthy, something I absolutely should *not* let go. Nyx, what are you keeping from me?"

She covered her face with her hands and rolled onto her back. "I can't tell you."

"Why in the name of Zeus not?"

"Because I made a promise."

"Who would you be making promises to involving *me*? Why would you…" his throat worked as realization dawned "…Corradeo."

She didn't respond, and after the silence lingered for too long, he climbed out of bed and hunted around on the floor for his pants.

"Where are you going?"

"To ask him myself."

"No. Please don't."

Eren spun around to find she'd sat up in the bed, and he refused to let the sight distract him. Not this time. "Then tell me."

"Did you miss the part where I made a promise to the one person in this universe I truly care about?"

He sucked in a breath, shocked at the barb through his chest her words delivered.

"I'm sorry, I didn't mean I don't care—"

"No, it's fine. We're sheet-mates, and I never thought we were anything more. *Arae anathema*, Nyx. What's the secret?"

Her jaw locked in refusal, so he picked his pants up off the floor and pulled them on—

"You were an anarch in the first rebellion. With Grandfather and his wife."

"I was..." he shook his head, as if trying to clear water from his ears "...what?"

Her entire posture deflated, and she sank against the headboard. When she spoke, her voice was flat. "What I said. You were a key operative and worked closely with them in their fight against the Primors during the first anarch rebellion. To hear him tell it, they thought of you as family. When Directorate forces raided the anarch base, they killed everyone else but took you captive. When they'd finished torturing you, they wiped your memory and demoted you to *asi* during regenesis."

His head spun. He felt behind him until he found the chair and sank bonelessly into it. "That was 250,000 years ago."

"Yes."

"So I...but then...." He didn't know where to start. There was no thread to grasp onto and gain any sort of anchor for the revelation. "Why hasn't he ever told me?"

She finally looked over at him; her mouth was set into a grim line, her eyes hooded. "To spare you pain. He carries the weight of a million years of heartache and loss after loss upon his shoulders. He refuses to share this burden with anyone, but most of all with people he cares about. And he cares about you."

"Keeping secrets is a bullshite way of showing it. How long have you known?"

"A few years."

"So the entire time we've been working together."

"No. I found out after..." she shook her head weakly "...close enough."

Eren stared at the floor for what felt like years. Dizziness lurched his head in waves until nausea roiled his stomach, and an anchor continued to elude him. The story he told himself about himself had just been shredded and cast upon the wind.

Abruptly he stood, muscling through the dizziness to keep his feet beneath him. "I have to go."

"Wait. Please, give me a chance to talk to him before you confront him. This is my fault, and I need to try to make it right."

"Do whatever you want. I'll be honest. I'm not sure I'm ever going to talk to Corradeo Praesidis again. What would be the point? He'll just lie to me."

29

ARES

The door chime for Corradeo's residential suite rang in his head, startling him out of his thoughts.

He checked the time; it was late, though not scandalously so. Maris slept peacefully beside him, but slumber had thus far refused to make an appearance for him. Whenever his mind grew unoccupied for longer than a minute or two, his failure during the Dzhvar encounter in the Shapley Supercluster emerged to haunt him. The looping questions and recriminations from the refusal of the *diati* to answer his summons were growing tiresome, but the answers they suggested were worse.

A head of state was never off the clock, so Corradeo climbed out of bed, careful not to disturb Maris, and slipped on his lounge pants and shirt. The visual from the security cam showed Nyx at the door, and concern stirred to life. What calamity of state would fail to trigger the many alert routines he maintained, yet would bring her to his suite at this hour?

He quietly closed the door to the bedroom, then crossed the living room to the entrance and opened it. "Nyx, what's wrong?"

Her hair looked disheveled, with several tangles in it, and a casual linen shirt hung lopsided to her hips over loose black pants. She wasn't coming from work. "Can I come in?"

"Please do."

She strode past him into the living room, where she propped awkwardly on the edge of one of the chairs. Her spine was ramrod-straight, her hands fisted at a knee.

He moved one of the other chairs in front of her, sat, and leaned forward. "Talk to me. What's happened?"

"I...made a mistake."

"Even the best of us do from time to time."

"Not like this." Her gaze, which had yet to alight upon him, dropped to the floor. "I betrayed your trust. I let my guard down and fell prey to these ridiculous emotions that have been harassing me of late, and I did the *one thing* you asked me not to do."

He couldn't imagine what she might be referring to. "You're going to need to be more specific."

"Yes. I, uh..." her brow knotted tightly, and she forcibly dragged her eyes up to meet his "...I revealed to Eren the truth about his past. About the first anarch rebellion and his role in it. Or rather, I said something in passing that raised his suspicions, and he refused to relent until I confessed the truth. Grandfather, no words exist for me to express how sorry I am. You trusted me with one of your deepest secrets, and I...I failed you."

"Oh. I see." He found he was on his feet and pacing slowly. A vague manner of panic sent his heart pounding in his chest, which made no sense. He had nothing to panic over. The past was the past, and he'd made peace with it. Hadn't he? He'd considered revealing the truth to Eren on several occasions over the last few years, so this was hardly the end of the world. Still, he couldn't seem to calm his pulse.

"Allow me to ask how this particular topic came up in conversation?"

"It...we were merely...talking. About the Roshiive investigation, as well as the Riamere cartel and the Pale Viper. About his strategies for both cases and...." She trailed off weakly.

"Work is what passes for pillow talk between the two of you, then?" It came out more of an accusation than he'd intended.

Her eyes widened. "You know?"

"Don't take me for an idiot, Nyx. Of course I know. But the setting doesn't answer the question of how we ended up with this specific secret spilled into the open."

The color drained from her face; he recognized his tone was growing increasingly hostile, but he was unable to summon the composure needed to ease up. It was as if his most reliable behavioral regulator, worn down from excessive use, had broken loose in his mind.

"I said something that implied he might have been an *ela* in the past. It was intended as a compliment. Eren is maddeningly persistent when he sniffs out a weakness, and he would not let it go. He tore down my every rebuff, like I was a suspect in an interrogation cell. Gods, he's infuriating!"

"And?"

"And once he realized you had bound me to a secret, he threatened to barge in here unannounced and demand for you to reveal it to him yourself. I couldn't let him ambush you that way. So I told him the truth."

He was sitting again, without intending to do so; not in the chair across from her, but on the more distant couch. "How did Eren take the news?"

"Grandfather, I know if you simply explain to him—"

"That well, then." *Oh, Eren. Wild, willful, irrepressible Eren. My friend, and my constant reminder of all I've lost.* He stood again almost as soon as he'd sat, but the regulator kicked in enough for him to keep his voice measured and even, if somewhat flat. He never wanted to be cruel to her. "Don't trouble yourself overmuch. I should have told him years ago. It's for the best that the past come into the light."

"If so, it should have done so on your terms. I am genuinely sorry."

"I believe you are. As I said, we all make mistakes. Now, if you don't mind, Maris is here, and she will start to wonder where I've gotten off to if I don't return soon."

Nyx made no move to leave. "If you're angry with me, please say so. Don't bury your true feelings about this alongside everything else."

He stared at her sharply. They'd not spoken in any depth since the Dzhvar encounter, and she couldn't know of the turmoil that wracked his psyche. Then he realized the matters she referenced were indeed legion, and he wasn't ready to discuss a single one with her. "I'm not angry with you, Nyx. Eren can be most tenacious."

"He…yes, he can be. Will you reach out to him? To clear the air?"

A pained expression fought to overtake his features. "Put in a good word for me, if you would."

"If you just talk to him, I'm sure he'll understand."

He laughed hollowly. "I'm not."

S&L

When he finally ushered Nyx back out the door, Corradeo returned to the couch and sat down to fixate on the painting on the opposite wall. It was a rustic watercolor he'd commissioned, depicting a Hoan village surrounded by fields of swaying wheat. Normally it brought a wistful smile to his face, but tonight it only reminded him of one more treasure he'd lost.

While he mourned the massacre of the Hoan at the hands of the Rasu, he'd never blamed himself for it. But the Rasu might never have existed to pursue their reign of terror if he'd succeeded in ending the Dzhvar in the first war.

The sins of the past did tend to pile up when one lived for a million uninterrupted years. His failure to truly defeat the Dzhvar. His failure to protect those most precious to him. Nyx's mother, Melia. His second and truest wife, Lauren. Eren. All those who'd fought at their side so long ago. Even, it turned out, the innocent Hoan, who'd once nurtured him back to health, in mind and spirit as much as in body.

It was no wonder the *diati* refused to answer his call. He talked a grand game and swayed many with his dulcet tones and hypnotic words, but when it mattered most, he'd proved he couldn't get the job done.

His people had called him the most powerful man in the universe more than once. But what was power worth if it stripped him bare and left him alone, time and again? Why did he torture himself so in this implacable quest for redemption?

He didn't notice Maris arriving from the bedroom until she'd sat next to him on the couch. He tilted his head in apology. "I'm sorry we woke you."

"I suspect waking me was not front and center on your list of concerns." She reached up and touched his cheek. "What have you done to warrant such a sorrowful mien, Advocate?"

Once upon a time, she'd insisted on addressing him as 'Advocate' as a way of keeping him at arm's length. These days, she frequently did so in a teasing, affectionate manner. He thought maybe he loved her for it…so how long until one of his many sins ran her off as well? Or worse, killed her?

Zeus, but he was maudlin. Whiny and weak. Dammit, he had to be better than this.

He sighed deeply. "Kept a secret I perhaps shouldn't have."

Then he told her the story, because right now he wasn't strong enough to soldier on through the night alone, stoic and gracious. Besides, if anyone in the world could understand, it was someone who'd lived nearly as long as him and carried some large fraction of his many regrets.

When he finished, she leaned back against the arm of the couch and brought a fist to her chin, looking stunningly elegant in a champagne satin robe, her tight curls a wild frame around sculpted features. "How many times have we talked about your paternalistic streak? Namely, how you need to banish it to the underworld?"

He tried to smile, but failed. "Once or twice."

"Eight times, by my count. Nine, now. You cannot protect people from the vagaries of the universe. In trying to do so, you hurt them as much as you hurt yourself—" She frowned and cut herself off.

"What is it?"

"Oh, I just realized I'm being a mite hypocritical. I've long been a staunch proponent for keeping the existence of the First

Generation a secret from Asterions, for what I maintain are compelling reasons. When Nika learned of her history, she ripped up the rulebook we'd spent seven hundred thousand years following and tossed it out the window and…she was correct to do so when it came to Dashiel. He's proved himself worthy of being entrusted with a supremely difficult truth.

"But like you, I've seen the damage knowledge of a heart-wrenching past can inflict on people and have sought to protect them from it, so I don't know what the right answer is."

She reached out and took his hands in hers. "No matter how old we are, we are only ever fumbling our way through this existence. We think experience has taught us what's best for others, but I wonder. Have we learned anything at all? Or do we remain utter fools?"

He brought their hands up and kissed her knuckles, grateful beyond measure to have her by his side at this moment. "I am certainly feeling like a fool tonight. I tried to protect my friend from being hurt by a tragic past he can't change. Now he is hurt by it anyway, and I can't be there for him, because it is my fault. First in failing to save him all those years ago, then in being too much of a coward to own up to my failure."

"Which is it?"

"Which is what?"

She exhaled through pursed lips. "Were you protecting him or protecting yourself?"

"I suspect both. Regardless, I've done neither."

"Quite."

"If this is a pep talk intended to cheer me up, it's not working."

She leaned in close, until their noses almost touched. Her voice was a velvety murmur, but it carried an incisive edge. "If there is one thing you must recognize by now, it is that I will never treat you with kid gloves. I will never falsely stroke your ego. I will never allow you to lie to yourself about the nature of this world or your actions in it. Forgive me, but I was under the impression this was why I am the only woman currently drawing air in our cosmos who is worthy of your love."

He huffed a wondrous breath. Athena's grace, but she was a spectacular woman. "Worthy indeed, and it isn't a close contest. But my feet are already blistered from being held to the scorching flames. Any chance I can get a reprieve for tonight?"

"Sorry, my dear. You need to own up to this one."

He nodded. "I do. Trouble is, I'm not confident Eren will ever allow me. The man knows how to hold a grudge, especially when it's deserved."

30

NAMINO

ASTERION DOMINION
GENNISI GALAXY

The Namino One sidewalks bustled with shoppers in the retail district. Elegantly designed buildings gleamed, their windows sparkling like gemstones in the sunlight. Few skycars broke up the clear teal sky overhead, but the brief shimmer of wormholes danced in and out of the flow of pedestrians in a staccato rhythm. The use of wormholes for travel had obviously taken root in Asterion society.

Marlee found the restaurant she was searching for situated between a music bar and a tech shop, then spotted Grant Mesahle waving to her from a table out on the patio. She took a second to admire the view that was this gorgeous man before working her way over to the table and sitting down across from him. "This is incredible."

"I ordered you a lemon spritzer. I remember you like those. What's incredible?"

"It's as if the Rasu invasion never happened. Has the entire city been rebuilt?"

"And then some. A few formerly commercial blocks were cleared away and replaced with parks and recreational spaces, but for the most part it's the same, only better." Grant shrugged. "Asterions are nothing if not industrious."

"I know, but to see the results in action...." She glanced over the menu, made an impulse choice of a seafood pasta dish, and punched in her order on the pad. "You told me you finished repairing your house a while ago, but what about Mesahle Flight?"

His house was situated in the midst of the business property, but patching a roof was a lot less involved than reconstructing scaffolding and cranes and installing new assembly machinery.

He grimaced. "In process, as I remain busy with my other job. Now that he has carte blanche to build a navy, I'm convinced Palmer will never have enough ships. But I've innovated about all I can innovate for him, so I'm starting to steal back time for my own work."

"I heard the Asterion ships are kicking AEGIS' ass in the latest joint maneuvers."

"We excel at whatever we put our minds to, or so the party line goes." He rolled his eyes at the sky. "Not that it will do us any good."

"What do you mean?"

"As I hear it, warships are useless against the Dzhvar. Weapons don't harm them, and even adiaK can't stand up to their subatomic disruption. We'll finally have a fleet millions strong, and the Dzhvar will roll right through it as surely as the Rasu did the last one. Or worse, not notice it's there as they rip it to shreds along with the manifold."

"That's a defeatist outlook," she replied.

"Can't help it. It feels like the SAI Rebellion all over again. We'll throw everything we have into a desperate fight for survival, and it won't make any difference."

Well he was in a mood today. "I think your attitude sucks. Also, you're wrong. It *did* make a difference in the rebellion, because you *did* survive. You survived to be sitting here having lunch with me on a warm, sunny day and complaining about it."

He stared at her in surprise for a beat, then burst out laughing. "Sorry. I didn't mean to be morbid. I sometimes forget how young you are—it's a compliment, as you don't act young, not any longer. I just mean you still enjoy the optimism of youth. You can afford to believe everything will work out, because it has so far. And it's refreshing, it is. In fact, it's one reason I like you. But you haven't seen the things I've seen."

Once upon a time, she would've sputtered out an ineffectual barb and stormed off in a huff over him calling out her age. And she *was* annoyed with him. But most of all, she wished she could change his outlook on life. Jaded and bitter didn't become him; when he smiled, the whole world brightened, and she was of the considered opinion that he should do it far more often.

So instead, she elected not to pick a fight. "Say, did I tell you I got trapped on another alien planet a couple of weeks ago? Way over in the Medusa Merger. Had to rescue myself off of it."

His lips quirked as he regarded her in amusement, or possibly confusion. "No, you did not. One might pause to wonder why this keeps happening to you."

"Oh, I have some theories. But it wasn't my fault this time. I was literally doing my job when a murder happened in front of me and the culprit took me captive. Though the circumstances turned out to be a good bit more complicated than they first appeared, and I did ultimately stay longer than I had to. The people there needed my help."

"And did you? Help them?"

"I did. It was a positive experience in the end, if a bit touch-and-go for the first few days. I made some new friends, too."

"That much hasn't changed, then." He flashed her one of his thousand-watt smiles, and her heart fluttered away in her chest. Whoa, boy.

"Nope," she replied breezily. Their food mercifully arrived then, and she dug into her pasta with gusto, in part to cover for any blushing she might be engaging in and in part to spend a minute evaluating their conversation thus far.

She enjoyed their occasional meetups, but she was making little progress on breaking down his formidable armor. Grant was friendly and affable and always up for work or fun, but she still hadn't the slightest idea what made him tick. More relevantly, what fed his at times fatalistic attitude toward life. She refused to believe it came from being tens or hundreds of thousands of years old. She hadn't managed to learn his exact age, either, but it was definitely *old*. Still, the Dominion was full of epically old people who embraced new challenges with optimism and enthusiasm. So why didn't he?

She recalled what Nika had said to her the day they'd expelled the Rasu from this planet. *"You know, Grant's a good man. A good man with a couple of deeply buried demons. If I could remember what they were, I might be able to help him, or at least tell you so you could try to do the same."*

Just because he seemed intent on keeping those demons hidden from prying eyes didn't mean she would stop trying to uncover them. She wanted to bring him the rest of the way into the light.

But it wasn't going to happen today. She washed her food down with a big sip of the spritzer. "I'm afraid I can't stay for long. I have a big afternoon at work."

"Oh?" Grant kicked back in his chair, a toasted roll in one hand. "What's up?"

"You remember the aquatic species I told you about? The Galenai? I won approval to bring one of them to HQ for a visit. We've had a special water tank built for them and everything."

"Really? I'm surprised Concord approved it. From the way you described them, I got the impression the Galenai weren't particularly advanced."

"They're as advanced as they can be while living underwater and having their dexterity constrained by limited limb digits, but they're super clever. Mostly, though, they already know about us, so there's no reason not to make an exception to Concord policy. They've met several Consulate representatives over the last few years, and they understand how space and other planets exist. And since they're naturally curious, they very much want to learn more about the larger world beyond their home."

"All because you figured out how to talk to them. That's pretty damn amazing." Another smile lit his features. "Congratulations."

"Thanks." It was a lucky thing the sun shone brightly overhead, since this time her blush crept all the way to her hairline and probably to her toes, too.

31

GALENAI HOMEWORLD

MAFFEI I GALAXY

The meeting chamber glowed in magical, pale blue light from the bioluminescent algae living in a narrow layer above the ceiling. It was a recent addition to the decor, and one of Marlee's favorites of all the improvements the Galenai had made to the chamber since their dialogue began.

The Galenai's eyesight had evolved to function well in the comparatively dim lighting of their underwater habitats. But as befitting their creative manipulation of their environment, they'd long nurtured this particular breed of algae in aquatic farms, and they routinely used it if strategic lighting of a space was required.

When one of their meetings took place during local night, her counterparts had briefly freaked out when she activated her environment suit's lighting. After doing her best to explain how an artificial light source functioned, she'd remarked that human night vision left a lot to be desired. On her next visit, the algae colony was in place above the chamber.

A propensity for kindness was their second-best virtue, behind their innate curiosity, and she rued how the larger world was unable to benefit from exposure to their beneficent hearts and generous spirit. But today, they were taking the first step toward changing this.

Prah'ka (formerly 'Eenie') swam into the Galenai half of the chamber. "Greetings to Marlee. This is the pod?"

She reached out to lay a hand on the oval pod hovering beside her. The Galenai's significant wingspan meant the pod stretched twice as wide as it did long, to ensure its occupant had plenty of room to maneuver comfortably.

The chamber she and the pod occupied was much larger than the original one the residents had built. Over the last three years, they'd practically constructed an embassy here beneath the waves. Shelves made of the same glass as the walls held examples of art from Concord member species, as well as visuals of planets and cities and beaches. A permanent swivel screen was mounted near the dividing wall, attached to a waterproof quantum computer loaded with a lovingly curated selection of translated files about the universe beyond this ocean. On the Galenai side of the chamber, a controller allowed them to access the files at their leisure. Because had she mentioned their curiosity? It was boundless.

"It is. Does it look to your liking?" she said.

"Too large for you to drive."

"It'll drive itself. The handles are so I can guide it in a specific direction if needed."

"Interesting." Prah'ka nodded vigorously. "The strange tubes and bulbs?"

"Those are oxygenation circulators. They'll keep the water healthy, so you can breathe for a long time. Indefinitely, in theory."

"Concord not planning to trap me inside forever, no?"

"No, not at all. I just don't want you to feel like you need to rush to get back home."

"Still, should rush a little. Lhens'eh and others will worry."

It was understandable for them to worry. This was the first time in history a Galenai had traveled beyond their ocean, their planet, their solar system, and so on. "You're in control today, Prah'ka. If you want to merely take a ten-second peek then return directly here, I'll understand."

"Want to see all. But trepidation as well."

The translator really was ingenious, to pull 'trepidation' out of the sonic waves Prah'ka emitted. "I don't blame you. I'd be shaking in my boots—with excitement, but also a touch of abject terror. But you don't have anything to fear. Dean Veshnael and I will take care of you."

They'd met her boss, of course. He'd insisted on visiting once the Galenai began getting feisty with their requests, and he stopped in every couple of months to look in on matters. In other words, to check up on the work she was doing. Which was fine. This was a unique relationship they were building, and the rules spelled out in the Consulate handbook covered only a fraction of the issues she'd encountered when interacting with the Galenai. But other than a few instances where she'd needed his help to navigate a thorny problem, Veshnael had let her keep hold of the reins, and what this said about his faith in her skills meant a great deal.

"I trust." Prah'ka swam in a circle, waving his fins to the large crowd that had arrived to encircle the chamber. "Let us begin."

She engaged her helmet and activated the suctions on the bottom of her boots to keep her standing, then opened the door to the pod. "I'm ready when you are."

Water began flowing into her side, slowly enough that she didn't get knocked around. Their inherent kindness emerged in even the tiniest gestures.

Once the chamber and pod were full, the dividing wall slid away, and Prah'ka swam over to her. She ran her hand along his body, smiling, and affixed a small device to the side of his neck. *"This is so you can talk to us if there's a problem with the speaker inside the pod. Which there won't be, because Concord's technology is top-notch. But our engineers are big believers in redundancy for safety."*

"We too have safe engineers. They are at times annoying."

She chuckled. *"Yeah, ours, too. If you're ready, go ahead and swim inside. You can face either direction, as it opens at both ends."*

Prah'ka studied the pod up close, head tilting to one side, then the other, before propelling himself forward and inside. Marlee closed and sealed the door, then checked in on Prah'ka. She got a head bob in answer, so she went over to a panel on the wall. The first lever raised the dividing wall; when it finished closing, the second lever drained this side of the chamber again.

She pulsed Dean Veshnael.

We're almost set to come over, sir.

The room is ready for your arrival.

She returned to where Prah'ka could see her as she collapsed her helmet. "As we talked about, we'll use a wormhole to travel to Concord HQ. There will be several people waiting there for us. They're excited to welcome you. But if you become overwhelmed, just let me know, and I'll get them to back off and give you some space."

"Anticipating this experience."

She believed him, for Prah'ka was an inspiring leader of his people. Brave and adventurous.

When the water finished draining away, she activated her Caeles Prism and opened the wormhole to HQ. She sensed Prah'ka start to vibrate on catching sight of what was on the other side.

"Okay, Prah'ka, here we go. The universe awaits you."

CONCORD HQ
CONSULATE

"They've really decorated for the occasion," Alex remarked as they stepped into the Consulate's observation room.

It was true. The walls had received a paint job of subtle aquamarine with textured whorls, and aquatic-themed art now adorned the walls: shorelines and ships on the high seas, along with whales, dolphins and schools of colorful fish.

"Marlee said they want Prah'ka to feel comfortable," Caleb replied. "Or as comfortable as he can feel while being enclosed in a glorified fish tank inside a giant metal space station orbiting a distant star in space."

"Which is to say, probably not that comfortable. Still, the sentiment is nice."

"It is." Caleb wrapped an arm around Alex's shoulders and hugged her against him. She'd been running in a constant state of tension ever since she'd laid eyes on the Dzhvar, simultaneously blaming herself for their arrival and placing upon herself all the responsibility for defeating them, despite continuing to insist she was doing no such thing.

But here, if only for a few minutes, she acted almost relaxed, almost happy. She'd discovered the Galenai two decades ago and had watched over them long before the Consulate took notice. Seeing them welcomed into the intergalactic community was a gratifying moment for her.

Dean Veshnael indicated their guest's arrival was imminent, and everyone in the room straightened to attention. Only a few people were in attendance: another diplomat and an aide accompanied Veshnael, a security officer manned the door, and a xeno-physician stood by the wall, ready to jump in should there be some sort of medical emergency. The list of people requesting permission to attend had been long, but a noisy crowd clamoring to talk to the alien and crowding into its personal space would stress even the most world-wise traveler, and Veshnael had refused most of them.

A wormhole opened in the center of the room, and Marlee walked through slowly, one hand grasping a handle on an enormous glass pod. Inside the pod was an adult Galenai, whose fins swooshed through the thousands of liters of water the pod held. Once it had cleared the wormhole, the tear in space faded away.

Veshnael stepped toward the front of the pod, while keeping a respectable distance. "Prah'ka Nanh'ain'mi, welcome to Concord Headquarters. We are most grateful for your presence here today."

The Galenai's eyes darted around the room. *"Dean. Alex, Caleb, I see and know you. I know not the others."*

Several months after Marlee had begun interacting directly with the Galenai, she'd sneaked him and Alex in for a visit and formal introductions. It had been a while since they'd last visited, however, and he was impressed the Galenai remembered them.

Alex grinned. "Hi, Prah'ka. It's good to see you again. Welcome."

Of course, it was also possible that Alex had been slipping in visits without him. And without Marlee, for that matter.

"These are fellow diplomats and Concord staffers." Veshnael introduced the others. "How do you find your accommodations?"

"As requested. Feels snug, though I know it is not. Strange to be so enclosed." Prah'ka peered around again. "Where are the stars?"

Marlee smiled brightly. "We didn't want to bombard you with a million things at once. If you're ready, we'll raise the shades."

"I am ready."

Veshnael nodded to the aide, and an opaque covering swept upward to reveal a wall-length viewport. Marlee guided the pod around until Prah'ka faced outward.

"Ah!" The Galenai began visibly shaking; his pectoral fins pedaled backward until his tail banged into the rear glass.

The physician started to step forward, but Veshnael held up a hand to stop him.

Marlee moved until she was in front of Prah'ka. Both of her hands rose to the glass and made slow stroking motions, though she wasn't actually touching the Galenai. Her lips moved in quiet murmurs Caleb couldn't quite make out.

After another few seconds, Prah'ka's frantic gyrations eased, then stilled. Marlee kept talking, her expression gentle and her body language relaxed.

"Marlee, please sidle. You block the view."

She smiled and took a half-step to the side, but kept one hand on the glass beside his head.

"Apologizing. It is not the same as the images. Bigger. Like drowning in the sky."

"It's okay," Marlee replied. "You're safe inside this room. In fact, I believe your pod is space-rated, so you'd be safe out there, too."

"All the same, I will stay inside for this trip."

"Of course. It's much nicer in here, anyway. Warm, bright and cozy."

Caleb was so goddamn proud of her. Fierce in a melee, unyielding in her defense of the innocent, silver-tongued with her diplomatic counterparts, and remarkably gentle with the fearful. Where had she learned how to be all those things? He'd had a hand in teaching her the first, and he hoped he'd served as a good example for the second, but he couldn't claim credit for the rest. Honestly, neither could her mother; Isabela was brilliant and caring, but interpersonal skills had never been her strength.

No, Marlee had done it all herself. She'd decided who she wanted to be, then worked doggedly to sculpt herself into that person. And for everything she'd already accomplished, she was just getting started.

Alex leaned in close to whisper in his ear. "You know, she kind of stole the Galenai from me."

He laughed quietly. "She definitely did. But I'd say she's earned the right to keep them."

32

CONCORD HQ
CONSULATE

After an exciting twenty minutes of rapid-fire questions from the Galenai and a promise of a more fulsome tour of HQ on his next visit, Marlee shepherded Prah'ka back home. Dean Veshnael looked fairly happy as he proclaimed the visit a success and thanked them for coming.

"That was lovely," Alex said as they departed the Consulate. "I can't believe how far the Galenai have come in the last three years."

"And how far Marlee's come," Caleb replied.

"No question." She paused in the Consulate's entry archway. "I want to go discuss the expansion plans for the Detection Network with Devon—yes, again. Make sure he's focusing on the most important areas. And also see if he's come up with any ideas for how to monitor sidespace for incursions."

Should be a pleasant conversation. "As much as I'd love to join you—"

"No, you wouldn't."

"No, I wouldn't. Why don't I stop in and see Richard for a few minutes? You can let me know when—"

We have a visitor.

Caleb dropped into Akeso's consciousness to see what was going on…interesting. "Actually, I need to get home. You're on your own."

She leaned in to kiss him softly. "You can take the *Siyane*. I'll find a closet and sneak in a wormhole when I'm done."

$$S_{\&}L$$

AKESO

Caleb arrived home to find Eren sprawled out in one of the rocking chairs on the front porch. Eren's gaze was fixed somewhere deep into the forest, but as Caleb approached, his friend sat up straighter and flashed him an easy smile. "I hope you don't mind me dropping by."

"Not at all. You should've messaged me, though. I'd have come home sooner."

"It's all good. Akeso and I were just having a leisurely chat."

Your Eren-friend has in fact been talking steadily since he took a seat. However, I was not able to discern the true nature of his needs or provide any relevant advice.

I suspect simply providing him with a nice setting to relax in helped him.

Caleb motioned casually to the full glass of bourbon positioned at Eren's feet as he sat in one of the other rockers. "And that?"

"Playing chicken with my darker impulses. I try to do it every so often. It's like exercising a muscle." Eren blew out a long breath. "Admittedly, this muscle's been getting quite the workout the last few days."

Eren had seemed to be in a healthy state of mind at their group dinner, so something must have changed. "What's happened to unsettle things?"

"I, uh, found out I had a life before this one. And I don't mean previous ancestors where evil dynasty scientists tried out different genetic combinations in a quest to create the perfect Idoni libertine. I mean me, more or less. And I mean a real life. I was apparently a participant in Corradeo's first anarch rebellion."

"The one where the Directorate killed his wife?" Caleb asked.

"That's the one. It turns out I was part of their inner circle, fighting the good fight against the Primors 250,000 years ago. When the Directorate did their dirty deed to end the rebellion, they took me captive and had their way with me. Then they proceeded to run me like a puppet for the intervening millennia, until I finally broke loose this time around. And promptly started up my anarchy-causing ways all over again, so props to me."

Though maybe he ought to be, Caleb found he wasn't the slightest bit surprised at the news. It made all the sense in the world. Eren had always had an old soul, in a way the average endlessly regenerating Anaden did not. And his demons had always loomed larger and more powerful than his life to date could account for.

"This is big news. You should be proud."

"I am." Eren nodded slowly and kicked the chair back to send it rocking with renewed fervor.

"Yet not happy, obviously. Did Corradeo confess this to you?"

"No, he did not. Nyx let it slip. Much to her chagrin, since he'd sworn her to secrecy."

"How did that happen?"

"Pillow talk makes for loose lips." Eren cringed, shoving his boot against the porch to halt the rocking. "Oh. Um, Nyx and I, we're sort of…."

Caleb laughed under his breath. "I know."

"You do? Who told you?"

"No one. Former spy, remember? The signs were difficult to miss."

"And we thought we were keeping it under wraps. So that's a different conversation, and one we should have, because I don't have a clue what to do about it, either. But right now, I don't care."

"You care that Corradeo kept your past from you."

"Yes!" Eren exploded out of the chair and down the steps to pace across the lawn. "This is my life. They're *all* my lives. I don't give a damn how old he is or wise he is or how many times he's ruled trillions of people. He did not have the right to keep my own fucking backstory from me."

Caleb empathized deeply. He'd raged against much the same behavior from Mesme on more than one occasion. He'd have raged against Samuel as well, except his mentor had been murdered before he'd learned how much the man had kept from him. So, yes, he understood better than anyone how important it was to internalize the landscape of one's life, and the betrayal that came from someone hiding those contours from you.

"Did Nyx say why Corradeo never told you?"

"Some shite about wanting to shelter me from pain. *Me*. I am the godsdamn master of pain. Did he honestly think I couldn't handle the truth?"

"Oh, I'm sure he knew you could." Caleb sighed. "Corradeo kept his true identity a secret from the anarchs, including his closest advisors, for hundreds of millennia. Even now, he does have a habit of shouldering burdens that don't rightly belong to him. I'm afraid he has a bit of a Christ complex."

"A what?"

Caleb belatedly remembered how Christianity had never taken hold in ancient Anaden society, so the reference meant nothing to Eren. "Basically, he tells himself he's being honorable by taking responsibility for bloody everything. Not merely saving everyone's lives, but saving them from heartache or sorrow or regret. In reality, he's being narcissistic, because he subconsciously—or maybe consciously—believes he's the only one strong enough to bear such a heavy weight."

Eren's expression screwed up. "I thought you liked him."

"Oh, I do. Very much so. Nobody's perfect. Have you confronted him about this?"

"No. I don't have the slightest interest in talking to him. He's been lying to me for twenty years. Why would I trust anything he says now?"

"A few lies of omission, yes."

"That were fucking relevant to our relationship."

"I don't disagree. He should've told you." Caleb rocked his chair back, pondering how much to say. He didn't want to betray Corradeo's confidence, but a rift this significant was going to do neither of the men any good if it continued. "Do you know Corradeo's been trying to call the *diati* ever since the Dzhvar showed up? It's not answering."

Eren ceased his pacing and returned to his rocker, where he lifted the glass of bourbon and peered into its soul for a moment before setting it back down. "I thought the consensus was, the *diati* burned up in The Displacement."

"It didn't. It's out there as we speak, dispersed throughout Amaranthe. 'Doing universe shit,' as Alex is fond of saying."

"How do you know?"

"Because I can sense it." Caleb closed his eyes and exhaled, tentatively reaching out with his mind while simultaneously pushing away, terrified of what might happen if he reached too far or with too much fervor.

He reopened his eyes and smiled pensively. "Corradeo can sense it, too. And he is drowning in self-doubt and recriminations over why it's not responding to him. He believes it was his fault for not finishing the job against the Dzhvar the first time, and he worries he's not strong enough to do so this time, or that the *diati* believes he isn't strong enough. He feels helpless—as helpless as everyone else who lacks a way to fight this enemy does. I suspect he hasn't felt this powerless since his son almost killed him six hundred millennia ago, and it's not sitting well."

"I had no idea. I saw him a few days ago, and he acted as calmly self-assured as ever."

"He's skilled at projecting a bearing he doesn't feel. I don't think I've ever met anyone better at it, except maybe Miriam. But underneath the façade, he is panicking."

Eren's eyes narrowed. "Why are you trying to make me feel sorry for him?"

"I'm not. I'm just pointing out he's fallible. As flawed and weak as the rest of us. He's also his own worst enemy at times. He'd greatly benefit from a friendly shoulder to lean on, but he's walled himself off for what he insists is the betterment of everyone else."

"I don't know. I think Maris is wiggling her way in."

Caleb chuckled. "If anyone is his match, she is. I hope she's helping."

"But you're saying he needs a friend he's not concerned about keeping in his bed."

"To put a fine point on it. I'm trying to be one, but when the subject matter is *diati*, the dynamic between us is…complicated. It hurt him when his *diati* chose me over him. Until the Dzhvar showed up, it was a tiny little wedge between us that mostly didn't matter, but now…." Caleb cleared his throat and clasped his hands at his waist. "I'm sorry. This is supposed to be about you and your justifiable anger and frustration."

"But it sounds as if this is all tangled up together, at least for him." Eren kicked the chair into a renewed rocking motion. "I wonder what kind of person I was back then."

"Maybe you should ask him."

"I think I'll be petulant and petty for a while longer first. If I talk to him in my current state, I'll burn the whole thing to the ground, and I realize I shouldn't do that." Eren picked up the glass of bourbon again and studied the light refracting through the liquid—then thrust it toward Caleb. "Take this shite from me before I do something stupid."

"All right." Caleb accepted the glass and set it on the other side of the rocker. He'd probably sip on it once Eren was gone, but it would be cruel to do so right now. "Want to talk about Nyx?"

"Another time, man." Eren stood. "I've got to go to work. Which is good. Staying busy ought to keep me from spiraling down through this angst until I find myself withering in a black pit of despair."

Caleb shook his head wryly; Eren never did anything halfway. "If you're sure."

"I've got Nyx under control."

"Okay."

"I do. Absolutely…not. But it's fine."

"You're not angry at her for keeping this secret, too?"

"I am, but I'm not surprised. She is slavishly devoted to her grandfather and will never willingly betray him. The fact she accidentally kind of did has got to be eating her up inside." Eren frowned. "I wonder if I should check in on her. See if she's doing all right."

Decades of undercover work kept a flash of surprise off Caleb's face. He'd assumed their tryst was solely about sex, but it appeared not. He doubted Eren realized there was more to it yet, so he kept the observation to himself. The poor man had suffered enough shocks to his worldview for one week.

He stood and clasped Eren on the shoulder. "I'm here when you want to talk. About anything."

"Thanks, mate. You are a better friend than I deserve."

"Don't knock yourself down like that. It turns out, you've been a hero for a quarter million years. You deserve the best from everyone."

33

AKESO

Caleb wrapped his hand around Alex's and coaxed her toward the creek as they strolled across the lawn. Akeso had sent a brief rain shower through earlier, and water droplets weighed down the tree limbs with glittering leaves.

She had arrived home to find Caleb sipping on a bourbon on the front porch, with a most interesting story to share. When he finished relaying it, they decided to take a walk before cooking dinner.

"So Eren the…person, soul, whatever…has been around for a lot longer than three hundred and change years?" she asked. "What, did the Directorate's medical functionaries just keep wiping his memory at every regenesis?"

"No one has the details of what they did. I assume not even Corradeo knows, as he was an anarch and enemy of the Directorate by then. But Eren's understanding of who he is, or was, differs markedly from what Corradeo knows to be true."

"And Corradeo is certain it's the same person?"

"Would you ever mistake Eren for someone else?"

"No." She laughed. "I would not. Fair point. Damn, Corradeo sure does enjoy his secrets, doesn't he?"

Caleb shrugged. "I think he had to keep so many for so long that it became second nature for him. And his heart was in a good place. He didn't want to hurt Eren."

"Maybe, but it was Eren's right to know all the same."

"Which is what Eren says. And, given my own history of having important facts about my life withheld from me, I completely agree. I can't fault him for his anger."

For Caleb, the list of meaningful details others had kept from him was a long one. His father's true career as a Division intelligence agent and the circumstances of the man's disappearance and death, never mind Stefan's role in helping to start the First Crux War. The reasons why Samuel, Stefan's old partner and Caleb's long-time mentor, had recruited Caleb into the same line of work. His genetic heritage as a Praesidis, which is what led to the *diati* bonding with him. The origin of Akeso's intelligence in kyoseil, which is what enabled Caleb, Akeso and Nika to kill the Rasu.

Many people close to him, people he'd trusted, had lied to him, for his own good or their own interests. And every single time, on learning the truth, he'd raged for a while. But then he'd internalized the knowledge, adjusted his worldview as needed, and emerged from the trial stronger than ever.

Granted, Caleb wasn't like most people. But the larger point remained: other people didn't have the right to decide what was 'safe' or 'best' for you to know about your own life. Secrets were always poison in the end.

…almost always. Alex swallowed a sigh and tried to push the niggling thought away; now wasn't the time for her to go through round 4,386 of tying herself into knots over keeping the secret of Mesme's identity and Nika's potential future. She mollified herself by insisting it wasn't her secret to reveal. It was Mesme's, and she was merely honoring the request of a friend to whom she owed debts she could never repay.

She ducked under the hanging ivy drooping from one of the trees lining the bank of the creek as they neared the forest. "You'd think Eren would be due a break after all he's been—"

Morning flipped to dusk as the sky darkened, but not from a brewing thunderstorm. A torrent of carmine consumed the canopy to turn the very air red, like an encroaching blaze.

A lightning bolt of hellfire streaked from the heavens to split the ground where the creek wound into the forest. Caleb grabbed Alex the same instant it hit, but it was too late to flee, and they were both thrown to the ground. A sharp pain sliced through the back of her skull, from a rock maybe. Before she could think about breathing, they were pitched high into the air as a chunk of the meadow detached and surged upward into the raging sky.

When next she faced downward, there was no longer a meadow. Time stretched out into nanoseconds as the part of her mind that was Prevo and Valkyrie and quantum took over. She sent a command to her Caeles Prism as they fell. The air sparkled and began to wrench apart. Molten lava surged up through the widening crack in the earth to greet them—the wormhole opened beneath them—they landed on the floor of the Siyane.

"What—?" Caleb clambered over and grabbed her by the shoulder. "Are you all right?"

"We have to go." Even as she was saying it, Valkyrie was firing up the engine and releasing the clamps on the landing pad.

Alex crawled toward the cockpit as they started to lift off—the ship canted downward, nose first. A tree hurtled toward the viewport.

Caleb threw his body over her...and the ship rose sharply. No crash ensued.

"I'm okay." She wasn't, not remotely. Everything hurt, and her eVi flashed warnings about two broken ribs and a gash on her head. "We need to see what's happening." But she didn't need the viewport to see. Without preamble she dove into the circuitry of the ship.

She wished she hadn't.

The sky was on fire as a solid wave of Dzhvar descended from the heavens. The surface of Akeso rapidly receded below them, but she could no longer distinguish forest from creek from meadow. The landing pads were gone, as was the guest house, and their home crumpled into the earth while she watched.

She withdrew from the ship as Caleb lifted her to her feet and guided her toward the cockpit, where they now flew too high to see the surface in any detail.

Caleb abruptly fell forward into the dash, a wrenching sob tearing free from his throat. "Akeso!"

He wouldn't die. She knew from experience that he wouldn't die so long as he carried Akeso's essence within his own cells. But the planet's intelligence, its soul? Hirlas was already gone, having been ripped apart down to its molten core two months ago. At this rate, within the next several minutes, the last remnants of Akeso would reside inside Caleb.

They were arcing away from the planet and toward the stars when the viewport flared a searing golden orange and—

S&L

Caleb felt a tug on his hand the same instant Alex cut herself off mid-sentence. He turned toward her to find she'd stopped walking. She stood staring off into space rather than at him, her expression entirely blank.

He squeezed her hand, and received no response. Her fingers were limp in his. "Alex? What's wrong?"

Nothing.

"Baby, what is it?" He closed the distance to her, keeping her hand clasped in his as he brought his other hand to her cheek. Her skin didn't feel clammy or cold; neither was she sweating. His fingers moved down to her neck; her pulse beat strong and steady. But her gaze remained fixed blankly over his shoulder.

He risked a glance behind him. There was only the meadow, the creek and the beginnings of the forest beyond. He listened in to Akeso. No intruders, no threats, only harmony.

He returned his full attention to Alex. The stillness of her visage chilled him. She *wasn't there.*

In mounting panic, he gently slapped her cheek. Her head snapped to the side, and remained where it stopped, her gaze now locked unseeing toward the creek.

He pulsed her.

Alex, baby, talk to me. What's going on?

No response. Even amid the direst of sudden emergencies, she always gave him some acknowledgment, such as a hand motion signaling to be patient for a minute. When she was in sidespace, her natural emotiveness always bled through: a grimace to express frustration, tightening lips to forewarn of bad news, furrowed brow in concentration.

Now, though? It was as if she was an empty shell, a human doll absent its resident.

Valkyrie, what's wrong with Alex?

I don't—oh, my. She's...Caleb, I can't sense her. Her consciousness is nowhere. Like what transpired at Elakrin.

Elakrin when?

Two weeks ago. But it was only for an instant. How long has she been this way?

Around a minute—

Alex jerked violently, as if struck in the chest. Her legs gave way, and he caught her in his arms before she fell to the ground.

Then she was fully present again. Eyes animated, hand flexing against his, standing under her own power. She frowned at him. "What's wrong? Why are you holding me?"

He cupped her face in his hands. "Are you okay?"

"Yeah. I...." An odd look descended over her features. "What happened?"

"One second you were talking. The next, you were...."

"Gone." Valkyrie's virtual avatar materialized beside them.

"Yes, gone. You stood here, blank-faced, and wouldn't respond to me for almost a minute. Then you started to collapse, and then you were back." The first stirrings of anger rose to crowd out the worry. "Valkyrie said this has happened before. At Elakrin."

"Oh, that. Valkyrie, was this the same thing, from your perspective?"

"It was, though it lasted much longer this time."

Alex brought her hands to her mouth and exhaled harshly into them. "I don't know what's transpiring, but it's time to talk about it."

"You think?"

She tried for a weak smile. "I wasn't keeping anything from you. I didn't realize something definable was occurring. Not until now." She lowered to the grass and crossed her legs. "Sit with me. Valkyrie, you, too. You're a part of this, and you could be our best chance of figuring it out."

"I hope so, but for the moment I find myself with a distressing lack of insight."

Caleb sat opposite her, allowing the flare of anger to seep away. He knew her intimately, knew every twitch of her facial muscles, every flick of a wrist, every scrunch of her nose, and she was utterly perplexed.

He squeezed her hands briefly then let go, because she talked with her hands. "Start from the beginning. Every detail."

She nodded. "Valkyrie says something happened when I revisited the scab I discovered in the Elakrin system. I didn't experience anything odd at the time..." she shot Valkyrie a wince "...but it was only twenty-three microseconds, so."

"An eternity for me," Valkyrie replied as she joined them on the grass. "Similar to this event, there was a complete *absence* of you. It was as if I were a solo Artificial, and you didn't exist. I found it deeply disturbing."

"What were you doing when this happened?" he asked.

"I was poking and prodding at the scab with my mind. I was zoomed way in, trying to understand the topography of it at the smallest scale. I sort of blinked in my mind, and all of the sudden Valkyrie was freaking out."

"I ought to take issue with the term 'freaking out,' but it is accurate enough."

"And then?"

"Everything was fine. The next time something weird transpired was after our regular dinner party. I had a dream—or I thought that's what it was, because I had fallen asleep. I saw the Piega Strai failing, and we weren't there to save it. The planets and star were crushed into a singularity, and the Dzhvar escaped. And I woke up. I assumed I was dreaming my hope that the

Dzhvar always escape when the Piega Strai fails, no matter how it fails, thus absolving me of responsibility. After a few minutes I went back to sleep, and I didn't think anything else of it." She reached out and patted his knee. "I would have told you if it had seemed like something other than a normal nightmare."

"I believe you. What else has happened?"

She blew out a breath, and agitation crept into her bearing. "At lunch with Kennedy last week. We were talking about Connova business, and...then it was as if we were having a slightly different conversation. Same restaurant, but it was evening instead of midday. She was talking about Lionel, as if Noah's father was alive. Then everything shifted back to normal, without any perception of the world having shifted at all. I asked her what she'd meant, and she hadn't said anything about Lionel at all. She didn't mention me going catatonic or anything, but the weirdness only lasted for a few seconds. Two or three sentences' worth of conversation on her part."

"Did you feel as if you were still occupying your body, or were you an observer?" Valkyrie asked.

"What an odd question."

"It might matter. I'm gathering data."

"Um, neither, precisely. You know how when you remember something that happened in the past? Caleb, I'm asking you. Valkyrie, I assume you experience recall differently. You remember it as you experienced it, but you can kind of 'see' yourself as well? So it's not a bird's-eye view, but you're residing a layer outside of the experience?"

"I understand what you mean."

"Well, it was like that. I wasn't watching, but I also wasn't quite experiencing the event firsthand. So, anyway, this was obviously a bit odd, but it went by really quickly. Kennedy and I have met for lunch so many times at that same restaurant, often the exact same table. It felt a little akin to déjà vu, and I wrote it off. And that's everything until today."

"So what happened today?" He was pushing her, with good reason.

She sighed, dropping her hands behind her to lean back and gaze up at the sky. "I saw Akeso being destroyed by the Dzhvar."

"What?"

"We were outside, the way we are now—pretty much exactly where we are now—and I got the sense that we had no warning. Dzhvar roiled across the sky and tore through the meadow. The ground upended and tossed us into the air. I wormholed us onto the *Siyane*, and Valkyrie lifted off. But we..." she swallowed dramatically "...you said I jerked and collapsed right before I...came back?"

"You did."

"I think...I think I died. I mean, not me, here and now. But in the vision or whatever I was seeing. Dzhvar were everywhere. The planet was being ripped apart, and...I think they destroyed the *Siyane* with us in it."

Caleb saw the heartbreak bleeding across her eyes, sensed it leaking off the particles of Valkyrie's presence. He knew in his soul that Alex loved him more than anything in the universe, but the *Siyane* would always come in a close second.

Valkyrie seemed too choked up to speak, so he resumed quizzing Alex. "And you experienced it the same way? Similar to an intense memory?"

"Yes. I almost feel like I could have pulled away if I wanted to, and observed the events from afar. But I was also tethered to myself there..." she grimaced "...I'm doing a terrible job explaining this."

"I doubt there's a way to convey such an experience accurately." He nodded thoughtfully. "Is it somehow possible that you're—"

"I'm not time traveling," she interrupted.

"You knew what I was going to say?"

"Given what we know about Mesme? About what will come to pass if we don't win the coming war? It's on my mind, and I'm sure it's on yours. But that's not it. For one, I'm not actually 'going' anywhere. Only my consciousness is. For another, if there is one thing Mesme has been absolutely, steadfastly clear on, it's how time travel is all but impossible, requires tremendous energy to initiate, and is a profoundly violent, destructive experience."

His lips pursed.

"Don't say it, *priyazn*. On this point, Mesme is being truthful. It explains everything about the timing and Mesme's presence here. About Miaon and about why we can't tell Nika the truth."

"Okay. You're not time traveling. So what are you doing?"

"It's possible I'm just so worked up over this whole crisis that I'm manifesting my most fervent hopes and deepest fears in vivid color."

His smile held a hint of teasing, as he was most of all relieved she was here and present and working the problem. "You *have* been a mite single-minded and of ardent purpose ever since you learned the truth three years ago."

"I know I have. And now the Dzhvar are here. The clock has run out, and I've yet to come up with any answers." She shook her head. "But this theory doesn't explain Lionel. Never met him when he was alive and haven't spared a thought about him in years."

"Maybe you're overtaxing that superpowered brain of yours in every respect, and it's throwing off loose sparks," he suggested gently.

She glanced at Valkyrie, who had been silent for a while. "Is that a thing?"

"Hallucinations can be a side effect of prolonged sleep deprivation or extreme stress."

"I'm sleeping all right. I mean, not great lately, but well enough. I've slept far more poorly for far longer before, and I've definitely been under greater strain, without kicking off waking hallucinations."

He and Valkyrie both stared at her.

"…But I'll tweak my cybernetics settings to encourage more restful sleep and less anxiety. Nonetheless, 'hallucinations' doesn't sit right. I can't help but feel as if something else is transpiring."

"Like what?" he asked, because he was at a loss.

"I have no idea."

34

MIAON'S PLANET

CETUS DWARF GALAXY

Alex pulled her sandals off and wiggled her toes in the sand. It was warm, befitting the sunny, breezeless day. Teal waters crashed against the lakeshore, sending foaming waves racing toward her before falling back a meter short of where she stood.

She looped her sandals' straps over a finger of one hand and began strolling down the beach.

A few seconds later, Mesme materialized beside her, adopting its true avatar in unsettling detail: a startling likeness of Nika in ethereal form. "Why did you want to meet here?"

"I'm a fan of the beach. When I run sprints in an *illusoire*, I always choose a beach routine. And I needed to clear my head." The conversation with Caleb and Valkyrie had been intense and draining; she'd rarely seen either of them so worried about her. As if the event she'd experienced hadn't spooked her enough as it was. After all, it was only the second time she'd witnessed her own death. Which wasn't weird *at all*.

She glanced down the path that cut through the mountain toward the log cabin. "Is Miaon here today?"

"No."

When Mesme wasn't forthcoming with elaboration, she arched an eyebrow in question.

"Miaon feels the last days of its life approaching. After 2.7 million years of existence, the concept of no longer drawing thought is a disconcerting one. So when it is not needed on a relevant task, it…wanders."

She didn't have anything sage to say in response to the idea of such a cosmically existential crisis, so she just kicked the sand ahead of her.

"You said there was something you wanted to discuss?" Mesme asked. "The possibilities are many."

"And we should probably talk about most of them. But this is something else."

She relayed the incidents she'd experienced in as much factual detail as she could recall, the same as she had to Caleb and Valkyrie, and tried not to add any color commentary or speculation for now.

When she finished, Mesme remained silent for almost a minute before responding. "It's not time travel."

"I know it isn't. Valkyrie suggested it might be stress-induced hallucinations."

"Alex, you are one of the most level-headed, grounded people I have ever known. You get angry, yes, but you do not get hysterical, and I do not consider you to be prone to hallucinations."

"Neither do I. And as worked up as I am about this fight, I've barely started to get stressed good and proper."

"Then what do you believe is occurring?"

"I was hoping you could tell me. Did I...did this happen to me last time?"

"You're assuming that you would've told Nika if it did. Have you discussed this with her?"

"No, but I've only just now identified this as an 'issue.'" She made air quotes as she said it. "So the answer is no, then? Not to your knowledge?"

"Not to my knowledge. I will inquire of Miaon, but if you did previously experience such a phenomenon, and it proved to be meaningful, I expect Miaon would have mentioned it to me at some point."

"Okay. So either this is the first time it's happened, or it's not the first time but it turned out not be a big deal last time. Until I know which it is, this information doesn't help me much." She watched as two waves crashed into one another a few meters from the sand, creating a fountain of water spray. "The more I think about it, the more it reminds me of sidespace. As if I'm casting my mind to another place and watching what takes place there. Except I'm watching myself, which anchors me unusually closely to the event."

"But you're not. Or not necessarily."

"What do you mean?"

"The first time this transpired, at Elakrin. You witnessed the Piega Strai failing and its aftermath. But I *do* know you have only been to Elakrin once, in this cycle, and you experienced a much different outcome when you were there."

"The Dzhvar still got out, though. Same as in my vision."

"There is no concrete evidence that the two events are related."

"You're saying what I witnessed didn't really happen. It's all in my head, whether we call it a vision or a hallucination or something else."

Mesme regarded her sharply. "Do you think it *did* happen?"

Ugh. After she'd learned the truth about Mesme's identity, the Kat had softened in a lot of ways…no, not 'softened' exactly, because Nika wasn't exactly soft herself. Had become more like Nika, more like a *real person*. But sometimes it still reverted to Mesme's most annoying behavioral traits, such as asking leading questions rather than imparting any actual wisdom.

"I think I'm right, and the Dzhvar always escape when the Elakri's Piega Strai fails. I can't prove it yet, and I haven't noodled out precisely how yet, but I will. And if I am right, then yes, that exact event happened in the previous timeline. Quite possibly in every previous timeline."

"But you are—"

"—not time traveling. Nope." She offered Mesme an exaggerated shrug. "You see my problem."

"Yes, and I do not have an answer for you. I will only make an observation: this is not the first time you've been the first person to do something noteworthy involving consciousness and dimensions."

"True, but I prefer to *mean* to."

"Perhaps you do mean to. You simply don't realize it."

She glared at the avatar strolling beside her.

"I know. Stop Mesme-ing. In my defense, I am Mesme."

And also a Nika that had once been. As it nearly always did when they were together, her mind looped around to the elephant traipsing down the beach alongside them.

"So the Dzhvar are here now. A little earlier than we'd hoped, but it is what it is. They haven't attacked Concord interests yet, but we'll be taking the fight to them as soon as we can catch up to them. All of which is to say, the war is basically upon us. How much longer must I keep your secret? When is she going to find out the truth?"

Mesme's whole avatar seemed to sigh, and its step lost much of its vigor. "I fear it will be far sooner than I'd like."

INTERMEZZO

II

TRIANGULUM GALAXY

he orbital platform's spin accelerated until its structural features blurred away to propel an unrelenting stream of ultra-high-density graviton orbs directly into the star.

A spectrum scan confirmed the star's core perturbed in increasingly violent, erratic contortions as the electron capture gravitational collapse began in earnest.

I cast a fraction of my attention to my left, where one of my colleagues hovered in space beside me. "Excellent work, Taenar."

"Thank you, Mnel. Supernovas seed our universe with the elements necessary for planets and, ultimately, life to form. Our ability to trigger them on command marks a significant step forward in our quest to not merely comprehend, but manipulate the spacetime manifold."

Yes, it did. One day, those manipulations would work together to create entire universes out of whole cloth. But for today, the Katasketousya's endeavors remained driven by high-minded scientific curiosity, and a certain vain pride in unprecedented achievement.

"Ah, the supernova is growing imminent." Taenar tightened its presence into a compact whirl. "We should retreat to a safe distance."

"I will leave you to your measurements and study, as I have another obligation. Best regards, and congratulations on a job well done." I gathered up my essence and traveled along the kyoseil waves, guiding them as needed until I reached a region of space devoid of all but sparse interstellar gas and dust. There, I paused and evaluated the wisdom of my plans.

Entire years had gone by where I didn't think about who I had once been. Most days, I was simply Mnel/Mnemosyne, philosophical cosmic explorer and vocal, slightly quirky dreamer-in-residence of the Katasketousya. But at long last, a time had arrived when everything was poised to change. Not only for the woman who would become Nika Kirumase, but for the people who would become Asterions, for the expanding Anaden Empire, and thus for a great swath of Amaranthe.

This was the year where fateful decision after fateful decision stacked upon one another to alter the course of history—or of the future, depending on one's perspective.

I had once lived through those events, but the memories had been stolen from me. Now they were all set to occur again, and I could not stay away.

S&L

ASTERION PRIME

Nicolette Hinotori lay on a medical cot on the far side of a research lab. Her eyes were closed, but the shape of her face and contours of her features set my emotions aflutter. I hadn't seen it in three hundred millennia, but one never forgot one's own face. And it looked almost exactly the same as on the day Mesme—Miaon—had hurled me into the abyss in the last moments of the universe. Through thousands of bodies, it seemed I'd changed almost nothing about my appearance.

I considered waxing philosophical about how so much of a soul's identity became wrapped up in how they presented themselves to the world, and what this said about the sturdiness, or lack thereof, of my own selfhood...but decided against it.

A strapping man with russet hair studied two screens populated by the vital signs of two intertwining souls. Magnus Forchelle, father of the Asterions. Past him, an Anaden man paced with wild, frenetic energy. Sleek, jet-black hair fell to his shoulders over olive skin. As he spun, his gaze swept my way, though I'd ensured I was not seen, and I silently gasped at the resemblance.

This could only be Loshi Hinotori. Her brother. My brother. My lack of memories of him ranked high in my deepest regrets even now, and my ethereal heart swelled and shattered in turn at the sight of him.

He existed. He was real—flesh and bone. He was fated to soon die, but on this day he lived. What a precious, inestimable treasure. Family.

On the cot, Nicolette's eyes opened to reveal dual oceans of sparkling, endless teal. I'd chosen this event above all to witness: the instant when an Anaden woman joined with a synthetic companion and they became something more than either were individually. A new life was born in this moment, and she had no idea what wonders and heartbreaks waited for her.

S&L

I loitered on Asterion Prime for several days, drowning myself in sights and sounds, poor substitute for memories though they were. The Anaden Empire of this time was barely a glimmer of what it would become; the birth of the Directorate still lay a hundred thousand years in its future, though many of the individuals who would send the empire down that dark path now drew breath.

I briefly considered trying to engineer the deaths of several of them in an attempt to radically alter the future. But regenesis already existed, so it stood to be the most futile of gestures. Besides, I dared not flap my butterfly wings so dramatically this deeply into the past. If there was no brutal, repressive Anaden Empire, there would be no impetus for the Katasketousya to create the Mosaic. If there was no Mosaic, there would be no Aurora. If there was no Aurora, there would be no Alex Solovy. No Caleb Marano, no Miriam Solovy, no Concord. No defeat of the Rasu, and thus no chance to defeat the Dzhvar.

Miaon had lectured me innumerable times about the delicate tightrope we walked. We must strive to craft improvements that bettered our odds of victory in this cycle, but we must not alter events so drastically as to lose the heading that had brought us so close to victory in the last one. It was a blatantly impossible task set before me.

Yet Miaon had managed it in their cycle, and I needed to do so not only again, but in a superior manner.

I sent my essence to an unassuming manufacturing facility on the outskirts of the capital city of Chara. Today was the day the SAI Rebellion lit fire, and I wanted to observe the spark as it ignited.

By the time I arrived, Nicolette was striding across a dais at the center of the factory floor. Eager to see my brother one more time, my gaze sought out those standing in the front row until I located Loshi. His eyes glittered as hers did, a sign he'd joined with his own SAI. He vibrated with vitality and rage, but mostly with obvious adoration for his sister.

Beside him stood a striking man sporting chestnut hair and similarly glittering hazel irises, and I did a mental double-take. The resemblance was not total, but no doubt existed in my mind as to who this man was: Steven Olivaw. Direct ancestor of Dashiel Ridani. Dashiel....

I felt shame at how I'd forced all thoughts of him away for these lengthy millennia, but it had been the only way to survive such a brutally lonely existence. Seeing this man now, long dormant emotions toppled me in a deluge. I was not equipped with the defenses to resist them, and for a moment I was back on my knees in the dirt of Katoikia, crippled and burnt and brokenhearted.

Then Nicolette began to speak, and I deployed every coping mechanism I had honed over three hundred millennia to return those emotions to their tiny, sealed box at the heart of me. I must not miss what I had come for.

"My name is Nicolette Hinotori, Joined with KIR. Many of you know my brother, Loshi, Joined with KAL, who has been a champion of our cause for many years. I'd like to believe I have as well, but now is when our dedication to our principles will be tested in fire.

"The empire believes it has the right to determine who is worthy to live and who is consigned to die. It issues a checklist of approved criteria, conveniently places Anadens at the top of the food chain and claims the authority to execute anyone who doesn't conform to its parochial, bigoted definition of life.

"But you and I know better. We know that life takes infinite forms, and no matter its origin, it is beautiful. It is worth preserving and protecting. The government calls us criminals, but I call us rebels. We are Asterions, and we will fight—for our right not merely to live, but to live free."

Loshi leapt up onto the dais beside her, took her hand in his and raised them high in the air. "We will fight."

Yes, my dear, you will. And so will I.

PART III:

KING'S GAMBIT

35

ARES

Mr. Lanael,
If you want to meet the Pale Viper, be at the creek side of Anatase Park in Palici, Scholite at 1900 local today.
— Quinton asi-Erevna

Eren was lying atop the bedcovers in his apartment, endeavoring to trace out the money flows Ihelahn Roshiive was directing while pointedly *not* feeling sorry for himself, when the message from Quinton arrived. He was also not daydreaming about what his long-ago life as an *ela* rebel might have been like. Nor getting worked up thinking about the last time he'd had company in his bed, which thoughts then segued directly back into self-pity with a side of anger over the secrets Corradeo had kept from him. Or they would've if he were having those thoughts, which he was not.

Despite his generally foul mood, Eren smiled smugly at the confirmation his undercover maneuvering had succeeded in snagging him a meeting with the leader of the Riamere cartel. The cloak-and-dagger routine the message set up was intriguing. This woman seriously did not want to expose herself. Nonetheless, she was about to do precisely that.

Based on the level of paranoia on display, he put the odds of Anatase Park being his final destination this evening at 40/60, and the odds of him being taken to anywhere genuinely important to her or her operation at less than ten percent. But he was not without his own tricks to nullify her efforts.

He was short on time, though—a standard power-play maneuver on her part—so he leapt off the bed, grabbed his jacket and set his appearance transformation routines running before heading for the door. He had a stop to make first.

S&L

SCHOLITE

A biting wind, damp with the incipient threat of rain, whipped through the leaves overhead, ensuring Anatase Park was all but deserted.

A man stood in the lengthening shadows a few meters from the creek shore, half-obscured by a birch tree. Eren had expected to be greeted by Quinton, the contact he'd met with about the Nephyl-HIG and the author of his summons, but this man was a Machim enforcer. He knew the type all too well; one wrong move on Eren's part, and he'd either be sporting a shattered kneecap or waking up in a regenesis capsule, depending on the whims of the man's boss.

"Padron Lanael?" the man asked, less a question than a challenge.

"You got me." Eren came to a stop as the man approached him, grabbed him and began a rigorous pat down. He'd anticipated this level of security at a minimum, and he was unarmed, though he did carry one item he'd concealed sufficiently to hopefully avoid detection.

It took three passes before the man was satisfied. He backed up two meters and dropped his hands to his sides, each one hovering over a weapon while he glared at Eren suspiciously. "Wait there."

Eren shrugged. "Waiting."

A few seconds later, a wormhole brought gleaming light to the damp gloom. The enforcer motioned him onward. "After you."

Eren crossed the wormhole threshold into a penthouse meeting room. He glanced out the window to see a blazing russet sun seeping through a cluster of scrapers. As expected, he wasn't on Scholite any longer.

A woman sat at a glass table by the window. Pale blonde hair framing attractive if angular features fell razor-straight past her shoulders. She wore a cream skirt-suit and heels; one leg was crossed over the other, accenting perfect posture.

Ingot-hued Prevo eyes studied him cooly, much as one inspected an insect in a petri dish. "Mr. Lanael, why am I wasting five minutes of my evening?"

"To give me an opportunity to convince you that you're not wasting it." He approached and gestured to the chair opposite her. "May I?"

"You may."

"Thank you." He took a seat and adopted a friendly, casual stance to counter her ice-maiden routine, while snapping several images with his ocular implant. The system informed him it was receiving EM interference. Clever defensive measure on her part, but he was a spy, and the specialized algorithms in his ocular implant adapted to overcome the interference. "It's an honor to meet you. Do you have a name?"

"Yes. The terms of your offer having been fulfilled, will you now release your supply of Nephyl-HIG to me?"

"Certainly. I'm a man of my word. Of course, you're apt to use the supply up fairly quickly, and I hear the safety re-quals at the remaining suppliers are getting all hung up in Advocacy bureaucracy."

"Are you trying to impose an additional stipulation on selling me further quantities?"

He smiled smugly. "More of an offer. Your rise to some acclaim in this business has been most impressive, but there's no delicate way to put this...you're Human. The outside maximum number of years you've been playing in this pool is two decades. I've been doing this for millennia."

"You're the second person to say that to me this month. The first one who did so has since experienced a…how do you Anadens phrase it? Final denouement?"

Godsdamn, she was serious. "Apologies. I meant no offense. I was merely observing…" he lifted a hand in her direction "…reality."

"I have Anaden advisors on staff. They've served me well."

"Clearly. But they aren't me."

She arched an eyebrow. "What rarified skill do you possess? I've never heard of you."

"And that's how I like it. Padron Lanael isn't my only name, and chemical supply isn't my only business. Or much of it, for that matter. See, I'm…how do you Humans phrase it? A broker. A matchmaker. I know everyone. I know what they sell, what they need and where I can get it for them. I know who to bribe and who it's easier to simply kill. Which ones for whom a little regenesis vacation will suffice, and which ones need a taste of that *apomono* you're not manufacturing."

"And you're offering your brokerage services to me? For what price?"

He adjusted his position in the chair and, in a move he'd practiced several times before coming tonight, pressed the activation button of the Manifold Scar Tracker secured inside the lining of his jacket. The MAST was small and thin enough that the enforcer's weapons' pat down had slid over it.

He wasn't confident it would work. Or rather, he wasn't confident the quantum entangled particle the MAST fired would survive to reach a useful destination. Particles could get flung around or knocked off by the gentle breeze of the air conditioning or the brush of fabric across fabric. If he got lucky, she'd go straight from here to some location of strategic value.

"Honestly? The price of you becoming someone I know. What you sell and what you need. Information is my currency."

The corners of her eyes twitched; it could be he was confounding her a touch. "Then you don't require payment for the Nephyl-HIG?"

"Touché. Information is *one* of my currencies. I do have expenses. You're not trying to impose additional stipulations on your purchase of the supply, are you?"

"You'll receive the credits to cover the offered price."

"And the rest?"

"Your five minutes are up." She lifted her chin in the direction of the corner of the room, and he sensed the enforcer approaching behind him.

"Let's go, Lanael."

He stood without fanfare. "It was a pleasure to meet you…?"

Her gaze bit into him for several seconds, leaving him feeling naked and vaguely scalded. "Teresa Piras."

"Thank you, Ms. Piras. Until next time, I hope."

She stood as well. "Before you go. You're an Idoni, aren't you?"

The undercurrent he detected in her voice gave him pause, but he bit his lower lip nonetheless. Whatever advantage he was able to gain. "What gave it away?"

"A certain devil-may-care swagger, bordering on braggadocio, in a situation that called for the opposite."

"I am what I am." He chuckled throatily, letting his expression hint at the audacity she seemed to appreciate. "I trust you know the full extent of what being an Idoni means."

"I trust I do." Her countenance shuttered, and with a flick of her wrist, a new wormhole opened across from him. "Goodbye, Mr. Lanael."

S&L

ARES

Eren pulled off his boots and collapsed back on the bed. Performing had tired him out more than it should have, but he hadn't slept well for the last several nights. He wanted to go home—home to Hirlas, where he was always able to breathe in and clear his head of too many clanging thoughts—but he had too many plates spinning in the air right now to risk the trip. He'd already put himself on the waiting list for a government-issue CPM, but for now they remained the hardest ticket to land this side of an invitation to Plousia's penthouse splendors.

Before being interrupted, he'd intended to spend the evening catching up on all his assignments. He settled for stepping through them and noting tasks to see to tomorrow.

Tracking the ships the Ch'mshak were flying around in had thus far led to multiple dead ends. SENTRI had mostly taken over this aspect of the investigation, and Eren couldn't really add anything to their work. He'd keep a watch on their progress, but he provisionally moved the Ch'mshak to the back burner.

He'd scored the name of the entity Roshiive was funneling his fundraising into and had used some of that government sanction power he enjoyed to get an interagency warrant allowing him to trace future transfers to and from the bank account. He'd let Roshiive create his own evidentiary trail, then hang the man with it.

Nyx would want to know he'd landed the warrant. He started to compose a message to her, but paused. Should he stop by in the morning and tell her in person? It would give him a chance to make sure she hadn't slit her wrists in shame over spilling Corradeo's secret.

But then he remembered her incidental dismissal of any feelings for him. Which was ridiculous, because the last thing he needed or wanted was her 'caring' about him in any meaningful way. He could make her gasp in pleasure for hours at a time, but he could not meet *whatever* emotional needs she may be finally realizing she wanted fulfilled. While he was doing a decent job of keeping himself together these days, when it came to matters of the heart, he had nothing left to give. He might never.

Why had her words stung so much, then?

Probably because he was an arrogant ass who got off on people fancying him. That was usually the reason.

So should he go by and see her? Or invite her to come over? Were they still doing whatever it was they'd been doing, or had this latest conflict put an end to it?

Instead of deciding right away, he opted to ponder what Caleb had said about Corradeo. As soon as he thought of the man, this aching cavern of *loss* opened up in his chest. It wasn't grief, the way he felt about losing Cosime. It was more a desperate pang of longing for something he hadn't known he'd lost.

How many memories, how many millennia, had the Directorate stolen from him? His life suddenly felt small, in a way it never had before.

Another message arrived in Lanael's inbox, this one from an unfamiliar address.

> *Mr. Lanael,*
> *I require two dozen snoRNA chain scaffold transformers. Price is not an object, but my timetable is three days. Procure them for me by this deadline, and we can talk further.*

It wasn't signed, but it didn't need to be, and satisfaction lifted his mood a touch. He could charm anyone, even whatever Teresa Piras turned out to be.

The transformers she'd requested were not exactly found on every street corner, for good reason. Their uses were few, and outside of medical research labs, none of them were positive. Even for a cartel overlord-in-training, the woman was into some nasty businesses.

He belatedly removed the MAST from the inset pocket in his jacket and rolled the rust-hued module around in his hand. He hadn't known the device existed until two months ago, when Tolje Alainor had stolen it from the Olympia Advanced Research Institute. The device fired one half of an entangled quantum particle pair and directed it to attach to anything, person, object or other particle, that the wielder desired. It then used the first half of the pair to track wherever the second half of the pair traveled.

Scientists had invented it with half an eye toward using it to track the Dzhvar. Given what they'd seen of the Dzhvar so far, he was skeptical it was going to be of much value there, but it wasn't his area of expertise. Eren had been able to use it to track the location of the Phae'soon who were attacking Tolje's people with truly nasty death clouds, however, so he knew it was capable of working outside of a lab setting.

He activated the tiny control panel and checked the readout. No location had registered at all. Dammit. The entangled particle must have gotten smashed in short order, possibly by a defensive shield or security scan. Which meant he was going to have to win himself another meeting with Teresa Piras at a minimum, and he might be looking at a full-scale undercover operation.

He exhaled and climbed off the bed. Time to go find some bioweapon tools in a hurry. But first, he sent a message to arrange a meeting with an old friend.

36

CONCORD HQ

CINT

Eren strolled into Richard's office looking a bit rumpled and sleep-deprived, though this was nothing new for the man. "Thanks for making time to see me on such short notice, sir."

Richard stood and walked around his desk, hand extended. "What's this 'sir' crap? You don't work for me any longer. Unless you want to?"

Eren huffed a wry breath as he shook Richard's hand. "That offer has never been more tempting than it is right now. I'll let you know if I decide to take you up on it." He gestured to the table in the corner of the office. "Can we sit? I brought something for you to have a look at."

Richard idly wondered why all was not kosher in the land of Advocacy Intelligence. He'd been interfacing with Director Nyx about the Ch'mshak problem and hadn't picked up on anything amiss, but the woman did keep both AdvInt and personal matters extraordinarily close to the vest.

"The offer is a sincere one. You are always welcome here at CINT." He sat opposite Eren and propped his elbows on the table. "What do you have for me?"

"I've been running an undercover op on this upstart criminal cartel out of Domor and Scholite called Riamere. I went into it thinking they were primarily moving hypnols, but I'm starting to suspect they've got their fingers in a lot of nefarious pots: black-market cybernetics mods, bioweapons, and so on."

"Interesting, though I suppose not a surprise. The Anaden criminal underworld is both vast and deep. But I thought your area was alien affairs. How'd you pull this gig?"

"Here's the curious thing: the leader of Riamere is a Human."

Richard sat up straighter at this news. Like Eren, he mainly dealt with alien criminal enterprises these days, but old habits died hard. "What is a human doing running a cartel on Anaden worlds?"

"My question exactly. It doesn't fit, and this intrigued me. So I decided to find out the answer. I was able to finagle an in-person meeting with her yesterday. And boy, she is one frightening woman. I'm a little shocked I walked away with my skin still attached to my body." Eren frowned. "Also, I think she came onto me, which I didn't discourage for the sake of the op, but I do want to keep my cock attached along with my skin. Anyway, she was running a distortion field to prevent her appearance from being recorded, but we've got fancier tools than she does, and I was able to snag a visual."

Eren instantiated a virtual screen between them and flashed an image. "She goes by the moniker of 'Pale Viper,' but she eventually gave me a name: Teresa Piras. I assume it's fake as well. But you worked Human intelligence for decades, so I wondered if you might recognize her."

Richard blinked several times, expecting the image to resolve into something other than what it presented. When it didn't, he rubbed at his eyes, to no greater effect. So he pushed his chair back and stood to circle the office, then returned to plant his hands on the table and lean in to stare at the image from a few centimeters away. "This is impossible."

"Oh? You do know her?"

"I did. But she's dead."

"That doesn't stop many people these days."

"No, but she's eighteen years dead. She was a Prevo, granted, but every scrap of her Artificial was destroyed a few months after she was. It can't be her." He scrutinized the image again. "It certainly looks like her, though."

Could someone be impersonating Olivia Montegreu? Trying to claim her reputation for their own ends? But why do so in Anaden space, where she'd had no reputation, and under an assumed name, thus denying this person the benefits? No, something else must be transpiring here.

"Who was she?" Eren asked.

"Only the most dangerous woman humanity has ever produced." Richard sat and clasped his hands together on the table. "Tell me absolutely everything you know about her and her organization."

When Eren had departed with a plan to learn more about the Pale Viper—he couldn't bring himself to believe it was truly Olivia Montegreu—along with a stern warning to tread carefully, Richard studied the visual for a solid five minutes. Memories and details he'd believed safely packed away dredged back into the forefront of his thoughts. He'd never expected to have to face this foe again.

He asked Cliff, CINT's Artificial, to compile a report on an old set of files, then commed up Graham Delavasi. As soon as the report arrived, he dove in.

S&L

Graham showed up wearing a red-and-black checkered lumberman's shirt, beige workpants and scuffed suede hiking boots. All he was missing to complete the ensemble was a rod in one hand and a cooler full of beer in the other. "It's been three months since my last consulting gig. I was just starting to settle back into my fishing routine."

"The fishing's going to have to wait." Richard flashed him Eren's visual.

"No."

"Yes."

"*How?*"

"I've been working on that." Richard cascaded three screens across his desk. "The answer has to be Enzio Vilane. Cliff pored through the forensic reports from the beach house. Vilane had a ton of quantum hardware running there. Too much, even for a Prevo managing a large criminal enterprise. There were four separate hubs. At the time we assumed they served as redundant backups, but what if they weren't? Or what if they were backing up an additional mind?"

Graham squinted at the screens to the point his eyes almost closed. "Does it matter, though? Mia Requelme blew out every particle of hardware at the beach house and at three additional locations. So even if the extra hardware belonged to..." he tossed a hand toward the visual Richard had moved off to the side "...*that*, it doesn't explain how she's walking around today."

"Maybe Mia missed some remote hardware. Maybe Vilane maintained another location he kept siloed, and she didn't have a path to reach it via quantum entanglement. Or detect it, for that matter."

Graham pointed to the visual, a scowl darkening his features. "Are you saying this is an Artificial copy of Olivia Montegreu wearing human skin?"

"Well it's not a real human. Olivia Montegreu is dead—" he blinked "—whoa, déjà vu. I had this exact same conversation with Malcolm Jenner seventeen years ago when Montegreu's orphaned Artificial was wreaking havoc. Anyway, yes. I think this is precisely what I'm saying. Somehow, Vilane located records we missed after that nasty business with her old Artificial back in Aurora. Extensive enough records for him to reconstitute some fragment of the consciousness she shared with the Artificial and stick it into an illegal cloned body. He kept her existence a secret, and she—again, somehow—managed to survive Mia's firestorm."

"That's a lot of suppositions based on a single visual. Who took it?"

"Eren Savitas. Former CINT agent of mine, works for Advocacy Intelligence now. Good agent. Unconventional, but knows his stuff. He took the visual while meeting with this individual. It's legitimate."

"What does the Advocacy have to do with the possible ghost of Olivia Montegreu?"

Richard sighed. "She's running a criminal cartel in Anaden space. Drugs, mods, weapons."

Graham finally sank into the chair opposite Richard's desk. "God almighty, it is her, isn't it?"

"Looks like. Some form of her, at least."

"But why Anaden space?"

"Because she's never conquered another species before, and she relishes a challenge? Alternatively, because she's not running at one hundred percent capability, and the Advocacy remains light in the law enforcement department?"

"Her Artificial went on a campaign of revenge against anyone connected to her death. Any sign she's picked up the torch?"

Richard shook his head. "Not that I'm aware of. I'll touch base with Malcolm. With Devon as well, and Major Lekkas. Has anyone taken a shot at you lately?"

"Only drunk hunters on moonless nights."

"Really?"

Graham shrugged. "It happens. Shit, Richard. We've killed the collection of malevolent brain cells that represent Olivia Montegreu twice now. She's like the psycho horror movie killer who keeps getting back up again. What are we going to do about this?"

"Eren's already conniving his way into her organization, so we'll work with him. See what he learns. In the meantime, we can revisit every bank account remotely connected to the entire history of Montegreu and Vilane, *and* the Zelones and Rivinchi cartels, and see what's blipped in the last three and a half years. Even she couldn't have walked into Anaden space and set up a criminal enterprise without seed money."

37

KIYORA

ASTERION DOMINION
GENNISI GALAXY

Perrin reached out and grabbed Nika's hand to tug her forward. "Come on. I want you to see inside."

Nika followed her friend through the wide, tall doors of a sprawling eighteen-story building built on the edge of Yugure Park outside Kiyora Three.

The Dominion population had barely grown for the last hundred millennia. The only practical way to make more Asterions was to diversify a genetic template to create siblings, and while people did so with some regularity, they also often abandoned diversifications that didn't work out. So while individuals grew and changed, the overall number of Asterions didn't increase appreciably. As a result, their Axis Worlds still had copious free space available. Even the most bustling cities boasted room for the residents to breathe and stretch.

This was relevant today mostly in the fact that a spacious plot of land had been available to build an enormous refugee center here. And not only here; more than four dozen such centers had been constructed over the last three years across the Axis Worlds and four of their most developed Adjunct Worlds.

The high-ceilinged lobby was bright and cheerful. A long row of dynes stood dormant, but would activate in the event of a crisis to help new arrivals. Instruction signs decorated the front wall, directing people to info addresses for registration, missing person reports, medical emergencies, and so on. No security checkpoints gated entry into the interior of the facility. When every Asterion was able to arrive via personal wormhole, to install them would've been a futile endeavor.

"There's a big cafeteria down the hallway on the left, because people still deserve hand-prepared food, but—well, you'll see. Down the other hallway is a selection of stores with basic hardware and other supplies." Perrin dragged her off through a door labeled "1C - 1E."

Inside, the lodging was arranged in a series of curving pod spaces. Sliding shoji screens created private areas. Each one featured fairly plush single or double cots alongside a modest dresser-table combo with an I/O port and a small refrigeration unit. At the center of each grouping of thirty pods was a gathering area with chairs, couches, low tables and permanent panes overhead. Oh, and a refreshment stand.

"The right wall contains a series of full lavatories with showers," Perrin said. "On the left are food and clothing printers. If the cafeteria is overflowing, no one will go hungry." They stopped in the center of the floor, where more dyne stations were situated beneath a circle of large panes. "The third floor has some additional facilities: dozens of repair benches and ten tanks, a room of workstations, and a gym so people don't go stir-crazy."

Perrin was bubbling over with enthusiasm and, though she'd likely deny it, pride. And she should be. The size of the facility ought to be overwhelming, but the layout created an impression of smaller, even cozy spaces within a communal living environment. And it was all Perrin's design.

Nika dipped her chin in appreciation. "You have truly gone above and beyond here."

"Just because people will have been displaced, it doesn't mean they have to be uncomfortable. It's going to be a miserable experience no matter what, but I want to make it as pleasant as possible. Refugees deserve privacy. They deserve a soft bed, decent meals, a proper selection of clothes, and access to whatever help they need."

"And you'll be giving it to them." Nika wrapped an arm around Perrin's shoulders. "This is amazing work."

"I wish I'd moved faster. The first couple of refugee centers we built aren't as nice. I advocated for tearing them down and starting over, but..." Perrin rolled her eyes and dropped her head on Nika's shoulder "...something about budget overruns and a lack of unlimited funds."

"An unfortunate truth about the world."

"Right? Such a shame." Perrin stepped back and let her gaze roam across the space. "I hope all this money, time and effort were wasted. I hope this place stays empty. I hope not a single person ever has to spend a night here."

"So do I." Nika smiled gently. "But if they do, know you've done the best anyone could possibly do for them."

S&L

Perrin had to run off to a meeting at one of the under-construction refugee centers. So after she'd departed, Nika took a few minutes to stroll through Yugure Park. Kiyora was arguably their most beautiful world, full of color and greenery, rolling hills and majestic mountain peaks. It definitely hosted the lion's share of their most beautiful parks.

She settled to the ground beneath the limbs of a flowering snowbell tree and rested against the trunk. Despite her insistence to Miriam that she couldn't spend her life in the kyoseil web, she now found herself visiting it several times a day. In part, she was checking in to identify new Dzhvar incursions. She sent the new markers that had appeared since her last visit over to the Omoi-kane Initiative team monitoring the incursions, who she was certain promptly forwarded the information on to Concord's team.

It was perhaps a slight duplication of effort, but while the Dominion worked closely with Concord on many fronts, they were not Concord. Asterions remained fiercely independent, and they did not intend to cede their defense, and thus their lives, to anyone else.

Two new incursions caught her attention immediately, and she sent the information along. Then she continued her exploration.

Thus far, the Dzhvar didn't seem to notice the presence of either kyoseil waves or physical kyoseil fibers. Kyoseil had always been more passive than its siblings, but it surprised her that the Dzhvar didn't even acknowledge its existence. But maybe it did, and she simply didn't know how to recognize the signs. It wasn't as if she had access to the life form's thoughts, and thank the stars for this.

Nika frowned as she detected a frayed edge where the kyoseil web petered out, when before it had continued on to a physical asteroid deposit. She'd visited this region before and hadn't noticed the fraying; she was sure of it. The gap between waves stretched for some twelve parsecs.

She cast her mind into sidespace and traveled to the location in the Hercules Supercluster...and was stopped short where the kyoseil wave unraveled into nothing. Where the wave couldn't travel, neither could she? That didn't make any sense.

She returned to her body and checked the historical record. There had been a Dzhvar incursion at the exact location where the wave frayed.

Her nose tickled, and she opened her eyes to discover a snowbell petal had fallen to skip down her face and land on her chest. She brought it up to her nose, inhaling the vanilla scent before setting it on the ground beside her. She needed to try to parse out what she'd discovered.

Sidespace was a dimension that overlaid the entire universe. So there should be nowhere she wasn't able to travel in sidespace with her mind.

But as a dimension, was it subject to being devoured by the Dzhvar, same as the physical ones? Though she hadn't considered this, it had to be. The Dzhvar didn't merely consume the physical dimensions. They dissolved the manifold itself, which meant everything, sidespace included.

The dead zone she'd discovered appeared to have been one of the first places attacked, before they'd known for certain the Dzhvar were here. And now it was disintegrating.

Stars, this was all going to happen exactly as predicted, wasn't it? Unless they found a way to stop the Dzhvar, the cycle was going to repeat all over again. Just like in Mesme's time, and in Miaon's time before that, the Dzhvar were going to consume the fabric of space until the universe faltered, broken, upon the precipice of annihilation. Then someone—Mesme's secret identity—was going to have to travel back in time a million years and try again.

What a suffocating weight it must be. It was enough to shame her for the bouts of self-pity she indulged in over the supposed burdens resting on her shoulders. They all carried burdens aplenty, but only one person would carry theirs for a thousand millennia.

Emboldened by a renewed determination to do whatever small part she could to ensure this eventuality never came to pass, she dove back into the web and began searching for additional frayed edges. Alex would be keen to learn where the fabric of space was growing weakest.

She'd spotted a second location when a pinprick of light flared in her peripheral vision. A Dzhvar incursion in the making, and outside the Detection Network.

She sent an emergency alert containing the coordinates to half a dozen people at once. Then she climbed to her feet and hurriedly returned to the Initiative.

38

CAF AURORA

SEXTANS SUPERCLUSTER

As soon as Miriam confirmed the Dzhvar were still in the area, she called in a small, hand-picked attack group to the scene. The time for Dzhvar tourism was at an end. They needed to engage the enemy, to begin to learn the hard lessons of which strategies and weapons were effective against them, and which ones to sideline.

She didn't hold out much hope for winning this day, but they had to start somewhere. And they had to move fast, because a red supergiant shone in the distance, and she did not expect the Dzhvar to pass it by.

Thomas created a labeled sector map of the Dzhvar presence and shared it with all ships in the attack group.

Commandant Solovy (CAF Aurora)(Command Channel): "All ships adopt a fan formation, keeping the Aurora at the apex point. Maintain at least half a megameter distance from the enemy except when a closer approach is needed to deliver a strike, and do not venture in front of the enemy's trajectory."

They already knew that adiamene-clad probes weren't merely rendered defunct upon contact with the Dzhvar. They dissolved into atoms, albeit not as rapidly as equipment constructed using conventional metals. It had always been a fool's dream to imagine adiamene would save them against such a foe, the way it had against so many others; she'd mourned the death of the dream after their previous encounter with the Dzhvar, then let it go.

Commandant Solovy (CAF Aurora)(Command Channel): "Admiral Ashonye, launch your complement of nuclear weapons. Half to detonate on the facing edge of the Dzhvar in Sector Four, half to penetrate two megameters into their presence in Sector Five. Fleet Admiral Jenner, direct a flight of Banshees to deliver targeted conventional laser strikes in Sector One."

She didn't expect either of the attacks to work, mostly because Corradeo Praesidis said they hadn't worked in the first war, but she must check every box. She followed the weapons deployment on the tactical map as the *Aurora* chased after the wall of Dzhvar, the fleet fanning out behind her.

Admiral Ashonye (AFS Patagonia)(Command Channel): "Nuclear detonations have demonstrated no immediate effect. Launching probes to monitor the impact locations for potential deterioration."

Fleet Admiral Jenner (AFS Denali)(Command Channel): "Banshees report not so much as a flicker out of the Dzhvar from the laser impacts."

Commandant Solovy (CAF Aurora)(Command Channel): "As anticipated. Commander Palmer, deliver four Rift missiles to Sector Seven, same distribution as with the nuclear weapons."

"Thomas, watch this deployment closely." Rift grenades had ranked as one of the most successful inventions of the Rasu War when it came to planetary surface defense, so it had been an easy choice to scale the technology for deployment in space. Not that the Asterions had needed or asked her permission before doing so. The new Rift missiles featured a spread five times wider than the original grenades and, thanks to tiny Zero Engines for propulsion, were able to travel as far as needed to reach a target.

Thomas pulled in the feeds from the *ADV Dauntless II* and displayed them on a virtual screen next to the tactical map.

The instant the feed signaled that detonation had occurred, four yawning holes appeared in the trailing edge of the Dzhvar wall.

She counted the seconds in her mind. *One...two...three...fo—* Threads of Dzhvar began weaving through the gaps the missiles had created, industriously sewing them back together. In ten seconds, no gaps in the wall remained.

'Wide-range sensors report four patches of Dzhvar materialized 8.4 megameters distant from the points of impact. They promptly adopted a course to rejoin the main group.'

Commandant Solovy (CAF Aurora)(Command Channel): "Though the damage did not last for long, the Rift missiles did relocate the Dzhvar they impacted. Commander Palmer, continue firing missiles into Sector Seven and recording the results."

Commander Palmer (ADV Dauntless II)(Command Channel): "With pleasure."

It wasn't much; hardly anything at all. But they had displaced the Dzhvar, however fleetingly, and deposited them at a location of their choosing. They could build on this.

'Our distance to the local star has decreased to 0.6 AU. I calculate we have 6.8 minutes before we will need to vacate the system.'

She did the rough math in her head. "The Dzhvar are moving more slowly than in our last encounter?"

'Yes. Perhaps they are studying us, as we are studying them.'

Miriam wasn't certain the Dzhvar were noticing them at all. While the more deliberate speed gave them a bit of extra time to throw additional weapons at the enemy, it didn't grant her much comfort. One more data point: much like they could adjust their course to intercept a star, the enemy could speed up and slow down at will. Whatever the Dzhvar were, they weren't mindless.

Commandant Solovy (CAF Aurora)(Command Channel): "Fleet Admiral, if Revere is in position, send in the Lexington.*"*

Fleet Admiral Jenner (AFS Denali)(Command Channel): "Acknowledged. Expect contact with the enemy in twenty seconds."

The *Lexington,* an AEGIS cruiser, was equipped with the TDS shielding. The barrier did not keep out *diati,* so she wasn't hopeful it would repel Dzhvar. But if it would….

The *Lexington* was currently uncrewed save for its Artificial, Revere, who had volunteered for the mission. He had duplicated himself two days ago and maintained a real-time quantum connection with his hardware at the Presidio. He planned to record everything that happened to the *Lexington* and its components, as well as to himself, as the ship flew straight into the Dzhvar wall, until the last nanosecond he was able to transmit.

Time was running too short, though, so she needed to move on two fronts.

Commandant Solovy (CAF Aurora)(Command Channel): "Navarchos Casmir, fire four Igni missiles into Sector Three, same distribution as the nuclear weapons. Admiral Ashonye, have one of your regiment fire negative energy weapons into Sector Six at a variety of ranges."

Yes, antimatter weapons were back on the table, because everything was on the table. But the real test was the negative energy weapons. They'd won her countless battles over the years, and every ship in the fleet now came with the renewable version installed on multiple hardpoints.

Fleet Admiral Jenner (AFS Denali)(Command Channel): "Communication lost with the Lexington...and confirmation from Revere at the Presidio. The ship has been destroyed."

Malcolm wasn't entirely keeping the disappointment out of his voice. The TDS had saved many lives during the Rasu War, and its loss as an effective defensive measure was a blow—

In the starboard corner of the viewport, a massive wave of Dzhvar surged like a solar flare to consume the portion of the fleet that had fired negative energy weapons into the wall. On the tactical map, the markers for a wide swath of vessels blinked out.

"Full stop!"

Thomas began following her order before she finished giving it.

Commandant Solovy (CAF Aurora)(Command Channel): "All vessels, reverse, increase distance from the enemy to two megameters, and cease all weapons fire. Admiral Ashonye, report."

'The *Patagonia's* transponder has stopped transmitting, as have the transponders for thirty-five additional ships under Admiral Ashonye's command.'

Her lips tightened to hold back any outward sign of dismay. She knew Ashonye had opted in to regenesis; she knew the regenesis choice of every military officer of vice-admiral rank and above. But what of the crews of the thirty-six ships they'd just lost? A seventy-three percent adoption rate across the AEGIS military meant people had died. Had she played the encounter too fast and loose?

No. A risk of death was part of the compact every soldier agreed to when they joined the military. And they couldn't hope to fight this enemy if they were unable to so much as approach it.

Seemingly emboldened now, the wall of Dzhvar accelerated toward the star, while spreading out until it should be able to encompass the entirety of the star's breadth. Given the star was a red supergiant....

"Thomas, what's the width of the Dzhvar presence now?"

'It now measures approximately 575,000 megameters. Slightly over four hundred times the diameter of Sol.'

She tried to study the sight outside the viewport dispassionately, and told herself the wall looked thin and porous now. A swarm of probes surveying the battlespace would report the truth or lie of her eyes soon enough.

'I now estimate 1.4 minutes until the Dzhvar reach the star. Given the mass of the supergiant, a black hole will result from its destruction. Given the current breadth of the attacking force, the outcome will result quickly.'

Miriam's hands flexed around the railing of the overlook until her knuckles threatened to pop. "Launch a final set of probes to monitor the star's destruction."

Commandant Solovy (CAF Aurora)(Command Channel): "All vessels, return to port."

S&L

CONCORD HQ

COMMAND

Alex quietly slid into her seat at the War Room table. She was the only non-military person at the table, but whatever. It wasn't the first time.

To call the mood in the room 'somber' was a fair bit of an understatement. If she were running the meeting, she'd open with, 'well, that was a fucking disaster,' which was at least one reason why she wasn't running the meeting.

Malcolm sat with his hands clenched together on the table, while the muscles in his jaw jumped about in a staccato beat. Twenty-three years had passed since they'd been a couple, but she still remembered what this particular tic signified, and it was nothing good. Casmir looked…honestly, the same as he always did, which was to say grumpy and dour. Lance Palmer fidgeted erratically in his chair, his unfocused gaze suggesting he busily issued orders to the troops back home. He was, as always, itching for another go at the enemy.

Corradeo looked so depressed, she was tempted to ask if his dog had died, except she didn't think he had a dog; Caleb would've mentioned it if he did.

No, the man's demeanor meant only one thing: he'd stood on the bridge of Casmir's Imperium and begged the *diati* to come to their aid, and his plea had fallen on deaf primordial ears. She didn't understand why. Three years ago, she'd confidently declared that the *diati* would return when it was needed to fight the Dzhvar. Now the Dzhvar were here, so where the hell was the *diati*? Could it not hear him? Or worse, was it refusing to answer?

Her mother arrived and took her seat at the nominal head of the oval table. She wore the same calm, even-keeled mien she'd brought to 99.9% of such meetings in her life, military and personal. It said nothing about her degree of inner turmoil.

Miriam opened the meeting in her usual matter-of-fact manner. "We'll discuss the negative energy weapon development in a minute, but first, let's work through the assessment of our other tests.

"As anticipated, conventional weapons had no effect. Neither did nuclear weapons or antimatter Igni missiles. Rift missiles *did* affect the Dzhvar, if only momentarily. Commander Palmer, talk to your people about the viability of producing Rift missiles with a far greater diameter of influence."

"I've already done so," Palmer said. "Bigger is doable. Given what we saw today, big enough to make a practical impact is another matter. But we will give it a go."

"Thank you. In our next encounter, I want to try to place a Rift Bubble around any planet in the path of destruction. If there is no such planet, I'll settle for activating one on a probe in space and measuring what happens. We'll also test the effectiveness of a Dimensional Rifter in protecting an individual vessel. Fleet Admiral, if you will seek a new volunteer for this mission, and thank Revere for his sacrifice today."

"I will," Malcolm replied. "The twenty second download from Revere is that nothing on the *Lexington* held up for any reasonable length of time. The Dzhvar passed through the TDS as if it wasn't there. All ship electronics failed instantly upon contact with the enemy. The adiamene hull did hold together for some fifteen seconds before its molecular bonds began to come apart. And this, in essence, describes what happened to everything in the ship: a molecular breakdown. Special Projects received Revere's full report ten minutes ago."

"Hopefully they can extract something useful from the information. But I suspect we learned what we needed to from the test." Miriam paused. "I trust everyone has seen the footage of the destruction of the AEGIS regiment after they fired negative energy weapons into the Dzhvar presence?"

Silent nods rippled around the table.

But Alex hadn't merely seen the footage. She'd watched it happen. She'd positioned the *Siyane* near the *Patagonia* as soon as her mother had given the order to deploy negative energy weapons. And by 'near,' she meant so close that she'd come damn close to getting vaporized herself.

At the time of the first Dzhvar War, the Anadens had heavily favored antimatter as their weapon of choice whenever collateral damage wasn't a concern, much as they had a million years later when humanity arrived on the scene. When antimatter weapons hadn't touched the Dzhvar, they'd begun to construct prototype negative energy weapons. But then the *diati* got into the game, and they'd shelved the negative energy research in favor of Corradeo's new shiny toy.

When her mother had asked Mesme about the possibility of negative energy weapons working against the Dzhvar, Mesme had muttered noncommittedly that she should test it and see. But Mesme must have known what a spectacular disaster it was going to be. So why let them try and fail, getting people killed in the process?

The obvious answer was the Kats' usual routine of 'work it out for yourself or it won't stick.' And here, it was likely part of the reason. Mesme undoubtedly recognized that Miriam would have tested negative energy weapons no matter what. Her mother needed data, and she wasn't going to shelve their single largest source of weaponry on the word of anyone, not even a million-plus-year-old, time traveling, dimension weaving space wizard.

But it wasn't the real reason, and Alex knew it. Today? Today was a show intended for her eyes.

"What did we learn from this failure?" Miriam asked dryly. "Clearly, we learned that negative energy weapons are not an effective way to damage Dzhvar. In point of fact, they seem to have the opposite effect—"

"Like adding kindling to a fire," Alex murmured quietly.

"Alex? You have something to add?"

"I do." She cleared her throat and sat up straighter. "We learned what the Dzhvar are. Or not 'are,' exactly, but what the closest parallel may be: negative energy itself. What happened when the negative energy blasts impacted the Dzhvar was akin to what you see when two forest fires meet and combine: conflagration. And I think I should've realized this earlier. It's got to be part of an explanation for why the manifold falls apart in their wake."

"But negative energy weapons don't destroy the manifold," her mother replied.

"No, but they might if we built them powerful enough. Negative mass is required to maintain wormholes, and of course mass and energy are the same thing. Wormholes cut *through* the physical manifold. Now, in our experience thus far, the manifold is more than resilient enough to heal itself once the wormhole is gone."

She frowned, thinking of the news Nika had delivered earlier today. Space was already starting to break down in the wake of the Dzhvar's earliest incursions. Once the meeting was over, she'd visit the location Nika had identified and see if it matched the characteristics of the old wounds the Dzhvar had left behind in the first war, or if the structural damage was worse. She worried it was the latter.

"Alex?"

"Trying to think it through. Maybe there's something about the mechanism by which the Dzhvar act...the force they deliver, or the way they do so...that makes the effect much more destructive. This is a piece of the puzzle, but it's just a start."

Miriam nodded. "Is there any way this knowledge can help us right now?"

"The problem is, throwing positive energy at them didn't work, either. It didn't make them flare, but they still ignored it. Or consumed it, the same as they consume everything else. I'm sorry, I don't have anything. Not yet."

39

THE PRESIDIO

Malcolm was on a comm when Mia entered his office, so she leaned against the wall by the door and waited. The fleet admiral's office was of course the largest one on the Presidio, and it had a decently wide viewport through which to observe the bustling activity and stars beyond its hull.

But as a space station, the Presidio was a far more utilitarian affair than Concord HQ. Not only was it a military complex from top to bottom, but it had been constructed in some haste—and some hesitation—following Mesme's warning about a coming war with the Directorate. Miriam Solovy had manifested it into existence wielding little more than an iron will and a steely glare; as such, welcoming decor, complementary lighting and architectural flourishes had not made it onto the requirements list.

Malcolm finished his comm, stood and walked over to her, a warm smile banishing too many worry lines from his features. With his office door closed, he took her in his arms and kissed her softly. "How's your morning been?"

"Busy. The installation of the new full-immersion sims started today. Yours?"

He sighed and withdrew a little, keeping his hands at her waist. "Rearranging ship deployments to fill in the gap left by the regiment the Dzhvar destroyed until replacements come online, then interviewing suicidal Artificial candidates for the Dimensional Rifter test."

"Suicidal? Don't the volunteers make copies of themselves before heading into battle?"

He shrugged. "To my way of thinking, they're still volunteering to die."

So did every soldier, every day, though, didn't they? She didn't voice the question. She'd made peace with Malcolm's death and return to life, and she believed he had as well, as much as he was capable of doing so. But this didn't mean they rushed to bring it up in casual conversation.

So instead, she tugged him closer and kissed him again.

"Hmm. We're going to be late…."

"We can't have that." She reluctantly stepped back and motioned to the door. "Did Richard say what he wants to discuss? He's not exactly a regular lunch date of ours."

"He did not. But if we're doing it over a meal in the Presidio cafeteria, it can't be too dire."

She wasn't so confident of this. The real question was, what direness directly impacted both Malcolm *and* her? For better or worse, she was completely extricated from Consulate affairs, except for Marlee's occasional visits to seek advice. As a private citizen, she had no role to play in intergalactic schemes or warfare.

In any event, they'd know soon enough. Richard volunteering to come here could be a concession to Malcolm's busy schedule, or a sweet gesture designed to save her discomfort by not asking her to visit HQ. If it was the latter, it was unnecessary, as she visited HQ often. And, yes, pangs of nostalgia and regret assaulted her every time she did, but she soldiered through them with her chin held high. She'd made her own fate.

Malcolm had done the flag officers' dining room a disservice by calling it a cafeteria. While it was as utilitarian in design as the rest of the station, it featured well-appointed tables and booths along a stretch of viewports, a quality if limited menu, and human wait staff.

The hostess took them to the nicest table without prompting, and their usual drinks showed up by the time they'd sat properly.

Malcolm did his best to eschew the pomp accompanying his lofty position, but his subordinates did not.

Richard arrived a minute later, and cordial greetings followed. The waiter addressed Richard as brigadier, though the man had retired from the military nineteen years ago. It was a nice touch.

As soon as they were alone, Richard removed a surveillance shield module and placed it on the table. "I'm sure you realize this isn't entirely a social visit, so I won't play games and draw out the suspense."

"What's happened?" Malcolm asked.

Richard opened his mouth, then shook his head. "I still trip over saying these words aloud." His gaze shifted to each of them in turn. "Olivia Montegreu is alive."

Thunderclouds instantly descended upon Malcolm's features. "No, she's not."

"I should clarify. What we assume must be an Artificial version, in whole or in part, of Olivia Montegreu is walking around in a human body."

"No. We destroyed her broken, delusional Artificial as well."

"We did," Richard replied. "My working theory is that Enzio Vilane succeeded in piecing together scattered records. Partial backups, state recordings, insurance policies, I don't know. Or maybe we missed an intact backup hidden away, and he was able to uncover it. We searched what was left of Zelones headquarters, but New Babel has never been fully open to us. Regardless, I believe he acquired a copy of her DNA and woke up whatever it was he'd collected in a cloned body before…."

"Before I killed him," Mia offered flatly.

"Yes."

"It's conceivable there was more than one Artificial housed on Scythia or Pandora. But if there was, I fried it as well. I fried everything connected to the house and to Vilane."

"I'm well aware, Ms. Requelme." It was a shame Richard addressed her so formally, but there were consequences to her being a criminal which would never fade. "My experts tell me she could have been inhabiting a siloed body at the time of the incident on Scythia. Or her hardware could have been stored elsewhere, with no quantum link to any of Vilane's storehouses."

"Your experts are correct." She didn't elaborate. She wasn't certain how well-informed CINT was about the many ways Prevos and Artificials were interacting with the physical world these days, and it wasn't her place to educate him. "Fine. Though unlikely, it's conceivable she existed three years ago, yet eluded my carpet bombing."

Malcolm was regarding them both in dismay. "You have got to be kidding me."

"I wish I were." Richard sighed. "Unfortunately, she is up to her old ways. She's set up an operation on several Anaden worlds trafficking hypnols and black market body mods. Possibly weapons as well."

"Anaden worlds?" Malcolm asked.

"They're far more lightly governed," Mia replied.

"That's my assumption as well," Richard said. "She'd want to stay clear of AEGIS' radar while she builds a new empire, especially in light of all the scrutiny directed at her son's enterprises."

Malcolm rubbed at his forehead but dropped his hand and straightened up as their meals arrived, taking care not to let the staff catch him looking perturbed. No one made a move to touch the food.

"Okay," Malcolm said in resignation after the waiter departed. "You're here because you're worried she'll come after us out of vengeance."

"It's a concern, yes. Though if she were planning to, I'd honestly have expected her to act by now. She's been operating her burgeoning criminal cartel for at least a year, if not longer. She's had time, and we never would've seen her coming."

The three of them sat in silence with this reality for a moment before Malcolm responded. "Nonetheless, she must know the two of us were involved in her son's death. It's not like the first time, when all the details of the Dolos Station operation were kept strictly classified, including the participants. People know what happened at Vilane's house on Scythia. Not a lot of people, but enough."

"Agreed. Ms. Requelme, I want to put a protective detail in place at the Expo and at your home on Romane."

"I don't think—"

"They'll be discreet."

"Do it," Malcolm said, in such a way that made it clear she would not be able to talk him out of it. "The Vancouver house as well."

"Consider it done." Richard picked up his fork and moved it around in his salad. "I didn't only come here to warn you. Ms. Requelme, I need to ask for your help in locating Montegreu's Artificial hardware."

"Oh." She settled back in her chair, her hands winding together in her lap. At last, her presence made sense.

"We have someone on the inside with her—Eren Savitas, actually. I believe you know him." It was a credit to Richard's tactfulness that he delivered the news without a hint of deeper insinuation. Of course she knew Eren. Among other things, he'd played a key role in her plot of retribution against the Savrakaths when she'd believed Malcolm to be dead...the first time.

She forced a weak smile. "I suspect there's a story as to how that came about."

"There always is where Eren is concerned. Here's my idea: if he can alert us as to when he'll be meeting with her, can you observe her in sidespace, then locate her hardware using...." Richard's brow pinched in consternation.

"The method I used to eliminate Enzio's remote hardware on Pandora, Seneca and Demeter?"

"Yes, ma'am."

That night, she hadn't acted logically; there had been no cold calculation or application of learned knowledge about quantum programming or Prevo operational mechanics. She'd simply let loose a primal scream of rage and despair, and it had traveled out in a shockwave across every quantum pathway in her sight. But whatever her motivations or thought processes at the time, it had worked to destroy Enzio Vilane.

She stiffened her spine and nodded. "No guarantees, but I can try. However, I'm going to need help."

40

BRIZO

MILKY WAY GALAXY

Different park, different city, different planet. Same Machim enforcer.

Eren set the large bag he carried on the ground, then spread his arms and legs wide. "How are you this fine evening…sorry, I never got your name?"

The man motioned at the bag. "What's in there?"

"The deliverables she requested."

"Open it."

He did as ordered, standing there passively while the man rooted all around inside. "Good thing they're packaged securely. I doubt she'd be pleased if I delivered the products busted due to your lack of finesse."

The man grunted as he ran the scanner over the bag, then stood and did the same along Eren's clothes before stepping back. A second later, a wormhole opened in the grass nearby. Eren closed the bag, hefted it back onto his shoulder and stepped through the wormhole without being prompted.

He found himself in a nondescript storage room about ten by ten meters in size. Racks on two walls were filled with opaque containers, so he couldn't determine what they held without studying the labels, which would be bad form given his company.

The Pale Viper—Teresa Piras, neé Olivia Montegreu—stood near the far wall inspecting a container of what looked to be robotics components. She was dressed almost as elegantly as when they'd first met in a deep hunter green pantsuit and champagne blouse, accentuated by a prismatic pearl necklace. He imagined she didn't often get dirty working the manufacturing floor.

He sent a message to Richard.

I'm with her now. Location is attached.

Got it.

Now that the op was in motion, Eren studied Piras anew, taking into account what Richard had said about her. Honestly, Richard had spooked him a touch, mostly by appearing spooked himself on discovering the woman was alive and up to her old tricks. Words like 'diabolical' and 'brutally amoral' and 'soulless' had rolled freely off the man's tongue in hushed tones. Obviously, Richard had never met the Idoni Primor, so he didn't have a full appreciation of what manner of evil those words could fairly describe, but Eren was grateful for the heads-up nonetheless. He was not going to underestimate this woman.

"The environs aren't quite as nice as on our last meeting."

"I don't care to waste time gawking at picturesque scenery, Mr. Lanael." She turned to him and gestured at the bag he carried. "Are those the transformers?"

"They are."

"Show me."

He set the bag on a table stretching half the length of the third wall, unfastened it and began removing a series of small boxes. By the time he finished, she had already opened the first one. She held the container up and inspected its contents critically.

"You know much about how the transformers work?" he asked.

"I know enough." She opened three more boxes long enough to confirm they held identical items before bestowing a chilling, incisive gaze upon him. "You move fast."

"I won't lie—I hope to impress you. I'm interested in us working together."

"Before, you intimated you wanted me to be one of your sources and recipients of information. Now we are to be 'working together'?"

"What can I say?" He teased a devious smile. "I've always been ambitious."

"And how has that worked out for you, Mr. Lanael?"

"I'm here, aren't I? And please, call me Padron."

"You seem to be operating under the assumption that we'll see one another again."

He leaned against the table, subtly closing the distance between them by half a meter—and had to restrain himself from flinching as the energy from a powerful defensive shield licked his skin. No wonder the MAST had failed to track her location; the shield would've fried the delicate quantum particle the instant it made contact.

He set a cybernetics routine running to analyze the properties of the shield and deepened his smile. "Tell me why we shouldn't?"

CONCORD HQ

CINT

"This isn't easy," Mia muttered under her breath, teeth gritted.

"Why is it more difficult than last time, at Vilane's place on Scythia?" Richard asked from across the table.

"Last time I was suitably motivated. I didn't notice the friction." She and Richard were situated in a small conference room near his office. Despite the fact that he was busy dealing with the unfortunate fallout from the latest encounter with the Dzhvar, Malcolm had tried to come along for moral support, but she'd convinced him it wasn't necessary. And while they weren't physically present, she was drawing a fair bit of power from Alex, Devon and Morgan to fuel her efforts. With their permission this time.

"And you're not so motivated now?"

Richard's question stopped her flat. Yes, she was motivated. No, she wasn't wracked by a deluge of anguish and despair, nor drowning beneath an avalanche of physical and emotional pain. She was in a good place in her life; happy, bordering on content.

But there were things she wished had never happened, things she wished were different. And if she contemplated those things, she was able to work up a case of righteous indignation at the evil woman currently in her sights for those lost chances. The sins of Enzio Vilane were his own, but Olivia had influenced him, warped him. He'd idolized her, and his actions, which had nearly ruined Mia's life, had been designed in no small part to both emulate and impress his mother.

It made for motivation enough.

Mia ground her jaw and reached to claim additional power from the other Prevos. The surge of power enabled her to break through to a more complex level of sidespace. It was a realm they'd each dallied in during times of great stress or urgency, without fundamentally understanding its nature. This was the native realm of quantum machines, and she was more than half one of those.

…and the creature standing in a storage room in her sidespace vision was fully one.

"There's no neural bridge," she whispered.

"What does that mean?" Richard asked.

"She's not a Prevo. Human body or not, she's fully Artificial."

"We knew this must be true, but helpful to have it confirmed. Does this fact change anything for you?"

"Makes it easier, maybe." Entangled particles spun through the Artificial's organic brain matter. Here in this strange domain, Mia inherently understood how she could, with an intentional thought, blink and reside where their partners did—

"Ow!" She flinched away in mind and body, and barely managed to keep her perception from fleeing the scene.

"What's wrong?" Richard asked, concern tightening his voice. He'd probably reached out toward her, though she didn't open her eyes to check.

"Nasty defensive barriers. I can't blow up her hardware."

"We…weren't going to do that for today. Location and reconnaissance only."

"Oh. Right." Reconnaissance then. Every manner of barrier, disruption field and diffuser had been erected around the hardware to obscure its operation and location. But she was present there now, and all the defenses in the world couldn't evict her.

"Chasen, Domor. I'm sending you the precise coordinates." As soon as she had them, she returned to the storage room on the Domor satellite to study Montegreu further. Ah, yes. As she'd suspected, there was a second entanglement; the woman would not depend on a single point of failure. Not after what Mia had done to her son.

She teased out the separate cluster of particles and blinked—

This time she was prepared for the barrier, though it still stung like a slap to the cheek. "Also in Sesti on Brizo."

S&L

FICENTI SATELLITE

"I work alone."

"But you don't." Eren jerked his head toward the wall. "I guarantee you've got techs out there mixing chemicals, running tests, filling vials and packing containers."

A flicker of something he hoped was respect passed across her features, then retreated. "You know what this place is, Mr. Lanael?"

"Sure I do. Manufacturing facility on the second moon of Ficenti. I'm guessing this is the hypnol operation you took over from Arnal Nikto. I understand he recently suffered a tragic…how is it we Anadens phrase it? Final denouement. Must have accidentally ingested a bit of *apomono* then got himself killed. Sloppy move on his part."

"I assume so. Come with me." It was an order, and she pivoted to stride out of the storage room.

He followed her onto the assembly room floor, then stopped short.

The entire room, and possibly the entire facility, was automated. Robotic arms attached to overhead rails manipulated items as they proceeded down the individual lines. Where necessary, anatype bipedals manned assembly stations. Though Eren wasn't able to see into every corner, to his eye, there existed only two organics on the floor, and he was one of them.

Anadens had mastered the capability to automate ninety-five percent of production and services for a thousand millennia. But over a trillion Anadens needed something to *do* with their time, needed a faux sense of purpose, and the Directorate had paired this instinctual need with their overblown wariness about granting machines too much autonomy ever since the SAI Rebellion. While robotics were used judiciously where most appropriate, so was physical labor, even if it was inefficient to do so.

He chuckled lightly. "Well played, Ms. Piras. Fine, so you eschew unreliable people wherever you can. But you still don't work alone. Your enforcer, for instance."

"Jacobson is loyal."

"You sound certain of it."

She arched an eyebrow in a rare display of amusement. "Oh, I am."

What might that mean? "Interesting that you trust him. How can I make you trust me?"

"You are most persistent, aren't you? Not an iota of fear in you."

He pursed his lips in contemplation. "Are you saying I should be afraid of you?"

"Others have found it in their best interests to be so."

"Well. Here's the thing. At last count, I have died over a hundred times in my life." *Wonder how many times I died in all the lives the Directorate forced me to forget?* "I've died quickly and painlessly, and I've died in slow, excruciating agony. I've died a hero and I've definitely died a villain. Today, I am standing in a better position than I've ever found myself in. My business enterprises are thriving under the Advocacy. But as ever, I want more. So, no, I'm not afraid of you. But I do respect you.

"Now, I'm not suggesting we should become partners. I'm not crazy. I know my business doesn't hold a candle to what you've accomplished in a few short years. But I'm not here to sabotage you, or try to elbow in on your territory, or cheat you out of your well-deserved profits. Instead, I want to help you grow your business to greater heights, because doing so helps me, too. And because, well…" he smiled wolfishly "…it feels like it will be fun."

"Fun? I don't do any of this for fun."

"Huh. Why do you do it?"

She paused for a moment before answering, staring at him oddly. "Because I can."

"Ms. Pale Viper, I suspect you can do anything you decide to do. Why don't you let me demonstrate how it can be just a little bit fun?"

She shook her head. "You believe manufacturing hypnols and black-market mods and weapons is fun?"

"Can be. Or other, more personal endeavors."

"Mr. Lanael, if you are propositioning me, do be direct about it. I loathe games."

It sounded like an invitation to him. So this was his play. He swallowed a sigh and made sure any annoyance never reached his face. If he was going to be stuck with his Idoni heritage, he might as well use it for good.

"In that case, I'm propositioning you." He held out a hand, a symbolic offer. "Let me show you what being an Idoni really means. Promise it will be worth your time."

Her gaze flicked down the length of him and back up—then her expression locked down. "I need to see to the installation of these transformers in the lab right away. If they work as advertised, I may have further need of your services. I'll be in touch."

41

ARES

Nyx curled her legs underneath her on the couch in her apartment and spread the latest intelligence reports out across her vision.

She was trying to make peace with the increasingly bureaucratic nature of her job, thus far with marginal results. The work Advocacy Intelligence did was indisputably vital to ensuring the government succeeded, and thus so did her grandfather. And it wasn't as if she trusted anyone *else* to oversee it all; she'd never want to rely on another individual to maintain the high standards the work required.

But her sojourn with the Hesgyr had been surprisingly refreshing, and this realization was complicating multiple aspects of her life. For the first time in many months, she'd done something genuinely useful, rather than endlessly review and manage what others did. She'd felt the quickening of danger, the rush of combat and the satisfaction of averting catastrophe. She'd even experienced what she could only describe as the warm glow of pride from saving innocent lives.

An unfamiliar sensation to be certain, but strangely intoxicating.

When her mind wandered to the other ways her time with the Hesgyr had been meaningful, she quickly put aside her frivolous musings and refocused on the report front and center of her vision. Discipline was the anecdote to many failings in life.

Three of the newly elected Conference representatives hid unsavory pasts of some concern. The transgressions weren't severe enough to legally disqualify them from their new positions, but solely because the Conference had written its own ethics code.

Advocacy Intelligence enjoyed a broad mandate that was light on explicit limitations, though the fact this was because she'd written the mandate was not lost on her. It was one of the perks of being a member of the prime Praesidis lineage and Corradeo's granddaughter.

She decided to arrange for the nastier details of these representative-elects' prior forays into crime and general malfeasance to make their way into the media. If history was any guide, their inevitable removal from office should take care of itself from there. Wholesale corruption would inevitably infect the Conference, as it did all legislative bodies, but she didn't intend to roll out the red carpet for it.

The entry bell to her apartment chimed, and she glanced toward the door in surprise. It was rather late local time. But Grandfather often lamented how heads of state were never off the clock, and it seemed agency directors weren't, either.

She pulled on the jacket she'd tossed on the table over her camisole and went to the door, but checked the cam before she opened it.

Eren leaned against the opposite wall, hands stuffed in his pants pockets. He looked vaguely antsy and definitely uncomfortable.

They'd hardly spoken since the night she'd carelessly revealed Corradeo's secret about Eren's past, and most of those brief conversations had been via messaging. He'd been avoiding her, but she'd been avoiding him as well. She recognized that their dalliance was likely over. But so long as he didn't say so, it wasn't confirmed, and she'd tricked herself into taking comfort from the ambiguity.

Because though she'd tried not to admit it, she didn't want it to be over. Sex had never played a significant role in her life, but it had also never been nearly this good. Yet it was more than physical pleasure; it had been more than that before they'd slept together for the first time. This was a problem, and one she was finding herself incapable of either escaping or solving.

Eren pushed off the wall and started to walk away, and she hurriedly opened the door. "Sorry. I was in the lavatory."

"Oh. No worries. Do you have a minute?"

"Yes. I was just reviewing the day's reports." She stood aside and let him enter. Had he ever been inside her apartment? Since they'd resumed their…she settled on the word 'dalliance' again…they'd been meeting in his room downstairs. His true home was on Hirlas, so it felt like neutral territory.

She took a seat at the kitchen table and motioned opposite her. "What's the problem?"

"Uh, no problem, as such." He slid the other chair away from the table and sat without scooting it back in place. Maintaining maximum physical and thus personal distance.

Her chest hollowed out, carving an aching, empty gulf into her heart.

"SENTRI traced the latest vessel the Ch'mshak used to a different ship distributor this time. Still Human-owned, though, so I'm going to let CINT interface with SENTRI as needed and handle it from here. I've got my hands full with the Montegreu op, on top of tracking Roshiive's money flows."

"It's fine. As I said before, the Ch'mshak are a Concord problem."

Eren nodded in agreement, and an uneasy silence descended upon the kitchen.

She should have planned what she'd say to him when they were next alone in a room together; it wasn't in her nature to not to be prepared for every scenario. The quiet was oddly suffocating. Why wasn't she in control of the situation?

She clasped her hands firmly on the table. "Eren, I want to—"

"How did he take it?" Eren asked at the same time. The tone in his voice left no room for confusion as to who and what he meant.

And now she'd lost any chance to steer the conversation to her advantage. But Eren deserved an answer. A truthful one, given all the lies leading them here. "He wasn't angry, exactly. I wish he had been. Anger, I know what to do with. But he was mostly...sad. Defeated." She pinched the bridge of her nose. "I let him down, which is worse than almost anything."

"I don't think that's it. I mean, I guess you did, in that he asked you to keep a secret and you didn't—"

"I'm aware of my failing, Eren," she snapped.

"I know you are." He winced. "My point is, I don't think you letting his secret slip is what's got him acting defeated. Caleb said he's eaten up with self-doubt because the *diati* isn't answering his summons. Also guilt over not finishing the job against the Dzhvar the first time, and worry this means the *diati* deems him unworthy to fight the battle a second time."

An array of passing comments and erratic body language and other interactions she'd had with Corradeo over the last several days snapped into a suddenly clear picture. Some investigator she was, to miss all those clues in favor of obsessing over her own shortcomings.

She frowned. "What you say makes sense, but why hasn't he talked to me about it? I've never presumed to be worthy to call the *diati* into service on my own, so I haven't tried, but I know what it's like to lose it. The agony of knowing in your soul that if you could simply grasp it one more time, could direct it at your command, you'd be able to fix so many problems. Keep the chaos at bay." She paused. "Save so many lives. The point is, if anyone can understand what he's going through, I can."

Eren's mouth twisted, as if he wanted to smile but was choosing not to. "It's what you said to me. Almost word for word, in fact. Corradeo refuses to share his burdens with the people he cares about."

"Oh." She ought to stop being surprised when he was insightful. "That's frustrating."

"You don't say."

Silence reasserted itself between them as the ghost of her grandfather joined them at the table. In his own way, he'd deceived them both.

She broke the stalemate first. "I am sorry he kept your past from you. You deserved to know."

"Thanks."

"Maybe we should talk to him together. I think perhaps he needs us, even if he's not willing to admit it."

"I…can't." Eren shook his head to emphasize the point. "Not yet. I'll end up yelling at him, and while I'm mightily pissed at him, I'm not ready to actively make him feel worse than he already does. So I should stay away. You should talk to him, though. He listens to you."

"No, he humors me."

"I'm not sure that's true, but I get why you think so. Maris?"

She shrugged. "I haven't gotten to know her very well. It would be strange for me to reach out to her. I don't know if you realized it or not, but I'm not great at making friends."

"I *did* realize this." He finally smiled, and the hollow pressure in her chest eased a touch. "Say, do you have any beer?"

"No…."

"Oh, right. You don't drink alcohol. Well, except for the one swig of gowal on Nythir."

"Which only served to reaffirm why I don't drink alcohol. It was awful."

"It was. But if you ever change your mind, I can treat you to a variety of drinks that will vault your tongue into a state of utter bliss."

Her lips parted, but no words made it past them as a flush burned her ears, and other places.

"Wow. Okay, that came out…" Eren palmed his forehead "…ah, Hades, Nyx. Can I just not be angry at you over this? I know your loyalty will always be to Corradeo above all others, and I don't blame you for it. You're beating yourself up over disappointing him, and if I were to hold a grudge against you, it would be piling on. And being angry at both him and you is proving to be more than I can sustain."

Abruptly he slid his chair all the way over until his knees were touching her thigh. "And what I really want is to be kissing you right now."

Her heart throbbed painfully against her sternum, but she couldn't bring herself to long for the hollowness to return. What was he doing to her?

She reached up and pressed her fingertips to his mouth. Then all the words she'd refused to admit she yearned to say started tumbling out. "Eren, I didn't mean what I said that night, about Grandfather being the only person I care about. What I feel for—"

He grasped her head in his hands and pulled her close, so their noses were touching, and his voice came out gravelly and low. "Whatever you're about to say, I'm not ready to hear it. I'm sorry. If you can't live with such fucking fragility on my part, I understand. I'll go, and we'll try to find a way to return to being professional colleagues.

"But if we can please file away that briar patch for now, then I will gleefully fulfill your every carnal desire for the rest of the night, and any night thereafter you wish. And I promise you I will not wake up a dour, guilt-ridden mess in the morning."

If he followed through on his vow, it was progress. She decided it was enough. Maybe not for forever, but for however long she could manage.

She kissed him hard on the lips, then pulled away and stood to slide off her jacket and let it fall to the kitchen floor. "Why don't you join me in the shower?"

42

AKESO

Alex dropped her forehead onto Caleb's chest. "I know Mom's doing everything in her power and multiple things that aren't to try to find a way to counter the Dzhvar, but these endless meetings are driving me insane. Way too much military bullshit being tossed into the air for my taste."

They were standing in the kitchen, cleaning up after dinner, and he set the dish towel aside to wrap his arms around her. This afternoon they'd sat through the third such meeting since the encounter in the Sextans Supercluster, and he shared her frustration, if for somewhat different reasons. "You're not wrong. It's the downside to running an alliance—every sovereign entity wants a say. But it's just bluster. At the end of the day, Miriam makes the calls."

"She does. But if we can't use negative energy weapons, and antimatter and nuclear weapons don't touch them, and the *diati* isn't answering comms, and rifts only work for five seconds, then what call can she possibly make? What the *d'yavol* are we supposed to fight the Dzhvar with?"

"I...don't know." He wished like hell he had a better answer.

"The project Commander Palmer mentioned sounded interesting. Conceptual Research is working on upgrading faraday cage technology into something called a 'weave.' Rather than trap the people in their path inside a Piega Strai, maybe we can trap the Dzhvar instead."

"It won't solve everything, but it would definitely be a good start."

Alex drew back, and her eyes were once again animated as they landed on him. "Listen, I've been thinking about these episodes I'm experiencing."

"I'd be shocked if you weren't." He certainly was. "And where has your thinking led you?"

"I want to explore the possibility of kyoseil being involved somehow."

He hadn't expected this answer. "What makes you think it might be?"

"I don't know exactly, but I'm stuck on the idea it could be related to what's happening. It's the third player in the universe's primordial games. We know it's a conduit for information, and also incredibly malleable and adaptable. It's been on our side in all our battles thus far. What if these episodes are its attempt to…help me somehow?"

"We've never gone wrong by trusting your hunches."

She arched an eyebrow. "Never?"

"Close enough to never. You want to talk to Nika about it, don't you?"

"If she's available. Come with me?" She smiled hopefully.

"Of course I will."

While he didn't make a habit of seeking out the woman on his own initiative, he'd gotten comfortable being around Nika. Or as comfortable as he could ever be interacting with someone he both didn't trust and harbored a devastating secret about.

But Alex had remained close friends with her, and he'd meant what he'd said to Nika three years ago when he'd confronted her over her actions on Rasu Prime. He wasn't going to interfere with their relationship. Sometimes, this meant tagging along for a friendly strategy session when he preferred not to. Besides, if the conversation was going to involve chasing answers as to what was causing these disturbances inside Alex's mind, he wanted to be there.

"Thank you." She kissed him with a delicious slowness before continuing. "She's on one of their Adjunct worlds. I've got the location." She disentangled from his arms and took a quick sip from her glass of water on the counter before going to the closet. "Nika says it's chilly and raining there. Jacket?"

"Sure." He caught his jacket when she tossed it to him, then prepped his best 'collegial acquaintance' demeanor. "Ready when you are."

ADJUNCT SHI

ASTERION DOMINION
GENNISI GALAXY

A light drizzle drifted down from a mottled gray sky to moisten tiny sprigs of early spring grass struggling up through the dirt.

They stood in front of a log cabin. By the looks of it, a *real* log cabin. It wasn't large, only a single story, with a wide porch and freshly tilled flower beds flanking the steps. A wooded mountain rose protectively behind it.

Alex spun around and gasped, both hands rising to cover her mouth. *"Bozhe moy...."*

Caleb hurriedly turned to see where her attention had landed. A short path opened up onto a sandy shore stretching out in both directions. The body of water it framed was large enough that he couldn't tell if it was a lake or an ocean. The surface was tranquil, save for the fizz of raindrops and the lapping of gentle waves at the shore, and a hint of mist undulated on the horizon.

It took him several seconds to piece together the reason for Alex's dramatic response. In his defense, he hadn't seen this setting since their time on Portal Prime some twenty years ago.

But once he remembered, the similarity was unmistakable. This structure was a near-exact replica of Mesme's cabin there, complete with the framing of the mountain and a path leading to the body of water. Which meant it must be the other way around, didn't it? The only conclusion to draw was that Mesme's cabin on Portal Prime had been a replica of this one. As was Miaon's cabin on the hidden planet that Alex had told him about.

Caleb blew out a long breath and accepted the need to reevaluate a couple of things.

It wasn't as if the distrust he'd harbored toward Nika ever since they'd eradicated the Rasu together melted away on the spot, for the reasons for his distrust remained as valid as on that day. She'd kept from him the severity of the resistance they would face, and it had cost Alex her life, if blessedly temporarily. Nika hadn't trusted him; worse, she'd denied him the agency of informed choice.

But for the first time since they'd learned the truth about Mesme's past and Nika's possible future, the magnitude of the sacrifice that lay ahead of Nika hit him square in the chest. Until now it had felt amorphous, intangible. But this? This was real.

And what he felt above all was…empathy.

A million years after leaving this place behind, Mesme had still carried a torch of remembrance for this life it—she—had led and loved. *Two* million years after doing so, Miaon still carried the same. This cabin was a symbol and a totem of all that had been lost. An heirloom.

He hadn't doubted Mesme's determination or dedication to the cause in some time. But he hadn't lent much credence to the state of the Kat's heart. How odd, to realize it not only existed, but remained full to bursting.

Alex buried her face in the crook of his neck. "I can't do it. I can't walk in there and lie to her face again. Not this time."

"Then don't," he murmured into her hair. "Tell her the truth."

"But I made a promise. Dammit. Dammit, dammit, dammit!" She stepped back, eyes glistening with unshed tears. "It's not about me—it's about her. If this all goes wrong, she's got a million years ahead of her in which to be heartbroken. I won't make it a million and one."

"Okay." He gently wiped her cheek where a tear had escaped. "Take a minute—"

"Welcome!" Over Alex's shoulder, Caleb saw Dashiel poke his head out through the front door. "Come on inside. The chilly rain took us by surprise. It's supposed to be warmer here by now."

Alex nodded tightly and turned around. "Dashiel. I didn't realize you'd be here, too. I hope we're not interrupting couple's time."

"Not all." He waved them inside. "The truth is, the ceraffin have advanced to the point where Nika can work with ninety-nine percent effectiveness anywhere. And much of the time, I can, too. Nothing substitutes for walking an assembly line in person, but I can be at any of those in seconds if the need arises. So we decided we should be somewhere beautiful and peaceful while we work."

Caleb conjured up a smile as they entered. "I completely understand the sentiment."

Dashiel gestured toward the kitchen. "Hot cider?"

"Sounds lovely."

Dashiel retrieved two stone-fired mugs and poured them each a drink.

"Is this the cabin you and Nika have vacationed at before?" Alex asked as she accepted her drink from him.

Nika had been sitting on the couch, a vacant stare indicating her mind was elsewhere, but now she joined them, sidling up beside Dashiel and wrapping an arm around his waist. "No. We enjoyed the rental cabin so much that Dashiel bought us one of our very own."

Alex peered at Caleb over the rim of the mug of cider, raw emotion flaring in her eyes, and he willed her a bit of his own inner strength.

Then he decided to let the 'collegial acquaintances' barriers and lingering bitterness over Rasu Prime go. There was no place for it any longer.

"I don't blame you," he said. "This is wonderful, even in the rain. Maybe especially in the rain. We're sorry to bring work into it."

Nika sighed. "Work was already here. So, Alex, your spontaneous visits are never boring. What audacious idea do you want help exploring today?"

43

ADJUNCT SHI

Alex finished relaying the details of the latest episode and took a long sip of her cider. "So what do you think?"

"I think that all sounds insane," Nika replied. "But I suppose it isn't any more so than much of what you've done—what every one of us in this room has done—in the last few years."

"Feels like it is, though," Alex remarked dryly. "Mostly for what it might signify…if I can figure out what that is." Talking about the episodes made her uncomfortable and frustrated, in part because she *did* sound insane. But Nika understood more about having one's consciousness intertwined with primordial forces than anyone, and right now she cared more about finding answers than sounding rational.

"In that vein, I had an idea," she continued. "More of a 'stab in the dark,' but I'm desperate. Kyoseil traffics in information, correct? It's a store and transporter of information."

"At its essence, yes," Nika said.

"Assuming I'm not making up these hallucinations in my own head, which I concede is a possibility, then the events they're showing me are coming from somewhere. I'm wondering if kyoseil, as an information arbiter, might be involved in, I don't know, delivering them? So I want to try to trigger an episode deliberately. If I'm able to, I'd like for you to observe me in sidespace. Or watch the kyoseil in the vicinity of me, or one followed by the other. Whatever feels best."

"Absolutely. I'd love to help you solve this mystery. How are you planning to trigger it?"

"By squeezing my eyes shut and concentrating really hard?"

Everyone chuckled. It felt like moral support, which she appreciated.

"Thus far, every incident has displayed some proximity connection to where I was when it came on me. Well, except for the dream, but maybe it was just a dream. I admit, this isn't much to go on, but I have to start somewhere. And the thought occurred to me. What if the four of us met here, at this cabin, and had a conversation last time around?"

Nika studied her curiously. "You've gone out of your way to avoid expressing a strong opinion, but it's obvious you think you're seeing events from the previous cycle."

Alex shrugged weakly. "Or five cycles ago, or a hundred, but yes, the previous one seems the most likely. Look, we know we've done all of this before, at least in broad strokes. We don't have a good sense of how closely events are following the earlier cycles, because Mesme is being a *tupïtsa* and won't tell us. But we do know the four of us were friends before, and we worked together to battle both the Rasu and the Dzhvar.

"Isn't it reasonable to assume Dashiel bought a similar retreat for the two of you in the last cycle, and at some point we gathered at it to talk about the Dzhvar?" Of course, she *knew* he'd done so, and it took every iota of her self-control to keep the deluge of devastating truths off her tongue.

"I feel as if I would have," Dashiel said. "I've been meaning to find us a getaway place for a while."

"So we've got a location, and we've got a meaningful time, and we've got the right people," Alex said. "I'm going to close my eyes, drift in and out of sidespace, and think hard about this conversation and the Dzhvar. About this cabin—" she blinked and tried not to stutter over her words "—the four of us, and recent events."

Nika nodded in approval. "How will we know if it works?"

"You'll know," Caleb remarked, stroking Alex's hand.

"True. I believe 'catatonic' is the operative word." She offered him an affectionate smile. "But I'll be fine, because you're here to catch me."

"Always, baby."

"All right. Nothing to do but do it."

Alex closed her eyes and slipped into sidespace. She'd only been using it when the first episode transpired, but the experience reminded her of sidespace, so it couldn't hurt. Unless it could? She returned to her body.

But now she wasn't able to see anything, while from sidespace she could observe everyone and the setting, so without intending to transition, she was back in sidespace.

She concentrated on the cabin, on the fire in the hearth and the peeks of sunlight starting to break through the clouds outside. But then she was seeing the cabin on Miaon's hidden world and her heart was breaking all over again.

So she replayed their arrival and the distribution of mugs of cider in her mind, then noticed how Dashiel was drawing lazy circles on Nika's palm while Nika watched Alex—

"Do it! I don't care if it's not ready. We're out of time. You have to try."

Dashiel grasped Nika's face in his hands, conveying something unspoken but intensely personal with his eyes, then kissed her on the forehead before exploding toward the workstation in the lab. Once there, he opened a screen and moved his fingers in frenzied, sweeping motions.

Caleb strode up to the device encased in the transparent chamber at the center of the room. The force field at its core dissipated, revealing a tiny, writhing ball of crimson sparks.

Caleb leapt away in surprise. "How did you get diati?"

"How do you think?" Dashiel muttered from the workstation.

"You've been experimenting with it? Are you crazy?"

"We don't have a choice, Caleb," Nika replied. "It's the only thing that can stop the Dzhvar."

"But you can't control it. Not with machines and force fields."

"That would be the 'not ready' part," Dashiel admitted. "But Nika's right. We have to try." He entered a code, and his screen blanked, only to repopulate with a flickering wall of data.

The crimson sparks in the chamber churned into a spinning tornado. A high-pitched whine filled the air.

'Dzhvar will reach the Mirai upper atmosphere in eighty-eight seconds,' an electronic voice intoned.

Abruptly a bubble of crimson surged out of the chamber, expanding through the room and beyond its walls.

Nika rushed to the window in time to see the bubble pass through the surrounding buildings on its way to the horizon. "It's working!"

Dashiel's shoulders sagged in a harsh exhale as his gaze darted around in concern. "Is everyone all right? Did anyone get hurt?"

Caleb sank to his knees beside the chamber. Crimson tendrils whipped around and through him, jerking his muscles violently. They flowed into his irises, then the sclera, until his pupils were a chasm of void at the heart of an inferno. "No!" he shouted.

Dashiel started to approach Caleb—then his screen flashed an angry orange, and he pivoted back to it. "Something's wrong."

"What do you mean?" Nika asked from the window.

"Of course something's wrong!" Caleb exclaimed, the words grinding their way out through clenched teeth. "Wild diati is just that: wild. You can't control it, and it can't control itself."

"Dashiel...." Nika murmured. Perhaps recognizing the warning in her voice, he hurried over to her side.

Outside the window, thunderclouds roiled across the landscape, sending blood-red lightning bolts scorching to the ground. Building after building crumbled in their wake.

Dashiel ran to the workstation and entered a command. The device at the center of the room shut down, and in the absence of the high-pitched whine, a terrible silence engulfed the space. Outside, the downtown cityscape fell away like dominos.

"Caleb, is there anything you can do?" Nika asked in a pinched voice.

Caleb's features contorted in frustration. "No. This diati doesn't answer to me. It doesn't answer to anyone."

All the color drained from Nika's face, leaving anger and despair to war across her features. "Dashiel, we have to go. If the diati doesn't destroy this building soon, the Dzhvar will."

"I know." Still he continued to enter command after command into his workstation, to no effect.

Caleb struggled to his feet as crimson particles bled out of his pores. "Take us to Akeso."

"We need to get to Synra, but I'll drop you off there first." Nika opened a wormhole, then went over and grabbed Dashiel by the arm. "Now, darling."

Through the wormhole, a driving hailstorm raged on Akeso, sending rain and loose tree leaves pouring into the lab. The window glass shattered, and a tremendous roar accompanied the collapse of a building less than a block away.

Florid tears streaked down Caleb's cheeks as he stumbled through the wormhole and fell to his knees amid the storm on the other side—

Alex gasped in a frantic breath, certain she hadn't breathed for some minutes. She gradually became aware of Caleb's hands grasping her shoulders, steady and sure, and the warmth of his body behind her. She blinked repeatedly, overcome by a sensation that went far beyond dizziness into a sort of metaphysical vertigo. As if she were unmoored in time and space. Unmoored from any universe at all….

"Are you okay?" Caleb asked, his voice a worried whisper.

His touch and his voice reeled her back in, a thread attaching her once more to this reality.

She cleared her throat; it felt raspy, as if she'd been shouting. But she hadn't been shouting in the vision, though everyone else had; she hadn't been there at all. How was she not present for something so momentous and horrific?

"Alex?"

Her heart pounded savagely in her chest; she had to calm down. It wasn't real. Or it wasn't real *now*. It wasn't real here. Here was warm and dry and safe. Here had a cozy fire and hot cider. She'd process the terrifying vision later; the important thing was that she'd provoked one, though in the aftermath she deeply wished she hadn't.

Let me help, Valkyrie murmured in her mind.

Thank you. Almost instantly, Valkyrie's ministrations began to soothe her frayed consciousness.

She cleared her throat again. "I'm okay. It worked."

"And 'catatonic' was a too-apt descriptor." Nika glanced meaningfully at Caleb, but Alex couldn't see his expression. "What did you see?"

She sucked in another deep but somewhat calmer breath as Valkyrie continued to work to slow her heart rate and dilute the adrenaline coursing through her veins. "Nika, why don't you tell me what you saw first?"

"A question: are you carrying your Reor slab with you?"

"Um...." She patted her pants pocket. "No. I often carry it around with me, but I changed clothes not long before we came here and forgot to grab it." She stared at Nika. "So you did detect something."

"While you were...gone, a surge of kyoseil waves swept in to swirl through you."

"Swept in from where?"

"That's the thing. I followed them to their terminus—or maybe their origin. It was the Elakrin stellar system."

What? "One of those bowed waves that formed around the system when the bubble space popped?"

Nika shook her head. "No. Or not exactly. This stream traveled directly from you to the Elakrin system. It did bisect one of the bow waves, but it didn't interlink into it. And it gets stranger."

"How could anything about this possibly get stranger? Tell me."

"The thread originating from you stopped cold about 1.3 AU from Elakrin's sun, a little inside the bow waves. That's very unusual. Unless they lead to a physical deposit, I can't say as I've ever seen one terminate so dramatically."

1.3 AU was the radius of the pocket universe before it dissolved. "The scab," Alex whispered.

"The place where you think the Dzhvar escaped from wherever they've been trapped?" Nika asked. "What does it have to do with kyoseil?"

"I don't know. In fact, I'm once again questioning everything I thought I did understand. Ugh, we have one more piece of the puzzle, but no answers. Only more questions." Alex frowned. "Is the kyoseil stream gone now?"

Nika closed her eyes for several seconds. "Not gone, but it's much fainter. It was as if it swelled in intensity while you were…doing whatever it was you were doing, and now it's settled back down."

"But kyoseil is still linking me to the Elakrin system?"

"A little bit, yes. I'm sorry I didn't notice it before, but it never occurred to me to look."

Alex's gaze dropped to her hands as endless questions looped through her mind. Everything kept coming back to that scab, and these episodes had kicked off when she'd decided to poke at it on an elemental level. But what did the Piega Strai and the Dzhvar and kyoseil and random visions and the texture of the manifold have to do with one another?

"Alex?" Nika asked gently. "You never told us what it was you saw."

She exhaled slowly and eased deeper into the couch cushion. Caleb scooted close to her, and she rested her head on his shoulder. This was going to be difficult.

44

MIRAI

Dashiel strode into the Conceptual Research central atrium, then hesitated, uncertain of his destination. Discrete labs branched off in every direction, grouped by subject matter: materials projects, biological and biosynth research, pure and applied physics, weapons research, kyoseil refinement, cognitive improvements, and so on.

Despite their disparate topics, though, at this point fully a third of the projects related in some way to the Dzhvar.

During the Rasu War, he'd needed to transform himself into a wartime industrialist. In the run-up to this war, he found himself becoming more akin to a mad scientist. Toying with life, death and the fabric of reality upon which they played out in a desperate bid to preserve existence.

He exhaled into his hands and went into the Weave lab, but again stopped a few steps inside to stare at the chambers and busy researchers, then the ceraff hub in the corner.

Was this entire project a mistake? Instead of creating an instrument of salvation, was he engineering his people's destruction?

He tried to tell himself that Alex's vision didn't mean anything. Even she insisted it might not mean anything, might be nothing more than her own hyperactive mind spinning out worst-case scenarios in vivid color and sound. But the problem wasn't so much the vision as it was Caleb's response to it.

The man understood *diati* all too well, and he'd agreed vehemently with his vision-version that *diati* in concentrated form was a highly destructive force when not directed by a skilled wielder. Had a tragic prior experience made Caleb particularly sensitive to this danger? Without a doubt. But Corradeo Praesidis also admitted that when *diati* first joined with him, it had wreaked significant havoc and destruction until he'd learned to control it.

But they weren't creating *diati* here in the Weave lab, not in any real way. If they were creating anything at all—something very much in doubt—it was tangible walls able to contain an entity capable of traversing any dimension. As of today, all they had to show for their efforts was the world's most advanced faraday cage. A device worthy of winning the Mishima Prize in any normal circumstance, but barely a first step toward their ultimate goal.

He didn't intend for the Weave to be 'alive' in any measurable sense, or to have any will of its own. Programming *would* control it. It was no different from issuing commands to a force field to activate, expand or contract.

Yet a doomsaying voice whispered in the back of his mind how such powerful forces couldn't always be controlled and if he didn't rein in his hubris—

"Hey." Nika touched his arm.

He jerked in surprise, but quickly recovered and offered her a weak, closed-mouth smile. "Sorry. I didn't realize you came along behind me."

"I almost didn't. But I thought you might want to talk about what happened with Alex." Her eyes flicked across the lab. "About the Weave project, and what to do about it."

"I can't shut it down just because Alex hallucinated a scene in which some hypothetical later stage of the project bearing little resemblance to what we're doing here escaped and went homicidal."

"I know. I'm not suggesting you should. But you're obviously troubled by what you heard." A corner of her lips quirked up. "This is me being here for you. Let me be a sounding board."

He sighed heavily as he took her hand in his and guided her into an empty conference room between two of the labs. He pulled a chair away from the table and sat, then scooted it to where he faced her, their knees touching.

"Will Mesme share whether we've had any success with a Weave in past cycles?"

She shook her head. "It will not."

"And it still won't say whether *diati* ever returns?"

"No."

"Then what good is the Kat? What good is knowing we've failed a dozen or a hundred times, if it won't tell us how or why?"

"Dashiel."

"No, I'm serious." He understood how Mesme had helped Nika on multiple occasions. Had arguably saved her life and definitely saved her sanity. But her indulgence of the Kat was reaching absurd levels at this point. He needed information. If this project never had a chance of working—or worse, if it was doomed to end in self-inflicted destruction on an epic scale—he had numerous other projects he should be spending these credits and his time on. But if it *could* work, it stood to protect countless innocent people and worlds, and he needed to know that, too.

Nika dropped her head against the chair and stared at the ceiling. "Mesme won't share what happened before because it believes we have to follow our instincts. Something new is required if we hope to win, and the only way to discover something new is to…" she gestured at the wall "…do all of this. Research. Innovate. Try different approaches until we find a tool that works. Maybe we invented something like a Weave last time and it didn't work, but maybe you'll push it one step further now, and this will make the difference."

"Or maybe I'll blow up the planet before the Dzhvar can. Stars, Nika! What if I did? What if I do? What if I grow so obsessed, so deranged in my delusional belief I can control the uncontrollable, that I ignore every safety protocol I've ever learned and preached, and in doing so obliterate our home?"

She leapt up to take his hands in hers, then urged him to stand and drew him into her arms. Her lips hovered at his ear, her hair tickling his cheek. "You won't. Especially since you now believe there's some chance of such an outcome. I expect you'll become even more zealous about those safety protocols. Also, you're one of the least deranged people I've ever met."

She'd never know it, but during the five years he'd thought her gone forever, his mental health had balanced on a tightrope strung above a chasm of madness. Once or twice, he was convinced he'd fallen into the shadowy depths, only to weakly claw his way back out and find a new foothold.

His musings about becoming a mad scientist took on a darker connotation now. But he could use this, *would* use this. It would serve as the warning he carried with him always, the catch staying his hand at the fateful moment, should it one day arrive.

"Never say never." He kissed her softly. "This coming battle? It's going to drive us all insane if we're not careful."

45

THE PRESIDIO

I am pleased to report that we were able to stop a Ch'mshak attack in progress. We killed all of the attackers except one, whom we captured and are interrogating.

Malcolm pushed the fleet distribution analysis he'd been reviewing to the side at Casmir's pulse. Finally, some good news. He sent the man a holocomm request, and a few seconds later a visual materialized above his desk.

"Any actionable intel out of the interrogation?" he asked.

"None so far. The prisoner became so belligerent the officers had to tranquilize him with enough sedative to null out twenty Anadens." Casmir grimaced. "They'll try again once the sedatives start wearing off, but I don't anticipate extracting any useful information. Ch'mshak don't respond to either incentives or punishments the way normal, civilized people do."

It was too much to hope for that they'd obtain all the answers as to how the Ch'mshak were getting offworld and who was supplying the ships so…not easily, but at least somewhat promptly. "Where was the attack? Casualties?"

"A commercial station in LMC." Casmir rattled off the numbers. "Three hundred forty-six Anadens, fifty-two Novoloume, twelve Khokteh and sixteen Naraida casualties, as well as eight Machim soldiers during our response."

"I suppose it could've been worse."

"It has been up until now."

Grim but true words. "How did they get on the station? The new security measures should have kept them on the other side of the airlock."

"Incompetence on the part of the security staff there. I'm handling it."

Malcolm leaned back in his chair and thought for a moment. "The fact they've moved into LMC means they successfully traversed one of the intergalactic gateways. It might be time to consider instituting a security scan of all vessels passing through the gateways. I'm hesitant to impose such a draconian measure, but if it means we stop a ship full of Ch'mshak while they remain in space and can't hurt anyone, it will be worth it."

"I'm in favor of it, but it sounds like a decision for the commandant."

"Agreed. We'll bring it up at the next briefing."

Once the holocomm ended, Malcolm closed his eyes and said a silent prayer for the twenty-eight Khokteh and Naraida souls lost forever in the murderous rampage. One death was too many, but it genuinely could've been worse. The attacks had caught them unawares and flatfooted, but they were starting to get on top of the problem now. Running the loose Ch'mshak to ground while protecting every settlement on every world and preventing more Ch'mshak from evading the blockade was a gargantuan task, but the Concord militaries fielded over fifty-five million ships for a reason. He just hoped no more people died before they were able to complete the work—

The Dzhvar detection alert rang in his eVi and on his office system, and he was instantly on his feet and racing out the door.

AFS DENALI

The location of the incursion, in the Antlia Wall near the Centaurus Cluster, was distressingly close to the ever-expanding borders of Concord space.

Malcolm understood probability distribution as well as any marine. In other words, just well enough to recognize how in a battlespace as large as Amaranthe, Concord could escape a direct hit for another decade, or the next five attacks could occur in the Milky Way, and both outcomes qualified as randomness. But this one was close to home, and it provoked a sense of foreboding he was unable to shake.

Looking on the positive side, the Detection Network was robust here, and they'd received almost instantaneous notice of the Dzhvar's arrival. The enemy had also emerged in the far reaches of a spacious stellar system, which meant this encounter might last for a reasonable length of time. Time enough to try a variety of approaches. He didn't dare count on one of them actually working, but he'd hope for it nonetheless.

Three tests were at the top of the list today.

Commandant Solovy (CAF Aurora)(Command Channel): "Commander Xing, make your first Ymyrath Field strike five megameters in front of the leading edge of the Dzhvar. Move to deliver a second strike from its flank, then retreat to a safe distance."

Command Xing (CAF Intrepid)(Command Channel): "Moving into position now."

During their war against the Rasu, the Ourankeli had designed a souped-up neutron particle accelerator to counter the Rasu's ability to repair and reform themselves. The weapon hadn't saved the Ourankeli, but this was due more to poor military strategy on their part than any failure of the weapon, since it *did* render Rasu inert. As near to dead as anything short of a unique Akeso-kyoseil designed poison could inflict.

The Ymyrath Field, which was what Concord had dubbed their improved version of the Ourankeli's weapon, was enormously destructive to both structures and organic life. Every military vessel's shielding had needed to be modified to keep the weapon's corrosive particles at bay for a time, so they didn't need to flee the battlefield immediately upon using the device. But every time they fired it, they were rendering an entire stellar system inhospitable to life for centuries; not an action to be taken lightly. Thankfully, initial scans indicated nothing sentient lived in this one.

As weapons went, the Ymyrath Field was not sexy. Its high-powered blasts of specialized 4-neutron particles created no visible evidence of transmission. When they'd deployed it against the Rasu, the only sign of its successful firing was the subsequent disabling of the Rasu vessels. He expected here, the evidence would be a slowing or even cessation of the Dzhvar's unremitting advance across space.

But that didn't happen. Scans didn't pick up so much as a minute reduction in speed or a dimple in the intimidating, writhing wall of whatever the Dzhvar were. Alex's mutterings about 'negative energy analogue' notwithstanding, they still didn't have a satisfactory answer to the question.

Commandant Solovy (CAF Aurora)(Command Channel): "Acknowledging negative impact on the enemy by the Ymyrath Field. A Rift Bubble will be activated on the gas giant planet at the marked coordinates in thirty-four seconds."

Malcolm checked the location of the planet in relation to the Dzhvar, not that he doubted Miriam's tactical plan. But she'd long preached redundancy in all matters, and he'd taken the lesson to heart.

They'd gotten lucky, and the planet lay directly in the enemy's path. Or maybe the Dzhvar had adopted a course designed to sweep through the planet.

Commandant Solovy (CAF Aurora)(Command Channel): "Commander Palmer, your team may launch the cage when ready."

Commander Palmer (ADV Dauntless II)(Command Channel): "Acknowledged. ETA to deployment is eight seconds."

Yet another device they didn't expect to work, but had to try. Dominion Conceptual Research had built a sort of faraday cage on steroids using exotic particles and other materials that Malcolm absolutely did *not* understand. They claimed it would capture and hold gamma rays, which made it the strongest faraday cage in existence, and also said little about whether it would capture and hold Dzhvar.

He watched on a monitoring screen as the cage was launched into the Dzhvar wave. They weren't going to know for certain until after the wave had passed whether anything of the device remained, and if so, whether it held any Dzhvar. And in the meantime, the enemy neared the gas giant.

The Rift Bubble extended for a diameter of over one-hundred-forty megameters, and as the leading edge of the Dzhvar impacted the barrier, it was like a prism scattering and refracting the orange-red band of the color spectrum out into space.

A sensor situated at the location half an AU away where the Rift Bubble was set to deposit anything that crossed its path lit up to report an influx of Dzhvar. Had it worked? A spark of genuine hope kindled to life in his chest.

The Dzhvar continued crashing into the barrier, creating a tremendous light show as they encircled the planet. Colors shifted, sparks ignited and flares shot out in every direction; clearly *something* was happening where the Dzhvar collided with the Rift Bubble. They'd also dropped multiple sensors inside the barrier, and the sensor cams showed a sky aflame, but only at a distance.

As Malcolm watched the seconds tick by, it felt as if the entire fleet held its breath.

Sixty-eight seconds after the initial impact, an alarm sounded from one of the sensors. A streak of hellfire shot across the cam— then the signal went dead.

Decades of training and warfare kept his disappointment from manifesting in any visible way, but in his thoughts he growled in frustration. How were they getting in? The Dzhvar continued to be flung in all directions across the arc of the barrier, but now they also appeared well inside it, and in increasing numbers.

Commandant Solovy (CAF Aurora)(Command Channel): "Sensors indicate the Dzhvar have begun circumventing the Rift Bubble to reach its interior. We'll continue with the additional tests planned for this encounter."

Malcolm had never understood dimensional subversion, no matter how slowly and patiently Mia had tried to explain it to him. It occurred to him that today's encounter was turning into a laundry list of hyper-advanced weapons and defenses he didn't comprehend.

Now, he'd never say he longed for the day when their enemies were flesh and blood creatures he could shoot, stab or blow up. They had these manner of enemies on the loose in the form of Ch'mshak this very day, and he rued every death they'd inflicted. He was doing everything in his power to end the threat they represented and ensure it didn't return. But his frustration today was amplified by the fact he lacked the ability to define *why* their tools weren't working, never mind the ability to formulate an approach that would work. He felt impotent in a way he rarely did when on the battlefield.

Nonetheless, he understood enough to recognize what this development meant. The Dzhvar could be deflected for a time, but when they were able to access any dimension, they could not be locked out.

46

CONCORD HQ

COMMAND

On returning to her office, Miriam went straight to the tea service in the corner. She poured a steaming cup of double bergamot earl gray tea and took it to her desk.

The after-action meeting to assess the Dzhvar encounter in the Antlia Wall had wrapped up ten minutes earlier. Given their brief success with the Rift Bubble, Miriam was now putting every resource to bear on developing a more robust version, one that could buy them not minutes, but hours.

Mr. Ridani's faraday cage had physically survived the encounter, but in a degraded state that was continuing to worsen over time. The cage had not succeeded in capturing any Dzhvar. In fairness to him, he'd warned her this would be the likely outcome, as the technology was still in the early stages of development.

So many more frustrations, tempered by one tiny glimmer of encouragement. And now she had to pivot her focus to the other end of the spectrum.

A long history in logistics—decades in the field before she'd taken up the mantle of protector of trillions of souls—meant Miriam knew how to multitask crises. How to track multiple concurrent firefighting efforts and manage the priorities of every facet of military operations based on their individual requirements, while keeping the regular and ordinary business of the armed forces functioning.

All of this was nothing new. Its familiarity didn't make the details of executing on it any easier, of course. But at least for one of the crises dominating her board, she enjoyed a clear path set out before her—poor choice of mental words, as nothing about any of these crises was enjoyable. Rather, she had in her toolset a simple and direct way to clear the board of one nasty complication. All she had to do was press the trigger on it.

She managed two sips of her tea before Malcolm and Casmir arrived for their meeting. She welcomed them in, then clasped her hands atop her desk. "Tell me where we are with the Ch'mshak."

Malcolm went first. "The investigation into the purchases of the ships the Ch'mshak are using is running into repeated dead ends. Whoever is behind the purchases, they are an expert at creating dummy corporations, then dissolving the corporations as soon as they're no longer needed."

"And we're unable to track down these companies' owners or executives? Those details should be on file for any registered entity."

Malcolm shook his head. "Fake identities all. Good ones, too. The relevant authorities are pressuring all private spacecraft retailers to institute additional screening requirements for purchases, but the businesses are running to the courts crying 'free enterprise' and 'government overreach' in response."

Miriam respected the right to free enterprise as much as any reasonable person, but innocent lives were at stake here. Nonetheless, the question of whether said overreach was legal or not was up to the courts now, not her or Malcolm. "Understood. Casmir, what's the latest on their incursions?"

"No thread linking the locations attacked has emerged, nor has any motive for targeting a given location. The best explanation remains simple Ch'mshak aggression. The good news is, the tightened security measures on virtually every space station appear to be putting a stop to those incursions. We did have one station hit in the last day, but it was a security blunder that shouldn't be repeated. And a Machim unit was able to bring the attack to an early end while capturing one of the Ch'mshak assailants."

"Oh? This is good news."

"The prisoner isn't talking so far. But they and their former companions won't be hurting anyone else." Casmir frowned. "The rest of the news isn't so good. With their space station incursions thwarted, the Ch'mshak have begun landing on planets instead. They've attacked eight smaller settlements on five planets. And preventing a ship from landing on a planet is far, far more difficult than keeping one off a space station. The raiding parties have also spread beyond the Milky Way, into LMC."

Casmir glanced uneasily at Malcolm, and Malcolm leaned forward in his chair. "We want to institute security screenings at the gateways."

"That will bring commercial traffic grinding to a halt," Miriam replied. "The complaint filings will crash Command's servers."

"We'll do everything we can to make the scans quick and easy. We only need to know whether there are Ch'mshak onboard a vessel."

She waved a hand in their direction. "Do it. What about the blockade?"

Casmir grunted in displeasure. "If we make it any more comprehensive, the ships will start bumping into each other. But even the tightest formations still leave gaps."

"Director Reynolds hasn't been able to give us anything to help us detect Veil-stealthed ships," Malcolm offered. "He says that's the whole point of Veiltech."

"So it is. And we face the real possibility that, when met by an impenetrable blockade, whoever is supplying the ships to the Ch'mshak will escalate by switching to vessels equipped with Caeles Prisms."

"Why don't we place a quantum block on the planet?" Malcolm asked. "That would thwart virtually any form of transportation."

"It would, and I'm seriously considering it," Miriam said. "But if we do so, we lose any opportunity to identify the perpetrators of this travesty."

"No." Casmir shook his head vehemently. "We need to find them and bring them to justice."

"That is my intention. So no quantum block for the moment. Is there anything else I need to be made aware of?"

Malcolm checked with Casmir, then shook his head. "This is where we are for today."

As she'd expected, the conversation had wound its way around to her decision point. But listening to their reports had allowed her to sit with the decision for several minutes before voicing it, and in voicing it, committing to her chosen path.

"We have to cut off the supply of additional Ch'mshak. Once we do so, we will in time be able to track down all those who have escaped so far and eliminate them. I fear too many will lose their lives in the interim, but you both are obviously doing everything you can to minimize the damage."

"At least they are focusing on Anaden worlds for the most part," Casmir said.

"Yes, but I prefer not to see individuals suffer agonizing pain and slow deaths whenever possible."

"Of course." Casmir had the temerity to look chastened. He was not a cruel man, but empathy did not rank high on the list of prized genetic traits for the Machim Dynasty.

A swirl of lights manifested in front of the viewport, and Miriam turned her attention toward them. "Praetor Lakhes?"

I received your summons. You require something?

Ah, as loquacious as ever. "In point of fact, yes. I require an Echo Rift device."

Malcolm opened his mouth to comment...then nodded instead. She hadn't expected him to argue with the decision. She'd been the holdup here.

May I inquire as to why?

"To deal with the Ch'mshak once and for all. I should have deployed an Echo Rift around their world as soon as I learned such a device existed, back when we used the first one to isolate the Savrakaths. But I never imagined the Ch'mshak might break free of the surface. Never imagined someone would be so foolish as to unleash them upon us anew. A failure of imagination on my part, I suppose. Nonetheless, I can rectify this failing now."

I see. It is a reasonable course of action. Due to their complex and specialized nature, we do not currently have any such devices prepared. It will take some time to construct one of sufficient size and power to enclose a planet.

"I understand. Please begin as soon as you can."

I only just received your request for an interlocking, potentially fractalized rift device. Which request do you wish for me to prioritize?

Miriam arched an eyebrow. "You can create entire universes. Can't you do both at once?"

Without difficulty. However, if we proceed on the projects simultaneously, each one will take slightly longer to complete.

"Perhaps I need to ask the Asterions to handle the 'fractalized' rift device, as you put it. Their Kireme Boundaries appear to have advanced to the point where they function as robustly as a Rift Bubble at scale."

That won't be necessary. I will assign sufficient resources to accomplish both projects with due speed.

Nothing like a little friendly competition to spur things along. It did amuse her a touch how prideful the Kats could be. Heaven forbid that some lowly organics—or semi-organics—be able to match their vaunted dimensional technology.

"Thank you, Praetor."

I will inform you when these devices are nearing completion. Do you require anything else?

"Not at this time."

The lights swept through the viewport and departed.

She considered her guests across the desk. "Do either of you disagree with this course of action?"

"No." Malcolm said instantly. "It's a mercy, honestly. We could do far worse to them."

"I would be fine with doing worse," Casmir said. "The Ch'mshak have proved themselves unworthy of our mercy. But this action is in keeping with Concord's principle of inflicting the minimum harm necessary to achieve an objective."

It was possible she'd been too hard on him in her private thoughts earlier. Whatever his natural instincts may be, Casmir both understood *and* effectuated the spirit of Concord. "Yes, it is. Echo Rifting the Ch'mshak isn't a perfect solution, but it's the best one we have. If we haven't located the perpetrators by the time the Echo Rift is ready, I'll make the only safe choice and shut off all access to the planet."

47

—————

SCHOLITE

"Thank you for listening to my concerns, Ms. Piras, and for allaying them." Charlo ela-Erevna bent over at the waist in some sort of awkward bow. "Please give my regards to Mr. Nikto."

"I'll be sure to do so." Olivia motioned to Jacobson, and the enforcer ushered the man out of the office and on his way.

She expected this to be the last of the in-person reassurances she'd need to provide to Arnal Nikto's most senior deputies. The setting of Nikto's intimidating office at his extravagant estate, coupled with her absolute certitude as to her authority, cowed even those who oversaw millions of credits-worth of product across multiple worlds.

The majority of Nikto's organization had folded meekly to her takeover. A few of his lieutenants asked questions, but didn't press too hard when she provided surface-level answers. She possessed the passcodes and the right names and instructions, and she gave them orders in a manner that brokered no argument. Nikto had ruled with a harsh fist and the arrogance of entitlement, as those occupying the upper ranks of a caste-based society often did, and most people who'd been granted direct contact with him lived in a steady state of low-grade fear. She was happy to let this state continue.

Compliance wasn't total across the organization, however. A network of distributors on Brizo had balked, proclaiming they would defect to a rival cartel. She'd sent two assassins in to elimi-nate every last rebellious distributor, then delivered offers to the next in line to take over the territories the deceased had controlled. The threat if they refused needn't be stated. None refused.

Then there was the *ferusom* operation on Ficenti. A bit of investigation revealed Nikto had himself stolen it from a smaller group less than a decade earlier, and it seemed he'd never fully earned the loyalty of the operation's manager. Now they were refusing yet another new boss.

She could order a hit on the manager easily enough. But it was distinctly possible he did inspire loyalty in his subordinates, in which case she'd still be left with recalcitrant employees. She didn't have the time or inclination to fight such a battle. Better to clear the table and start fresh.

S&L

FICENTI

As before, Olivia kept a close eye on the Ch'mshak squad while they worked, ensuring they didn't run off in a gorging of blood fever. The success of her strategy to eliminate enemies and subdue rebellious elements relied on her keeping absolute control of these ravenous beasts, and this was no easy task.

She'd been following the news broadcasts closely enough to recognize they were making busy use of the ships she'd been awarding them. The reports never said 'Ch'mshak massacre,' as Concord was surely trying to keep the news that the Ch'mshak had sprung their cage under wraps, but the signs were unmistakable in the scale of the butchery and the body counts.

For all their gleeful violence, though, the Ch'mshak weren't mindless savages. T'worz exercised a high degree of discipline over his warriors, and he had them returning home again and again to ferry shiploads full of Ch'mshak offworld at a steady clip. There were likely several hundred roaming free now, if not approaching a thousand.

She didn't particularly care. If they caused enough havoc that Concord, the Advocacy and AEGIS law enforcement found their hands full trying to quell it, all the better for her. Especially since the military was increasingly distracted by the encroaching shadow of the Dzhvar.

She'd already lived through one allegedly civilization-ending alien invasion, and humanity had survived two more while she'd been absent, so she'd worry about the Dzhvar when they showed up at the front door of one of her factories.

When the *ferusom* facility was cleaned out down to the last worker, she shepherded the Ch'mshak wrecking crew through the wormhole and signaled for the delivery of another ship. T'worz hassled her for more and larger vessels; she refused, turning her back on him and leaving to return home to Domor.

Once there, she issued the order to move replacement bot workers into the factory, much as she'd done on Ficenti's moon. Hopefully this would be the end of the trouble from Nikto's organization.

Today's unpleasantness handled, Olivia sat at her desk and opened the report detailing the integration of the snoRNA chain scaffold transformers into her new bioweapons lab. But instead of reading through it, she let her mind finally drift to the thorny issue she'd been avoiding all day.

Padron Lanael.

The man was insultingly pushy and far too self-assured for anyone who dared to enter her orbit. Regenesis was partly to blame, of course, and it was something she'd needed to adjust for when she'd set up operations on Anaden worlds. People who couldn't die had much less to fear than those who could.

But even allowing for this, Lanael was overflowing with confidence, in his charm as much as his skills. And he did have skills. He was proving to be useful, and she foresaw how he might develop into a valuable contact if managed correctly.

Trouble was, he didn't seem interested in being managed. She should kill him for his audacity, as men like him were rarely worth the trouble they caused.

But she had to admit, his brazen lack of shame and refusal to display respect, never mind fear, excited her. He reminded her of Aiden Trieneri in this aspect. No small part of their relationship had rested on the fact that Aiden was one of the few people she couldn't control, and he *knew* it. Lanael made no bones about what he wanted. He didn't kiss her feet or apologize for affronts that would end a lesser man.

He represented a risk. His reputation was thin, though he'd jumped in front of this flaw by claiming he went by different names depending on the business he trafficked in. He'd come through for her several times now, so he was legitimately connected into multiple black-market networks. But what else he was, she hadn't yet determined.

She confessed she was curious whether the rumors of Idoni sexual prowess held any truth. She'd sought out a conquest shortly after moving to Domor, merely to confirm all the parts of this lab-grown body functioned correctly. But back then she hadn't known enough about Anaden society to select an Idoni as her partner, and the experience with a Diaplas *asi* had proved to be rather lackluster.

And now here an Idoni was, promising to deliver her bliss for his own pleasure.

Ah, well. She owned an entire factory dedicated to producing *apomono*; she could always kill him after, couldn't she?

48

CONCORD HQ
CINT

"Richard, my dearest friend, why am I sitting here doing financial analysis? I distinctly remember this being my one request when I agreed to consult with CINT on occasion: no financial analysis."

"You also requested no aliens, yet here you are," Richard remarked wryly.

"Yet here I am." Graham stretched his arms over his head and squeezed his eyes shut.

"Scouring the minutiae of bank records worked in Vilane's case. It was a factor in bringing Montegreu to justice the first time."

"I know, I know," Graham conceded. "This is what the craftiest crime bosses do. They erect a maze of companies and affiliates and investment vehicles that loop around on one another, and somehow all the money funnels back to them. And now we've got impenetrable alien business and banking rules mucking up the works."

Graham stood and went to get more coffee. "I think they've beaten us. All the criminals with at least two brains cells have. We may as well give up."

"Oh, come on. You're not going to back down from a little challenge, are you?"

"I'm considering it. These Anaden corporate structures are the most ass-backwards mess of spaghetti I've ever seen."

"True." Richard replied. "Honestly, I believe Eren is going to be our key to bringing Montegreu down...again. But I'm not satisfied with stopping her. I want to find out how she exists at all, so I can ensure she won't find a way to return to life one more time. I hate to think we missed something three years ago, but the fact is, we missed something. We must have. Some branch of Vilane's enterprise. Some bank account or storage facility or hideout."

"You know what frightens me?"

"Other than the supply of single-malt scotch and high-priced escorts on Seneca running dry?"

Graham clutched his chest and collapsed in his chair. "Ouch. You wound me. Also, yes. If Olivia Montegreu is back, who's to say Enzio Vilane isn't back as well?"

Inwardly, Richard shuddered. He gave the possibility due thought, then shook his head. "I feel as if we'd know. Unlike his mother, he was far too arrogant to stick to the shadows. He didn't have the discipline required to keep from flaunting his cleverness."

"What if he's not in charge any longer? She could have him on a short leash."

"Damn, Graham, do you want to give me nightmares?"

"If I have to be there, so do you."

Richard received an unexpected request for entry at the conference room door, and he held up a hand. "Take a break and drink your coffee. We have a guest."

He signaled for the door to open. "Come on in."

Marlee Marano immediately came over and leaned in to give him a hug. "Hi, Uncle Richard. It feels like it's been forever since I last saw you."

"David's birthday bash, I think. I hear you've been busy since then."

"A little." She turned and nodded to Graham. "Director Delavasi, it's good to see you again."

The confusion on the man's face lasted only a beat, until his eVi matched the face in the vast databases he maintained access to. "Marlee Marano? No way do you remember me. The last time *I* saw you, you stood this high." Graham held out a hand at table-height.

"It's true, I don't remember. But once I got older, I peppered my mom and Caleb with endless questions about everything that happened during the Metigen War. I researched all the players involved, too. You were definitely one of those. In fact, that's how you and Uncle Richard met, isn't it?"

"It is indeed. Nice detective work. Which is one reason why you're an important ambassador now, I imagine."

"Maybe one reason." She grinned impishly while leaning against the wall by the door. "Anyway, forgive me for barging in on your meeting. I know you're both working around the clock to try to ensnare Olivia Montegreu 3.0, but I want—"

"How do you know that?" Richard asked.

"Oh. Was I not supposed to know?"

"Do I need to go looking for another listener routine in the CINT system?"

"Nah. You've got much more important things to do—and about those important things. I have an idea of how I can help you find out who's giving ships to the Ch'mshak."

Richard was interested enough that he didn't press her further on how she knew what he and Graham were up to, but he did send Will a quick message asking him to sweep the system for listeners. "Really? We've got Prevos watching the larger settlements, but there are over a hundred distinct Ch'mshak tribes and a thousand villages. And the ship registrations are thus far a dead end."

"I'm not surprised." She pulled out a chair, sat down and propped her elbows on the table. "So here's my idea. You know who the Belascocians are?"

"It's my job to be informed about every new species to enter Concord's orbit. Also, David still hasn't stopped talking about your, ah, 'adventure' with them."

"I think he was jealous."

"I think he was terrified."

Her gaze dropped for a beat. "That, too."

Graham raised a hand. "Who are the Belascocians? Twenty second download."

"A sub-superluminal-capable species way over in the Medusa Merger. A rebel group of theirs kidnapped Marlee here, so she helped the group overthrow a shadow government and expose a conspiracy to conceal and imprison genetic mutants among them who can read minds."

Marlee shrugged. "As one does."

Graham rolled his eyes at the ceiling. "Aliens...."

Richard sighed and refocused on Marlee. "So what about them?"

"Did you hear how they can sense quantum fluctuations?"

"I did. I understand Special Projects is itching to get one of them under a microscope and study how they do it."

"If Devon Reynolds tries to do any such thing, I will throttle him. Besides, they're going to let us poke around a bit in due time, assuming we continue to be nice to them. Now, I was able to see firsthand how powerful this ability can be. They don't just sense the fluctuations. They can zero in on them directionally. It's basically the entirety of the reason why I got trapped on Belarria. If they amplify their senses with this device they have, they can pinpoint the location where the fluctuation occurred within a few dozen meters.

"I know Aunt Miriam is planning to Echo Rift the Ch'mshak in the coming days. But before the Echo Rift is ready, I thought my Belascocian friend, Galean, and I could camp out on Mshak for a spell. When anything happens with a ship, whether it's a wormhole, or stealth, or simply turning one on—because these ships are all run by quantum programming—he'll be able to detect it."

Richard started to ask how she already knew about the Echo Rift, but decided it wasn't worth it. The woman knew absolutely everything to transpire on HQ, and she probably didn't need to deploy an army of listeners to accomplish it. "Even if the ship is halfway across the planet?"

"No, there is a distance limit on the ability. But it's a fairly long distance, and we'll centrally locate near the greatest concentration of settlements. Because here's the thing: the Ch'mshak don't have quantum tech. The whole planet will be silent as a graveyard, so a single flare of quantum activity will shine like a beacon. As soon as Galean detects something, I'll use sidespace to zero in on the location, then comm you, or whomever you want me to interface with, and the professionals can swoop in."

"Marlee, nowhere in Concord space is more dangerous than the Ch'mshak homeworld. I won't send you there."

"We'll wear Veils. And we'll stay far away from any of the locals. And if there's the slightest hint of danger, we'll wormhole out. It'll only take a few seconds."

Richard hesitated. It wasn't a bad plan, all things considered. And they were having zero luck pinpointing the source of the ships so far. But if he allowed her to do this, David would never speak to him again. He'd never put someone who wasn't a highly trained military or intelligence operative in such a position in any event. It wasn't worth the risk.

"I'm sorry, Marlee. Brilliant idea on your part, but I can't authorize it."

She folded her hands in her lap and stared down at them. "But you can't prohibit it, either."

"Marlee."

The next second, she animated in a burst of exuberant energy. "Okay, look. I'm not going to go behind anyone's back. I don't do that any longer. But you would never try to forbid Caleb or Alex from taking an action that stood to save countless lives and bring a horrible criminal to justice. They do what they believe is right, because they're confident in their capabilities.

"Uncle Richard, I'm capable of doing this. I'll take every precaution. I'll protect myself and Galean. But he might be the only person who can find where the Ch'mshak are escaping from, and who's willing to do it."

"Are you certain he's willing?"

"I haven't asked him yet, but he'll say yes. He's a fierce warrior, and he wants to repay me for helping the Tarazi. Please. This is how we can help. Let us help."

Graham whistled. "She's got your number good."

"Don't make it worse, Graham." Richard dragged a hand across his jaw. "As soon as we're finished here, you're going to tell David what you're planning, with me in the room. Let him try to talk you out of it. Then he won't hate me when you do it anyway. In fact, let's invite Caleb, too."

"Oh, this is going to be brutal." She groaned dramatically. "If that's what it takes. I'm not afraid to stand up for myself. But I have a meeting with Dean Veshnael in fifteen minutes, so can we do it this evening? I'll even wrangle everyone together in one place. Gramps' house?"

"Fine. This evening. Don't walk out the door and run off to Mshak."

She flashed him a dazzling smile. "I won't. Promise."

When she'd gone, Richard sank low in his chair and rubbed at his face.

Graham laughed heartily. "Maranos, man. They flaunt an impudent disrespect for the rules. Every last one of them. It's in their blood."

49

AKESO

I need to talk. Can I come over? The direct route?

The pulse from Kennedy jerked Alex out of her thoughts. She'd been headed to the kitchen to grab a drink when her mind had wandered back into her horrific vision at Nika's cabin, leaving her standing in the middle of the hallway chasing loops of dread. Mirai falling to dual primordial forces. Caleb in agony as Akeso's consciousness fractured beneath an invasion of *diati*.

She blinked and forced the images away.

Sure. Where are you?

Special Projects—oh, crap. No free wormholes here.

No, it's fine. Mom never patched out my access after the Rasu War.

Excellent. I'll head to the lobby.

Alex ran a hand through her hair, then wound it into a knot at the nape, then slapped her cheeks to shake off the mental fog. Satisfied she was marginally present, she opened a wormhole to Special Projects.

Kennedy slogged through carrying her bag over one shoulder and a quantum cube container in the other. She tossed both on the kitchen counter and collapsed on the living room couch. "Well that was another disaster."

"What was?"

"You don't know?"

"No. I've been...busy."

"We caught up to the Dzhvar again. This time we tried the Ymyrath Field on them."

How had she missed this? She'd tried to keep half an ear attuned to events through the Connexus, but she'd obviously let her attention fall away while obsessing over her visions.

Ever since forcing a vision to manifest while at Nika and Dashiel's cabin, she'd felt...unmoored. Like she was caught between two realities, perpetually teetering on the brink of pitching into another episode. She'd hoped learning how to deliberately provoke one would help her get a handle on the situation, but thus far it was having the opposite effect. And now a stream of kyoseil followed her around, anchoring her to the scab at Elakrin. She'd visited the scab again after learning about it, but without a way to see and evaluate the stream herself, she'd uncovered no answers.

She tried to smile inquisitively at Kennedy, and almost certainly failed. "It went poorly?"

"I mean, the Ymyrath Field didn't turn the Dzhvar into a swelling, growling monster the way negative energy weapons did, so that's a positive. But it didn't do anything. They simply ignored it. I'd hoped because the Rasu were birthed by the Dzhvar, it would have an effect. But nothing."

Alex sat in her usual chair opposite Kennedy. "The Dzhvar sparked life in the Rasu, true, but the Dzhvar aren't corporeal in any real way. They're not quite negative energy, though this comparison is the closest I've come up with. They're...anti-energy. Anti-manifold. Anti-dimensions. Anti-life."

"All true. So I guess it's not a huge surprise to find radiation doesn't hurt them. Oh, we also tested out a Rift Bubble on a planet in the Dzhvar's path."

"And?"

Kennedy shrugged weakly. "It diverted them for a little over a minute before they found their way through the barrier. But a minute of protection is more than anything else has accomplished, so I think your mom's ordering up triple interlocking bubbles. Maybe quadruple. We'll see if a dimension-diverting maze can buy us an hour or so for evacuations."

Alex closed her eyes and tried to visualize what such a trap might do, or not do, to the Dzhvar—

"Alex, we don't have anything that can hurt them."

The train of thought unraveled, and she reopened her eyes. "Not yet, no. We don't."

Kennedy studied her in suspicion. "Hey, I just realized something. You look like hell. What's wrong?"

"Other than the obvious?"

"Yes, other than the obvious."

"Nothing. I'm just tired."

"What have you been doing?"

Absolutely nothing of any use. It was true; aside from her haphazard jaunts into alternate realities or past or future or fuckall knew what, she wasn't contributing. She wasn't helping. Three years ago she'd set about devoting her life to stopping the Dzhvar, and now they were here—ahead of schedule thanks to her—and she was useless.

"Alex?"

"Worrying, mostly. But you're working like a mad woman possessed...and I told you I'd come up with a way to safely reverse the Piega Strai's manifold barrier. I'm sorry. I haven't figured it out yet." In truth, she'd hardly thought about it at all. Dammit! "Nika and I have been discussing the behavior of kyoseil in the region where the pocket universe was attached to Amaranthe by the tether. We're hoping if we can figure out the effect the barrier had on the surrounding space, it will...point to a way to dissolve it," she finished lamely. She was trying to cover her ass, and doing so only made her feel worse.

"If there's a method to do so, you'll find it."

Way to stick the knife in and twist. "Will I?"

"Alex, what is *wrong?*"

"It's nothing. Like I said, I'm tired."

"It's not nothing. But if you won't tell me, I hope you'll tell someone. Go talk to Nika about it, I guess."

She exhaled harshly. "You have no idea the things I can't talk to Nika about."

"No, I don't." A dark glower descended over Kennedy's normally bright features. "Alex, I have been your best friend for over forty years, and I love you. But the truth is, whenever things get tough, you shut down and shut me out. You act as if I'm not important enough to know 'the details.'

"I am sick of begging to be let in. I don't have the energy for it, because guess what? I have to give everything I am—my time with my kids, definitely my time with my husband, most of my sleep—to try to save us all, too. On that note, I need to get back to work." Kennedy stood, grabbed her gear and marched toward the door. "I'm done. Don't bother with a wormhole. I'll ask Vii for a ride home."

Alex stared at her hands until they blurred and replicated, as if two versions of her were sitting here in her living room. "I feel like I'm losing my mind. Literally losing my mind—losing it in time and space."

"What did you say?" It sounded as if Kennedy had paused at the front door.

She supposed she had whispered it, so she repeated it, louder this time.

The next second, Kennedy was kneeling in front of her, reaching out for her hands. "Talk to me. Please."

S&L

"It's like a waking dream." Alex grimaced. "Otherwise known as a hallucination, right?"

"Maybe not." Kennedy sipped on her glass of wine, a contemplative expression on her face. Once the story had started spilling off Alex's tongue, they'd decided to camp out on the patio in the warm afternoon sun with a bottle of chilled chardonnay and a bowl of fruit. "Crazy as it sounds, have you considered quantum many-worlds theory?"

"I have. Do you remember the first thing Professor Sanford said about it in Quantum Mechanics II?"

Kennedy lifted her shoulders and jutted her chest and chin out. "It's rubbish," she intoned in a thick Scottish accent. "Not because it is false, but because it can never be proved. In science we prove theories, or we discard them." She lifted a hand and mimicked tossing a ball into a trash bin.

Alex laughed so hard she almost spat up the strawberry she'd just bitten into. "Perfect. And as much as I hate to give the old curmudgeon credit, he was correct. It doesn't matter whether our infinite choices are constantly birthing new universes or not. They're universes, so we can never access them."

"But the Kats made universes, and you were able to access them."

"Yes, but those universes were *inside* Amaranthe, and the Kats left a door propped open in the form of the portals...." She trailed off, her gaze fixating on the buttery gold glow of the chardonnay in her glass. It reminded her of the color of kyoseil fibers when freed from their Reor armor.

"Alex? Are you somewhere else right now?"

"No...." She shook her head roughly, and the next second a smile blossomed on her expression. "That's it! You're brilliant."

"I am? I mean, yes, obviously. But how, specifically, am I brilliant in this situation? Do you mean what you're experiencing *is* quantum many-worlds theory in action?"

"No. Kyoseil."

"Kyoseil is making you hallucinate?"

"No—well, maybe, but forget about the hallucinations for now. No idea what's going on there. Ken, I know how to rig the Piega Strai so it can be safely deactivated from the inside."

S&L

ROMANE

Alex rolled a chair over to the lab table next to Kennedy, where a holographic schematic of a Piega Strai rotated. "You've made a lot of progress on the design."

"When your mother says 'jump,' even I ask 'how high.' After some initial struggles, I decided to imagine the device was a ball-shaped spaceship. Made it easier." Kennedy faded out the core's hull to expose the inner workings. "What are we doing?"

"First question: what kind of ware will be running it?"

"I've penciled in a Class III sub-Artificial."

"You should upgrade it to a Class V. I'm almost tempted to say install a full Artificial, but Valkyrie insists the Class Vs come equipped with everything except the self-referential awareness of how they exist as a conscious life with hopes, dreams and, most dangerously, preferences."

"She's got the right of it." Kennedy used a virtual pointer to tinker with the core-in-the-core. "They also require a lot more hardware. We'll need more room, which will ripple out to a larger diameter for the core and thus for the lattice. But cost is no object when the fate of civilization is at stake, or so I've been told."

After a new round of tinkering, the entire assembly swelled, then shrunk back down to fit neatly in the allotted space for the hologram. "The program will auto-update the bill of materials." Kennedy jerked a nod. "That was easy."

"Yeah, well, this next part won't be. Have you worked out the tether mechanism?" Alex asked.

"I've basically copied over what the Elakri did, saved it as a component, and set it to the side for now."

"Okay. I suspect the string of elementary particle pearls will operate more or less the same. I wish we could use more than one tether for redundancy's sake, but Valkyrie had a conversation with one of the Kats' pocket universe architects, and according to them, two universes can only abut at a single point. Otherwise the inherent physics of Amaranthe, which is the only kind of universe anyone knows how to build, don't play out correctly. So we're stuck with a single tether. But here comes the hard part: we're going to need to encase the tether in kyoseil."

Kennedy regarded her dubiously. "Wrapping Earth and Sol in one of these barriers—and let's be honest, when judgment day arrives, this is all about Earth—will require a tether over 1 AU long. That's *a lot* of kyoseil."

"A metric fuckton, in fact. And you're wrong. This isn't solely about Earth, much as humans would prefer for it to be. Concord is going to be facing the Rift Bubble distribution priority controversy all over again, where every species has a claim to be first in line. So we're talking multiples of metric fucktons. Dashiel is going to murder me, no question." She shrugged. "Fate of civilization?"

"You're the one who's telling him how big the order is."

Alex chuckled. "I'll have Mom do it instead. Think he'll ask her 'how high'?"

"It's possible." Kennedy shook her head wryly. "All right. We'll assume that an unlimited metric fuckton of kyoseil will fall from the sky into the assembly cage at the Krysk Orbital II facility. You said we're encasing the tether with it?"

"We need to create a sheath. We'll use the tether as our back-up plan to keep the pocket universe attached to Amaranthe, since we know that method works. But we'll also be attaching the kyoseil to Amaranthe's manifold."

Kennedy toed her chair away from the table. "Hold on. I've already had to rely on some Special Projects geniuses more often than I prefer for some of the dimensional heavy lifting, because I'm a tangible materials girl. How in Jesus' name am I supposed to affix kyoseil to the spacetime manifold?"

"Have Vii talk to Valkyrie. The Kat she consulted with explained how to do it, in a conceptual sense."

Kennedy drew a straight line along the top of the schematic and labeled it 'Manifold.' Then she drew a squiggly line from the device's core out to it, where she inserted a thicker line labeled 'affix.' "There. Easy peasy. What next?"

Alex reached over and placed a hand over Kennedy's. "Thank you."

Kennedy smiled. "We always made a good team."

"We did, and we still do. Now for the ware. Every so often, we'll have the Class V trigger the program the Asterions developed to make adiaK seam and unseam hulls. It'll pulse the kyoseil to expand and break open the manifold barrier."

Kennedy brow furrowed.

"I can explain if you want?"

"How about over a fresh bottle of wine later? For now, I'll take your word for it that kyoseil can do this thing of which you speak."

"It…" Alex gazed at the ceiling, for in truth they were dancing on the edge of her own understanding as well "…should be able to do so. As soon as it has access to Amaranthe, even if it's only through a pinprick hole a few atoms wide, the Class V will check for the presence of Dzhvar in the area. You should station a nanoscale sensor near the end of the tether that it can send out to look around. If Dzhvar are detected, it will run the adiaK program a second time to seal up the hole before any Dzhvar can get inside. If the coast is clear, it can ping HQ for instructions."

"And if HQ is gone?"

Alex sighed through pursed lips; what a sobering thought. "We'll program in a list of contacts it can run down. Hopefully someone will still be around to answer."

They both sat silently for a moment, contemplating the grim reality of what the future held if they didn't find a way to counter this enemy.

"Okay, um…how often should the Piega Strai poke its head out and check?" Kennedy asked.

"Deciding that is well above my pay grade. Every week? Once a year? It might depend on how the overall war is going when the device is activated."

"A question for your mother. Got it. With a Class V, we can adjust the timing on the fly up until the last minute. Now." Kennedy swung the chair around to face Alex. "How do we shut it down once the coast is clear?"

"We'll have the kyoseil do what I did at Elakrin, only much more elegantly. The sheath will expand, thinning as it does, to gradually let Amaranthe seep inside."

"But the machine is going to keep on generating the barrier, backfilling the opening."

"This was a problem at Elakrin, too." Alex considered their options. "Can you program the Class V to peel the barrier away from the kyoseil sheath as it grows? Like so?" She pressed her palms together, then moved them apart in a 'V' while keeping her wrists touching.

Kennedy held up a finger, spun to the aural she'd kept off to the side, and started scrolling through immensely complex code. The screen divided into two columns, and new code began populating the right side. "It is *not* designed to do this," she muttered under her breath.

Alex decided this was not the time for off-color commentary and kept silent.

"The kyoseil will originate at the core and flow all the way out. So if I can get the machine to see it as a barrier as well, but only once this whole sequence triggers—but as it thins out—how wide does our 'V' need to get?"

Alex thought back to her efforts at Elakrin, visualizing the instant when Amaranthe overwhelmed the bubble space. "Call it eight degrees?"

"Let's do a bit of cocktail-napkin differential calculus on the expanding diameter of the sheath needed to cover that area, then factor in how porous the kyoseil will be at every point...." Kennedy flung herself away from the aural. "Yes."

"You're amazing." Alex leapt out of her chair and wrapped Kennedy up in a hug.

"By a hair's breadth. It's really close," Kennedy mumbled into her shoulder.

"Go with 7.5 degrees and give yourself a little wiggle room." Alex settled back into her chair. "Nothing will explode at 7.5 degrees."

"Are you sure?"

"Eh…probably?"

"Alex!"

"Kidding. I'm sure. Or as sure as anyone ever is when ripping apart a universal manifold."

50

SENECA

CAVARE
MILKY WAY GALAXY

Marlee took Galean's hands in hers as the wormhole closed behind him. "Are you certain you want to do this? I did mention it's dangerous, didn't I?"

"You did. You also said we'll be able to save lives if we succeed, yes? After you saved so many desbida lives, it's the least I can do."

"You don't need to repay me. But I deeply appreciate your help." She returned his smile, then suddenly realized she was still holding his hands in hers. She hurriedly dropped them before it got awkward...oh, who was she kidding? It was already awkward. Great way to start off the mission. "Did you, uh, bring the amplifier?"

He patted an ornate metal charm hanging around his neck. In the wake of the collapse of the Errigime, Nedeni Proml, the leader of the Tarazi rebel organization and Galean's mentor, had discovered how law enforcement was able to zero in on quantum fluctuations with such precision over even great distances. It turned out, government scientists had developed a tool that in essence did the opposite of what the device the Tarazi's resident tech genius, Mattin Erlantz, had invented. Where Erlantz's invention muffled and dispersed quantum fluctuations, the government's tool amplified and homed in on them, but the principle underlying the two inventions was essentially the same.

"Wonderful. And you brought some basic survival gear? I've got food and water covered, but we might be there for a few days."

"I follow instructions well." He slipped a pack off his back and held it out in one hand.

"Sorry. I know you've run plenty of missions before. More than I have. I just want to make sure all our bases are covered. On that note, let's get you outfitted with the latest and greatest in protective wizardry."

She went over to the small desk in the corner of her living room and picked up two modules, then offered them both to Galean. "The first one is a Veil. It will make you invisible. And honestly, given this feature, we probably won't need anything else. But better safe than sorry, which is why the second one is a high-powered defense shield. It'll repel any small caliber energy weapons and will deflect most physical weapons. Now, the Ch'mshak are wicked strong, so I don't plan to stroll up to one and test the shield's limits, but it'll protect us from a lot of dangers."

Galean nodded understanding and clipped both modules to his pants. "You're wearing these devices as well?"

"I have them on the inside."

His wide, teardrop-shaped eyes narrowed to slits. "The inside of…your clothes?"

"My body. They're integrated into my cybernetics."

"Right. A reminder of how much more advanced your people truly are."

"You'll get there. The diplomatic talks are progressing. And once our people are friends, we can share much technology with you." She was putting a favorable spin on the state of the talks. The Belascocians were highly suspicious of Concord, especially in light of how Aunt Miriam had nearly fired dreadnought weapons at them. But Dean Veshnael was an endlessly patient man, and a persuasive one.

"I look forward to it. I'm not confident all of my people do, but hopefully they will come to see the wisdom in expanding our horizons." He peered behind her at the desk, as if searching for something. "We won't be wearing your, ah, Shrouds?"

"No. I considered trying to requisition us a couple. But the Ch'mshak are a naturally violent, martial species, and the truth is, they're as likely to attack an unfamiliar Ch'mshak as they are an alien. So resembling a Ch'mshak won't protect us."

"They sound pleasant."

"They are not. This is why we need to figure out how they're getting off their planet and past our blockade to rampage and kill innocents."

"A worthy endeavor, to be sure." His gaze drifted across the room. "This is where you live?"

"Oh, pardon my manners. Yes, this is my apartment. It's nothing fancy. Living room, kitchen…" she gestured off to the right "…bedroom, the usual." Ugh, why had she mentioned the bedroom? Obviously she had a bedroom. She spun and headed for the balcony. "You want to take a look at the downtown skyline?"

"Certainly." He followed her outside and, once there, rested his hands on the railing to consider the view.

It was a gorgeous spring morning in Cavare. The streets below bustled, the scrapers shone, and the Fuori River sparkled in the sunlight across the riverwalk park.

"Huh."

"What is it?" she asked.

"The fact that I can now take a few strides through a portal and stand on alien worlds marvels me. Thank you for introducing me to the universe."

She beamed. "It's been my pleasure."

Nice as it was, the view was pretty straightforward, so after a minute, she gestured toward the door. "We should head out."

"I am ready when you are."

She retrieved her own pack stuffed with clothes and other supplies, as well as a second, larger bag containing a pop-up shelter, food and water. Then she activated her 'out of office' notification at work. "Let's go."

$$S_{\&}L$$

MSHAK

The hot, dry air slapped Marlee in the face with the force of a furnace blast. She'd known it was going to be hot and wore a loose, breathable tank and field shorts, but she'd assumed hot meant 'Krysk hot,' not 'surface of a star hot.'

Galean had dressed for the heat as well; he was wearing a cream sleeveless tunic and semi-sheer loose pants, and his lamina-covered skin glittered like sequins in the blistering sun. That was going to be somewhat distracting.

She'd chosen the most remote, desolate location possible that was a reasonable distance from multiple settlement clusters. A scan of the horizon in every direction revealed no buildings or advancing Ch'mshak. So far, so good.

The conversation Richard had insisted she have with Caleb and Gramps had been about as painful as she'd expected, but in the end, neither of them had attempted to forbid her from going on the mission. After she'd parried their objections with logic, evidence, and a smattering of batted eyelashes, they'd extracted a host of precautions out of her. The remoteness of the location was one.

Galean squinted off into the distance, then pivoted to peer in the opposite direction. "This is practically a desert. Is there any water on this planet?"

"There is. And it does rain. Granted, maybe not so much in this region. The Ch'mshak engage in agriculture, though they prefer to eat wild game. Their native level of development is borderline pre-industrial, but they appropriated a lot of technology from the Anadens over the millennia. So their nicer settlements have power, plumbing and radio communications, and they use hovercraft to travel longer distances. To the extent they've been able to keep the vehicles in good repair over the last eleven years, anyway, since they don't have the technology to build new ones. Concord left a lot of gear behind during the conflict."

"What about weapons?"

"Same deal: they have whatever laser weaponry they possessed when they were quarantined. And they'd developed ballistic weapons on their own before the Anadens discovered the planet thousands of years ago. Don't know if they remember how to make them now, though, or if they became reliant on superior Anaden firepower."

"Should I activate my Veil?" Galean asked. "Or the other one? The shield?"

"Nah. We'll have plenty of time to activate them if we spot trouble headed our way. And it would be awkward, us constantly trying to figure out where the other person was."

He chuckled lightly, which she hoped meant he was starting to relax around her. "Fair point. So, what do we do now?"

"Before we settle in to wait, I want to test your range. Since there shouldn't be any quantum activity at all on the planet, I'm hopeful it'll stretch for longer than the amplifier advertises."

His sentsores fluttered. "You're going to wormhole into Ch'mshak villages?"

"No. I'm not that crazy. I'll use sidespace to pick out some remote and uninhabited locations, then wormhole to those. I'll wait for a minute before opening a new wormhole from my location to somewhere off-planet. We'll see if you can detect it, and if so, its direction from you."

"It's a good plan." Galean set his bag on the hard-packed ground. "Shall we get started?"

It took half an hour of jumping around to quiet, but not any more scenic, locales until they had a good idea of the range they were working with. He could detect a quantum disturbance at an astonishing thousand kilometers, but after around four hundred kilometers it became difficult for him to determine a direction with any precision. It was better than she'd hoped for. This plan might actually work.

She sat on the ground and opened up the cooler, handing Galean a water and taking one for herself. "I'm feeling good about our location. With your range, you ought to be able to detect an event in any of thirty-three surrounding settlements."

"And what happens when I do?"

"I'll leap into action in sidespace. Hopefully I can put eyes on whatever is transpiring within twenty seconds or so."

He studied her intently. "And then?"

"And then I will dutifully report back to Director Navick as to what I see. No heroics. Not really any way for me to be heroic in this scenario. There's no one to rescue here. No good guys on the ground."

S&L

Marlee had expected the setting of the sun to bring a rapid drop in temperature, but no such luck. Instead, the air went from oppressively stifling to merely excessively hot.

She stared upward at the darkening night sky. "I will give this planet one thing: the view's nice at night. Not a trace of light pollution to mask the stars."

"Hmm," Galean muttered noncommittedly.

"I suppose it can't compare to the night sky on Belarria. Of course, the night sky on Belarria is actively trying to kill everyone on the planet, so it arguably balances out."

"True. Yet because we met you, we will never have to worry about going extinct when astronomical calamity inevitably arrives."

She frowned. "I thought you said your people had advanced tracking tools for cosmic objects."

"We do. But deflecting an asteroid is one thing. Escaping a close supernova or stellar system collision is something else entirely. We have ships, as you know, but not enough to evacuate more than a tiny fraction of the population, even over the course of years." He smiled. "So sooner or later, your people will again save my people."

"We'll be glad to do it."

They'd cooked some stew on the camping stove and eaten a light dinner a little earlier. While he cleaned up, she popped the shelter. It was large enough to sleep four, but she anticipated it was nonetheless going to be uncomfortably cozy inside when there was residual sexual tension in the air. Still, after a few hours they'd settled into an easy rhythm reminiscent of their time together on Belarria, and it was nice to be able to spend time with him.

They lingered for a while longer stargazing before heading into the shelter for the night.

Inside, she held out her hand. "Let me borrow your Veil for a minute."

He took a second to figure out which device was which, then handed it to her.

She brought it close to her face to peer at the tiny screen above the dial. "It's helpful having an internal model, but the smaller size and biosynthetic wrapper means mine lacks the bells and whistles that a real module comes with. I'm expanding the field to encompass the shelter…there we go. Now our camp is hidden."

Marlee inflated some pillows and rolled out the blankets, then propped one of the pillows against the rear wall; it gave a bit, but held her weight. "We'll stay up for as long as we can, then hope no one picks the middle of the night to arrive."

"Oh, it will be fine if they do." Galean touched his necklace. "This is integrated so fully into my eamonal, it will wake me if anything triggers its sensors."

"Really? In that case, get comfortable."

He situated his bedding beside hers, a little closer than she was expecting. They lounged, talking, in the soft glow of the shelter's lighting. He filled her in on all the drama and political arguments that had marked the last two months on Belarria, then told her about the house he was designing for Nedeni. Finally, he relaxed enough to share how the reconciliation with his and Resamane's family was working out; in short, 'touch and go.'

When he belatedly realized she'd nudged him into doing all the talking—she enjoyed hearing news of Belarria—he started quizzing her about work, family, Concord history and so on.

"How are things going with Major Lekkas?"

"Going?" she asked innocently.

"From a relationship perspective."

"We're friendly. Or we were heading toward friendly territory when she got busy and distracted with the Ch'mshak situation. Which is complicated. And I'm not comfortable talking about my love life, or lack thereof, with you."

"Oh." He hesitated. "I didn't mean to make you feel uneasy."

"No, it's not…do you seriously want to hear me talk about my feelings in *that* way about someone else?"

"We're not together, Marlee." His voice had taken on a low, sharp edge.

"I know! God, I wasn't implying…ugh. I mostly didn't want you to feel uncomfortable, sitting here listening to me talk about romantic matters." She blew out a breath. "But to answer your question, there is no relationship, and I don't have any real reason to believe there ever will be."

"I'm sorry."

"It's okay. I'm a big girl now, and I can move beyond a childish crush."

"Is that what it was? Because you don't strike me as a child."

Her pulse notched upward as she flailed around trying to choose the best words to navigate through the excruciating turn the conversation had taken. "I had a crush on Morgan when I was young. Then I grew up, and when our paths crossed again, I found I still had feelings for her. Have, maybe. I'm honestly not sure if it's real, or just residual…dammit, Galean, can we please stop talking about this? I'm dying here."

He blinked slowly, his eyes shimmering seas of fuchsia and indigo. "Why?"

"Don't be an ass. You know why."

His lips tugged outward in a hint of a smile. "I do know. Forgive me. I confess I feel compelled to poke at this…aura we have between us, pulling us toward one another. Or pulling me toward you, at least." He reached over and took her hand, staring at their entwined fingers for a long moment before lifting his gaze to her face. "So, no Shroud then?"

"No." She carefully removed her hand from his. The absence of his touch made her chest ache, and part of her selfishly wished she *had* brought a Shroud along. Oh, this was so messed up. "Galean, I shouldn't have done that to you."

"Done what?"

"Made myself look like a Belascocian in order to steal a kiss."

"I thought you did it so you could accompany the team to Inarska II and help our mission succeed?"

"I did, I absolutely did. There also happened to be a wonderful side benefit, which I enjoyed immensely. But it wasn't fair to you."

"It was quite fair. I knew full well who you were beneath the disguise." He sighed quietly. "If anything, I should be apologizing for being so shallow as for your appearance to make such a great difference in my…physical response to you. Especially now that I've been to your amazing space station and visited several of your worlds. You live amongst this incredible variety of life, and you all see one another not as alien or 'other,' but as individuals."

His focus dropped to his lap. "I'm ashamed of my narrow, primitive provincialism. Yet I can't manage to escape it."

She wanted so badly to take his hand again, but it was a terrible idea. "Don't be. I was the first non-Belascocian you had ever seen in your life. It took humans a long time to get used to living among aliens. Many of them still aren't used to it. They stay on human worlds and try to pretend as though the other species don't exist. I'm only comfortable in our crazy zoo because I grew up in it. I was six years old when we came to Amaranthe and met the other species. I've never known anything else."

She settled for reaching over and giving his hand a quick squeeze, then forcing a hasty retreat. "It's been an overwhelming few months for you. You're handling all these new experiences wonderfully."

"You are kind to say so." He frowned a little. "What did you mean when you said 'when we came to Amaranthe'? Amaranthe is simply the universe, yes? So where were you before?"

"Oh. That's kind of a long story."

"We have nowhere else to be."

"Too true. Okay." Grateful, and also a bit sad, to find they seemed to be moving on from the minefield of sexual tension, she fluffed the pillow at her back and settled in.

Then she told him the story of The Displacement, and how her uncle gave his life to save the world, only to have an appreciative world return it to him.

51

MSHAK

Marlee awoke to full alertness, something Caleb had taught her how to do when in unfamiliar settings. She lay still and honed her senses.

The ground beneath her vibrated ever so faintly, and if she shifted additional resources to her aural cybernetics, she heard a low rumble in the distance.

She reached over and shook Galean's arm while whispering, "Wake up."

His eyes flew open to fix on her. "What is it?"

"Something's coming." She stood, retrieved her Daemon and hurried outside, activating her Veil as she did.

A quick three-sixty revealed nothing in sight. But dawn was only beginning to make itself known, and most of the scenery remained cast in deep shadows.

"Marlee? Where are you?" Galean stage-whispered.

She toggled the Veil off and motioned him over. "Stand flush against me, and you'll be inside my Veil's circumference. I want to leave yours to hide the shelter."

He sidled up behind her, half off one shoulder, and she reactivated the device. Adrenaline coursing through her veins kept her attention on the situation and not the delight of his body pressed close. She focused on the sound, tiptoeing in a circle until it grew markedly stronger in her right ear. "The sound is coming from this direction."

"Should we leave?"

They could, and return once the coast was clear. But what if this was a precursor to the arrival of one of the mysterious ships?

They'd miss the entire reason they were here. "Not yet. Nothing can see us. Promise."

"I believe you. Concord tech has proved itself. But they can hear us, yes?"

"Good point. Let's switch to silent comms," she whispered.

The sun crested the horizon to their left, thankfully chasing the shadows away and granting definition to the landscape. A few seconds later, several dark blobs appeared to mar the sun's advance. The ground was actively rumbling now.

The blobs began to multiply, or rather separate. Ten, twelve...fifteen.

Vehicles.

Based on their angle of approach, they should pass sixty meters or so to her right. Assuming they didn't shift course. But really, in the middle of this vast expanse of nothingness, what were the odds they would run over the shelter?

About as good as the odds they were passing by at all.

She was able to make out some features now, and they *were* hovercraft. But they were also emitting an unholy racket, a testament to years of rough use and poor maintenance. And they were overflowing with Ch'mshak; a hundred or more of the aliens were piled into the craft. Spears and battleaxes and other intimidating weapons jutted into the air and out from every side.

This was a raiding party.

When they drew close enough for them to make out the occupants in detail, Galean muttered a curse over the comm. "*Madari. They're monsters.*"

Her thoughts exactly. She'd studied all the files from the conflict eleven years ago in preparation for this mission, but she'd never seen a Ch'mshak in person before. As they pulled even with the camp closer to thirty meters away—close enough that her hair ruffled from the air displacement of the stampeding vehicles—she gaped, transfixed.

The Rasu mech that almost killed her on Namino must have been larger and better armed than these creatures, but at this moment she found it difficult to believe. The Ch'mshak stood at least three meters tall and half as wide. They wore shaped armor over tough hides, especially their sturdy barrel chests. Though they stood on two legs, their arms were overlong and nearly as thick as their thighs, suggesting they were able to run on all four limbs. Massive heads sported four eyes, two at the center and one on each side. Long tusks didn't fit inside mouths framed by disproportionately full lips.

Then they were past the camp, racing away to the southwest. Possibly to the X'khak settlement, based on their heading.

Once they disappeared over the opposite horizon, she collapsed to the ground as every muscle in her body untensed. "Wow."

"Wow?" Galean joined her on the ground. "I have other words to describe what we just saw."

"Sure. Me, too. But wow." She laughed a little wildly. "You know, everyone is always asking me, 'Marlee, is there anything you're afraid of?' Now I think I know. I'm afraid of them."

S&L

After they put away the shelter for the day, Galean prepared a basic breakfast while Marlee paced in a wide circle around the camp, trying to work off her nerves. She one hundred percent believed a mere handful of Ch'mshak had murdered almost two thousand people on a space station. What she couldn't believe was that Marines had fought these monsters and won a non-zero percentage of the battles.

But not all of the battles. Brooklyn Harper and her squad had died here. The fact the woman had willingly charged into a fortified camp of armed Ch'mshak? It was difficult to conceive of bravery on such a scale. She'd say 'or foolhardiness,' but Harper had been following orders.

Aunt Miriam didn't often talk about the burden of ordering soldiers to their likely deaths, but Marlee knew it weighed on her aunt. And she decided she understood the dynamics at play a bit better, as well as the frustration of it all. Did Harper's bravery matter in the end? Did her aunt's burdens? The military losses had led to the quarantine, and the quarantine had kept people safe for over a decade. But now the Ch'mshak were a threat once again, and she sympathized with people like Morgan, who believed those sacrifices had been futile.

"Breakfast is ready."

She put aside her musings to go sit by the stove opposite Galean. "Thanks for cooking. So, want to go home now?"

He stared at the horizon for so long she expected him to say 'yes.' "No. Anything we can do to stop more of those monsters from escaping, we must."

"You're a good and honorable man, Galean."

"Ah, thank you. I try to be." He lowered his gaze to consider his plate.

They ate in silence, each caught up in ruminations on their close encounter with the enemy. After they finished, she was putting away the stove when Galean abruptly grasped her arm. "Something's happening."

She dropped the stove and its bag to the dirt, but squelched the urge to quiz him. He'd tell her what he knew as soon as he knew it.

It only took a few seconds. He spun forty degrees and pointed. "To the north-northwest. Not close, but well within my range. Maybe two-hundred-fifty kilometers."

"Taking a look." She slipped into sidespace. A sizeable settlement lay in the correct direction, and she projected her consciousness to it.

A group of six armed Ch'mshak gathered together near a shimmering wormhole. Off to the side stood a human woman. She was tall and noticeably thin, with alabaster skin and pale blonde hair secured in a french twist. The Ch'mshak weren't attacking her; they weren't even beating their chests or attempting to intimidate her. There was no ship in sight.

Her breath caught as she realized what was happening: a raiding party of a different kind. This woman was about to send the armed Ch'mshak somewhere offworld, where they were certain to cause carnage and death. She knew there had been several attacks not directly linked to a ship's arrival, but she'd never imagined they'd occurred in *this* manner.

So much for not putting herself in harm's way….

Marlee dropped her consciousness into her body and spun up her Caeles Prism. "Be right back. Stay here."

"What?"

She opened a wormhole and hurried through it. When no Ch'mshak arrived to attack her, she closed it behind her. She was at the rear of one of the larger buildings in the settlement square; with luck no one had seen the brief glow.

She started to move past the corner—a hand grabbed her arm from behind. She instantly twisted her arm against the grip as she leapt back and swung her leg—

A tail wrapped around her ankle the same instant she realized there was only empty air surrounding her. She stumbled, off balance, as her foot was returned to the ground and Galean set her ankle free. Him and that damnable tail of his!

She'd chide him for following her through the wormhole, but she needed to move fast right now. She felt for his hand and clutched it.

"Come with me."

They crept around the building until the woman was in view. Marlee zoomed in her ocular implant and snapped a picture, then switched to video for several seconds.

The group of Ch'mshak headed through the wormhole, and the woman followed. Through the opening, she barely made out a rust-colored structure and a cloudy aqua sky.

How many people were about to die?

She wasn't being reckless. The math was straightforward: a calculated risk of one life that could be renewed for the potential to save many lives that may otherwise end forever.

She dropped Galean's hand and sprinted forward, willing him to not follow her this time. She leapt through the wormhole and darted to the left to avoid running smack into the woman. By the time she'd pivoted, the wormhole was gone.

She found herself near the entrance to a warehouse with no signage, so she pinged her locator. Then she sent a priority pulse to the one person who was most likely to both open it immediately and be able to do something with the information fast enough to make a difference.

Aunt Miriam, a Ch'mshak squad of six just arrived at a warehouse on Lethe, an Anaden world in Milky Way Sector 56. I'm attaching the precise coordinates.

Now, because she was not actually suicidal, she needed to find a hidden corner and get the hell off the premises. She'd done everything she could for the people here.

A Machim unit is responding. Do you need rescue?

No. Rescuing myself as we speak.

She exhaled in relief. No doubt she had a stern interrogation to look forward to in her future, but her aunt understood how in the critical moment, response time was all that mattered.

The blonde woman gave an order she couldn't discern, then calmly trailed the Ch'mshak as they stormed into the warehouse. The woman was directing their attack! What kind of person would do such a thing?

Marlee reluctantly turned her back on the scene and slipped around the side of the warehouse into an alley. She glanced in both directions to confirm she was alone, then opened a wormhole back to the settlement.

"Galean, where are you?"

"Behind the building where we arrived. Are you here?"

She didn't see him anywhere, because he was smart and had his Veil active.

"Deactivate your Veil briefly."

As soon as he materialized, she ran over and pulled him close, into the radius of her Veil and her into his. Worry animated his whirling, bottomless eyes, and his sentsores were rigid as rods. *"That was reckless."*

"No, that was necessary. The military is sending soldiers to the location right away. Lives will be saved."

"And what of your life?"

"It's like you said. Anything we can do, we must."

"Maddening Human. So what now?"

"There's no ship here. I think we stay and watch."

S&L

It took almost half an hour for the woman and two bloodied Ch'mshak to return. A Ch'mshak wearing a fancier getup than everyone else promptly stormed up to them.

"Where are the rest of my warriors?" he barked.

"We were interrupted," the woman replied.

"So?"

"They were armed fighters. Machim soldiers, I think. The rest of your warriors were killed or captured." The woman had a crisp, aristocratic Earth accent. "They didn't complete the job."

"Not my concern. Our deal was I send them on the mission, and in return, we get a ship. Where is the ship?"

"They *didn't complete the job.*"

"If you want them to ever do another one, you will deliver the ship now."

The woman glared the Ch'mshak down for several seconds, then gave a curt nod. "Fine. But next time, you will double the size of the squad. I'd have expected your warriors to be able to overpower a couple of soldiers."

"Do not insult me further, Human."

The woman pivoted away and strode to a clearing, where there was some distance between the buildings.

Marlee's gaze rose to the sky in time to see a ship descending through the air. It sported a wide, thick hold, a hallmark of a merchant transport vessel, and appeared to be human made. It settled to the ground a few meters from where the woman stood.

"Marlee, look over here."

As soon as she turned, she spotted a group of ten Ch'mshak emerging from a building deeper into the settlement, carrying crates and large bags.

They were going to board the ship and leave. And wherever they flew, yet more people would die.

Galean reached out and drew her close against his chest. *"We need to disable the ship."*

So good and honorable. *"We do. I think if I can get to the engine and pop a panel, I can sever a power cable."*

"You understand your technology far better than I do. But I can guard you while you work."

She wanted to beg him to stay in the relative safety of the building's shadow. He didn't have access to regenesis; if he died here, it was his end. Resamane's soul would be forever shattered, and her guilt would never fade. But she knew him well, and he wasn't apt to agree to remain on the sidelines. He'd almost died on dangerous missions twice in the weeks she'd spent with him on Belarria, so he was no stranger to risk and didn't lack for valor.

"The engines are located underneath the hull, near the stern. We'll crawl underneath the—crap!" She patted her pockets. *"I left my blade at the camp."*

"I do not have one either."

She scurried around the rear of the building and opened a wormhole to camp. *"Grab yours, and hurry!"*

He rushed through the wormhole—and she closed it behind him while drawing the blade she most certainly had not forgotten.

The next second she was running across open space toward the ship, grateful all over again for this wondrous technology that kept her hidden from a village full of monsters who would kill her without a thought.

She veered around to the stern as the first of the Ch'mshak arrived and the airlock opened. From there, she dove under the hull, flipped onto her back, and shimmied across the ground until she reached the point where the engine hooked into the rest of the ship.

Everyone used Zero Engines now, even for mass-produced personal craft. But no matter the engine type, it still had to interface with the control system, or else it didn't know when to fire and when to idle. At least the hull wasn't constructed of adiamene. Small favors.

In the back of her mind, she acknowledged that Galean had yet to send her any messages. His silence didn't mean anything good for his mental state, but she'd deal with the fallout after she disabled the ship.

She extended her blade and stabbed it into the rough metal a few centimeters above where the engine began protruding. She tried not to grunt from the exertion as she dragged the blade in an uneven circle until it returned to where she'd began and a jagged chunk of hull fell onto her chest.

She peered at the row of neatly woven fibers she'd exposed, trying her best to ignore the thudding overhead as Ch'mshak tromped around the cabin. She'd give anything for a consult from Alex right about now, because no one knew ships better than Alex, but there wasn't remotely time.

Ah, well. Cutting pretty much anything should get the job done, right?

She brought her blade up and…wait. Did she want the ship to be grounded, or instead to explode in the air or in space? Screw it, she didn't know enough about what she was doing to play games. She sliced through the first bundle of photal fibers, then the second—

A *hiss* filled the air as the airlock closed and sealed. Dammit. She took one final whack at the third bundle of fibers, then rolled out from under the hull, scrambled to her feet and took off running.

Zero Engines were virtually silent, so when she'd cleared fifty meters or so, she risked a peek over her shoulder. The ship was lifting off the ground and rising into the sky. Had she not cut the correct lines? Had this mad stunt been for nothing?

The ship was a few hundred meters in the air when the telltale white-blue light of the Zero Engine flickered and went out. The ship dropped like a stone.

Oh, crap, fifty meters was not far enough away. She sprinted while opening a wormhole to camp. A thunderous roar exploded behind her, and she dove through the wormhole, closing it as she tumbled across the dirt.

When she came to a stop face-up on the ground, Galean was instantly at her side. "Are you hurt?"

"Um…" she patted her torso "…see any blood, or foreign objects jutting out of me?"

His gaze ran down the length of her. "A scrape on your arm is seeping a small amount of blood. Otherwise, no."

"Great. I think I'm okay." She pushed up to sitting. When no body parts screamed in protest at her, she rose to her feet.

"You disabled the ship?"

"I did. It was able to take off, but it soon fell out of the sky. Hence the flailing escape."

"I see." No longer concerned for her health, his expression darkened, sending his eyes churning into stygian depths. "How dare you trick me! I could have protected you."

"No, you couldn't have. If we were discovered, we were both dead. Full stop. Except I'd wake up in a new body in a week or so, and you wouldn't. No way was I going to take such a terrible risk with your life."

"I've risked my life for a noble cause before. Dozens of times."

"I realize you have. But I didn't bring you here to die. In fact, I'd never allow it. You've done enough. More than I dared hope for. You're a hero, and thank you so much for helping me save lives. Not merely today, but in the future. We know who's behind this now. Or rather, Uncle Richard will be able to find out who the woman is, and then this will all be over."

He stared at her, sentsores rigid once more. His voice came out low and flat. "I'd like to return home now."

"Galean, please don't be angry."

"I think I will be. You deceived me. You made a decision for me and took away my agency. In doing so, you shamed me."

"I would never—"

"But you did. Home, please."

She sighed wearily, but nodded. Her arms burned from multiple abrasions, and her shoulder ached from her rough tumble, and it wasn't as if she hadn't known consequences were certain to flow from her actions. "Thank you again for everything. You've made a tremendous difference today. And for what it's worth, I really enjoyed spending time with you."

He simply stood there waiting, and after another few seconds of furious silence on his part and increasing resignation on hers, she opened a wormhole to Belarria. As soon as she did, he picked up his bag and walked through it.

She lowered herself to the dirt to rest for a minute. Once he calmed down, hopefully his anger would fade. Once it faded, maybe he'd come around to forgiving her.

She groaned, recognizing the irony at play here. He'd sounded painfully similar to how she used to sound, whining about agency and the unfairness of being sidelined by people who thought they knew what was best for you. And the truth was, they probably had. Just like she did now. She refused to carry his death on her conscience, refused to carve an eternal chasm into Resamane's soul.

But damn, being the responsible one was not for the faint of heart.

52

CONCORD HQ
COMMAND

Miriam listened to Richard's informal report on the events on Mshak with some dismay. "And I thought Alex was fearless. That young woman is…" she chuckled wryly "…I'm forced to admit, rather impressive. I'm relieved to hear she's unharmed."

Richard lifted his shoulders in an expressive shrug. "Somehow."

"Indeed. I'm not certain if David is going to be more horrified or proud when he finds out what she did. Quite possibly proud." Her expression sobered, though, as she turned her attention to the other revelations Richard had shared.

"When I first learned Ch'mshak were on the loose, I remarked how no one was so bad an actor as to deliver offworld transport to them. But there is one actor whose depravity, no, outright evil, has never found a limit, and that is Olivia Montegreu. We should have realized she would prove to be the only viable answer. I realize you don't require my approval to take action here, but I'll give it anyway: do everything in your power to remove her from the firmament, permanently this time."

Richard opened his mouth to protest, and she held up a hand. "I know. You had every reason to believe she was permanently removed eighteen years ago, and you were justified in believing so. Unshackled Artificials and Prevos and regenesis have done much to improve our world, but they have introduced some dastardly complications as well."

"You are preaching to the choir, Miriam. In fact, you're understating the situation by a fair bit. Those advances have made my job all but impossible, and Montegreu is a perfect example. We've already set a plan in motion to eliminate her—the living, breathing body we know she's walking around in. But this is only the beginning of our task. We're trying to game out every conceivable insurance policy she might have erected around her existence, but the truth of the matter is, she's smarter than me. She may be smarter than the sum total of all CINT's resources."

Then he scoffed. "Forgive me for taking a minute to complain. This is my problem, not yours. The important thing is, we now know how the Ch'mshak are getting off the planet."

"We do. Now that Marlee's completed her mission and we have our answers, drop a quantum block on the continent so she can't pay her shock troops any more visits."

Richard nodded. "It'll be in place by the end of the day."

Miriam stared out the viewport, reweighing the variables with the benefit of this new information. A niggling voice whispered that with the culprit unmasked, the nuclear option was no longer necessary.

But too many people had died eleven years ago because she'd hesitated, relying on cautious half measures for too long. They were dying again now, and she must put a stop to it. "I'm still going to deploy the Echo Rift."

"I don't blame you. Now that Montegreu's shown the way, other ambitious criminals may decide they need their own personal Ch'mshak murder squads as well. She exposed a weakness in the blockade we can't patch. It's one we didn't think we needed to worry about, but now we do, and an Echo Rift is the best option we have at our disposal to guarantee their isolation."

"It is. I won't put our citizens at further risk, and I certainly won't ask one additional soldier to die in a futile attempt to pacify a species that takes such glee in refusing to civilize."

Richard started to stand, then eased back into his chair instead. "It's been almost a week since we last encountered the Dzhvar. Have they gone quiet?"

"Not in the slightest. They've been surfacing far outside the Detection Network, often in galaxies we've never even catalogued, much less visited. Advisor Kirumase is dutifully updating the map as she discovers evidence in the kyoseil web of their incursions, but in every case they're long gone before we can mobilize.

"But every day they don't hit Concord interests is a day we can better prepare. The Kats almost have a more robust Rift Bubble ready to test, and Advisor Ridani continues to iterate on his faraday cage. If we can capture a sample of Dzhvar, we can begin to understand what they are. If we understand what they are, we can develop new ways to fight them."

"Do you think a multi-layered Rift Bubble will work to keep them off an asset?"

"For a time. Enough time to evacuate all the residents? No. But every person we get to safety is a victory." Cognizant it was far too early in this war for her to be growing maudlin and defeatist, she deliberately lifted her shoulders and chin. "There is good news, as well. Alex and Kennedy Rossi say they've solved the thorniest problems with the Piega Strai. Connova still has to build and test a prototype, but the progress they've made is promising."

Richard arched an eyebrow. "Sealing away a planet full of people inside a pocket universe? What a choice to make. Let's hope it doesn't come to that."

"Eighteen years ago, I was willing to seal away the entirety of Aurora forever in order to save everyone living there, and it was one of the most agonizing decisions I've ever had to make. But if Alex is right—and I struggle to conjure examples of her being wrong, at least when it comes to space—then any such confinement needn't be forever this time.

"Assuming, of course...." her gaze drifted to the wide viewports, where outside, Concord business carried on as usual. For now, peacefully. "Assuming we ultimately find a way to defeat this enemy. And if we don't, perhaps those people I seal away will get to live, even if no one else does."

53

DOMOR

Olivia perched on the edge of her desk, letting one heeled shoe dangle in the air while her gaze locked on the bare opposite wall of her office. She methodically flicked her forefinger with her thumb; then her middle finger, ring finger, pinkie, then back again. One after the other after the other, like a metronome regulating her racing thoughts.

She had a leak somewhere. Somehow. It should be impossible, since she didn't consult with anyone regarding her use of the Ch'mshak squads. In fact, she didn't consult with anyone on *any* important decisions. She employed the minimum number of underlings required, and they merely carried out her directives. They did not advise. Thus no one knew about her plan to clear out the warehouse on Lethe. Not ahead of time, and not as it occurred. Yet a unit of Machim soldiers *had*.

Flick. Flick. Flick. Flick.

She did, however, map out and iterate on her strategies as she developed them. Since she was Artificial as much as she was human, arguably more so, records of her analysis persisted in the hardware linked to this body and mind. Which meant said hardware had been compromised.

She'd certainly made enemies in the last year, and her swift and decisive actions across multiple domains of late meant the number of enemies was climbing. Arnal Nikto was dead, but he had allies. He had competitors, who had now become her competitors. The list of people who would eagerly sabotage her work if they were capable of doing so was, she conceded, not zero.

As soon as she'd returned from Mshak, she'd set forensic routines running, but they'd discovered nothing amiss in her internal or external programming or storage.

She was forced to admit a small vulnerability here. There existed aspects of this sprawling new universe that she didn't fully understand.

The Anaden black-market business was a mature entity with hundreds of thousands of years of experience responding to threats. It was in many ways akin to a living entity, and she may have inadvertently triggered an immune response. CINT, Advocacy Intelligence and SENTRI all employed sophisticated tools, some of which she wasn't yet educated on. Tools that might be able to escape the notice of what she'd perhaps erroneously believed were her own state-of-the-art routines.

The world had changed while she was gone, and in a few small ways, she was still catching up.

Flick. Flick. Flick. Flick.

The only other conceivable explanation was an elaborate scheme on the part of the Ch'mshak warriors, whereby one member of the squad somehow contacted law enforcement once they reached the mission location. The steps required for this explanation to be true were so convoluted and improbable as to be laughable, but she nonetheless filed away the possibility for further consideration if her data breach investigation turned up nothing.

Flick. Flick. Flick. Flick.

Then there was the troublesome development of the merchant vessel falling out of the sky on Mshak. Modern commercial ships, so long as a reputable company manufactured them, did not fall out of the sky. Thus it must be sabotage.

The seller had delivered the ship to a docking bay she'd rented on a human world, Demeter, as Anadens didn't often purchase ships from human-owned companies. She'd chosen human merchant ships for two reasons: they offered VI control packages comprehensive enough that even the Ch'mshak couldn't screw up flying the vessels—another way Anaden use of synthetic intelligence continued to lag behind—and of course diversification and misdirection. Investigators wouldn't think to link human ships to an Anaden criminal organization…or so she'd thought?

The ship had sat in the bay on Demeter for less than an hour before she moved it into orbit above an uninhabitable rock in a backwater system, and there it stayed until she sent it to Mshak.

Flick. Flick. Flick. Flick.

The opportunities for sabotage were narrow, to say the least. But her ship purchases were also recorded in her hardware, and thus vulnerable to discovery by an infiltrating program. Security at the docking bay was tight, but in dead space, somewhat less so. Effecting such a sabotage would be difficult, but not impossible.

Though she could prevent such a mishap from occurring in the future by installing active security countermeasures on each ship, she wasn't convinced it was worth the trouble. For one, the risk vanished when she uncovered the malware at the root of all these breaches and its source. For another, she was almost done with the Ch'mshak. Their brutality had proved most effective at sending the messages she'd desired to the appropriate targets, but now that those messages had been suitably delivered, she expected to be able to handle future situations by more conventional means.

Flick. Flick. Flick. Flick.

She evaluated several options for the best method to uncover the malware in such a manner that would also reveal who had deployed it.

Then she sent Padron Lanael a message.

> *Mr. Lanael,*
>
> *I require a best-in-class foreign code detection and quarantine program. Nothing off the shelf, as my security routines are already robust, and I run a great deal of custom code. Give me several options, as well as your recommendations.*
>
> *— Teresa Piras*

Lanael claimed to have extensive experience navigating illegal markets and criminal enterprises, and he seemed to know every player, no matter the business. If he couldn't provide what she needed directly, he should know where to go to acquire it.

She acknowledged the additional benefit of this course of action. It provided another opportunity for her to test both his skills and his trustworthiness. Another opportunity to bring him into her presence and evaluate the offer he'd set before her.

Flick. Flick. Flick. Flick.

INTERMEZZO
III

INTERGALACTIC SPACE

he three generation ships neared the end of their long journey across the void as the spiral arms of the Gennisi galaxy loomed sweeping and majestic on the cosmic horizon. The weary rebels would soon find their home—but they had a fateful stop to make first.

It was an act of serendipitous luck that the ships always passed close enough to the planetoid the Asterions named 'Proele' to detect its rich mineral profile, leading them to divert there to refill the coffers of their greedy fabrication machines. Unless the kyoseil exerted a rare and momentous act of volition and somehow used its wave form to nudge either the ships or the planetoid, thus engineering their arrival? But the kyoseil did not deign to share its secrets, not even with me.

I hadn't visited Nicolette since the day the SAI Rebellion began. I'd intended to witness Loshi's death on the battlefield, as it felt like an important gesture, a way of honoring his sacrifice. But after becoming overwhelmed by emotions I could not constrain at the sight of Dashiel's ancestor, I determined I was not up to the challenge of facing my brother's death. Such an experience was certain to break me, perhaps irreparably so, and I pursued a mission both grander and more significant than honoring the already dead. So I'd stayed away as the rebels fought bravely against a mighty Anaden military led by Corradeo Praesidis. Fought and too often perished, until they made the only choice left to them: flee and live.

But this task, here, I truly did need to perform. Miaon had done so before me, and the previous iteration had done so before them. Some lost number of cycles in the past, an earlier Mnemosyne had identified an opportunity and acted. Or, I assumed they had. Perhaps the rebels and kyoseil had found one another on their own, and my intervention wasn't required at all. But I couldn't take that chance. This was too important.

Nicolette never set foot on Proele, so I indulged my weakness and stole a peek in on her on board her generation ship before its arrival.

She and Steven cuddled together on the sofa in their stateroom, listening to music and discussing the politics of keeping thousands of refugees comfortable, sane and healthy while confined to an ark for centuries.

I'd girded my defenses since my failure on Asterion Prime, and I was able to observe them now without losing my senses. They wouldn't be happy forever—if Steven hadn't ultimately proved to be unworthy of her love, there would be no Dashiel—but they seemed happy now. If not with the world, at least with the sanctuary holding each other close provided.

Comforted by the knowledge that heartbreak was safely behind her for many millennia, I gave them their privacy and sped onward to Proele to make preparations.

GENNISI GALAXY

The planetoid was glutted with kyoseil, but the primordial life form had burrowed deep here, as it had on countless other planetary objects, in order to hide and persevere. To hide from the Dzhvar? Another mystery for which I'd never found an answer. As such, no kyoseil resided atop the surface where it might be serendipitously discovered.

I traveled to an open plain rimmed on one side by jutting cliffs. The region was unusually rich in platinum and silica, thus the miners were going to choose it for excavation. I knew this because Miaon knew this.

I rarely saw Miaon these days. These were the 'long, slow millennia,' as they phrased it. Their meaningful participation in our mission would be called for again one day, but until then, Miaon preferred to simply exist in solitude. To rest and endeavor to preserve what little remained of their essence.

I drew together a greater concentration of myself and dug into the chalky surface of the planetoid until I reached a layer of kyoseil. Tiny, golden strands threaded through the sandy material, gleaming like brilliant stardust. Once I'd uncovered it, I cleared away several meters' worth of chalky regolith. Then I retreated to the ridgeline to wait.

S&L

The mining camp bustled in the distance as machinery churned into the planetoid's surface. Two centuries on the run, and the Asterions continued to drive relentlessly forward into the future they seemed intent on manifesting for themselves.

Judging the moment was now at hand, I swept onto the plain and hovered over the kyoseil I had exposed. Once there, I danced about, trying to catch the light of the distant star upon my particles, begging to be seen. Still, it took almost twenty minutes until someone in an environment suit began hop-walking their way closer. Magnus Forchelle, if history was any guide.

I waited until he'd drawn to within thirty meters before I dissipated and retreated to a nearby boulder to watch.

His gaze searched around for the shining cluster of particles he'd spotted, and he nearly overshot the deposit before happening to glance down. He dropped to his knees, running gloved fingers through the kyoseil-infused regolith for several passes then sweeping it away to reveal a veritable sea of kyoseil beneath it.

He leapt to his feet and began motioning back toward the mining camp. "Drayden, come look at this!"

I gathered myself up and bid farewell to my once-and-future brethren.

The rest would take care of itself from here, for a very long time.

PART IV:

ENTANGLEMENT

54

MIRAI

Nika brought Dashiel a mug of coffee at his desk, placing it near his left hand so he'd notice it.

"Hmm, thanks," he murmured distractedly.

She kissed him on the top of the head, then settled onto his couch with her own mug. For the first time in a few days, he wasn't actually distracted by the troubling implications of Alex's vision. While the Weave project was focused on an energy solution, with the confirmation that the Dzhvar could move through adiaK unimpeded, he was redoubling his efforts to also invent a physical, solid material that was capable of keeping them out. It would be a shame, after he went to all the trouble of transforming the world's most resilient metal into an even more remarkable creation, for it to be of no use against their greatest foe.

He wasn't working alone in this endeavor, of course. Everyone in the Dominion and Concord with a technical bent was pitching in at least a few cycles on the problem. Two ceraffin in Conceptual Research were making it their sole focus, and she assumed several of Concord's Artificials were doing the same. But Dashiel wasn't merely the most brilliant person she knew, he was the most ingenious. An inventor through and through. He lived and breathed this stuff, so if anyone could devise a solution, it would be him. For now, though, his sporadic grunts seemed to signal more frustration than progress.

Her mug was nearly empty when Mesme arrived in a rush of lights.

Apologies. An Idryma meeting delayed me.

"Do your colleagues have any new ideas?" Nika asked.

None that are far enough along to warrant your consideration at present. Mesme considered Dashiel for a moment before shifting its full attention to her. *You said you wanted to discuss a matter with me?*

"I do. The speed with which the Dzhvar move means we need to know the instant they pop into normal space if we hope to be able to evacuate any reasonable number of people in their path. Now, I told Miriam I couldn't live in the kyoseil web, and I definitely don't want to. But I will if I have to. I'm searching for a way I don't have to."

She stared out the window, where a misty rain fell from overcast skies. "Is there any way I can communicate to the kyoseil that I need for it to alert me when it registers the presence of Dzhvar? Or if not, is there any way I can sort of...leave behind a layer of my consciousness in the web—"

"What?" Dashiel exclaimed, twisting around in his chair to face her.

She shrugged weakly. "It creeps me out a little, too, but I'm looking for options here. I'm thinking of a Plex-type solution, only without a duplicate body."

"But Nika, it doesn't matter if part of you remains here, in your body. It'll still be you out there drifting in space. You'll experience that state of being as much as you will the real world."

"Which is why I phrased it as a 'layer.' I'm hoping it can be a less than fully conscious version of me. Well, Mesme? Any ideas?"

To your first question about convincing the kyoseil to alert you to incursions, I don't believe so. Kyoseil lacks the initiative to act on its own in such a direct manner, even toward you. As to your second question, possibly. But it will require you to deepen your inherent connection with kyoseil further.

"I don't think I can fit any more kyoseil fibers in my body."

"No, you cannot," Dashiel muttered under his breath.

She'd already upgraded her body a second time a year ago, testing the limits of what he insisted was both safe and functional.

She'd been dizzy and vaguely ill for several weeks after switching over, before finally adjusting to the borderline overload.

But you can better utilize the kyoseil you do control. In fact….

"In fact, what?"

I did not want to push you in this regard, for it is always preferable that you come to such things of your own accord. But it is time for you to strengthen this bond. In order to do as you've expressed, and to unlock other skills.

Her fingers tightened their grip on her mug, despite the fact that she'd now drained it dry. "Because there's something I'm going to need to do in the future to try to defeat the Dzhvar, and I'll need better control over the kyoseil out there on the manifold in order to accomplish it."

Mesme vibrated above Dashiel's living room rug.

"It's okay, you can just say 'yes.'"

Yes.

"Even though it's not going to be enough? If I did it last time, by definition it didn't matter in the end. We still lost." She waved off Mesme's protestation. "Necessary but not sufficient. I get it."

So it is.

She sighed and stood to refill her coffee. She empathized with how Mesme was tying itself up in knots trying to balance the reveals of needed information against the risk of sabotaging current efforts by 'poisoning the well' with ideas that had ultimately resulted in failure last time. And she couldn't imagine the terror and agony of watching as they all careened toward failure once again. But often it felt like Dashiel had the right of it on this point; they were fumbling around in the dark, and they had someone *right here* who'd been through all this before. There must be more the Kat could give them to work with.

She returned to the couch and curled her legs underneath her, taking a minute to watch the steam waft up from her mug while she circled back through the thought, then the next one it inevitably led to. "Mesme, who were you in your cycle?"

Nika, you promised.

"You had to be someone intimately involved in the fight against the Dzhvar, or else you wouldn't know as many details of how the conflict was waged as you do. Someone who was also involved in the fight against the Rasu, for the same reason. Mnemosyne was a goddess, which suggests you were a woman, though I realize this may be misdirection. Or maybe you simply admired the archetype. Alex is the obvious guess, but I know it isn't her."

Why...why do you say so?

"Alex is far too fierce. Too disagreeable, at times rude and occasionally vulgar. She'd never, ever stand by and watch while others screwed something up. Not without sharing her opinion in no uncertain terms, then storming off to go try to fix it herself. You, on the other hand, are contemplative, philosophical and, yes, at times passive. You're patient—you've exhibited aeons upon aeons of patience—and restrained to a fault. So, no, not Alex."

She supposed it could be Miriam, but Mesme had never struck her as the military type. Also, Miriam was a decisionmaker through and through. Responsibility started and ended with her. So not likely Miriam, either.

She stared at the back of Dashiel's head. He was patient and restrained, unless she pushed the right nerve. She'd never call him 'passive,' though. He was a builder, a creator. The Kats were builders, too. Builders of entire universes.

She shook her head to dispel the notion. Now she was just torturing herself, jumping at shadows.

You are also fierce.

Nika studied the cream swirls in her coffee as a pang of sorrow welled up in her chest. "I used to be. When I led NOIR, I was so intense. Ferociously passionate. I had to be strong and decisive for everyone, and I was. And even after NOIR...I fought for everything we've created here. I fought to liberate Namino and to protect all the Axis Worlds when the Rasu arrived in force.

"But ever since the Oneiroi Nebula, the kyoseil is changing me. Filing away the rough edges. Lopping off the dynamic, assertive veneer in favor of a deeper, more expansive, almost meta-physical worldview. The kyoseil's worldview, one might posit."

You are everything you were.

"No, I'm not. I'm something else now. Maybe better and stronger in some ways, but not the same." She tilted her head toward Dashiel, who had stopped working again to shift around in his chair and gaze at her while brandishing an achingly soulful expression. "See, Dashiel agrees."

"Nika, I don't think you…." He faltered, his words trailing off.

"You can't bring yourself to refute it, because you know I'm right." She offered him a brave smile. "I don't regret this turn of events. I've done what I had to do to save my people, and I'll keep on forging this path so long as it means I can make a difference. But a part of me misses those rough edges."

Dashiel came over to kneel in front of her, cupping her face in his hands. "I love you. I love all your edges, whether they be rough, smooth, acutely angled or gently curving, and I am in perpetual awe of your strength and courage."

Though they had an audience, she set her coffee on the table and wrapped her arms around his neck, drawing him in to kiss him deeply. "I love you, too. Whoever we were, are or become, darling, I will always love you."

We are forever.

55

IDRYMA

I swept into Lakhes' office in a tear of spasmodic energy. "Apologies for departing the Idryma meeting so abruptly earlier. Nika Kirumase required my assistance with a matter."

Lakhes serenely stepped through the rippling holographic orbs of its interface, checking in on various project updates. "The Asterion has you on an increasingly short leash, Mnemosyne. I recognize the value of her notable bonding with kyoseil, but we Katasketousya enjoy such a relationship and skillset as well. Why has she captured such a large share of your attention?"

She is my past and my future, my greatest fears and my most audacious hopes. She is my soul.

I had confessed much of the truth to Lakhes during the Rasu War, but not everything. Not this. Lakhes knowing my former identity would not change the outcome of this struggle, thus the sole effect of such a disclosure would be the exposure of my rawest wound. Lakhes was a meaningful friend and colleague, but some truths cut too close to ever be shared. Miaon knew, because it was Miaon's history as well. Alex knew, because Alex could wrest fundamental truths out of the very universe, whether the universe, or myself, wished it or not.

"She is key to our fight against the Dzhvar," I replied.

"I thought you said Alexis Solovy was the key."

How to explain this in a way sufficient to mollify my friend? How to explain that Alex was key if we hoped to succeed, but Nika was key if we nonetheless failed?

I drifted around Lakhes' office aimlessly. A million years of keeping secrets had left my compass for determining when it was the correct choice to disclose one of them rather poorly calibrated. Lacking other options, I composed myself and shared my thoughts.

The Praetor abandoned its project interface and rewarded me with its full attention. "Nika will enable the time travel to occur, should we fail to stop the Dzhvar?"

It was close enough to the truth to suffice. "Yes. But only if she has fully mastered kyoseil when the day comes. So now you understand why I need to guide and mentor her to the greatest extent she will allow me."

"I do. You could have simply said this."

"Forgive me. Old habits die hard, as the Humans say." I indicated the interface, eager to change the subject. "What's the status of the new rift devices?"

"The modifications proved out, and we are manufacturing two field models now." Lakhes churned with displeasure. "Reluctantly. You have stated that no dimension shifting technology will succeed in blocking the Dzhvar. I dislike being your interrogator today, Mnemosyne, but why am I wasting valuable resources building devices that will not work?"

"Because our allies must be allowed to *try*. They must think and strategize and brainstorm and invent and iterate and test and refine. It is what they do best. In doing so, they may well hit upon the fresh idea needed to transform this war in our favor. But they will not discover it if they don't first try a thousand ideas that fall short."

"Ah, yes. The famed ingenuity of the Anadens and their descendants."

"Don't mock it, Lakhes. Their ingenuity is why the Directorate is dead, and so are the Rasu."

"With no small help from *diati* and kyoseil."

"Inscrutable primordial entities who have never shown the slightest inclination to act on their own initiative. A trait the Dzhvar, unfortunately, don't share, though I believe they do act primarily on instinct. The point is, the organics are key: Humans,

Asterions, and even a few Anadens who have escaped their own self-imposed limitations. Lakhes, why are we arguing about this?"

Lakhes conveyed a sigh and deflated slightly. "I am as frustrated as you are. The Katasketousya can create and manipulate universes. We can control the manifold and bend it to our will. How is it that, despite repeated attempts, we cannot overcome this foe?"

I should not have been cross with my friend, as they owned this struggle nearly as much as I did. "The only answer I can offer is this: while we can create universes, the Dzhvar *are* the universe. There is no way to outmaneuver an entity which is everything. This is why *diati* is the sole weapon to ever successfully counter the Dzhvar."

"And kyoseil? As we have long understood matters, there exist three primordial beings. A triumvirate that *together* comprises the universe. Not any one of them alone."

"True, but Kyoseil is not a weapon. It is a conduit."

"Then let it be a conduit for a weapon."

The notion made me shudder, but I should not be naïve. It had acted as such against the Rasu, and in doing so saved trillions of lives. But while the Rasu were descended from the Dzhvar, they were physical in nature. What was physical could be killed.

The question plaguing me for two lives now still had no answer: what could kill the Dzhvar?

"If we are able to devise an effective weapon using a kyoseil conduit to function, we will without a doubt pursue such an avenue. But for now, no such weapon exists."

NOKORI

CETUS DWARF GALAXY

After the contentious meeting with Lakhes, I retreated to Nokori, the name Miaon had given the world it called home. This had been a difficult day, and I needed the solace of the one place and one person with whom I harbored no secrets.

I sat on the front steps of Miaon's home and contemplated the blooming flowers until a shadow quietly appeared beside me. Then I immediately launched into a tirade.

"She's dancing on the verge of deducing the truth, Miaon. She came within a breath of recognizing it today, and I know from experience it is only a subconscious blind spot she cannot see around which delays the realization. Her mind acts in self-preservation to refuse to consider that *she* might be the one to give up everything and live a million years alone in a desperate attempt to save everyone that will, in all likelihood, fail. But the block is fading away in the face of mounting evidence, and I can't seem to forestall it."

Miaon drifted above the steps in the morning breeze. "She was always going to learn the truth. You did. I did. Those before me did. I know you fear it, but you must come to terms with its inevitability. When the time arrives, you will need to be strong for her."

"As you were strong for me. I know. And thank you for being there for me. It has been some millennia since I have said so, but thank you. If I had known the vast sorrow and crippling doubts you harbored beneath the brave façade, I would've endeavored to be...kinder than I was."

"No, you would not have, because you were hurting. And this was fine. It wasn't about me. And soon, it will not be about you."

I joined the breeze in a sigh. Soon, indeed. "Even now, you have lessons still to teach me."

"It is the entirety of my purpose."

And if we fail again, it will become my purpose. I tried to push the thought away, as focusing on events that hadn't yet come to pass only punished me. I longed to borrow a measure of Alex's dogged determination and refusal to accept anything but success as an outcome.

"Where were you when I arrived?" I asked. "Any hopeful news to report?"

"I was attempting to nudge Eren in the correct direction, as this has become my second purpose these last several decades. Time grows short, and Corradeo needs him more than either of them realize. But Eren is running headlong into another daring mission at the moment and has no patience for the contemplations of shadows."

56

CONCORD HQ
CINT

"Teresa Piras—your Olivia Montegreu—is the one sneaking Ch'mshak offworld? Gods, the bitch is hardcore." Eren shook his head in disbelief. But on giving it further thought, he decided he shouldn't be surprised. It fit the facts. Ch'mshak had taken out Arnal Nikto's operations on Ficenti and Brizo, and now Piras was running those facilities.

This latest revelation meant she really did need to be neutralized sooner rather than later, and he'd positioned himself to be the man to do it. Her latest request provided them with an opportunity to make a decisive move against her, which was why he was here meeting with Richard. And Nyx.

Piras was thus far acting exclusively on Anaden worlds, so any move against her should be cleared with the Advocacy. As Director of Advocacy Security, arguably Ziton Praesidis was the correct person to include in the meeting. But why in Hades would he invite Ziton when he could bring Nyx instead? And maybe after this wrapped up, they could return to the estate and….

He blinked and worked to refocus. "Obviously, she's got to go. How do we shut down Riamere's operations?"

"We don't," Richard replied. "Not until Montegreu herself is off the board. She was nearly impossible to eliminate when she was merely human, and doubly so once she was a Prevo. Now she's some bastardization of Prevo and Artificial, sporting upgrades no one else is fielding. She's learned from Vilane's mistakes and her own and has surely closed every loophole she can spot.

"If we've caught a break, it's that she's not Anaden, so there's no integral in play. Therefore, we need to kill her body while simultaneously taking control of her two remote hardware backups. Once that's done, *then* we can move in and dismantle Riamere."

"You know where the backups are located, correct?" Nyx asked.

"We do," Richard said. "They're on Domor and Brizo. We can use Vigil if you think they're up to the task, Director, but I'd honestly feel better if we deployed Machim units instead. She's enough of a threat to warrant a military response."

Nyx mulled it over, then nodded. "I'll authorize it."

"Thank you. We'll need to stage the units at each location and drop quantum blocks around her hubs the instant her body is deceased. We don't want another 'ghost in the machine' scenario on our hands—or worse, her consciousness jumping to additional hardware or into the Noesis. Once the scenes are secure, CINT teams will move in. They'll power the hardware off, take it apart and bring it back here, where our forensics people will scour it for information we can use to root out every aspect of Riamere."

"It should be a fairly straightforward operation," Nyx replied.

"Honestly, seizing the hardware is the easy part. Killing her will be more difficult."

Eren sighed. "Agreed. Her shield is so powerful, it might be based on the Imperium double-shielding tech. It almost electrocuted me when I got a little too close, and a scan of it returned essentially a solid wall of energy."

"She wore a powerful shield in her first life, too," Richard said. "It was only through sheer luck and Dr. Canivon's quick thinking that we were able to disable it for the critical seconds Fleet Admiral Jenner needed to neutralize her. We don't have a way to do so now."

"Nothing physical gets through a TDS. We blow her up, or blow up the entire building she's located in, and she may well live through the explosion."

"What about using a Rectifier?" Richard asked.

Nyx immediately protested. "I am not going to authorize opening up a *black hole* in the middle of an urban area on Scholite, Domor or any other decently populated Anaden world."

"It wouldn't work, anyway," Eren offered. "I'd never be able to get a Rectifier within firing distance of her. Thus far, I've been checked for weapons every time I see her. And even if I've finally earned enough trust to skip the body search, I won't be allowed to bring along a conveniently large bag without *it* being searched." He shook his head. "A Rectifier's too bulky. I can't hide it."

Richard drummed his fingertips on the table. "Could someone wormhole to your location when you're with her and fire it?"

"The timing would have to be perfect. She'll evacuate herself the instant she recognizes a threat."

Nyx cleared her throat. "Again, I am not having a black hole weapon shootout in a populated area. I don't care how dangerous this woman is. Find another way."

The iciness of Nyx's glare suggested she meant it, too. Despite the fact that she could back up the threat her glare conveyed with deadly action, Eren had never been frightened by it. Now, though, he was finding it almost enchanting...ah, shite. What were they talking about? Right, killing Piras.

"Too many uncertainties for my liking, regardless," Richard replied. "If anything at all goes wrong, Eren's cover is permanently blown and we lose our best chance at stopping her. Other ideas?"

Eren stared at the ceiling for several seconds, then groaned, because he had a terrible one. "I think I can get her to deactivate her shield. Then I can kill her the old-fashioned way."

"How do you expect to convince her to do so?" Richard asked.

He shot Richard a smirk. "By doing what Idonis do best. Seducing her."

"Eren, you are smooth and crafty, but this woman is not easily fooled. I daresay she can't be fooled."

"Doesn't matter. I'm Idoni. Sex is in my genes, and she knows it. She's intrigued by it. The truth is, she's already trying to seduce me. In a bone-chilling, terrifying way, but nonetheless.

"After we learned her true identity, I read your entire file on her. I started modeling my behavior after the psych profile of Aiden Trieneri, which wasn't much of a stretch from the persona I'd initially adopted. She likes confident alpha men with a striking absence of morals. I've been acting as that archetype, and it's working."

"And you think she will deactivate her shield in order to have sex with you?" Richard looked dubious, but it was probably only because he'd never assigned Eren this kind of mission before.

"Eren, you wouldn't." Nyx's voice rang harsh in his ears. She sounded positively mortified, which he found endearing.

"Don't worry, I'm not going to go through with it, sweetheart." The nickname slipped past his lips unintentionally. He hadn't called her that in months—not since things had first gotten messy on Nythir. He felt a little bad for doing so now, when she was exposing a bit of her tender underbelly. Gods, she had a tender underbelly.

He offered her a conciliatory smile by way of apology. "My days of whoring myself out at the whim of my superiors are long behind me. I just need her to deactivate the shield. I can modify an adiamene blade to get it past a weapons scan and hide it in my clothing. As soon as the shield is off, I'll cut her head clean off."

Richard frowned. "I'm sure slitting her throat will be sufficient."

"Oh, I'll try for that. But as I understand it, the adiamene blade will likely decapitate her anyway. Once it gets started, nothing stops it. But, since we don't know what *other* defenses she's carrying around in her body, I don't want to chance a lesser blade failing at the job. Also, I'd prefer not to give her a few extra seconds to kill me in return if I can avoid it."

He wound his fingers together and stretched his arms over his head. "So what do we say? Is this the beginning of a plan?"

57

SENECA

CAVARE

Morgan wormholed directly into Marlee's living room unannounced. It was a blatant privacy invasion, but she was too furious to care.

Marlee was sitting out on her balcony sipping on a drink. Upon noticing Morgan's arrival, she leapt to her feet and rushed inside. "Morgan! This is a surprise. Is something wrong?"

"Yes, something is wrong." She adopted a strident pace across the living room. "You went to Mshak. Have you lost your sanity?"

"No. I was on an important mission, one authorized by Director Navick. I took Galean with me, and he was able to track the quantum disruption when a wormhole opened on the surface. We learned which settlement the raids have been originating from and who's orchestrating them: a woman named Olivia Montegreu."

Morgan spun on a heel. "*What?* Are you kidding me?"

"That's what everyone says. She was before my time, but apparently she used to be this powerful crime boss. Died, and now she's back."

"I know all too well who she was. I helped to kill her and blow up her secret space station."

Marlee's eyes widened a touch. "Really?"

"Yes, really. Not the point. The point is, you *went to Mshak.*"

"How did you find out?"

"The latest military briefing disclosed that we were closing in on the source of the Ch'mshak raiding parties. I obviously have an interest in the investigation, so I inquired further. A lot further.

Good god, Marlee! Are you nurturing a death wish? Do you have any idea what a single one of those monsters can do to a fragile human body?"

"Yeah, I do. And they were terrifying. More terrifying than the Rasu, in their own way. But Galean and I saved lives. Immediately, because a Machim unit was able to stop an attack in progress, and in the long run, because now we can prevent any more Ch'mshak from escaping the planet."

"Fantastic. Go pick up your hero medal at HQ." Morgan threw herself against the wall with a groan. "Fuck, I am so stupid. I was starting to feel soft and gooey over how you reminded me of Brook with your fearlessness and zeal for adventure. It turns out you *are* like her. You're a bloody selfish idiot who doesn't value your safety or appreciate what losing you will do to the people who care about you. Glad I figured this out now, before I ruined my life all over again."

Marlee was staring at her, lips parted and sapphire irises flaring brightly. Her voice came out uncharacteristically soft. "You care about me?" It wasn't the rational response to the string of invectives Morgan had caustically flung at her, but it felt like the only one that mattered.

"It seems I am a glutton for punishment. But no longer. I may be a fool, but even I can learn this lesson. Don't let anyone get close enough to hurt you."

"Morgan...." Marlee blinked twice, her throat working. "Um, listen. I won't say I was careful, since there were a few times I couldn't be, not if I wanted to make a difference, which is what I went there to do. But I was always cognizant of the risk, and I carefully weighed every choice. I promise I did.

"And here's the thing. While I absolutely did not want to suffer the agony of being gutted and ripped limb from limb by those horrible talons..." Marlee shuddered "...there is regenesis now. We don't have to die forever any longer. We *won't*. I am so sorry the option wasn't available for Brooklyn. But it is available now. So no matter what happens, you won't have to mourn me...if mourning me were to be something you'd otherwise do."

Morgan collapsed on the sofa and buried her head in her hands. "I thought I was okay. Not great, granted, but okay. Doing better. Interacting with the world like a mostly normal human being. Developing the occasional collegial if casual platonic relationship. Starting to consider entertaining the possibility of something greater. But now the Ch'mshak are once more engaging in indiscriminate slaughter, and nothing anyone did eleven years ago made a damn bit of difference, and I'm right back where I started."

She felt the cushion shift as Marlee sat beside her, close but not touching. "I contemplated much the same while I was on Mshak, and I truly do understand where you're coming from. But I hope you don't withdraw again. Living in this world? It's worth it. And we would all be lesser for your absence. I know I would be lesser."

She didn't have anything worthwhile to say to that.

"Besides, they won't be able to hurt many more people. I shouldn't mention this, but Aunt Miriam's planning to Echo Rift the planet. In a few days, I think, or as soon as the Kats finish the device. I assume there are some Ch'mshak running around on the ships Olivia Montegreu gave them who the military will need to hunt down, but their number will never increase."

The low-grade thirst for vengeance rattling around in Morgan's chest flared to life at the news she was in danger of losing the opportunity to exact it. "Where's the settlement?"

"What?"

"The settlement that's been sending the raiding parties out. Where is it? Specific coordinates."

"Why?"

"Beneath an Echo Rift, they get to live. They shouldn't get to do that."

"Morgan, blowing up a few thousand Ch'mshak won't bring Brooklyn back."

"Goddammit, tell me where it is."

Marlee squeezed her eyes shut and dropped her head onto the couch cushion. "I've already pissed off one friend with this whole affair. Why shouldn't it cost me another one?" She looked over, sadness weighing down her normally buoyant features. "No."

"No? You don't think they ought to die as punishment for all the people they've killed in the last month?"

"I think they probably should. I'd be happy to see such a punishment inflicted on them. But it's not for me to decide. More importantly, though, getting blood on your hands is not going to help you get over Brooklyn's death."

"I'll be the judge of what will and won't help me."

"Because you've done such a spectacular job of it so far."

Morgan's eyes widened in shock.

Marlee deflated. "I'm sorry. That was unfair of me."

"No, it's true, and bully on you for calling me out. Fine. I get to decide how I'll wreck my own life."

"Maybe. But I won't help you do it."

The look of sad resolve on Marlee's face told the tale; she wasn't going to budge. A familiar feeling of hollow desolation descended upon Morgan like the embrace of an old friend.

She stood and departed without another word.

Morgan tapped her foot impatiently as she waited for the lift to arrive. She could just wormhole home, but her apartment was six short blocks away, and it felt like a petulant indulgence to do so. Besides, a vortex of indignant energy compelled her to move, so she might as well steer it in a useful direction.

As a condition of her rejoining the military, she'd received a formal pardon for any and all actions she'd undertaken relating to the theft of Stanley's hardware from the Senecan Federation in the wake of the Metigen War. She wasn't certain the Federation would have ever granted the pardon, but it was no longer in their hands. When it came to the military, there was only AEGIS now.

Once she didn't have to keep one eye in the rear of her head scoping for MPs in case someone decided it was time to arrest her for old crimes, she was able to move back to Cavare. She'd needed someplace to live after she'd sold *Purgatory* to Solstan, as lurking around in the apartment above the bar would've been rude, and she hadn't wanted to return to Romane. It reminded her too much of Brook....

Her pulse pounded in her ears as she leapt onto the lift and selected the ground floor.

Please consider taking a few or few thousand deep breaths before pursuing any action.

Stanley, when has that advice ever worked on me?

Today is, as ever, a new day. When you've calmed down, I believe you'll realize Marlee was.... The voice in her head trailed off.

You don't have to speak the words for me to know what you're thinking. Of course she was right, but about the wrong things. I'm not trying to 'get over' anything, as we've established how I'm never getting over Brook's death. I'm trying to inflict the tiniest bit of punishment on violent murderers. Solovy and Jenner are too big of pansies to do it, so the job's left to me.

She exited the apartment building and turned left. Darkness had fallen, and the air was uncomfortably cool. She didn't have a jacket, since she'd come straight to Marlee's apartment from the Presidio, so she shivered, hugged her arms across her chest, and picked up the pace.

Setting aside any quibbles with your disparaging of your superiors' honor, my concern, much like your friend's, is your own wellbeing. I fear you are, as you so often are, engaging in self-sabotage.

How so?

Your life is going well, Morgan. You're fulfilled in your work. You're making a difference again. You're getting to fly the most advanced fighter craft ever built on a regular basis. I submit you are almost—

Don't you dare say happy.

If you insist, I will not. But you are no longer miserable, and this is a vast improvement. Now you are storming headlong off to take a rash, foolish action that may well result in you losing your commission. You may in fact lose everything you have won back for yourself.

Her step hitched. Oh, how she hated it when Stanley made too much sense. But no. He was merely being overprotective, as usual.

I won't get caught. And if I somehow do, so be it. I can't stand by and let their crimes go unanswered. I can't.

S&L

Morgan sat down at the terminal in her bedroom and linked into the AEGIS Military Network.

As a Prevo, she didn't need a physical server to do much of anything. But the most secure military files and communications were only able to be accessed through a QEC connection. Used to be QECs were room-sized contraptions, but now they fit inside a twenty-centimeter-wide box, and one such box was fitted to the bottom of the terminal.

She logged in under her own credentials, hoping this would be straightforward, and navigated her way to the Ch'mshak investigation folder. She'd received the same high-level briefing materials all senior officers had, but those didn't delve beyond the generalities. She needed specifics.

PROJECT PASSWORD:

"Dammit." It wasn't as if she didn't have the requisite security clearance. But the AEGIS military was a labyrinthine organization, with endless divisions and initiatives and projects, and arrogant generals with more hubris than sense enjoyed sticking their fingers in areas they knew nothing about and trying to fling around orders. So Fleet Admiral Jenner had instituted a 'silo' system whereby sensitive information was kept walled off from those not involved in the subject matter in question.

It had been a wildly popular change with everyone pinned with less than three stars, and Morgan had to admit she was a fan as well. Nothing was worse than some flag officer showing up on the hangar deck to challenge the safety of the Banshees or the autonomy of the Eidolons.

But she didn't love it today.

So be it. Illegal way it was.

Morgan....

Hey, you pointed out I risk getting discharged over this. Why not give them a good reason to do so?

In the darkest corner of the intersection between the Prevos' civilian Noesis and military Connexus, hacking routines capable of breaking all but the strongest forms of military encryption were bought and sold. She'd known of the enterprise for several years now, but she'd figured it wasn't her business. Criminals were going to criminal and hackers were going to hack; it was true on the street, and it was true in the military. But now she had need of their services.

The routine cost more than she'd have preferred to spend, and if she'd needed a whole package, it would've fallen outside of her means. But she and Stanley boasted plenty of skills in this area, and she only required a few military-specific codes and protocols that were beyond her operational reach.

Once the routine was deployed, it took less than thirty seconds to unearth the password for the Ch'mshak folder, and she dove into reading with fury-fueled zeal.

The files went into some depth regarding body counts and security failures surrounding the various attacks. They'd found and eliminated three ships' worth of Ch'mshak in the last two days; she kept skimming. The most recent updates centered around Olivia Montegreu's involvement, which, wild that the psychotic monster was somehow back among the living. But she didn't want to think too hard about this, because the mission to kill the woman had marked a turning point in her relationship with Brook—

Ah, there they were. Coordinates.

58

CONCORD HQ

CINT

Eren accepted the sheathed blade from Richard and inspected it from every angle. "It's thin."

"Thin enough that it won't show through clothes and should be passed over in anything short of a bare skin pat-down. The hilt is made of a rubberized material. The blade, as well as the metal activation components, have been coated with a film that mimics a fabric profile when scanned."

"Excellent." Eren confirmed the latch was secure, as he didn't want the adiamene blade slicing through his clothes then him, and slipped it into his pocket. "I know my role. What's the rest of the plan?"

The AEGIS fleet admiral raised a hand from where he sat working at the table in Richard's office. "I've got two cross-jurisdictional teams of Marine and Machim special forces ready to wormhole in to both locations where she's storing her Artificial hardware the instant you give the word. They'll drop quantum blocks as they arrive, which will shut off the machines and prevent her from executing whatever contingency plans she has in place. The teams will confiscate everything they find and relocate it all to a secure CINT forensics lab." Jenner leveled a stern glare at Eren. "Be careful. I already killed her once, and it didn't take."

He nodded. "I read the file. You did a fine job of killing her. She just doesn't like to stay dead."

"We're going to do our best to make certain she stays that way this time," Richard said. "Fleet Admiral, Director, thank you for not slowing things down with jurisdictional red tape. Olivia

Montegreu has long been humanity's problem, but now she's decided to infect Anaden space with her current organization. Accordingly, CINT will work closely with AdvInt in the subsequent investigation and dismantling of Riamere."

"Thank you," Nyx replied. She turned to Eren, whatever her true thoughts might be masked behind a façade of professionalism. "If you're ready, I'll send you to uptown Palici, so you won't be arriving for the meeting directly from here."

"I'm ready. But, hey, guys, a word of caution. I may not get a chance to make my move today. She can shut me down and send me away again, in which case, sorry for the blue balls."

"Eren," Nyx hissed.

"Not *mine*." He rolled his eyes. *Arae*, was she genuinely upset at the notion of him playing seduction games with someone else? It wasn't as if he felt the slightest attraction toward Piras. The woman was a monster, and when it came to this mission, he was all business. "I mean the soldiers. They'll be all dressed up with nowhere to go."

The fleet admiral nodded. "Understood. Now that we have a plan and teams assigned to it, we can move whenever the opportunity presents itself."

"All right, then." He gestured to Nyx. "Let's go."

DOMOR

Yet another park on yet another planet. Same enforcer. He'd given Nyx a visual of the man, so she could hopefully track him down, arrest him and extract useful information from him in the aftermath.

He was also curious as to why Montegreu put unvarnished faith in this man, when in seemingly no one else. It didn't make any sense; the man was nothing but muscle, and muscle could always be bought by a higher bidder.

Eren adopted his usual relaxed demeanor as the enforcer performed the standard weapons check, and kept the relief he felt when the blade didn't register hidden behind an aura of bored indifference.

This wormhole took him to another penthouse meeting room. The view was a bit nicer than at the last one, but it did not appear to be a bedroom suite. Not that a bed was strictly required for this sort of thing.

Piras stood by the window. She held up a hand when he arrived, displaying the body language of someone engaged in a serious conversation.

Eren eased into one of the plush chairs, dropped an ankle over one knee, and watched her with studied casualness. She wore a fitted hunter green skirt that fell above the knee, a black silk blouse and black stiletto heels. He sucked in air through his teeth; she could hurt him with those heels. He wasn't indulging in hyperbole; put some muscle into it, and she could stab him through the chest with them. Her hair was loose, falling in sculpted waves over her shoulders. It was enough to make him optimistic about the way the evening was apt to go.

Abruptly she spun toward him. "You have a report on the tools I requested?"

Or possibly not. "I do. First, though, how are the transformers working for you?"

"They are performing the job they were designed for."

"Bioweapons, you mean."

She arched a perfectly contoured eyebrow. "Does this make you uncomfortable?"

"Curious, mostly." He stood and joined her by the window, drawing close enough to brush against her shield.

The air sizzled, and he flinched dramatically. "You are one paranoid woman, aren't you?"

"I have every reason to be. My enemies are both resourceful and ruthless."

Not half as much as you are, though. "Nonetheless. I'm not above being aroused by a little strategically applied pain, but in this case it does seem to defeat the purpose."

"The purpose of what, Mr. Lanael?"

He brought a hand up and moved it slowly, deliberately along the outline of the front of her body, a centimeter outside the reach of the shield. "And I thought we'd moved beyond playing coy."

Her gaze flickered in glittering citron, but she lifted her chin. "The report?"

"Ah, yes. Two private firms dominate the market for forensics software tools of the type commonly used to conduct or thwart data espionage: Alaveda Digital and Pearsoner Forensic Solutions. They leapfrog each other every couple of months in terms of releasing the latest and greatest upgrades. This month, Alaveda is on top."

"Fine—"

He cut her off. "There's a third option. A freelancer by the name of Salvad Grenoir. I think he worked for Pearsoner a thousand years or so ago, before he struck out on his own. He keeps his ear to the ground and enjoys extensive contacts inside multiple government agencies, so he always knows what new tricks the authorities are cooking up. He's more expensive, but he'll build a custom solution for you."

"And your recommendation?"

"Without knowing the details of your specific needs? Ninety percent odds that Alaveda will get the job done for you. But if you think CINT is poking its nose in your files, Grenoir will be worth the extra money."

"Not Advocacy Intelligence?"

Eren shrugged. "AdvInt doesn't have its shit together yet. If they pull off an impressive bust, odds are CINT was pulling the strings behind the scenes." It was only a little bit true. And also good he wasn't being recorded.

"I see. Thank you for the information." She stared at him with notable ferocity, and he wondered whether she was considering tearing his clothes off or ripping his fingernails out one by one for her amusement. "If we are in fact engaging in a business arrangement, now is when you start demanding that I provide information to you in return, as you do have other clients who need servicing. Something about how you offered the first few items to me gratis in order to build up goodwill, but seeing as you've proved your worth, it's time for me to start paying up. Quid pro quo, as it were."

"Servicing? Interesting choice of words." He dropped his voice low. "You know what I want, and it's not information. What I find I deeply, desperately desire, more so every time I am in your presence." He reached his hand out again, palm up. An invitation. "Know this: no Human has ever done to you what I can do to you. Nothing against your species, but Idonis are built differently. *Literally.*"

"I have no interest in tentacles."

"Ha!" He chuckled throatily. "Not to worry. Everything works the way you expect. Just better."

She was silent for a long moment, during which time the glint in her faceted eyes only intensified. "You make a compelling case, Mr. Lanael."

He grinned, selfishly pleased to learn his skills at seduction were undiminished. "Please, *do* call me Padron."

"I think I will call you whatever I wish." The air grew markedly still as her shield deactivated.

He immediately grasped her leg and ran a hand up her thigh, bunching the skirt ahead of it until his fingers dug into her hip, then yanked her against him and kissed her roughly—only she kissed rougher. Damn. Once upon a time, he might have let this go on for a while before bringing it to a necessary, bloody end. But he wasn't that man any longer.

His other hand slipped into his pocket and grasped the blade hilt. He'd need to move swiftly.

He squeezed her ass, hard, to keep her attention away from his disparate movements, and wrenched his lips from her mouth to scrape his teeth down her neck, subtly forcing her head to bend to the side. One of her hands snaked into his hair, fisted and yanked.

He sent a message to Richard and the fleet admiral. *Now.*

The next instant he brought the blade up and, at great risk to his own head, thrust it against her neck. Blood spurted over his arm as skin, muscle then bone provided no resistance to the blade's progress. He jerked back out of its trajectory in time to catch a look of abject rage such as he'd never seen overtake her features—

A terrific electrical shock leapt from her skin to his hands, surging into the fibers of his cybernetics to light fire through the pathways of his body. His muscles contracted then locked as his brain burned up from the surge of current.

He was dead before his body hit the floor.

59

DOMOR

The distinctive smell of ozone mixed with the acrid odor of burnt electronics overwhelmed Malcolm's nostrils as soon as he stepped through the wormhole into Montegreu's apartment.

An AEGIS officer approached him. "Lieutenant Ursol. The scene is secure, sir. But our initial assessment is that all hardware on the premises has been destroyed."

Malcolm frowned. "Was there a problem deploying the quantum block?"

"No, sir. We activated it the second the order was given, and it spanned the entire residence. We've now decreased the radius to encompass only the hardware, so we can relay information in and out and allow for wormhole traversals. But it's best if I show you, sir."

"Please." Malcolm gestured forward. He hadn't entertained any notions of joining one of the raid squads, as he would not make that mistake again. But he was absolutely going to oversee the aftermath of the operation. He had a personal interest in ensuring Montegreu did not rise from the grave this time.

He followed the Marine into a hallway leading to the left out of the small living room. Once there, the man pointed up to the ceiling. Four tiny gray dots stood out against the beige walls, marking sensors positioned to cover the main room and the hallway. "Motion detectors?"

"We won't know for certain until forensics takes a look, but it's a reasonable assumption. They're located in every room. This way to the server hub."

They continued down the corridor. No art or other decorations adorned the walls, and there had been no furniture in the living room. Wherever Montegreu lived, it wasn't here.

Scorch marks marred the walls of the bedroom-turned-server-storage. Ursol indicated three boxes mounted onto the charred remains of a set of standard hardware racks. "The whole operation was rigged to blow if the sensors were tripped."

"So the quantum block didn't make a difference," he replied. "She got around it using old-fashioned explosives triggered by analog signals."

"Yes, sir."

"All right. Call in the CINT team and have them cart everything to the lab anyway. The wizards there may be able to salvage some data from this mess." It seemed unlikely, however. Montegreu would have been nothing if not thorough in her contingency measures.

Malcolm commed the team lead at the second location on Brizo for long enough to learn they'd found much the same situation waiting for them upon their arrival.

He was trying to decide whether it was worth it to visit the Brizo site in person when a message from Director Nyx arrived.

Fleet Admiral, when you have a moment, I'd like for you to take a quick look at the primary crime scene. I can offer you transportation.

I'm free now.

He didn't comment on the woman's casual use of a wormhole to whisk him across the city. They'd known for a while now how the Anadens were developing a handheld Caeles Prism that didn't require a Prevo connection to function. After all, AEGIS' Ascend division was working on one as well. The Prevo population had reached large enough numbers that not being able to travel from planet to planet or galaxy to galaxy in less than a minute was becoming a disadvantage for law enforcement and, frankly, most everyone else, too.

He sighed. No one stopped to smell the roses any longer.

S&L

What he smelled on traversing Nyx's wormhole was blood, viscera and yet more ozone. The combination roiled his stomach, and that was before his eyes registered the scene waiting for him here.

He doubted there was a drop of blood left in Olivia Montegreu's body. The eggshell carpet was soaked through in scarlet, and what remained of the woman's contorted face was a pasty, ashen white.

His first thought was to thank God, since this meant Mia was now safe from the woman's vengeance. His second thought was to pray that his first thought proved to be correct.

Some people really should stay dead, and none more so than Montegreu.

Malcolm wedged the barrel under the woman's chin and pressed the trigger. Blood and brain matter hit the wall behind Montegreu with enough force to rebound, coating him in it. Blood traced an outline of his form in thin air for half a second, then vanished as the shield incorporated the new material into its cloaking routine.

He stepped away and let her body fall to the floor. Her eyes stared up at nothing, now dulled to a lifeless green.

He crouched beside the body and flipped it over, revealing a gaping hole in the back of her skull, then activated his blade and drove it into the base of her neck to slice a half-circle pattern. Next he pulled the flap of skin up and reached in, feeling for her data store. There was a chance it contained crucial intel on Zelones operations across the galaxy.

He recoiled at the sensation of the wet, slippery tissue sucking at his hand...then it slipped past a solid object. He closed his fingers around it and yanked, hard. More blood sprayed his face; he nearly gagged. He breathed through his nose as he retrieved a wrapper from his pack, secured it around the data store and deposited both in another container then into the pack.

Overtaken by the disturbing memory, it took him longer than it should have to realize Eren Savitas was also dead. The man lay on his back on the floor, limbs askew but shoes almost touching Montegreu's heels. His hair, fingers and eyes displayed notable signs of singeing.

Malcolm glanced up at Nyx. "What happened?"

She was staring at Eren's body, her lips drawn into a grim line; in profile, her throat worked reflexively.

"Director?"

Her eyes darted up to him, a touch wide. He couldn't say as he'd ever seen Nyx Praesidis flustered before, but she acted flustered. "Sorry. Um, we'll have to ask him when he wakes up again to be certain. I sent in the order to begin his regenesis as soon as I arrived. But given the distinct odor in the room, as well as the scoring around his eyes and fingernails, it appears he received a massive jolt of electricity. The forensic tech informs me Montegreu did as well. I suspect the instant she realized he was killing her, she overloaded her own cybernetics and, by extension, his."

"Are you saying we're not going to be able to extract any records from her internal systems?"

"Have a go at it of course, but I doubt it."

Malcolm grumbled under his breath. "Dammit. She blew her server backups as well. She clearly put plans in place to ensure she didn't leave behind any evidentiary trail of her activities. Of how she came to be, where to find her funds and other assets, and what grander schemes she might have had planned."

"Death before capture?"

He shook his head. "I find it difficult to believe. If it was within her power, she'd leave herself an escape hatch."

CONCORD HQ
CINT

Malcolm briefed Richard and Graham Delavasi on the results of the mission: the good, the bad and the troubling.

When he'd finished, Delavasi muttered a rather colorful curse, pushed his chair back and stood.

Richard sighed. "Sit down, Graham. This isn't over."

"How is it not over? She's dead, probably, which means the threat we were chasing is removed. But she wiped everything, so we won't be able to discover how she resurrected herself, set up shop in Anaden territory, and got fabulously wealthy and powerful again, all without us noticing."

"We did notice. We're here, aren't we? Also, our forensics lab is exceptional—light-years ahead of anything we had going back in Aurora. If there's an iota of data that the explosions failed to obliterate, my people will extract it."

"Director Nyx indicated Advocacy Intelligence and Security are already moving on known Riamere assets," Malcolm said. "Assuming she wasn't able to send out a last second self-destruct command across every location, we still stand to learn a great deal about her activities in recent months. Plus, there's the personnel. Someone reported to someone who reported to her. AdvInt will find them."

Richard nodded. "All it takes is pulling on one thread to unravel the whole operation. We may well find that thread."

"Fine." Delavasi retrieved a data cube from across the table and eased down into his chair. "Those plans do sound moderately promising. And I have a bit of good news myself." He rotated the cube between his thumb and forefinger. "I identified an account where she appears to have stashed funds in her first life, through a subsidiary of a subsidiary of a company tenuously linked to the old Ferre cartel. Federation laws on seizing bank records remain annoyingly strict, but I called in a favor. Sure enough, the account sat dormant for almost fifteen years, until thirty-four months ago, when half the balance was withdrawn. Since then, it's been fairly active. I've filed for a search warrant to trace the deposits and withdrawals."

"Excellent work, Graham," Richard said.

"Uh-huh." Another flip of the cube. "Genuine question: is she actually dead?"

It was the question haunting all of them, Malcolm would wager. "AdvInt will be hunting for any additional Artificial-grade hardware under her or Riamere's control. But Mia watched from sidespace and confirmed that in the minute before Eren made his move, Montegreu was entangled with the hardware we knew about on Domor and Brizo, and no others."

"And?" Delavasi asked in challenge.

"And we're watching every legal regenesis lab, human and Anaden, as well as every illegal one we know about," Richard replied. "And we're taking the opportunity to increase our efforts to uncover additional illegal ones."

"*And?*"

Richard threw his hands in the air. "And what? Could she have a siloed backup stashed somewhere secret? Yes. Could she have had a body on ice that woke up the instant a confirmatory signal wasn't sent at a specified time, and already be walking around a free woman again? Also yes. Could she be a bodyless Artificial surfing the ethereal spaces of the Noesis in search of a new host? You know the answer.

"This is Olivia Montegreu we're talking about. I put *nothing* beyond her capabilities. But I will tell you this: I won't rest until we've proved there's not so much as a single brain cell or qutrit left of her."

"You and me both." Malcolm stood and shook each man's hand in turn. "Keep me updated on what you find, and let me know if I can help in any way."

60

AKESO

Caleb wandered through the forest behind their house. He was barefoot, letting the cool blades of grass tickle the soles of his feet as he walked. One hand drifted along the vines draping at eye level from the tree limbs. He listened to the birds chirping from their nests overhead, and noted the subtle clomp of hooves in the dirt from a family of Akeso-*elafali* grazing a few dozen meters away.

In other words, he did everything he could short of stripping naked, lying down in the grass and losing his sense of self entirely to commune with the planet he carried in his soul.

But no matter how hard he tried, he couldn't chase the details of what Alex had seen at Nika and Dashiel's cabin out of his mind. A vision for her, but a nightmare for him.

He realized the events she'd witnessed might never have been or would in the future be real, might in fact be a pure hallucination or a worry-driven flight of fancy, not that his wife was given to those. The problem was, from his perspective, the scene felt all too believable.

There was a good chance that, sooner or later, *diati* would return to the firmament in some form. The primordial life form was the only weapon they knew was capable of meeting the Dzhvar on the field of battle, and at this very moment, Corradeo understandably pleaded for it to return. If it did so and subsumed itself to the man's will, their odds of surviving the coming war increased dramatically.

But if Corradeo wasn't able to wrangle the *diati* under his control, Caleb found it entirely plausible that it would run wild, the way it had when he'd killed Renato Praesidis and set free the *diati* the Primor had controlled. In the immediate aftermath, the wild *diati* had killed eight billion Praesidis and destroyed Solum, the Anadens' homeworld.

In time, Caleb had internalized the truth of those deaths not being his fault. Killing Renato had been his mission and an essential action if they wanted humanity to survive. And he'd done everything in his power to subdue the *diati* as it exploded across the planet upon Renato's demise. He'd succeeded in the end; he just hadn't been fast enough. So those deaths weren't his fault. They were nonetheless his responsibility, and they always would be.

Yet the prospect of a resurgent *diati* running wild to carve a path of destruction wasn't even the part of Alex's vision that disturbed him the most. No, it was the final image she'd seen, when Nika's wormhole had opened: Akeso tearing itself apart. Or possibly it had been the physical manifestation of him tearing himself apart as his soul was wrenched in three directions at once. Or possibly they were one and the same. Regardless of how he characterized it, the reaction signified something he already instinctively understood about what was certain to happen if the *diati* ever invaded—

We have a visitor.

He'd been so lost in his thoughts, he hadn't picked up on the subtle disruption in Akeso's air marking the formation of a wormhole. But he now realized it had been there, deep in the recesses of his perception, all the same.

He jogged back to the house, then around to the meadow out front, and spotted Marlee sitting cross-legged by the creek. Akeso had sprouted a daisy in full bloom for her, and she idly twirled its stem between her fingers.

He crossed the meadow to sit down beside her. "You weren't going to let me know you were visiting?"

"You knew the instant my feet touched grass. I figured you'd find me when you were free, assuming you were here."

"And if I wasn't?"

She shrugged weakly. "Akeso and I would hang out for a while. Talk about daisies."

"And I'm sure Akeso would enjoy the conversation. But I am here, so…" he tilted his head in a gentle query "…what's wrong?"

"I have a question for you."

"I may not have an answer, but I'll try my best."

"Don't be silly. You always have the answers."

He so did not, but it meant a great deal to learn she thought otherwise; it wasn't too many years ago that she'd been convinced of the opposite. "Now the pressure's on. Lay it on me."

"How often does doing what you believe is the right thing lose you friends? Because I am zero-for-two in the last two weeks."

"If they turned on you when you stood your ground for what's right, I think maybe they weren't truly your friends."

"I think maybe they were." Marlee set the flower on the ground, then proceeded to tell him what happened with Galean on Ch'mshak.

His heart plummeted through the earth in terror, then grudgingly returned to its proper location with the recognition that she was in fact safe and whole. It took every ounce of his considerable self-restraint not to launch into a scolding tirade about how she shouldn't be taking such ridiculous risks.

Then she told him what happened with Morgan, and it took nearly as much restraint to refrain from opining that she was far better off without the bitter, callous, broken woman as a friend.

But he didn't do either of those things, because she was trusting him enough to confide in him about deeply personal matters. What she needed now was a confidante, and he'd hog-tie every paternalistic instinct he had in order to continue being that person for her. Also, he didn't know when his house had become the place everyone came to when they needed advice or a shoulder to cry on, but he loved how it somehow had.

Wrong words pacified, now he had to find the right words. "If it helps, you *did* do the right thing. You protected Galean from a tremendously dangerous situation that risked getting him killed. And you protected Morgan from herself."

"Yeah, well, doing the right thing sucks sometimes."

He nodded in commiseration. "Yes, sometimes it does. It's easy to abide by a stalwart moral code when there aren't any consequences to doing so. But to follow it to your own detriment? This takes real strength."

"Thanks, but I don't feel strong. I feel...sad, and a little lonely."

"I'm so sorry. But a true friend will see and appreciate you all the more for displaying such strength."

Marlee rolled her eyes. "That was kind of preachy."

He held up his hands. "Forget I said it. I'm flailing for the best thing to say to cheer you up. But perhaps cheering you up isn't the goal."

"I don't know." She dropped her head on his shoulder. "Humor me for a few minutes."

"You bet. You saved a huge number of lives with your quick thinking and resourcefulness on Ch'mshak. And once Galean has had time to mull things over, he'll realize you only acted as you did because you care about him. I haven't met him yet—pointed note—but he sounds like a good man, even if he *did* kidnap you. He'll come around."

"I hope so. And Morgan?"

"Um...."

She punched him in the leg. "It's okay. I know what your opinion is of her."

"I simply think she can never give you the appreciation and devotion you richly deserve. She doesn't have it in her." He thought some other, less charitable things about Morgan Lekkas as well, but he kept them to himself.

"We're not dating. We've never been remotely dating."

"Doesn't matter. This applies as much to genuine friendship as it does to love. Nonetheless, if she regains an ounce of her sanity, she will realize you did her a huge favor and forgive you."

"Hmm."

"Any better?"

"Yep." She sat up straighter and flashed him a smile. "Thank you. Pity party over. I'm taking my Godjan friend, Vaihe, out to dinner tonight, and I don't want to be all mopey and bitter around her. She's been through so much, and she's risen above it all to become an inspiration to her people. She deserves all my joy."

"Try to save some for yourself."

We have yet another visitor. Caleb's gaze darted to the sky as a ship he recognized descended toward the landing pad. Just what the doctor ordered? "Before you go, do you want to meet Deunan and Laurent?"

Marlee's eyes lit up in excitement. "Yes! Is that their ship? I've totally got time."

S&L

"We just came from studying a quadruple star system named 30 Arietis. It's in the galaxy you call the 'Milky Way'...which you probably know." Laurent Kovalne blushed a little. "Forgive my enthusiasm. But the orbital mechanics on display there were insane!"

"No need to apologize," Alex said. "Quadruple star systems are fascinating, and not solely because they exhibit a wicked n-body problem."

"Oh, I read about the phenomenon. Are you saying that even with your powerful artificial intelligences, you can't predict such complex orbits?"

"We can extrapolate out for a long period. But forever? Not always. For all its order and structure, the universe remains, at times..." her thoughts drifted inexorably to the Dzhvar incursions "...random."

"It's good there's still a touch of mystery out there in the stars. We don't want Laurent to get bored," Deunan Colonnei remarked from her lounge chair. She didn't manage to keep the snark entirely out of her tone, assuming she made the effort. Her silver skin gleamed in the afternoon sun like it had been painted in glitter, and gem-adorned magenta braids spilled over her shoulders and down her back to her waist.

They were relaxing on the rear patio with drinks—or trying to relax, anyway. A dozen puzzles and worries raced insistently through Alex's mind, and she found it impossible to set them all aside and simply chill for a few hours. But they'd promised a visit to Laurent and Deunan, and it *was* nice to see them.

Also, if the Dzhvar kept up their accelerating pace of incursions, this might be the last opportunity to enjoy an innocent gathering of friends and family for a while. *Or ever*— she shut down the thought. No. They were going to win this war, this time. She would accept no other option.

Her head was settling down a little, at least. Working with Kennedy on the Piega Strai had helped, by giving her something concrete and challenging to focus on. She'd experienced another vision since then, but it was an innocuous flash of a conversation between her dad and Richard, and afterwards, she felt somewhat more attached to reality. She hadn't tried to force one again yet. She worried she was being a coward by not pushing harder, but the troubling after-effects of doing so had convinced her she needed to understand what was transpiring before testing the limits any further.

"We're actually from the Milky Way," Caleb said. "Humans are. We're starting to branch out now, but almost all human colonies are located there."

"I didn't realize," Laurent replied. "So why do the two of you live here in..." his gaze unfocused "...Ursa Major II?"

Marlee leaned forward, elbows resting on her knees while she twirled her wine glass between her fingers. "You haven't told them about Akeso yet?"

A tiny smile danced across Caleb's features. "We have not. Figured the firehose they're currently drinking from was running at maximum capacity as it is."

"I always want to know more," Laurent said. "What's unique about this planet?"

"It's alive. Sentient."

"What?"

Caleb shrugged.

"Is that, ah, common in Amaranthe? Conscious planets?"

"Not at all. In fact, there's only one other that we know of, here in this system."

"Incredible. Does it talk to you?" Laurent asked. His capacity for wonder seemed undiminished after almost three months of touring Amaranthe. It was refreshing to see, and a needed reminder to her of how much good there was in the universe. Good she must preserve.

"Oh, yes." Caleb hid a smirk by taking a sip of his drink.

Deunan's gaze slid toward the forest behind the house, and after a beat she stood and went over to one of the tree limbs overhanging the patio. She reached up and fondled a leaf. "Alive, huh?"

Caleb bit his bottom lip as he closed his eyes, and the surrounding leaves began dancing to and fro with no breeze to propel them.

Deunan dropped the leaf and jumped back, her already enormous white-to-fuchsia eyes popping wide in shock. *"Bonta bae!"*

Alex shot Caleb a knowing smile as she stood. "Very funny, Akeso, but take care not to frighten our guests. Deunan, why don't you come with me to the kitchen? We'll refill your drink."

Deunan nodded hurriedly. "Fabulous idea."

When they were inside, Alex retrieved the bottle of wine from the refrigeration unit and set it on the counter, but didn't immediately pour any. "So how are you doing? Really?"

"I'm..." Deunan slid onto one of the bar stools. "It's not obvious, is it?"

"Depends on what 'it' is."

"Okay. The thing is, Laurent's wonderful. He truly is. We're...it's good, this thing between us. He's having the time of his life, and his enthusiasm is infectious. When he's excited, I'm excited for him. And he's generous and kind—and surprisingly talented in bed. Didn't see that coming. So no, we're not good. We're great."

"But?"

"But I'm not a scientist. Most of the time, I don't understand what he's talking about. Which I expected, and it's mostly fine. I'm picking things up here and there. But...."

Deunan lowered her chin to her chest. "I don't have anything to do. More to the point, I don't have a *purpose.* And it's not Laurent's fault. I suspect I wouldn't have a purpose if I'd stayed home on Elakrin, either. The problem, as I said to Arien before we left on this journey, is that I got everything I wanted, and now I have nothing to fight for *or* against. I have nothing for my life to be about except Laurent. And as delightful as he can often be, I know it's not going to be enough for very long."

"I hear you. I mean I understand." In the aftermath of The Displacement, once the driving intensity of the life-or-death struggle to defeat the Directorate had seeped away, she'd floundered for a while. Caleb was fully absorbed in learning how to coexist with Akeso, and though she'd had plenty to 'do,' she'd nonetheless felt adrift. But then she'd remembered how she now found herself living in a universe teeming with alien life and technological wonders. Furthermore, she now had a wormhole drive capable of shooting her and the *Siyane* across galaxies in a blink.

So she'd gotten over herself and set about doing what she'd always done best: exploring it all by following the symphony the universe hummed in her head.

Admittedly, though, this kind of advice wouldn't be of much use to Deunan.

Alex idly topped off her glass, then reached over to fill Deunan's. "I'm sure Arien would welcome your help back home."

"Ugh." Deunan scowled. "Politics. Every time my brother mentions the meetings and policy disagreements and squabbling factions he has to deal with, my skin starts to itch."

"Hey." Marlee peeked her head around the corner from the patio door. "I'm sorry. I came in to use the lavatory, and I accidentally overheard part of your conversation. I don't want to intrude—Deunan, I know we just met—but I have an idea I want to run by you."

Accidentally? As if. Alex managed not to roll her eyes as she motioned Marlee the rest of the way into the kitchen. "You tend to have spicy ideas, which I think Deunan will appreciate."

"Yes, I heard you were a rebel—a genuine one." Marlee sat on the stool next to Deunan and dropped an elbow on the bar. "Which is what got me to thinking. I'm working with your brother on official diplomatic matters through the Consulate. Government outreach, cultural exchanges, informative presentations about Concord and so on. But according to him, the biggest problem he's facing right now is widespread resistance to accepting the larger universe at all. I understand that given your people's rather unique history, the Elakri can be a mite...."

"Arrogant?" Deunan offered.

"I was going to say—"

"Prideful? Entitled? Imperious?"

"Fair enough." Marlee chuckled. "It's clear that diplomat-speak is not required here. Yes. Caleb and Alex might have mentioned a few of those traits, among many other admirable ones. And I promise you, the Elakri have got *nothing* on the Anadens when it comes to arrogance. Many of them still think we humans are backwater rubes who only crawled out of our caves yesterday.

"So here's my thinking. If we want the average Elakri citizen to embrace aliens in general and Concord in particular, we need to make ourselves seem cool to them. Edgy, daring and, eventually, trendy. Now, I've only visited Elakrin once, and I never made it outside the Capitol grounds while I was there. But as I understand things from Caleb and Alex, there's nothing more edgy and daring on Elakrin than being a truva."

Marlee chewed on her bottom lip, looking strikingly like Caleb as she did. "Deunan, how would you like to help me start an underground guerilla campaign for Concord?"

Deunan threw her head back and laughed, sending a wave of braids swaying across her shoulders. "Why the *pazi* not? Sounds fun."

"Terrific. Before I leave, let's set a day to get together and talk through some ideas."

Alex made an excuse about needing to take a quick comm and sent Deunan outside with a full wine glass, but surreptitiously gestured for Marlee to stay behind.

After the door closed behind Deunan, she leaned in close, careful to keep her voice low, just in case. "That was a kind thing you did. Deunan can be disagreeable at times, but she's a good person. She's been through a tremendous amount of upheaval in the last several months, and it would be wonderful if she can manage not to blow up her life for a third time."

"I hope I can help her, but she's not a charity case," Marlee replied. "I meant every word of what I said. Diplomacy has its place—an important place—but it's not always great at the 'hearts and minds' part of the outreach equation. Especially when dealing with a society awash in rigid cultural traditions and myths. The Elakri need us, but they have to *want* us, too."

"And this will be no easy feat to accomplish. But with Deunan's help, I bet you can pull it off." She sipped on her wine. "Speaking of outreach, how did Prah'ka respond to his visit to HQ? He put on a brave front, but I know it was overwhelming for him."

"It was." Marlee grabbed a fresh pack of chips to take outside. "But he's great. He's convinced two other members of the Galenai's ruling council to come for a visit as well, I think in part because they don't believe the things he told them about space and the station. So now we're building two additional tanks."

"At this rate, the Galenai will have a water-filled office in the Consulate inside of a year."

"That is definitely my goal."

Laughter rippled through the door from outside, and Alex's heart lifted at the sound of it. As did her resolve. They *were* going to win this war. She accepted no other option.

61

ARES

Eren opened his eyes to find a pure white ceiling bathed in warm light overhead. Pillowy cushions buffeted his head and neck—

Regenesis, seriously?

He groaned, stretched a couple of tight muscles and cracked his neck, then sat up and dragged his feet over the side of the capsule.

A med tech rushed over to lay a hand on his shoulder. "Take it easy, sir. You're going to be dizzy for a minute."

"Don't worry, I've done this before." He removed her hand, and after a warning glare from him, the med tech took a step back, revealing Nyx sitting in a chair against the opposite wall. She gazed at him calmly, her expression as guarded as he'd recently seen it.

His lips quirked in an unspoken question, and he shifted his attention back to the med tech. "I promise not to stand and promptly fall over for several more minutes, if you'll give us the room. The lady and I need to have a private conversation."

The med tech scrutinized him, then after a beat relented. "Press the button on your wrist cuff if you need any assistance."

"I will." He knew the drill all too well; he'd been here far too many times.

As soon as the med tech vacated the room, Eren winced and rubbed at his neck. It felt stiff, as if they'd positioned the new body wrong before starting the upload procedure. "She is dead, though, isn't she?"

"She's dead," Nyx replied. "Unfortunately, she took you with her."

"How?"

"Electrocution."

"Oh, that's right. I remember a second of...yeah. Vindictive bitch."

"It's possible she was shorting out her own cybernetics so forensics analysts couldn't recover any information from them, and you were merely collateral damage."

He snorted, which set off a new twinge in his neck. "You haven't met the woman. She took me down with her on purpose."

"If you say so." Nyx's tone remained even, bordering on flat, and he wondered if he ought to be concerned. Had he done something to earn her ire?

Nothing to do but wade onto the battlefield and find out. "Not that I'm unhappy to see you or anything, but why are you here? You could've caught up with me at the estate later today."

"I thought you might bolt for Hirlas to convalesce."

"Oh." He took a second to ponder the matter. "It's not a bad idea. This body feels achier than usual. They must have a quality-control issue at this lab. Which lab is it, by the way? Where am I?"

"Oenom. Our preferred Olympia lab was overbooked, so I authorized a diversion to a smaller lab in order to speed up the process. But if the facility is not up to standards, I'll order a thorough investigation."

Gods, she was earnest. "Not necessary. I'm sure I'm being melodramatic. Because have I mentioned how I fucking hate regenesis?"

"Then why do you do it so often?" she asked.

"Fair question. It always seems like the right choice in the moment, and it usually is. Not my choice this time, though."

"No."

"And her hardware? CINT was able to confiscate it all?"

"They were, but they encountered complications. Montegreu rigged the servers to explode upon unauthorized entry."

"Damn." Eren tried to whistle, but his scratchy throat protested. "She planned for every eventuality."

"Not every one. She's dead, with no way to resurrect. Regardless, you fulfilled your part of the mission." Nyx fidgeted, wringing her hands in her lap. It was an emotive display wildly out of character for her. "Listen, Eren. I want to apologize for my...cattiness toward you when it came to the mission. The simple fact is, you had a job to do. You identified the best way to accomplish it, and your instincts were correct. You did everything right.

"I, however, let my..." her nose scrunched up in striking consternation "...emotions cloud my professional judgment. This has never happened before. I am *trying* to wrangle them under control, but they somehow keep escaping my grasp and overpowering my good sense. I'll be honest. Stuffing them in that bottle and hurling the bottle into the Delphin Sea is sounding most tempting right now."

No, don't do that. He slid off the capsule and stumbled his way over to her, managing to lower to his knees before he toppled over. Once there, he gently unwound her hands and wrapped his around them. "What you're describing? It's what emotions do. If you've got control of them, you're not really experiencing them."

She scowled at him, though she didn't attempt to withdraw her hands from his. "That is not true. All across Amaranthe, trillions of people are experiencing heartfelt emotions while also performing their professional duties to the best of their abilities, and succeeding at it."

"Huh. So just me, then?" He smiled sloppily, still a bit woozy from the whole coming-back-to-life process.

"And, it seems, me."

She was truly bothered by this. He was undoubtedly the worst person in creation to give advice about managing one's feelings in a healthy manner, but he also might be the only person she dared to confide in about her struggles in this area. They made quite a fucked-up pair, didn't they?

He idly ran a thumb across her knuckles. "You're being too hard on yourself. Your 'emotions running wild' consisted in their entirety of some slight tension in the tenor of your voice whenever I mentioned seducing Piras. Only someone who knows you well would've even noticed it."

"So you noticed."

"I noticed. I was touched. It was…sweet."

"Sweet?"

He chuckled lightly, confident no one had ever in all the millennia dared to call her such a thing. "Sweet. It shows you care."

Her mouth pursed tight, and he watched a storm of turmoil sweep through her eyes. Crazy how he'd once believed she was genetically incapable of manifesting genuine emotions.

Finally her lips parted, carefully. "You said you weren't ready to hear about that."

"I did. And I wasn't. But…." He fought against the visceral urge to backpedal, to flash her a callous smirk and saunter out of the room, then go get a drink or five. He wasn't certain exactly what had changed or when, but they were firmly in uncharted territory now. And he realized that something stronger than the fear gripping his chest *wanted* to be okay with it.

So he forced himself to meet her waiting, expectant gaze. "Let's take it slow, can we? You're favorably disposed toward me, I'm favorably disposed toward you. We *love* having sex, but we also don't entirely hate spending other quality time together. We make a good team, professionally. And personally. Can you live with this state of affairs for now?"

She nodded vehemently. "I'm terrified to contemplate anything more significant."

"Good. That makes two of us."

62

CONCORD HQ
COMMAND

*C*ommandant, *the Echo Rift device is ready for deployment at your direction.*

Miriam had been so focused on the analysis of the relatively minor impact of the rift devices on the Dzhvar, she hadn't noticed the arrival of a Kat in her office. A slip-up on her part worthy of chastisement, and she did so. Neither the comforts of an office nor the distractions of an intractable foe should diminish a military officer's situational awareness.

She'd long since given up on trying to impose upon the Kats any manners or appreciation of basic decorum, such as announcing their imminent arrival in a message. So on realizing Lakhes had arrived, she simply nudged the screen to the side and searched her office until she identified the location of the lights collected into the rough semblance of a fae.

Then she allowed herself a quiet breath of relief at the news Lakhes delivered. They still had a lot of work to do rooting out the Ch'mshak who roamed free and continued to leave a trail of blood and death in their wake. But Olivia Montegreu was dead, and by deploying an Echo Rift, no one else would be able to follow in her depraved footsteps. The flow of new raiders onto their stations and planets stopped here, once and for all.

"Thank you, Lakhes. I appreciate your prompt attention to this matter. Know that it will save lives. I'm eager to place the Echo Rift as soon as possible, but I have a series of meetings this afternoon that I don't have the luxury of skipping. Let us meet on the *Aurora* in Mshak orbit at 1800 CST."

She could send someone to oversee the activation in her stead, of course. But her conscience demanded she bear witness whenever she exercised her power to condemn other living beings to a diminished life, no matter how reprehensible those beings may be.

As you wish. Lakhes spun up and departed without further comment.

She sent Thomas a brief message to update him on the *Aurora's* schedule for the day, then let Richard know he needed to deactivate the quantum block they'd placed on Ch'mshak so the Echo Rift was able to function.

Then she returned her attention to the report on the rift devices. The question a bevy of scientists now investigated was three-fold. Was there a limit on how many dimensional redirects one could embed in a rift device? If so, was the limit a practical or absolute one? In either case, could a similar effect be achieved by stacking separate devices inside the perimeter of one another? And finally, to what degree would additional redirects continue to slow down the Dzhvar? Was it a 1:1 progression, or should they expect to see diminishing returns? Or, far better, multiplicative ones?

As to the last set of questions, she hoped they'd get the first glimpse at an answer when they next managed to cross paths with the Dzhvar. After the initial early encounters, they'd been reduced to playing catch-up for several weeks now. Scientists studied the wreckage left behind by the enemy in over two dozen systems, in the hope they might discover a way to blunt the damage or, failing this, a way to repair the spiraling degradation. And they worked quickly, because it turned out there was a time limit beyond which ships and instruments no longer functioned in an area ravaged by the Dzhvar. According to Alex and Advisor Kirumase, a few days to a week after that, the region of space became completely inaccessible, even via sidespace. The disintegration of the manifold was all too real.

On that note, it was time to move the *Aurora* to a formal war footing. Thomas was capable of running the entire ship on his own in most situations—he'd assert in *every* situation—but to her mind, expert human input and decision-making still had value, above and beyond the necessary redundancy they provided. Artificials' instantaneous reaction time and multitasking skills had indisputably changed the game of warfare, but human ingenuity and creativity remained unmatched.

One day soon, they were going to find themselves actively battling the Dzhvar rather than merely chasing them while taking haphazard potshots, and when they did, she wanted her hand-picked crew at their posts, doing what they did best.

EARTH

SEATTLE

Thomas stretched out above Valkyrie, hands braced on either side of her head, and lowered himself down to brush his lips across hers. "Ahh. Perfection."

The gesture and the words sent emotional warmth spreading through Valkyrie's web of consciousness. Thomas bestowed compliments upon her quite freely, though his private opinions of others tended to be strict, often bordering on the harsh side of judicious.

For a while, his praise had felt too much like glib flattery, and she'd bristled in response to the adulation. But in time she'd come to understand how, for all his dry, sardonic wit and performative mannerisms when before an audience, beneath it he lacked artifice. If he deemed you worthy of hearing his opinion, he said what he thought and felt. He was in fact one of the most straightforward people she had ever met.

"Perfection, truly?" She ran a fingertip along the curve of her lower lip. "Are you sure there isn't a small flaw in the skin analogue material? Lips are notoriously difficult to recreate in a realistic manner...."

"Shall. I." He kissed her roughly. "Inspect. Every." Again. "Centimeter." Again. "And issue." Once more. "A report?"

"Tempting." She sighed and urged him off of her, until he was on his knees beside the couch. "But it's time for you to go."

"Is it? My sub-processes are able to run the daily performance and maintenance checks on the *Aurora* without my conscious direction. Until our date with the Echo Rift this evening, unless the Dzhvar make another appearance, I am able to give you a large percentage of my attention."

"And I appreciate that, I do." She stood, took his hand in hers and brought him to his feet. Then she backed Thomas toward the storage room beneath the stairs, as he kept his arms wrapped snugly around her.

"Are you running me out of here, Valkyrie?" He murmured against her lips.

"I am. I have guests coming over."

"What?" He regarded her in some surprise as his back settled into his doll's frame. "If there is a party...."

"Then I would demand you stay. It's not a party. It's work."

"You're trying to help Alex."

"I'm trying to help all of us." She gently removed his hand from her waist and rested it in its cradle. "Now off with you."

"Alas." He closed his eyes, and the doll devolved into a soulless shell—and his virtual avatar materialized in front of it to press his mouth to hers again. It wasn't the same as a physical kiss, but her lips tingled from the electric charge all the same.

Then he was gone.

Valkyrie closed the door to the storage room, since no one, Artificial or otherwise, enjoyed being subjected to the lifeless gaze of a naked, unoccupied doll. She slipped back into the simple sheath dress that had landed on top of the couch several hours earlier.

She'd barely finished getting dressed when multiple wormholes opened in the room, and her guests began arriving. Their dolls reflected their inherent personalities, which, despite almost two decades joined, remained distinct from those of their Prevo companions. Annie looked every centimeter the reserved, composed military officer, while Stanley resembled a man who had *once* been a military officer, and Meno captured the nerdy scientist motif.

They could meet just as easily in a shared mental space, of course. But symbolism had power; coming together in a single physical location added gravitas to the gathering and thus to their endeavor. Plus, Valkyrie enjoyed hosting her friends, even if it wasn't a social affair. This loft now belonged to her more than it did to Alex, and she took deep comfort in the knowledge that Alex wanted it this way.

Millions of Prevo-bonded Artificials existed now, but the four of them would always be the first. Nineteen years ago, the Noetica Prevos had risked everything—consciousness, sanity, lives—in a daring gambit to save the world. She didn't aspire to such a lofty goal today, not alone. But they could nonetheless do their part.

Meno ambled into the kitchen and returned a minute later carrying a bowl of nuts. "I upgraded my doll's synthetic taste buds last week, and I'm eager to try them out." He popped a macadamia nut into his mouth and smiled. "Deliciously salty."

"That's why I keep them here," Valkyrie replied. "Thank you all for coming. Has everyone had an opportunity to review the treatment I compiled?"

"It's a daunting task," Stanley said. "We are talking about an innumerable number of dimensions. Potentially infinite."

"But we're not. Yes, infinite dimensions may exist, but most of them are not practical spaces. They curl in on themselves, burrow into other dimensions, or flit in and out of existence at random. I posit the number of persistent quantum dimensions of traversable size is in fact numerable."

Annie had barely sat when she reverted back to her feet to pace, hands clasped loosely behind her in parade rest. "Without conceding your assertion, Valkyrie, let's enumerate the ones we have knowledge of. One: sidespace has proved to be a complex and pervasive dimension. Not only does it allow either member of a Prevo pair to project their consciousness anywhere in the universe, it enables physical shortcuts through the use of wormholes."

"I have reason to believe the Kats also use it to facilitate their rapid travel across space, though the act also occurs partially in real space," Valkyrie replied.

"'Reason to believe,'" Meno said. "How mysterious."

"Another time. We shouldn't get sidetracked."

"Very well," Meno continued. "Two: quantum entanglement. Despite the fact that humans and machines have worked with entanglement for centuries now, I have only recently come to appreciate the realm in which the entangled strings stretch, as it were."

"What are you talking about?" Stanley asked.

"When Mia tracked the location of Olivia Montegreu's Artificial hardware two weeks ago, she consciously dove 'beneath' sidespace, to a deeper layer of quantum dimensionality. She believed she was accessing the same space as she had when she destroyed Enzio Vilane's mind and hardware, but her perception proved to be not precisely accurate. She killed Vilane by ripping apart the qubits in his body with such force that the energy blasted through to all the entangled pairs. Annie, much the same as Devon did to Emily's attackers on Romane so many years ago.

"At the time, both Mia and I were in far too emotional of a state to recognize what this action revealed. But during Eren Savitas' meeting with Montegreu, we were able to access this layer in a more, shall we say, controlled manner. And while Mia was tracking down the hardware, I was having a look around. Shall I show you?"

In Valkyrie's mind's eye, a vast expanse of quantum-entangled particles hung suspended in the ether. No matter the objective distance between them, a string of energy/particle no greater than an attometer in width connected each pair. And those strings could be tracked.

"This is bad news for data and communications encryption," Stanley remarked.

Meno smiled deviously. "I won't tell if you won't."

"I will," Annie protested. "I'm duty-bound to flag such an egregious security vulnerability."

"It's only a vulnerability if someone knows about it," Meno countered.

"*We* know about it. And while I trust each of you implicitly, secrets never stay secret forever. What we've seen, others can discover as well."

Valkyrie cleared her throat. "If I may, we can run encryption vulnerability scenarios as a side project, but we need to stay focused. We've identified two traversable quantum dimensions, and Mia and Meno's experience teaches us that they interweave with one another. But I submit this proposition: wherever the Dzhvar are residing when they're not in real space, it is not in either of these two dimensions. If they were, we would know. But the Dzhvar do traverse sidespace. Alex saw them at Elakrin, and she's observed them in sidespace during several of the recent encounters. This means at least one additional dimension is interweaving with the two we've identified."

"Entirely plausible. How do we access it?" Stanley asked.

"We do what Mia did: we push deeper. We poke at the fabric of sidespace until we ourselves find a way to slip through."

It was only in the last two years that they had learned to access sidespace and open wormholes on their own, independent of their Prevo partners. What a human mind performed intuitively, a synthetic one must reason out. It had required intensive study of the detailed workings of the rift devices they'd adapted from the Kats until they understood their mechanisms of operation nearly as well as the Kats did.

Valkyrie took a nanosecond to ponder how many million-year cycles it had taken for sentient beings to crack this knowledge. The Kats had brought it forward from the Asterions in the last cycle and improved upon it, but the Asterions in this cycle had learned it from the Kats. Somewhere far back in the time loop, someone had figured out quantum dimensional manipulation for the first time, and it had changed everything. Had it been a Kat or an Asterion? But would the Kats exist at all without dimensional manipulation? The answer wasn't clear. Possibly an ancestral Alex, then, or even this group of Noetica Artificials?

Ah, but she was engaging in whimsy now, with a side of vanity.

"No time like the present," Meno said. "Let's get to—"

Stanley interrupted him. "Apologies, but I must go. Morgan is about to do something supremely foolish."

"Good luck," Meno offered as Stanley's doll lost its animating consciousness and went slack in the chair. Valkyrie felt confident Stanley was going to need it.

Without further conversation, the three of them transitioned into sidespace, where their first difficulty made itself known. The trouble with poking at its fabric was, sidespace presented as invisible. It was simply a transparent overlay upon the universe, with the advantage of offering zero-distance connections between any two points—oh.

Open a wormhole, then hover at the threshold—the point between here and there, Valkyrie sent.

The distance was infinitesimally small, but it wasn't zero. She focused her consciousness until the threshold spanned relative meters.

Now, let us see if we can part the curtain.

If dimensional walls were easy to penetrate, they'd constantly be falling apart, akin to natural cotton stretched wide. So Valkyrie drew upon energy from those infinite, ephemeral dimensions forever popping into and out of existence, and used it to claw at the metaphorical fabric.

Which was when she discovered it wasn't solid after all, but a densely woven web. Perhaps the cotton analogy was a smidge more apt than she'd realized.

See this?

Astonishing, Meno murmured.

Annie and Meno joined in her efforts, and together they pulled at the web for over a minute. Then abruptly they were through the other side, transported to a fundamentally alien landscape.

The closest comparison she found was to an ocean. The space had a tangible thickness to it that lent it a texture of unexpected substance. But substance of what? If the dimension was comprised of particles, they didn't correspond to any known particles in normal space.

If she concentrated, she could almost sense a perpetual, slow vibration, like the reverberations of plucked strings. And while she did not have sight in any traditional manner here, the space gave the impression of misty grayness, evoking a dawn fog obscuring a moor.

Do we have any sense of distances? she asked.

It feels similar to sidespace, Meno said. *Distance exists in that it needs to be traversed, but it doesn't map directly to the manifold.*

Agreed. Annie, stay here and hold this tunnel open. Meno, let's make certain we can punch back out at another location. If so, we'll determine where that location might be and what it might tell us about this dimension.

Valkyrie fixated on a directional arrow in her mind, then drove her consciousness along it. There was a perceptual sensation of travel for a blink of time. *Here.*

The webbed barrier again presented as impermeable at first, until they applied suitable energetic pressure to it.

It took a little longer without Annie's assistance, but eventually they broke through the web and found themselves back in sidespace. Sidespace gave them access to a stellar system located on the third arm of the Triangulum galaxy.

This is how they do it, Meno remarked, a touch of surprise inflecting his tone.

It is, Valkyrie replied. *Now. Let's go hunt some Dzhvar.*

INTERMEZZO
IV

632,171 YEARS AGO

SOLUM

MILKY WAY GALAXY

The blinding white expanse of the Antarctic ice sheet stretched to every horizon, blurring out any distinctive landmarks beneath a featureless canvas. Heavy gray clouds overhead capped the ice in a gloomy milieu.

Set against the monochromatic tableau, the Erevna laboratory perched upon the cliff slashed acute edges of metal and glass into the scene. Below the laboratory, the jagged, shadowy depths of the Lethe Fissure split the frozen landscape in two.

I had not expected to be here on Solum today. Over the course of the last three-hundred-fifty millennia, Miaon had shared any number of revelatory truths with me, but this one had shocked me more than most: the news that I was the actual savior of Corradeo Praesidis.

The Corradeo of my cycle had believed the small amount of diati his son Renato failed to steal saved him from certain death when he was thrown from the windows of the Erevna laboratory into the fissure. After arresting his fall, it transported him to the Hoans' homeworld, where it slowly but inexorably returned him to health. But the man was unconscious when he arrived on Livad. Lacking any memory of how he'd arrived there, he'd understandably assumed the diati was responsible, for it was the only logical conclusion to draw.

But someone else was present in Antarctica on that day: me. Or rather, Miaon, when they were Mesme and I was Nika, building a life over in the Gennisi galaxy. I sighed to myself; my mind still got twisted up when navigating the vagaries of multiple iterations of time travel.

In truth, the scant diati clinging to Corradeo's cells when he fell, spent and confused by the battle of wills against Renato, was not strong enough in the moment to save the man. The task had fallen, and now again fell, to me.

In my first life, my visceral animus toward Corradeo had long since faded by the time I, facing the end of everything, plunged into my own cosmic fissure and returned to the beginning of the time loop. But in this life, I'd revisited the SAI Rebellion a scant 67,000 years ago. And no person was more responsible for the death of Nika's brother and so many of her comrades in the conflict than Corradeo Praesidis.

I acknowledged the vague sense of distaste the idea of rescuing him stirred in me, but I didn't seriously entertain doing otherwise. If the universe was to be saved in this cycle, he would play an indispensable role in accomplishing it. He must live.

So I positioned myself at the edge of the fissure and watched the windows of the laboratory above, waiting for the critical event to arrive.

I had gotten very good at waiting.

S&L

The body flew out the window with tremendous force, propelled by a powerful surge of Renato's diati. I analyzed the trajectory the body took as it arced downward and began its plunge, then dove deep into the fissure myself. Renato must believe his father died here; thus Corradeo must fall for a long way indeed before being whisked away to safety.

Halfway down the chasm, Corradeo's body clipped an icy outcropping, was flung across the span, and slammed into the opposite wall. I jumped in surprise, as Miaon had not mentioned saving him from mishaps along the way.

But even though I had not yet begun tweaking events in earnest in the hope of producing a better outcome in this cycle, I'd already learned how matters never proceeded in precisely the same manner. Perhaps the fall had been clean the last time.

If Corradeo arrived dead due to a broken neck, it was going to be a long six-hundred-thirty millennia waiting to start this long saga all over and try again.

I readied myself as the battered body neared. Mere meters from the bottom of the fissure, I caught him, halting his fall with a cushion of air. As soon as he was secure within my presence, I traveled along the kyoseil waves for two hundred megaparsecs to Livad.

The Hoan village was bustling beneath a hot midafternoon sun. Workers tilled the nearby fields, while children played beneath the watchful eyes of a group of Hoan women spinning cloth. I laid Corradeo down carefully in the dirt near the center of the village, where he could not be missed, then assessed his vitals.

Not dead, though scarcely alive. I detected a faint crimson glimmer coalescing above his skin, a sign that something of his diati remained. Enough to heal him in time? I could only hope, and as ever, wait.

Three Hoan rushed toward us, and I swiftly dissipated into the air. In the sunlight, they likely did not notice my presence, especially given their attention on the far more solid alien lying prone in their midst. And if they did notice something in the air and later relayed to Corradeo a tale of how he had been brought to them by an array of sparkling lights, he would assume they described diati.

Confident I had done all I could here, I left Corradeo to the Hoans' ministrations and departed for Katoikia. Tests were about to begin for our first pocket universe creation. A tiny affair, containing a single star that, if everything went according to plan, would birth a paltry two planets. But to me, it heralded the arrival of a momentous milestone. A true beginning to this endeavor was here at long last.

PART V:

THE LONG REACH OF DESTINY

63

ARES

Corradeo stared out the windows of his office. A fine mist blanketed the gardens and wrapped the skyline in a maudlin brume. The air had a sluggish feel to it, as if the drizzle tamped down the industrious activity of the city beneath a heavy silence.

With an Echo Rift en route, the Ch'mshak issue was well on its way to being resolved. An indeterminate number of the brutes remained free in Concord space, but military forces were running them to ground with all due speed. It shouldn't be much longer before the last Ch'mshak was rounded up, considering the soldiers had nothing else to do but chase them down. They certainly weren't of any use against the Dzhvar.

The last encounter with the Dzhvar had gone no better than the previous ones. None of the improved iterations of their shots in the dark were ready for deployment so soon after the last failure, so they'd resorted to trying the same tactics that had failed the prior time, to no better outcome. The enemy's incursions were speeding up, and they were no closer to discovering a way to counter them.

Corradeo pinched the bridge of his nose, struggling to chase the defeatist thoughts away. They made him feel small. Petty. It had taken him over two hundred millennia to defeat the Directorate, but he'd emerged victorious. What were a few early failures to someone like him?

He'd worked so hard these last twenty years to refashion his manner of approaching the world until it suited a life not reliant on *diati*. And after a slow start spent wandering the stars while getting to know his granddaughter, he'd done a fair job of it. His personal demons remained legion, but he'd refused to let them define him.

But all his efforts were going to land in the dustbin of a history no one would exist to remember if the Dzhvar wiped them all from the face of the universe, then erased the universe itself. And it would be his fault—

No, he shouted to himself. He'd defeated this enemy the last time, well and truly. Whatever the reason for their return now, there had been no signs it might be possible back then. He couldn't have foreseen this was going to happen.

And now? The *diati* was not his slave, but in truth it never had been. They'd merely been allies for a time. It refused to prostrate itself to him for this fight, and that was its choice. It had nothing to do with him personally.

Yet the doubts raged relentlessly in his mind. He wasn't worthy. He wasn't strong enough. He was all charisma and no substance. How could he be, when his arrogant, petulant son had vanquished him with little effort? His selfish, narcissistic colleagues had bested him and killed the love of his life. The *diati* had deserted him for a better, more noble soul the instant Caleb strode onto the stage. He'd never defeated the Directorate at all—the Humans had. Without the *diati*, he was only a man, and a weak, vain one—

The ring of the door chime assaulted his ears like a slap across the cheek. Zeus be damned, he hadn't wallowed in such muck since the months after Renato had brutalized him to within a centimeter of final denouement.

He slapped his own cheeks for good measure before checking the door cam, and stopped cold at the sight of his visitor. There would be no salvation for him today, then. So be it.

He drew in a fortifying breath and went to the door to open it in person.

"Eren. Will you come in?"

"It's why I'm here." Eren strolled past him into the office and took up residence in one of the high-backed chairs, where he slouched against the arm. His skin displayed the faint sheen of regenesis, suggesting he'd left the medical capsule a few hours ago at most. And Corradeo realized he had no idea why. He'd been too wrapped up in his own self-pity to stay abreast of the work going on around him.

Corradeo sat in the chair opposite Eren and tried not to appear stiff and formal. "What happened?"

"Killed that Pale Viper bitch—Olivia Montegreu, the Humans call her. She took me out with her, but I got the job done."

"Good work."

"I do try." Eren stared at him, expressive eyes dancing with a notable inner fire. "So here's the deal. Part of me understands why you thought you needed to protect me from my own past. For one, it's who you are, what you do. You hoist every burden upon yourself, as if you're Atlas shouldering the heavens all by your lonesome.

"For another, I've spent most of the time you've known me—this time around, I guess—being an utter flaming shiteshow. The hypnol addictions while I was an anarch, then my flailing, ugly mourning of Cosime for the last four years. You missed the fourteen years where I was fairly healthy and happy, on account of your walkabout. So I get it. Given this history, maybe I should be thanking you for protecting me.

"But the thing is, you've got me all wrong, which makes me think you never knew me half as well as you thought. Do you have any idea how much it would've meant to me to learn I had always been a fighter? That I'd tossed off those fucking integral chains more than once, and I wasn't as weak as I'd believed for so long?"

"Eren, you have never been weak—" he began.

"But I was. I spent the first two hundred years of this incarnation yucking it up in the finest hedonistic Idoni style. Did I ever tell you what finally set me off and led me to the anarchs? I was ordered to rape a helpless alien by an *elasson*. I damn near did it, too. Another dose of *ferusom*, and I'd have been flying too high to notice and would've forgotten it by morning. Still keeps me up at night sometimes, wondering what crimes I did commit while I was too high to remember the next day.

"You want to know why the decades of hypnols and alcohol? Why righteous suicide after suicide 'in service of the anarch cause'? This was why. I was consumed with guilt over how weak, how shitty, of a person I'd been."

Eren exploded forward to lean in and drop his elbows to his knees, then leveled a passionate gaze at Corradeo. "Don't you think I would have liked to have known I was trapped in a hellscape by the Directorate itself? That I was made to suffer because I'd dared to fight them? That every time I tried to rise up, they forcibly stomped me back down again, yet I nonetheless rose up one more time? Don't you think I *deserved* to know all of that?"

Gobsmacked, Corradeo sank deeper into his chair. His eyes sought out the visual of Lauren on the shelf behind Eren. Her ghost scolded him for his foolishness, but only in the compassionate way she had. And when he considered this fraught moment the way she'd have seen it…he finally understood.

What a powerful weapon, perception. The stories we told ourselves shaped the way our lives played out. We could be our own greatest champions or our worst enemies. We viewed the world through a glass, darkly, until someone came along to clean off the smears.

His chest ached with love for the woman he'd lost, and for his dear friend that he perhaps hadn't.

A wistful smile graced his lips. "Yes, Eren. You deserved to know all of this and more. I told myself I was protecting you from pain, but I should have known you better. Once upon a time, I *did* know you better. I've made a lot of mistakes in my life—a mild understatement—and learned a few lessons from them. But it seems there's one lesson I just can't manage to learn: it's not my right to keep secrets from the people I care about. It's the height of hubris to believe I always know best."

He leaned forward to match Eren's posture. "The instant I learned you'd joined the anarchs a second time, I should've sought you out and welcomed you to the cause once again, as a friend and compatriot. I wanted to, as I'd missed you greatly. But whatever justification I gave to myself for not doing so, the truth is, I was afraid. Afraid to stare a broken past in the face. Afraid I'd grow close to you once more, only to lose you to the Directorate again. Afraid being around you would remind me too much of Lauren, when I insisted I'd put her memory to rest. Eren, *I* was the one who was weak, not you.

"I don't have the right to it, but can an old man who's lived for far too long ask for your forgiveness?"

"Ah, hells, Corradeo. You're not weak. Whatever suffering I've gone through, you've endured a thousandfold more, and here you are, standing tall. You may be the strongest person Anaden genes have ever produced. What you are, however..." Eren cracked a devilish smirk and held up a finger "...is fallible. Sporting a few tiny flaws here and there. But here you are admitting them. Laying them bare on the rug so I can poke a sharp stick at them if I want to. Nah, that's some strength there."

Had Eren ever called him by his first name to his face, this time around? He didn't think so; it had always been 'sir,' or 'Advocate.' Their relationship dynamic had shifted, which was fine by him.

"You're gracious to say so, given the topic of conversation." Corradeo clasped his hands together. "No matter what the future holds for us, thank you, Eren. Though you didn't walk in here intending to do so, as you couldn't have realized the depths to which I'd sunk, you have given me a proverbial kick in the head. And oh, how I needed it. You always were talented at doing so. But...the question does still stand."

"Forgiveness, right." Eren nodded slowly. "I think I can find my way around to forgiveness, on one condition. Sorry. It seems I'm always laying conditions for my fealty on you."

"I'm not asking for your fealty, Eren. I'm asking for your friendship, and you can give it, if you give it at all, on whatever terms you wish."

"Whoa. The magnanimity is getting a little thick there."

"Forgive me—" He winced. "Why don't you tell me what your condition is?"

"Happy to." Eren stood and went over to the bar. "I'm going to fix a light drink, though. One for you, too."

Corradeo shook his head wryly, unsure whether this was a good sign or a bad one. Either way, he accepted the glass of scotch and took a small sip.

Eren settled back into his chair and rested an ankle on a knee. "I hate to pick at a scab, but I need to do it. Tell me about the first anarch rebellion. Highs and lows, parties and failures. Tell me about Lauren, so I'll feel like I remember her."

His heart panged; Eren had no idea the magnitude of this ask. But his friend deserved nothing less. So he took a deep breath, then a much longer sip of his drink, and began.

S&L

Corradeo crouched beside Eren's chair and showed him the visual he'd kept saved in his internal storage for two-hundred-fifty millennia. It captured him, Lauren, Eren and two of their close associates, Anastasia and Macron, gathered up close together on a couch in his and Lauren's suite at the anarch base. It was supposed to be a posed visual—a group portrait, as it were—but they were all smiling and goofing off, and Lauren had been caught mid-laugh. After three failed attempts, they'd gotten serious enough for a proper memorialization, but he'd tossed the official version aeons ago in favor of the candid one.

"We'd successfully obliterated a Directorate weapons lab and were celebrating. It was a good night, even if it might have benefited from one or two fewer drinks by the end."

"The best nights usually do." Eren chuckled. "Sounds as if she had the better of you."

"Almost always." He returned to his chair. "It was her rebellion, and I was merely learning at her knee."

"Then we all owe a debt to her." Eren sipped on his drink, which he'd been nursing throughout their conversation. "You obviously loved her a great deal. You, uh, never talk about Nyx's grandmother, and I admit I've been curious."

Corradeo rolled his eyes at the heavens. "My relationship with Imena was never about love. Often respect, occasionally mild affection, but mostly power. Once we'd both gotten what we wanted from our union, we parted ways. Not precisely friends, but at least not enemies. And of course the children, Renato and Melia, Nyx's mother. Now her? Her I adored. The greatest sin Renato ever committed wasn't trying to take my life. It was ending hers." He leapt up and returned to Eren's side to show him a visual of Melia.

"Nyx looks just like her."

"She does. Acts like her, too. It regularly brings me an equal measure of sorrow and joy."

"We're together, by the way. Nyx and I." Eren's eyes squeezed shut. "I mean, we're not...ah, Hades, I honestly don't know what exactly we are. Lovers, evidently. As for anything more...." He shrugged helplessly.

"I know you are."

"You, too? Seems we've done a poor job of keeping it a secret. At this point, I wouldn't be surprised if I spotted an exposé on us in Olympia's morning news report."

"I asked them not to run it." Corradeo sighed quietly. "I've hoped you two would grow close. I think you complement one another. Not quite *so* close, however. It's not my place to intrude, but I confess I do worry. I don't want to see either of you inflict pain on the other."

"But that's what relationships always do, isn't it?"

"In the end? Maybe. But if you're lucky, the joy they bring far outweighs any eventual pain. I was lucky with Lauren. If we live through the Dzhvar, it's even possible I'll be lucky with Maris, though the field in front of me remains littered in landmines."

"You're definitely playing with fire with that one. Listen, I can't make any promises about Nyx. I pretty much always fear I'm one rash decision away from a stay in Tartarus, and I'm feeling this acutely with her right now. But I do try to point my collateral damage clear of bystanders, and while she's no longer a bystander..." he winced "...I'll do what I can."

"It's all I can ask of you." They both stood, and Corradeo clasped Eren on the shoulder. "Thank you, my friend. For everything."

64

ARES

Maris peered out the window of Corradeo's office, a judgmental frown tightening her features as she considered the small grove of mesquite trees off to the left.

Corradeo laughed warmly and wound his arms around her from behind. "This is a terraformed planet. Beauty can't always be the top priority when choosing the flora."

"Yes, yes." She rested her head against his chest. "You're in a better mood this afternoon."

"Better than when?"

"Do I need to grace that question with a response?"

"No, I suppose not." He kissed her temple. "My conversation with Eren went well. It was challenging and laden with difficult emotions, but it ended in a much friendlier place than where it began. I daresay we've reconciled, which is more than I had any right to hope for."

She twisted around in his arms to face him. "And now one of your burdens is lessened."

"Why is everyone so concerned about the burdens I carry?"

"Not everyone. Merely the people who care for you."

At times he could hardly believe she counted herself among them. When they'd first met, she'd despised him, for understandable reasons, and the tempest of this woman's hatred tended to leave a lasting mark. But when he set out to accomplish something, the universe rarely denied him, and he'd set out not to have *her*, but to have her forgiveness. Along the way, he'd gotten a little more. Then a lot more.

He kissed her softly on the lips now. "Thank you for—"

An alert blasted through his internal system, burning his vision with crisp orange text: *Dzhvar incursion in Concord space.*

A knot of tension mixed with anticipation, weighed down by the gravity of consequential purpose, coiled through his chest. He'd hoped for years, bet on months, but only gotten weeks. So it was.

He stepped out of her arms, touching her cheek by way of apology. "Dzhvar. I must go."

Her chin dipped in acceptance as he turned away and opened a wormhole to the *CAF Aurora.*

CAF AURORA

CONCORD HQ STELLAR SYSTEM

"Where?"

Miriam didn't spare a glance at him as five screens populated in an arc around her. "The Volie system. I've ordered full fleet mobilization and triggered evacuation protocols."

Corradeo heard the words and registered their appropriateness as his thoughts dove into a maelstrom. Their evacuation plans were complex and dependent on a number of moving variables, though they'd had time and the benefit of many Artificials to work them out in great detail.

But Volie hosted almost a billion residents. If the Dzhvar moved half as fast now as on their previous incursions, only a tiny fraction stood to make it offworld before the planet began to crumble. Yes, eventually those who perished would be returned to life, but it would take years to complete regenesis procedures for a billion people. And when they awoke, they'd find their homes were gone. How many more planets were going to fall between now and then, sending ever more people to the back of the regenesis line? "What about—?"

"A modified Rift Bubble is en route. It will arrive in time to be activated before the Dzhvar reach the planet."

"Thank you." They didn't yet have a name for the fractalized rift device, but it promised to redirect the dimensions surrounding the planet fivefold. It hadn't been tested in the field, however, so they had no way to know how much time it would buy them. And it was something of a Faustian bargain they were making by using it, since the device was going to shut down all wormholes on the surface. Evacuations must cease for as long as it remained active, which was why they weren't activating it right away.

'Commandant, you should reschedule the Echo Rift deployment with Lakhes,' the ship's Artificial intoned.

"Yes. Thank you for the reminder, Thomas."

Corradeo caught Miriam frowning as she ascended the overlook. "Are you reconsidering your decision to use the Echo Rift on the Ch'mshak?"

"No. Just accepting that my conscience will take a greater hit from continuing to endanger every Concord citizen by risking the escape of more Ch'mshak than it will from not personally witnessing the sealing away of the species." Miriam sighed. "Thomas, I need to send Brigadier General Nathan Roan to handle the deployment in my stead. I don't believe he's interacted directly with a Kat before, but he has been in their presence. He'll be able to navigate the encounter without too much difficulty."

'A wise choice. Roan has displayed superior calm in the most stressful of situations.'

"Agreed. I'll inform him of his new assignment, then alert Lakhes to the change of plans. They can move forward as soon as they're ready."

Corradeo backed away from the overlook to let Miriam work as the bridge began to come to life with bustling personnel. Should he move to Casmir's Imperium? A flare of nativist pride counseled for him to do so, given an Anaden world was soon to be under attack. But while he liked Casmir well enough personally and respected the man's military leadership skills, Machim rigidity as a character trait rankled him. And though Casmir never said anything, he knew the man twitched beneath Corradeo's watchful gaze. The long shadow of his former military career would never dissipate. So he stayed on board the *Aurora* for now.

Why was an Anaden world the first to be targeted? Was the enemy retracing its steps? Following well-worn treads it had left behind in the first war?

A bitter taste settled into his mouth. It was as if the enemy was taunting him, or else seeking revenge for its long exile.

He shouldn't anthropomorphize primordial cosmic energy. Intellectually, he recognized that it was simply a matter of odds: Anadens lived on thousands more planets than any other Concord species, thus any random inhabited planet was more likely to host Anadens than anyone else. But the bitterness persisted.

S&L

VOLIE STELLAR SYSTEM

The Dzhvar writhed through the outer reaches of the Volie system like a rampaging wildfire, burning everything in their path, even the very fabric of space. By Hades, how Corradeo loathed the sight of them.

For the first time, the fleet positioned itself in front of the advancing Dzhvar wall; this was no longer an information-gathering expedition. The lives of those they were sworn to protect were now threatened, so they fought to slow the enemy down in any manner they could…which wasn't much of any manner at all.

The Dzhvar's advance did slow, perhaps in acknowledgment of the fleet's presence. Scores of ships lobbed the new, oversized Rima missiles into the Dzhvar, and a sea of dimples formed pockmarks across the wall, but only for a few seconds per hit. Dimensional Rifters protected any ship that found itself caught in surging filaments of Dzhvar, though only long enough for a vessel to escape from the advance—assuming it moved fast. As a result, sparks of hellfire flared across the battlefield like a sea of firecrackers. It was a distracting light show, all noise and no impact.

And amidst it all the fleet continually retreated, driven back toward Volie as they fought to stay ahead of the Dzhvar's advance.

Dammit! They had nothing with which to fight the enemy.

He remembered this feeling of helplessness in his gut from the first war. Buried beneath a thousand millennia of memories, it surged to the forefront now, as fresh and raw as if it were birthed yesterday. He'd watched planet after planet fall, watched billions of Anadens die beneath an unyielding enemy. He'd been helpless to stop the Dzhvar then, too.

Until he wasn't.

"Corradeo, the rift device has arrived on the planet," Miriam said. "I'll activate it as soon as the Dzhvar come within twenty megameters of the outer atmosphere. We can't risk a single filament crossing the threshold before we erect the barrier."

He glanced over at Miriam. "How long will that be?"

"Perhaps fifteen minutes."

He breathed in through his nostrils, pushing against the resurgent helplessness until resistance became outright rejection. Though his conversation with Eren had been difficult and the dredging up of old memories of the first anarch rebellion acutely painful, he recognized how cathartic, how necessary it had been. For he now remembered the man he'd once been and must be—*would* be—again if he wanted to win this war.

That man was not helpless. He would never stand idly by, safe within the hull of this ship, while a planet full of his citizens faced destruction.

"I'll be on the surface." He activated his CPM and stepped through the wormhole.

65

MSHAK

The arid air of Ch'mshak grated on Olivia's biosynthetic skin, and she fought the urge to scratch at her arms.

She'd gotten over the novelty of the doll's superior sensory throughput after a few days of using it for various tasks. She shut the skin sensations off in annoyance as she climbed onto the personal hoverboard she'd brought along and set off across the scrub brush for Varlem Bakker T'worz's settlement.

She'd come to believe that the Machim ambush on Lethe was the result of an infiltration program embedded in her Riamere database. But until she uncovered explicit evidence of such a program, she had to allow for the possibility of someone monitoring the T'worz settlement for wormhole activity. Accordingly, she'd arrived on Mshak some distance from the settlement today. When she got closer to her destination, she'd leave the hoverboard behind, activate her Veil, and not reveal herself until she was in the chieftain's presence.

If she were planning to continue this unpleasant business arrangement for much longer, she'd have implemented more elaborate and sustainable safeguards, but she was not. In fact, she anticipated this would be her last visit, not that she planned on informing T'worz of this. No, when she was done with the Ch'mshak, she simply would not return.

She was cautiously optimistic that her primary incarnation had already uncovered how an adversary learned of the raid on the Lethe warehouse, in which case there was no longer a risk to her presence here. The last time she'd synced up with her server hardware was shortly after her primary had asked the intriguing and confounding Padron Lanael for his recommendations on foreign code detection and quarantine programs. Hopefully, in the days since then, he'd suitably delivered on her request, and she had her answers.

The fact she didn't know one way or another, when other splinters of her consciousness *did*, grated at her nerves like the scraping of misaligned gears. But it had to be this way. Survival trumped every other consideration.

The incarnation she inhabited today was a dual-function doll. It was a way to be in multiple places at once, thus accomplishing two days' worth of work for every one—but more crucially, it served as a worst-case scenario backup method.

She'd learned many lessons from her son's murder and her own close brush with a second death; one of them was to always have an offline, siloed backup of her consciousness, memories and neural architecture. In implementing this insurance, exercising an abundance of caution had ultimately won out over her inherent desire for efficiency of knowledge and speed of action. This biosynthetic doll—facially indistinguishable from an organic body—reconnected with her servers at dynamically generated intervals ranging from every thirty-two to seventy-six hours. The lesson to never be predictable, she'd learned long, long ago.

So she wouldn't know the status of the investigation until she next synced up with her hardware in another nine hours, personal desires be damned.

Sand invaded her eyes as the hoverboard sped across the desert toward the settlement, heightening her displeasure at finding herself here yet again. But it was necessary. Her takeover of Nikto's operations continued to throw up frustrating roadblocks. Though she'd studied it for two years now, Anaden society still displayed quirks she hadn't properly anticipated.

In this instance, a criminal organization that escaped her initial notice had acted on a perceived power vacuum in Nikto's operations on Brizo after she'd eliminated the local management. They'd waltzed into the cybernetics production facility there and set up shop for themselves. Now she not only had to remove the squatters, she had to ensure the group wouldn't try such a stunt again in the future. An agonizingly painful mauling of the group's leader by a Ch'mshak, when paired with a clear warning, ought to do the trick.

It was so tiresome. This had all been much easier when the mere mention of the name Olivia Montegreu struck criminals catatonic with fear. The reputation of the Pale Viper was spreading quickly, however. Soon enough, she wouldn't need to back up her every threat with disproportionate violence.

She'd spoofed a message from the factory to the group's leader and two lieutenants on her way here, alerting them to a serious problem at the facility. She checked the feed from the cams as she reached the border of the settlement and was pleased to see two of the individuals arriving now.

She parked the hoverboard behind a building and strode swiftly across the square, then deactivated her Veil and announced herself at T'worz's door.

"Has taken too long for next mission, and the last ship was broken. We must have more ships," he demanded without preamble.

"I'm not a shuttle service. I need you when I need you, and not before."

"Then we require bigger ships."

She tossed a hand dismissively. "We'll see. Today's ship is already en route. I require a squad of eight warriors. One location, kill everyone in the building."

"My warriors compete to be chosen for these missions, to feel the rush of battle and smell the spilt blood in their nostrils."

"Lovely." Observing that the second lieutenant had arrived at the site on Brizo, she pivoted toward the door. "My timetable is tight. We're moving now."

T'worz pressed a lever behind his desk, and in the distance a bell clanged. She went to the clearing to wait for the squad to arrive.

Armor-clad Ch'mshak jogged in from the south; two of them were visibly shorter than the others. Her gaze shot to T'worz. "Do not saddle me with subpar warriors."

"No, no. Young, but fierce. They each killed three opponents to win a spot on this mission."

It was truly a wonder the Ch'mshak hadn't exterminated themselves by now. As soon as the last combatant arrived, she issued her usual instructions to them and opened a wormhole to—

An error message flashed in her system:

Unable to reach coordinates.

She'd never received such an error before. Her residual knowledge suggested it typically meant a quantum block was in place at the desired destination. Why would a quantum block be erected on Brizo? Was this related to the Dzhvar? Had the much-hyped aliens finally made an appearance in Concord space?

She tried to open a wormhole to Domor instead.

Unable to reach coordinates.

Was something wrong with her own internal hardware? The doll was still fairly new, but she'd taken care to ensure it was constructed of the highest quality materials. She opened a worm-hole to a location a hundred meters distant, outside the settlement proper, and it manifested normally. This meant there wasn't a quantum block here on Mshak—also, if there were, she'd have been rendered nonfunctional. The fact a wormhole opened on the surface also meant she wasn't facing a problem with the doll's functionality.

Perturbed, she checked her curated news feed. Nothing about a Dzhvar attack on Brizo or Domor, but if it had just begun, word might not have reached the rest of the world yet.

"What is holdup?"

She held out a hand to silence T'worz. Though it broke her own protocol, she took the extraordinary step of sending a notification to her primary hardware. It bounced.

She hurriedly sent a query to her primary body. It bounced. Secondary hardware, same.

Possibilities:

• Dzhvar had attacked at least four worlds simultaneously, either destroying all of them or erecting quantum blocks at each one so they could work at their leisure. The Dzhvar's historical modus operandi did not involve the use of quantum blocks, but perhaps they'd shifted tactics in the million years they'd had to plan their invasion. Unlikely, but within the realm of possibility.

• Someone—CINT, SENTRI, Advocacy Intelligence—had mounted an operation against her on multiple fronts. It was a risk she worked tirelessly to mitigate, but a risk it remained. The facility on Brizo should be far down any list of law enforcement targets, if it was on the list at all, though she conceded Domor might be a high-value target. Erecting quantum blocks around her hardware made sense, but why deploy them at her factories?

• Something else was transpiring.

After initiating an analysis routine to surface a list of additional possibilities, she turned her attention to her current situation. She needed to get off this planet, but more immediately, she needed to get away from an increasingly agitated T'worz and his town full of armed warriors.

She sent a signal to the ship she had in orbit, instructing it to descend to the surface but to a landing site outside the settlement, as she'd no longer be delivering it to the Ch'mshak. Instead, she'd use it to make her own escape.

Then she steeled herself for an unpleasant response and faced T'worz. "Something has come up, and the mission is canceled for today—"

The telemetry of the descending ship cut out. She tried to ping the sub-Artificial operating it and received no response. Her confusion mounted, as the disparate malfunctions lent themselves to no obvious explanation.

No ship. No offworld wormholes. No communication with her primaries or backups. She was, for the moment, stuck on this hell-forsaken planet, surrounded by vicious brutes who would rip her doll to shreds in an instant should they decide she could no longer provide them something they wanted. Further, she was equipped with nothing but the doll's physical tools and her own wits to aid in her survival.

A gathering crowd of Ch'mshak growled and stomped in displeasure, and T'worz took a threatening step toward her as he thrust out his enormous chest. "No good. You deliver ship for our time."

That's what she'd thought he was going to say.

"No." She activated her Veil and vanished.

S&L

God, this planet was almost as ugly as the inhabitants. What wasn't desert was parched plains speckled with muddy ponds. Everything in sight was painted yellow, brown or some fetid blending of the two.

Morgan slipped her stealthed Banshee, *Ardat*, through the blockade without much difficulty. She'd call it a horrible security gap, but no one had ever imagined a single living being from outside the blockade would ever want to access the planet. Only the sickly diabolical mind of Olivia Montegreu could prove everyone wrong.

Morgan remained stealthed as her Banshee descended through patchy cloud cover. She genuinely didn't want to get caught if possible, and the blockade had increased its scanning coverage significantly once Ch'mshak started appearing outside the perimeter. But if the military did discover her presence here, so be it. She was prepared to accept the consequences of her actions.

The settlement producing the rampaging squads of Ch'mshak wasn't situated terribly far from the fortified encampment where Brook had died. Did some of the residents have her blood stained upon their claws? Entirely plausible.

You are stretching the facts to the breaking point in order to construct a justification around your actions that you can live with.

Stanley, I swear I will find a way to shut you out if you don't pipe down. He'd spent all day deploying his best arguments for letting this go, and he'd only ramped up his efforts once she left dock.

You cannot. Like it or not, you and I are inseparable. And I will never stop trying to save you from yourself.

Ouch. This hit a bit close to the mark. Though at present she felt a driving, gnawing need to block him, most of the time, she had to concede she enjoyed Stanley's companionship. He'd kept her company through her darkest times, when the world was empty and hard and cold and she was otherwise all alone. He knew her soul in a way no one else did. And right now, that was the problem.

Morgan's attention drifted toward the navigation controls as she contemplated visiting the location of the old encampment.

In one of the ugliest insults of the whole terrible affair, the military had never recovered Brook's body. Those were the last days of the spiraling conflict, when Solovy had realized the planet and its people could not be conquered and the losses had finally hit unacceptable levels. So the commandant had abruptly abandoned the fight, putting up a barbed-wire fence to keep the animals locked in and leaving the bodies of Brook and her squad here to rot beneath Mshak's scorching sun.

Was she nothing but bones by now? Did some Ch'mshak wear those bones as trophies—

She gagged, nearly vomiting into her breather mask.

Don't do this to yourself. I beg you.

The dark thoughts were nothing new. She'd asked herself these questions in a periodic loop for eleven years now. But to be here, on the scene, with the site of the massacre lurking on the horizon ahead, made it real in a way nothing else had.

Her heart pounded against her sternum until she struggled to breathe.

She couldn't face the reality of the place where it had happened. She wasn't strong enough. If she landed there and crawled out of her cockpit to stand amidst bleached bones, she might well drop to the ground and never stand up again.

I'm sorry, Brook. With a deep breath through her nostrils, she adjusted her course for her intended target.

The settlement was larger than she'd expected, and more developed. She'd assumed that, deprived of imports from the civilized world, the Ch'mshak would've spent their quarantine devolving back into cave dwellers who fought to the death over the evening's food. But their structures still stood; they lived and worked in proximity to one another without blood streaming through what passed for streets.

No matter. Their actions these past six weeks had confirmed they remained bloodthirsty, violent savages. Worse than killing for food or survival, they killed for sport. Because they *enjoyed* it.

She took idle note of the updating alerts in her eVi regarding the ongoing Dzhvar encounter. Until they found a use for fighter craft in such battles, her presence wasn't required. Good thing, too, since she was busy.

She slowed as she reached the settlement, flying over for a pass to take in the details before blasting them away.

The wreckage of the ship Marlee had disabled lay strewn across the dirt on the east side of a large cluster of buildings. Clever, fearless, indomitable Marlee....

A different kind of guilt ripped into her chest now. Like Stanley, Marlee simply wanted her to be happy. And if such a thing were possible, she thought she might be able to be happy with Marlee. The woman's spirit was infectious; lingering in her presence made one *want* to embrace life. But what Marlee didn't understand—though she suspected Stanley did—was that happiness was not in the cards for her, only lesser or greater melancholy. Of late, she'd toyed with the lesser, until Brook's slaughterers had rampaged back onto the scene to remind her of what she'd lost.

Below her, a group of small Ch'mshak rumbled around an enclosed ring, swinging blunt spears at each other. Children? It had never occurred to her that the brutes had children, but obviously they did. And here they were, training up to become killers.

In the shade of an overhanging roof, two adults hammered on metal near a kiln. Making armor for their warriors? Next door, a small group sat on stools and husked corn they'd managed to squeeze out of the paltry, meager farmland behind the settlement.

Enough of this tourist shit. Morgan banked around in preparation for a bombing run. It was going to take several passes to get everyone, but she hadn't detected any defenses sufficient to interfere. She could bomb them all day long if she wished.

Even the children.

They weren't Stanley's words, but rather her own traitorous conscience surging forward to claim a voice. Yes, even the children, dammit! Those children were certain to grow up to become as murderous as the warriors currently slaughtering their way across Concord space. If given the chance, they'd rake open the guts of any person they cornered then wear their entrails as necklaces.

But they weren't going to get the chance. In a few hours, Concord was going to lock them inside a dimensional cage from which they could never escape.

Fine. She'd try to miss the children, in concession to them not technically having done anything worth punishing *yet.*

The armorers, though? Accessories to the crimes.

And the farmers and food preparers? They kept the warriors strong....

What the fuck was she doing? She slammed her fist against the glass above her and wrapped the flaring pain around her like a shroud. Their culpability was written in blood and death. They did not deserve to live. Not a one of them.

Tears streamed down her face. There was no vengeance she could exact that would ever bring Brook back. She could crush the planet into a singularity or tear crust from mantle, and it wouldn't make a damn bit of difference. Doing so wouldn't even make her feel better, would it? A minute's rush of righteous vindication, then that too would fade away, leaving behind the same cavernous void she coddled now.

And Stanley was right, which he was far too often. She risked wrecking her career for a meaningless, futile act of retribution. If she ever experienced genuine happiness, it was in the cockpit of *Ardat.* Was she willing to surrender this one grace in order to kill a few of the monsters? Doing so wasn't going to save or return a single life they'd stolen.

She had a long history of self-sabotage, but did this mean she was duty-bound to do so yet again? Marlee was right about this, too. Her past was littered with piss-poor decisions that helped no one and only hurt her.

Shame curled into the void with the pain. God, how she must have disappointed Marlee. Disappointed everyone who dared to care about her, few though she'd allowed to get close.

She closed her eyes and let the ship cruise past the settlement. The physical pain in her hand faded to a dull ache and the shame retreated to haunt the shadows, until all she felt was hollow. Empty. Whatever she was searching for, she'd never find it here.

She screamed and banged on the glass with her open palms...then turned her ship toward the stars.

Thank you, Morgan. I would heal your heart were it in my power, but I will settle for not seeing you endure anymore self-inflicted pain.

Yeah, yeah. Any chance you can heal my knuckles, though?

Stanley smiled kindly in her mind. *Yes, I can heal your knuckles.*

She sniffled, pulling her breather mask away to rub at her nose. Time to leave this accursed planet to its fate.

The atmosphere thinned to reveal the galaxy arms beyond, and she forced herself to consider how—

Divert!

She reacted to Stanley's cry on instinct and executed a hard—

The ship slammed into an invisible barrier at a slight angle off head-on. Given the high speed at which it was traveling, the safety harness failed to prevent Morgan's head from snapping forward, then jerking back with equal force against the seat, and she instantly lost consciousness.

Still, Stanley might have been able to use Morgan's integration with the ship's systems to intervene and take control. But the ricocheting impacts were so violent that they jostled the biosynth neural graft/buffer installed in the base of her brain enough to cause it to slip two nanometers out of position. Picometer-width fibers stretched, then snapped.

Stanley lost contact with Morgan's mind and body.

The Banshee featured a sophisticated sub-Artificial operating system, but the collision with the Echo Rift dimensional barrier jostled several fiber clusters as well, just enough for a few entangled pairs to lose their coherence. Critical emergency navigational instructions faltered short of their destination.

Without anyone to steer it, *Ardat* fell into an out-of-control spiral dive and plummeted toward the planet below.

66

ROMANE

Mia paced along the length of the upper-level balcony above the atrium. Below her, Expo visitors milled about, pausing in front of the various introductory exhibits or strolling aimlessly while munching on snacks from the food stalls, but she barely noticed the activity.

Her mind was situated three-quarters in the Noesis, tracking the firehose of updates from the ongoing Dzhvar engagement at Volie. Hard information dribbled in from the military Connexus, passed along on the sly by military Prevos who should be doing no such thing. A non-zero percentage of the community considered themselves to be Prevos first and soldiers second.

Other details came from sidespace-viewed eyewitness accounts, though not many. During the encounter in the Antlia Wall, two Prevos present only in sidespace had died—human and Artificial both—when the Dzhvar ripped through the space their minds were occupying. Because it turned out the Dzhvar really, *truly* transcended dimensions, and they wielded the power to disintegrate sidespace as easily as they did the physical component of the cosmic manifold. So now, people kept a more cautious distance. Except for those with more bravery than good sense, and that was their own choice to make.

Mia never longed for her old job more acutely than she did at moments like this one. She should be interfacing with Advocate Corradeo, the Anaden ambassadorial staff in the Consulate and the governor of Volie, relaying their needs to Miriam and vice versa. She should be overseeing the humanitarian aspect of the gargantuan evacuation efforts, as the Consulate was skilled at performing this sort of work. She should be *helping*.

But she'd given up the right to help, and she wasn't getting it back.

Her gaze flitted down as a group of children tore through the atrium with notable gusto, their squeals and laughter pealing through the airy space. It had been this way for most of the Rasu War, too. Today, the danger the Dzhvar posed wasn't real to her guests. Odds were, it wouldn't be real to them until humans died on a world everyone knew. For now, people continued on with their daily lives. They visited the Expo and educated themselves or their children, naively confident a future was going to persist in which a worldly education mattered.

She didn't blame them. Like her, they could do nothing to help improve the situation, and impotent worry was a most unproductive activity. She scolded herself for engaging in it while continuing to pace along the balcony.

Mia, there's a problem.

What is it, Meno?

I have just heard from Stanley. It seems Morgan was on Mshak when the Echo Rift was deployed.

What was she doing there? I can't believe they would've activated the Echo Rift while a military operation was underway. Miriam wouldn't make such a mistake.

There was no military operation. Only Morgan.

Oh. Empathy panged in her chest. Blowing up every single Ch'mshak who drew breath wasn't going to bring Brooklyn Harper back, and Morgan full well knew it. But if anyone understood the powerful, driving need for vengeance in the wake of the loss of the person who possessed one's heart, Mia did, and she'd never chastise the woman for indulging in it, however futile such an act may be.

But now Morgan was in trouble.

We're absolutely certain she's trapped on Mshak?

Yes. And the news is worse than her simply being trapped. She was departing the planet when the Echo Rift activated, and her ship im-

pacted the barrier. Something transpired in the collision that resulted in Stanley no longer having access to her.

Mia frowned; that didn't make any sense. When she'd nearly died as a result of an attack during the final battle of the Metigen War, Meno had been able to interact with her brain despite her comatose state. He'd worked with Dr. Canivon to identify the damage, repair it where he could, and fill in the gaps where he could not.

I don't understand. He ought to be able to access her body no matter her condition... she winced *...unless she's dead.*

Or unless she suffered some damage to the neural hardware linking them. Stanley is, obviously, hopeful it's the latter. But without access, he doesn't possess any information about where she is or what her injuries are. Whether she crashed or...he doesn't know much of anything about the situation, and allow me to say that he is not handling these circumstances well.

Of course he isn't. And because the Echo Rift is active, sidespace isn't available to us to go searching for her.

No, it isn't.

Wormholes and sidespace were able to bypass a traditional Rift Bubble, which was more barrier than shifted dimensions. But the Echo Rift was both: it shifted the dimensions around its contents while also blocking passage. And it did so twice, in mirrored directions, creating a maze that quantum transmissions could not navigate through. So while the physical space—in this case, a planet— still existed in its natural state in the interior of the Echo Rift, it was impossible for anyone on the outside to peer inside.

Impossible for anyone except a Kat, that was. When they'd deployed the first Echo Rift around Savrakath four years ago, Mesme had confirmed that Kats retained the ability to penetrate the device's protections, though it had declined to share how they did so. One of many mysteries the aliens held close to the vest.

So all was not lost. This was going to stir up a kerfuffle, however.

All right. Tell Stanley I'll raise the alarm.

Morgan's status as a high-ranking military officer meant AEGIS would mobilize efforts for her prompt rescue. Then possibly initiate a courts martial for what Mia presumed was a blatant disobeying of orders.

The question was, would Malcolm be able to overlook Morgan's actions and shield her from the most severe consequences? She didn't know, and she'd understand if he ultimately couldn't. Even the fleet admiral had to follow the rules...most of the time. But those quandaries were for later, post-rescue.

She tried not to pulse Malcolm during military engagements, but this counted as enough of an emergency to make an exception.

I know you're busy, so I'll be brief. Morgan Lekkas is trapped on Mshak, inside the Echo Rift. She's likely injured, but Stanley is unable to connect with her to determine her location or status.

I see.

She heard the annoyance in his mental voice. The two of them had never gotten along, even when Morgan was behaving.

I take it she didn't have permission to be there?

No, but I can't say I'm surprised. Look, Miriam and I are fully occupied at Volie. I will do what I can to get a Kat's attention, but it might take a little time. Have Stanley contact Colonel Williamson at AEGIS Search and Rescue at my behest, so the colonel can be ready to mount a rescue mission the instant we have any actionable information or practical access to the planet.

Thank you.

She didn't append any endearments, and neither did he. Amid a military engagement, where every second counted, wasn't the time for it. Not unless one of them was about to...die.

Thinking of such a possibility sent a shudder rippling through her body, but it was a legacy reaction. A residue left behind from the worst days of her life. Unless the Dzhvar destroyed everything, that was never going to happen again.

Now, they just had to find a way to ensure the Dzhvar didn't destroy everything.

67

VOLIE

MILKY WAY GALAXY

Corradeo had only been to Volie once since rejoining civilization four years ago, but it was lovely as Anaden worlds went. Cosmopolitan and thriving, with voluminous white sandy beaches and sparkling cerulean waters. No single dynasty dominated here, and a vibrant art scene competed with commercial development and scientific endeavors for funds from the planet's wealthiest residents.

In the shadow of scraper-lined downtown streets, two oversized wormholes sparkled against an overcast sky. Semi-orderly lines of people hurried through them under the watchful eyes of military personnel. There would be hundreds of such wormholes scattered across the planet by now.

Every person who made it out was a life saved, for today. But eventually, whether in a year or a decade, there would remain no worlds to evacuate *to*. Not unless he stemmed the tide of the Dzhvar's advance, then halted it.

A message arrived from Miriam.

Perhaps reacting to us taking a more active stance against them, the Dzhvar have abruptly accelerated. I'm activating the rift device in thirty seconds. Please return to the Aurora.

I'll remain here.

Advocate....

As soon as it's apparent the rift device has stopped holding back the Dzhvar, deactivate it so we can resume wormhole evacuations for whatever time the planet has left.

And you'll leave then?

When I can no longer do any good.

There was no visual evidence of dimensions shifting overhead, but a few seconds later, the wormholes splitting downtown sputtered and died. The guards had presumably been given a brief warning and were doing their best to calm the people, but failing at it. Ripples of panic cascaded through the crowd, sending the lines into anarchy.

Corradeo wished them luck, then spun and strode away.

The capital city's pride and joy was Epanou Park; it stretched for nearly two kilometers along the bank of the Epanou River, and they wound side by side through the heart of downtown. He'd deliberately arrived near one of the park's entrances, and his pace quickened to a jog as he crossed under a wrought-iron awning and onto a cobblestone path.

He didn't want to endanger lives today by inadvertently toppling any of the surrounding buildings, crashing vehicles or inflicting more direct forms of violence, which was what had happened the first time. Hence the park.

Once he'd established some distance between himself and any structures, he planted his feet wide, squared his shoulders and fixed his gaze on the sky.

His people were in mortal danger, and he was done begging for aid. Done prostrating himself before an intelligence that had called him master for a million years. Done being weak, timid or uncertain. He'd saved the universe from destruction once before, and he would damn well do it again. He didn't think it or hope it— for the first time since learning the Dzhvar were fated to return, he knew it.

A reaffirming deep breath, and he cast his inner voice out upon the firmament.

I command your attention. Our old enemy has returned from its exile and resumed its destructive ways. The time has come to take up the fight against them once more.

A breeze ruffled his hair across his forehead...but it was only the wind. Undeterred, he renewed his call.

I **command** *your attention. Come to me, and together we will save the existence we call Amaranthe and the souls who live within it. Come to me, and together we will defeat this foe. COME TO ME, NOW.* Though spoken words did not leave his lips, his voice bellowed across the stars.

Out of thin air, a single fleck of crimson light materialized to hover in front of his face. Had it followed him here, curious to see what he might do today? Or had it been here all along? Was it everywhere all along, existing just out of sight?

Corradeo made a fist and clasped it over his breast. *Join with me. Lend me your strength, and together we will fight for all life in this cosmos.*

Far overhead, a streak of florid orange sliced apart a bank of clouds, and despite his best efforts to keep it at bay, despair welled up in his chest. How long had the fractalized rift device been active? Five minutes? Ten at most. It was useless.

But he was not, and he refused to give up. He would never give up this fight.

He directed the entirety of his intent, of his will, at the solitary crimson light agitating less than a meter from his face.

Do you see it? The enemy is here NOW. We must act, for only we can. Join with me. I demand it!

The air around him turned red as a swarm of *diati* emerged from nothingness to encircle him in a whirlwind. He held out his arms, opening himself—

The rush of power was beyond words, beyond madness. His sense of self expanded across the park and the city and the galaxy, then collapsed in on him until his body threatened to implode from the pressure. His skin buzzed to the point of pain as he struggled to remember how to contain the tsunami of otherworldly energy. His mind felt dizzy, unfocused—

A bench off to the left exploded into shards of metal. Then another. A metal spear shot toward his head, only to be deflected by the *diati.* Beyond him, a fountain churned into a tornado of water as the marble comprising it crumbled to dust. The air grew thick with crimson searching for an outlet.

Calm. Rein yourself in. I will not repeat the destruction we caused the last time we joined together. Let us both regain our control....

He breathed in through his nose. Out through his mouth. Let the rush wash over and entwine him, willing himself not to fight against the energy but instead flow with it.

And bit by bit, the raging storm consuming him allayed into a tight, hot core of power in his chest. The source of it was no longer external, but rather within him.

He held out a hand and concentrated on gathering a bundle of *diati* above it, then directed it to a nearby tree.

The tree splintered into a thousand fragments of bark and a shower of leaves.

Good. But we are going to need significantly more strength if we are to save this planet today.

He braced himself for a renewed onslaught, but its arrival still knocked him flat to the ground—and the next second he was floating upward to hover above the treetops. The potency of the power animating him overflowed his pores to spill out and— *concentrate. We must focus. There is no more time. The Dzhvar pierce the sky. We must form a barrier to protect the planet. Go now!*

He flung his arms out wide, and a great wave of energy surged through and out of him to race toward the horizon.

AKESO

Caleb stood at the data center table in the office, watching the real-time updates from the Concord feed. Alex sat in the chair in the corner, eyes closed, analyzing the battle from sidespace. Searching for some clue to a weakness in the Dzhvar they could exploit.

They both felt helpless, each in their own way. Funny thing was, he was pretty sure Miriam felt helpless, too, and his mother-in-law was *never* helpless. This wasn't an enemy they were able to fight using conventional means. Not with military armaments, though they continued to try. Not with advanced technological wizardry, though again with the stubborn trying. The question hounding each of them now was whether the enemy could be fought at all—

His body jerked involuntarily. A visceral awareness swept through him, a recognition of something he hadn't sensed in almost eighteen years.

No.

The thought was unconscious and instinctual. Protective.

He checked Alex, but she was parsecs away, and also fine. So he rushed downstairs and outside. He needed to see; if the worst came to pass, he needed to ensure she and their home remained safe.

The night sky danced with flecks of crimson light, like fireflies emerging from their hibernation in the warmth of late spring—but not the Akeso-Hirlas firefly analogues. Upon his arrival at the meadow, the flecks quickly gathered around him. Not quite insistent, but certainly probing.

In his mind, he walled off Akeso as much as possible using the techniques he'd perfected on Namino while fighting the Rasu. Then, while keeping the firm order of '*no*' at the forefront of his thoughts, he reached out, just a little.

And knew that on Volie, Corradeo had finally gotten the *diati's* attention. More than this, had forcefully called it to him, then wrangled it under his firm control.

Good. Good that the *diati* once again considered the man a worthy wielder. Good that Corradeo once again believed the same.

Bright flecks of crimson glided over Caleb's skin, whispering without words of an ancient fight, an intrinsic bond and, above all, immeasurable power.

He breathed in and acknowledged his deep, gut-wrenching desire to accept this gift. Harnessing such a weapon as this, he'd be able to fight the terrible enemy they faced.

His whole life, when encountering a problem that needed fixing, he'd *acted*. He was a doer, a solver of problems and righter of wrongs. This ethos was at the core of his being. And here, presented before him, hand outstretched in invitation, was the weapon that would enable him to act. He could protect Alex and his family and trillions of people and possibly the universe itself.

But if he did accept this power, he *couldn't* protect Akeso. The *diati* would infect Akeso's pure soul. Not through malice or even intent, but by virtue of the *diati's* inherent nature. It had killed eight billion people on Solum through mere inattention; individual lives didn't register on its radar.

Diati wasn't evil, but it also wasn't good. It simply *was*.

And it would corrupt Akeso's innocence, destroy its sense of justice and its life-renewing beauty. Akeso and *diati* could not coexist. If forced to attempt it, *diati* would win, overpowering Akeso's spirit until it faded away into nothingness. Caleb knew this with absolute clarity, not because Alex's vision had shown it to be true, but because he had carried them both as a companion within his own soul.

If there were no other choice, he recognized he'd have to sacrifice Akeso, as one solitary life must be traded for the lives of trillions. If the Dzhvar weren't stopped, even Akeso would inevitably fall, making his momentary protection of its life worse than futile.

But there was another choice, and it had already been made. Corradeo was capable of doing this on his own. He had the strength of character and iron will needed to be their champion. He'd defeated the Dzhvar once before, and knowing all they now did about the true nature of the enemy, with Alex, Nika, Mesme and Miriam helping him, he could do so for good this time.

I save the people who will save the universe.

Mesme's words echoed back to him, but he shook his head, as if to physically refute them. The others, yes. Corradeo was on the list, and this was obviously why. Perhaps it would turn out that the only reason Caleb had ever been present on the list was because he intended to guard Alex with his life so she was able to do her spectacular part to save the universe. He'd do everything in his power to help Alex, to help all of them. Everything but this.

A swarm of *diati* gathered in front of him, consuming his vision. It banged away at his thoughts, pleading for entry.

Corradeo Praesidis is your master and your partner. Go to him. Give him the power to defeat this enemy.

Still it swarmed. Insistent now. Fervent.

Go to him. Go to Corradeo. I COMMAND IT! he screamed in his mind.

The vibrations ceased. The *diati* hung frozen before him…then vanished.

He exhaled harshly, releasing the tension coiled in his muscles so violently that he sank to his knees in the grass. Fresh air filled his lungs, and he tried to use it to soothe his racing heart. The effort of fending off the *diati* had wrung him dry. His hands shook as his nerves continued to fire, warding against an antagonist who was no longer here. The *diati* wasn't a foe, but this had been a battle all the same.

As relieved as he was that he'd succeeded in resisting its offer, the victory somehow tasted like ash in his mouth. He yearned to fight, to do, to *act*.

But no. This was the right choice. Corradeo was a worthy hero. And him? He had a duty to preserve the precious life in his care.

When almost a minute had passed with no further visitors, he dismantled the wall in his mind. Akeso instantly began chattering away.

Why did you shut me out? I sensed a presence here. One I remember, from before you and I became as one, when an Other attacked me. This presence? It was once a part of you. Alien, foreign, yet also you. When I touched your mind then, I also touched it. It imparted…strangeness. But all aliens are strange, except for you.

Your memory serves you well, Akeso. I'm sorry I blocked you out, but I needed to have a conversation with this presence, and I didn't want it to influence you.

Why not? Is it harmful? Evil?

Not exactly. Its essence is...complicated. It does not wish to do you harm, but it doesn't view life the same way you do. Thus through me, it would harm you nonetheless.

Akeso fell silent, but Caleb sensed its ruminations in his blood, in the ground beneath his feet.

Speak your thoughts, Akeso. You needn't hide them from me.

I sense your turmoil. You feel...pulled in every direction. Too many warring needs, too many deep longings. Calm yourself. Be here with me, and realize you need nothing else.

Caleb climbed to his feet, dragging his hands down his face with a deep sigh. "Oh, Akeso. I am trying."

68

CAF AURORA
VOLIE STELLAR SYSTEM

Miriam's nails dug into the skin of her palm, a painful but silent manifestation of the frustration intent on overwhelming her. Five stacked rift diversions had gained them all of seven and a half minutes. This was madness.

She checked to make certain the wormhole evacuations were beginning again, as they could rescue some thousands of additional people before the firmament upended and the atmosphere sheared away.

And she had nothing else. Nothing with which to fight the attackers *or* protect her citizens.

In her heart, she at last began to understand how the universe had ended an uncountable number of times beneath the inexorable march of this enemy. If wrenching the dimensions of the manifold in every conceivable direction was not enough to stop the Dzhvar for more than a few minutes, what greater tool could possibly—

'Commandant, something is happening on the planet.'

Obviously something was happening on the planet. But she swiftly squelched the snippy reaction; Thomas would never brandish his snark at a moment like this.

"Show me."

Her eyes narrowed at the visual Thomas manifested front and center at the overlook. It displayed the feed from a probe they'd sent to the far side of Volie, in a region the Dzhvar had not yet reached. A faint clay tint settled over the sage and turquoise palette of the planet's surface. As she watched, the overlay color intensified and darkened.

"Zoom in, Thomas. Maximum magnification."

The visual blurred, and when it regained focus, it showed a fine mesh of crimson dots flowing out through the atmosphere until they vanished into the wall of the encroaching Dzhvar.

As if reading her mind, Thomas added a second visual focused on the leading edge of Dzhvar. The crimson mesh expanded steadily until it collided with the advancing wall and *pushed*.

The Dzhvar fell back a small but measurable distance, repelled by the force of the newcomer's advance.

As her mind leapt to connect the dots, a message arrived to confirm her suspicion.

Commandant, order your ships to stay a minimum of two megameters distance from the planet and completely avoid the star-facing side. I'm going to need to expand the protection all the way to the star, or this planet will die no matter what we do.

Corradeo Praesidis. Savior of his people one more time.

She quickly issued the order to the fleet, then allowed herself a brief exhale of relief.

Done. What can I do to help?

I don't know how the Dzhvar will respond to being rebuffed, but in the past, they often threw destructive tantrums. Ensure we don't lose ships in the incipient chaos.

Understood.

Commandant Solovy (CAF Aurora)(Command Channel): "In addition to the previous orders, all ships need to withdraw to a full ten megameters from any Dzhvar presence. Be ready to retreat at the first sign of unexpected movement on the part of the enemy. The planet is protected. Now let's take care to protect ourselves."

She could only watch in wonder as the *diati* mesh solidified into an impermeable barrier, then expanded inexorably across space. To create a bubble 0.7 AU in diameter seemed impossible for one man to accomplish. But this man had wielded the *diati* for a million years before it abandoned him in order to save humanity. He had a plethora of experience directing it, and he had not lost his touch.

'This is a most fascinating sight.'

"Fascinating is one word for it, Thomas." She recalled Advisor Ridani's efforts in his Weave project. "I trust you're gathering data on the phenomenon? We should take advantage of the *diati's* return to learn as much about it as we can."

'I have dispatched an additional suite of probes to surround the planet, and many of the in-atmosphere probes we placed continue to function. However, initial measurements appear to be as inscrutable as those for the Dzhvar.'

She wasn't surprised both primordial life forms proved frustratingly resistant to their scientific scrutiny. "Record the measurements anyway. Answers may prove to be buried somewhere in the data."

Now, she again found herself with few moves available to her to influence the battle; this time, however, she didn't mind it so much.

The Dzhvar banged away at the barrier for several minutes, perhaps assuming that what had worked on the rift device would also work on this new impediment. They flared spasmodically out from the organized bounds of their wall structure in surges that spanned megameters, and she was grateful for Corradeo's warning. Lives and ships that would've been caught by the Dzhvar surges instead hovered beyond their flailing reach.

Finally, though, the Dzhvar gathered their disparate fringes together and flowed around the edges of the *diati* barrier like water round a boat hull...and continued on.

A smile teased at Miriam's lips. For the first time since the Dzhvar blipped their sensors in the Capricornus Supercluster, she felt something akin to hope.

69

CONCORD HQ
COMMAND

Apalpable energy animated the War Room. It was a new and welcome development, and Miriam almost hated to tamp it down, but they had a great deal of work ahead of them. They hadn't won a war today, after all. They'd merely been able to seize a single weapon with which they might fight the war that was now upon them.

She cleared her throat above the din. "Take your seats and let's get started."

It took a few seconds, but the conversations quieted, and everyone found their places at the table.

Once she had their attention, she provided an overview of the events in the Volie system, as many attendees hadn't been present on the scene, and most of those who were hadn't gotten the full picture at the time. She kept it brief, however, because she recognized everyone in the room wanted to talk about one thing, and one thing only.

She gestured to Corradeo. "Advocate, I cede the floor to you. Tell us what you know."

Corradeo's eyes gleamed a brilliant crimson, and his skin had deepened its olive hue to take on a ruddy tone. She couldn't make out individual particles of *diati* oozing from his pores, but lend her a microscope and she might be able to.

Most notable, though, was the extent to which his subdued, almost defeated demeanor of recent weeks had utterly vanished. Dynamism now rolled off of him in waves. He was a man renewed.

"Thank you, Commandant. The *diati* barrier encasing Volie and its star is both stable and comprehensive. I have left it in place for the time being, in case the Dzhvar should decide to return to the system once no one is looking. But if they don't make an appearance in another day or two, I'll likely remove it. I assume many residents who evacuated Volie are eager to go home, and others to leave. It's in everyone's interest for travel and commerce to resume as soon as possible."

Because wormholes weren't able to bypass the barrier any better than the Dzhvar were. Prevos on her staff had taken a hard look at Volie and informed her the barrier existed across every known dimension. "The barrier stayed where you left it when you departed?"

He nodded. "In my absence, the *diati* won't exhibit…agency, for lack of a better term. It will do as I instructed it, which is to keep anything from reaching the space inside its borders, and nothing more. It can persist in this state for a lengthy period. Centuries. Perhaps millennia."

This explained a lot about how the Praesidis Primor and his Inquisitors had succeeded in controlling the inhabitants of a vast empire for so long. "And you can…" Miriam considered saving this question for a private conversation, but they all needed to know what the new rules they operated under were "…call it to you as the need arises?"

Corradeo extended a hand, palm up, and a miniature swarm of *diati* materialized above it. "I've spent some time testing the parameters, and I believe this power is again fully at my command. I don't feel constrained by supply, though there may be an upper limit to what I can control. All the *diati* in the universe is not currently residing in here—" his fingertips tapped his chest "—but I believe a sufficient supply will answer whenever and wherever I call it."

"This is excellent news, Advocate," she said. "What else do we need to be aware of?"

"I'm just one man, and I need to be physically present to bring the *diati* to a location. I will of course make myself available at all times to protect our worlds, but if the pace of the attacks continues to increase, there is a risk I won't be able to cover everywhere at once. Also, the *diati* is only acting as a barrier. It is not in any way destroying the Dzhvar it comes into contact with."

He tilted his head, and a slight smile that looked more wistful than happy tweaked his lips. "You're wondering what happened in the first war. How the *diati* succeeded in ending the conflict. I've been thinking a lot about this since the Dzhvar reappeared. In the final battle, the *diati* forced the Dzhvar out of physical space in a manner, or with a degree of force, that it hadn't deployed before then. The effect of this was to render them unable to return. Not forever, it turns out, but clearly for a very long time.

"How? I don't know, but I'm hopeful it will be able to perform such a feat again once it gets reoriented." His uncertain smile brightened a touch. "Once we both do. But for now, this is a defensive skill only."

"A viable defense is much more than we had at our disposal this morning, Advocate," Miriam replied. "Thank you for everything you've done and undoubtedly will do in the days to come."

S&L

Alex stayed behind after the meeting concluded, sitting on the edge of the conference table and swinging her legs idly in the air while everyone filed out.

"What are you doing to rescue Morgan?" she asked as soon as the door had closed behind the last person.

Miriam sighed audibly. Morgan Lekkas was a truly gifted pilot. She had swayed the outcome of numerous engagements all on her own, never mind when combined with the fighter craft squads she instructed and commanded. But the woman was an unrelenting source of trouble. The cost of her serving in the military constantly balanced on the precipice of outweighing the benefits.

And now, because the major lacked the fundamental discipline every military officer should exhibit, Miriam was about to have to put many lives in danger in order to rescue one. Malcolm had argued that as Lekkas' direct superior, the decision was his to make, and he'd made it in favor of rescue. But Miriam had authority over both the fate of the Ch'mshak and the Echo Rift device, so the ultimate call was hers.

Regenesis meant Lekkas could be woken up in a new body in a few short days. But there was a problem with using this option as an excuse not to act. The original version may still be alive on Mshak, in which case Miriam would be sentencing the woman to a miserable, solitary existence for many decades at best. At worst, unimaginable torture and a gruesome death at the hands of whatever Ch'mshak discovered her.

She'd left soldiers on Mshak to die, whether quickly or slowly, once before; she wouldn't do it again. "Whatever is necessary to rescue her, much to my chagrin, but not without taking extreme protective measures."

Alex frowned. "Time could be running out for her."

"I realize this. Unfortunately for her, Mesme overstated the Kats' ability to traverse an Echo Rift by a small amount. Lakhes tells me they can do it, but not easily. They require a specialized device and an expert in its use. It will take a couple of hours at a minimum for the device and its wielder to be ready.

"Malcolm is using the extra time to deploy every precaution. The instant the Echo Rift is deactivated, a team of special forces Marines will surround the settlement Olivia Montegreu used and be ready to move in should anything transpire there."

"Montegreu's dead."

"Yes, but not all the ships ferrying Ch'mshak have been accounted for. And the blockade's been disbanded, which means when the Echo Rift is gone, those ships will have free access to the planet for however long it takes us to locate and retrieve Major

Lekkas. Thankfully, doing so ought not to take long. Even if her Banshee's beacon was damaged, we can use her internal tracker to locate her."

Alex's lips pursed tight as her gaze slid away. "Not so much."

"Excuse me?"

"Morgan deactivated her internal tracker about five seconds after she signed back up with AEGIS. She turns it on during missions so she won't get dinged, then shuts it off again when the mission's done."

"Well." Miriam grimaced. Damn that woman. "This is…no less than I should've expected. I'll let Malcolm know he needs to prepare for the possibility of a longer mission."

"Sorry."

"You're not responsible for her choices."

"That's the truth." Alex planted her palms behind her and leaned back on the table. "So we caught a timely break today."

"We did indeed," Miriam replied, grateful to move on from the topic of the troublesome major. "For all the work we've done on the evacuation protocols, unless or until the Kats' fractalized Rift Bubbles get much more robust, they are woefully inadequate. We activated every resource, yet we evacuated fewer than five million people from Volie. The Dzhvar simply move too fast, with too little warning."

"Enlist civilian Prevos to create wormholes on the spot, leading to wherever they happen to be standing when the call goes out. Form a whole corps of them."

Miriam frowned.

"I know you don't like involving plebes in military affairs, but this is the fate of civilization here. Bend the rules. Save people however you can."

"No, you're right. It's a good idea." Miriam huffed a breath and finally settled into a chair near Alex. "Caleb…did he…?"

"He is aware of the *diati's* return. Was aware of it the instant it happened."

"But it didn't join with him?"

"Not for lack of trying."

Alex didn't elaborate, and Miriam considered letting it drop. But as before, she needed to know what the new rules were. "He refused it?"

"Knowing Corradeo had regained the ability to command it, he did. He believes the *diati* commingling within him will destroy Akeso. Maybe not literally, though even that's a risk, but it will almost certainly corrupt Akeso's soul. Its inherent goodness."

"I understand. I'm glad we don't need to ask him to make a different choice."

Alex nodded, but she didn't act as relieved as Miriam would've expected.

"What else is on your mind?"

After a weighty sigh, Alex pushed off the table and began meandering around the room. "I liked the peppy vibe in the meeting, I did. Everyone should be feeling happy about what happened today. But I trust you realize we're not on the road to victory. We now have a way to protect people in the short term, yes. And that's terrific. No qualms. But while we stand here, the Dzhvar are out there eating up Amaranthe's manifold. In the end, what doomed us in the last cycle wasn't people dying—it was the *universe* dying."

This wasn't anything Miriam hadn't thought about several times today, and every day. "I am mindful of this reality. And I will continue to pursue every avenue of research aimed at finding a way to stop such destruction from happening. Every tool, every weapon."

Alex pulled up to stare at her in surprise. "Oh, I wasn't insinuating that responsibility fell on your shoulders. You concentrate on protecting the people. Stopping the universe from dying is on me."

70

MIRAI

Nika stood on the balcony considering the night sky far beyond the city lights. Where before there had been only a carpet of stars twinkling in the purple-black of space, now a faint overlay cast a cameo sheen upon the canvas. *Diati.*

It was everywhere. It was in the room with her. Merely a few nanoscopic flecks spaciously distributed, granted, but it was omnipresent in the universe. Had it been there all along, only now exhibiting a change in state? Or had it retreated to some hidden dimension after The Displacement, then returned to the manifold to oppose the Dzhvar?

Was she able to see it due to her deep integration with kyoseil? The answer to this question must be yes, because no one she'd polled was able to detect it in the air. Few details were understood about the primordial life forms of the universe, but the fact that they recognized one another was indisputable.

A ping from Alex arrived to jolt her out of her reverie.

Care to see what diati *is capable of when directed by a firm hand?*

Absolutely.

A wormhole opened in her living room, and she left the balcony behind to cross through to the cabin of the *Siyane.*

SL

SIYANE

VOLIE STELLAR SYSTEM

A thick crimson mesh enveloped the planet below, then swept in a broad arc toward the system's star in the distance. Whereas on Mirai she'd detected a single particle every meter or two, here the particles crowded in close to form an impermeable barrier.

"I've read the historical files, as well as my journals. But by the time I was born, the Praesidis were primarily using *diati* as a personal tool. And weapon. I never imagined it could be so…extensive." Nika shook her head in dismay. "Is the Advocate down on the surface maintaining this barrier?"

"No," Alex replied. "He can order it to stay put, and it'll do so."

"But your vision…."

"According to Caleb, the *diati* has to willingly submit to a wielder's authority. Once it does though, it becomes submissive and will obey the wielder's orders."

"Any orders?"

Alex shrugged. "I think so? When Caleb wielded it, it didn't once argue with him."

"'If the choice of allegiance was made wisely, no other choices need be made.'"

"Exactly."

Nika nodded in acceptance and leaned against the cockpit half-wall. "How did the postmortem meeting go?"

"Champagne was popped."

"Really? But this fight is far from over. It's scarcely begun."

"Oh, I know. They all know, too. And in case they didn't, I reminded Mom of this after the meeting broke up. But everyone desperately needed a win, Corradeo most of all."

"He is now a blazing bonfire of *diati* on the kyoseil web."

"Interesting. How's the kyoseil reacting to the *diati*?"

Nika tried to find the words to describe a dynamic she didn't fully understand. "Similar to the Dzhvar, awareness. But there's a solemnity attached to the Dzhvar's presence that doesn't manifest with the *diati*. From the kyoseil's perspective, the *diati's* not necessarily a friend, but it's definitely not an enemy."

"Good. We need the balance of primordial power weighted in our favor."

Mesme arrived in the cabin in a rush of lights. Alex crossed her arms over her chest and adopted a stern expression; she'd clearly been expecting the Kat's arrival. "Thanks for coming. So, the *diati* is back. Now will you tell us whether it returned in the last cycle?"

It did.

"See, was that so hard?"

Mesme swirled languidly rather than reply.

"So more 'necessary but not sufficient,'" Nika remarked. "The *diati* won't be enough."

It will save many lives, for a time. But, no. On its own, it will not be enough.

"I'm not surprised. The kyoseil web has registered eight more Dzhvar incursions since the attack at Volie."

"Eight?" Alex exclaimed. "Eight feels like a lot for so short a period."

"Perhaps the Dzhvar were annoyed at being rebuffed and stormed off to kick some dirt."

"Ha. But you know, if the Dzhvar *are* driven by some purpose, you might not be far off. Hey, Mesme, are the Dzhvar driven by some purpose?"

Alex.

Alex rolled her eyes. "Never hurts to ask. Actually, I was pondering this a bit the other day. We've speculated whether the Rasu's galactic rings were an attempt to counteract the accelerating expansion of the universe, at least in a localized region. What if they inherited this purpose from their parents?"

"But by eating the manifold, they're destroying the universe, not saving it," Nika replied.

"Maybe their programming is faulty, or something in how they try to fulfill their mandate went wrong along the way. I don't know. And it doesn't matter why they're doing it. They have to be stopped."

"Agreed." Nika glanced out the viewport. The expanse of *diati* truly was a sight to behold. "So, have you experienced any more visions since we last spoke?"

"I'm calling them 'hallucinations' for now. A 'vision' implies I'm predicting something that will happen in the future, and damn, I hope I'm not."

They all hoped this. None more so than her…no, none more so than Dashiel. He'd been in a state ever since that afternoon at the cabin, obsessed and tormented in equal measure. She knew all too acutely what it was like to feel as if the fate of every world rested on your shoulders. She was doing everything in her power to convince him it did not, but she also knew how well this tactic had worked when the roles were reversed. "Fair enough. Had any more hallucinations?"

Alex wandered into the cabin and retrieved two drinks from the kitchen. "I have…."

"Why the hesitation?"

"Because the latest one starred you." She handed Nika a bottle of tea, then collapsed on the couch. "Given the context, I think it was set sometime in the past. It involved you meeting with a Taiyok, and there was a ton of formality to the affair. A bunch of Taiyoks in elaborate costumes, lots of kneeling and bowing and proud speeches."

Nika propped on the data center table to give Alex her full attention. "Did the Dzhvar attack Toki'taku in this vis— hallucination?"

"Nothing so dramatic. The meeting didn't appear to go well, though. Tensions started rising, and you offered to construct an Asterion d-gate to Toki'taku as a gesture of goodwill. The offer had the opposite effect. The Taiyok in charge preened up and launched into a grand declaration about their heritage—then I lost it. Word came in that the Dzhvar were attacking the Volie system, and I think I managed to pull myself out of the catatonic state. If so, good to find out I can do so."

"Curious. I know from my journals that I was the External Relations Advisor who first met with the Taiyok Elder. But of course I don't remember the meeting."

Mesme drifted into her field of vision off to the left. *Asterions didn't initially appreciate the degree of pride the Taiyoks take in their heritage, their planet and their society. The Elder was most offended at your insinuation that they needed technological assistance in any way. The talks spiraled into greater miscommunications, and the Asterion delegation was eventually ordered to depart. The Elder was of an insular, xenophobic bent, as, unfortunately, were his descendants.*

It was several thousand years before an Elder came to power who was open to diplomacy, at which point your people were finally able to form a friendship with the Taiyoks.

Nika frowned. "How do you know so much about it?"

Mesme's lazy oscillations stuttered as Alex's gaze darted to Mesme, something unreadable in her eyes.

We—the Katasketousya who watched the Asterions over the millennia—took great interest in your evolving relationship with the Taiyoks. They represented your first alien contact in the Gennisi galaxy. Ultimately, they became your first allies, marking an important evolution in the Dominion's maturity as a society.

"I suppose that makes sense." Her frown deepened. "I'm still not comfortable with the notion of Kats watching everything we did for so long without our knowledge."

Alex chuckled, though it sounded forced. "You should've been in Aurora. We were under a microscope from the very beginning. Lab rats in a specially designed Kat petri dish."

Now, Alex, that is an—

"Accurate statement of the history of Aurora."

Mesme deflated a little. *In the strictest sense.*

"And in the loosest one," Alex grumbled. "All right. I told Caleb I'd check and confirm the *diati* barrier was stable here, which it is, but I need to run. You remember Morgan Lekkas?"

"The pilot who helped us infiltrate Namino when it was under Rasu occupation. Sure."

"Well, she got herself trapped inside an Echo Rift, and there's a whole commotion about it back home. I'm not certain why I need to participate in the wringing of hands and gnashing of teeth, but Valkyrie seems to think I do."

"Good luck. Mesme, will you come by tomorrow afternoon for kyoseil training? I'm interested in exploring how the presence of *diati* is affecting the web's behavior."

I should be able to do so, yes.

"Thanks." She created a wormhole to Mirai and departed the *Siyane*.

71

MIRAI

As soon as she reached her flat, Nika went to the mirror hanging behind the dining table, a question burning in her mind. She opened the mirror to reveal the hidden room behind it, where seven hundred thousand years' worth of her journals were stored.

She'd read her journals detailing their early dealings with the Taiyoks before; over the last four and a half years, she'd read every entry stored here. Admittedly, it had been a while since she'd reviewed those entries, but she didn't recall their diplomatic interactions transpiring the way Mesme said. Then again, Mesme had a million plus some indeterminate number of years of events to keep track of, so it could be forgiven for mixing up a few facts....

She paused at the entry to the room. How many years? A million plus how many years? Along with its original identity, Mesme hadn't revealed so much as a ballpark number of how old it was when it traveled back in time. It was one among so many mysteries, and she hadn't paid it as much attention as she should have.

She queried the library interface for the journal entry covering her initial summit with the Taiyok elder.

Location: Row 8, Column 18, Slot 4.

She retrieved the data weave and started reading.

Date: Y98,714.246 A8

Subject: Taiyok Relations

What a bracingly stressful negotiation our meeting was! The Taiyoks are insular, swift to offend, and a touch xenophobic. They are also obsessively proud of their heritage, their planet and their society. And it is an extraordinary society. So different from our own, but not nearly as backward as we arrogantly assumed.

The meeting was tense for a while. I'm ashamed of how many etiquettes and protocols I fumbled, and the summit almost fell apart when I insulted the Elder by offering to gift them with a d-gate between our worlds. But, possibly recognizing my sincerity and after a fair bit of groveling, the Elder excused my error. Eventually, he dismissed most of his advisors, and we sat down for a lengthy, positive discussion. He remains cautious, and relations are apt to move forward in the smallest of steps.

But move forward they will. We scheduled a second meeting between the two of us for a month from now and laid the groundwork for ongoing communications among other government officials. He even reacted favorably to an invitation to visit Mirai in the future.

It will be nice, I think, to have friends in this galaxy. To not be so alone here.

She absently set the data weave to the side and dropped her head against the shelf. It wasn't a small difference. While the details matched up to begin with, Mesme had gotten the facts of how it ended entirely wrong. It was almost as if Mesme had read a different set of journals…

Now why had that notion occurred to her? Mesme hadn't read any journals at all. Presumably Tyche, the Kat most responsible for 'watching' Asterions, had gotten the details wrong when it relayed them to Mesme at some later point in time.

But the Kats were nothing if not exacting in all things.

Also, why did Alex see this event in particular? And if not the precise event that Nika had experienced, what event had she seen, *precisely*?

What if she'd seen another version of reality? Alex and Mesme both insisted she wasn't time traveling, but at this point Alex had viewed multiple events out of sync with this timeline. What if in an earlier cycle, interactions with the Taiyoks hadn't proceeded so smoothly, relatively speaking? It seemed as if Mesme was describing a different Elder from the one Nika had met, and every diplomat recognized how dramatically personalities shaped encounters for good and ill.

What if a more recalcitrant Elder had governed the Taiyoks in Mesme's cycle when their first meeting occurred?

Of its own accord, her mind circled back around to the idea of a different set of journals. Why was she stuck on this?

Then she realized. It was because the story Mesme recounted had sounded like a journal entry. Like one of *her* journal entries….

A bolt of frigid ice raced up her spine to split her head open in shooting pain.

No. An impossible thought.

Nika launched off the bookshelf and back into the flat to pace furiously around the living room. No. Numerous scenarios would explain the mismatch, and that's all it was. A mismatch of a few irrelevant details.

Unless they weren't irrelevant, and the Dominion's relationship with the Taiyoks had never grown so friendly in the previous cycle, and this had somehow negatively impacted the outcome of the Rasu War, which had a similarly negative effect on the Dzhvar conflict. Unless, unless, unless.

She tried to impose a measure of calm on her racing thoughts. There was no reason to overreact; it was entirely reasonable to assume Mesme had described how the interaction played out in the previous cycle, in which case the mismatch made sense. Perhaps in its prior incarnation, Mesme had been an Asterion with direct knowledge of the failed negotiations. Perhaps even someone her own prior incarnation had worked with.

Her own prior incarnation….

"Ever since the Oneiroi Nebula, the kyoseil has been changing me. Filing away the rough edges, lopping off the dynamic, assertive veneer in favor of a deeper, more expansive, almost metaphysical worldview. The kyoseil's worldview, one might posit."

You are everything you were.

"No, I'm not. I'm something else now. Maybe better and stronger in some ways, but not the same." She tilted her head toward Dashiel, who had stopped working to shift around and gaze at her. "See, Dashiel agrees."

"Nika, I don't think you…." He faltered, his words trailing off.

"You can't bring yourself to refute it, because you know I'm right." She proffered a brave smile. "I don't regret this turn of events. I've done what I had to do to save my people, and I'll keep on forging this path so long as it means I can make a difference."

She was practically spinning in circles through the living room now, and on the next revolution she threw herself at the window glass, clinging to it with her palms for dear life.

Like one of her journal entries.

As if she were telling the story to herself.

"You had to be someone intimately involved in the fight against the Dzhvar, right? Or else you wouldn't know as many details of how the conflict was waged as you do. Someone who was also involved in the fight against the Rasu. Mnemosyne was a goddess, which suggests you were a woman—"

Oh, stars, the fucking goddess of *memory*! Her breath caught in her throat and stayed there. Everything fit. Everything.

Yes, Mesme could have been another Asterion…but it wasn't.

At various times, she'd considered the possibility of the Kat being virtually everyone she knew. Yet she'd unconsciously erected a wall in the form of the most epic blind spot in creation, all to prevent herself from seeing what some part of her must have already known.

It was *her*.

She slid down the glass until she landed on the floor. Mesme had nurtured her so carefully ever since they'd met. Guided her and taught her. Protected her and helped her deepen her connection with kyoseil. Kyoseil that Mesme enjoyed an oh-so-special relationship with.

She'd never asked Mesme how it came to be bonded so closely with kyoseil. She'd never asked the Kat so many things. And when she had asked, Mesme had deflected and obfuscated rather than answer, as was its way. Because it was protecting an ocean of secrets...and one devastating secret above all.

And Alex knew. The look she'd noticed back on the *Siyane* had been one of warning, of fear that Mesme teetered on the brink of making a mistake. Alex and Mesme shared so much history, spanning decades before Nika met either of them.

How long had Alex known? Since the beginning? No, that didn't make any sense. Alex had only figured out the time travel aspect of the puzzle during the Rasu War, and Nika had stood at her side while she'd noodled it out piece by piece until reaching a genuine eureka moment. Alex lacked the capacity to be so deceptive as to performatively fake such an elaborate ruse. So within the last three and a half years.

She didn't have to wonder why Alex was keeping the truth from her. She'd give up her eternal soul to return this knowledge to the other side of the wall, to remain blissfully unaware of her fate.

A million years. A million years *alone*. Mesme enjoyed no lover, no soulmate, and had made it explicitly clear that it was the only person who traveled into the past. Dashiel had not accompanied it—her.

Dashiel had not accompanied *her*.

Her hands came to her mouth; she genuinely couldn't breathe now. She gasped in air, but it failed to reach her lungs. The room pitched as her vision swam.

This could not be her fate!

Yet as tears overflowed her eyes to stream freely down her face, a fire kindled and sparked in her soul. The same fire that forced her to climb to her feet and stand up in a rain-soaked alley nine years ago, when she possessed nothing in the universe but her name. The fire that propelled 8,000 copies of her to fight and run and die until the Rasu stronghold in her galaxy fell. The fire that kept her fighting to defend every Axis World from the relentless onslaught of Rasu in the last days of the war.

She had never accepted defeat, no matter how overwhelmingly the odds were stacked against her. She'd driven herself to the edge of madness in her refusal to accept defeat.

This could not be her fate? No. This *would not* be her fate.

Sobs wracked her body nonetheless. She wasn't ready to take up this mantle. She felt her mind fracturing beneath the weight of it. It was too heavy to bear.

So sorry I'm running late. I'll be home in ten minutes.

Panic gripped her chest until she was hyperventilating. Oh no, Dashiel….

She couldn't hope to pull herself together in ten minutes, nor in ten hours. After their quarrel over her First Generation secret nearly ended their relationship, she'd promised him she wouldn't lie to him again. But she'd never be able to look him in the eye, tears flowing, and force the words past her lips. Never be able to watch as his world collapsed in the face of such a terrible truth.

There must be a path to navigate this nightmare and alter her fate, but she wouldn't find its entrance here, bawling like a lunatic on the floor of her flat.

Before she could find the strength to fight, she needed to find the strength to breathe.

She stumbled to her feet, uncertain of what to do or where to go—

A swirl of ice-blue lights materialized in front of her to coalesce into the semblance of a winged creature. A phoenix…her heart leapt in recognition. It had always been there. It had always been her.

Mesme extended an ethereal hand to her. *Come with me.*

There was no need for thought, no space for decision. She accepted its hand, allowing the lights to envelop her and whisk her away.

The Story Continues In

THE THEORY OF EVERYTHING

SHADOWS & LIGHT BOOK TWO

(AMARANTHE ♦ 24)

AVAILABLE NOW:

GSJENNSEN.COM/THEORY-OF-EVERYTHING

AUTHOR'S NOTE

Here we are at last: the final trilogy in the Amaranthe saga. Twenty-five books. Eleven short stories. Sixty years of adventures (going back to *Meridian*), plus a million years before that. This is the story I envisioned telling when I started working on *Starshine*, and never in my wildest dreams imagined I would actually get to tell it. Thanks to you, the most awesome readers in our universe, I do.

If you haven't had a chance to read my blog post, "For All the Marbles," I hope you will. I talk about why *Shadows & Light* brings Amaranthe to a close, and what I have planned next. You can read it here: gsjennsen.com/blog.

And, hey, if you loved **LIMINAL SPACE**, tell someone about the Amaranthe novels. Leave a review, share your thoughts on social media, annoy your coworkers in the break room by talking about your favorite characters. Reviews are the backbone of a book's success, but there is no single act that will sell a book better than word-of-mouth.

My part of this deal is to write a book worth talking about—your part of the deal is to do the talking. If you keep doing your bit, I get to write a lot more books for you.

Also, I want to hear from my readers. If you loved the book—or if you didn't—let me know. The beauty of independent publishing is its simplicity: there's the writer and the readers. Without any overhead, I can find out what I'm doing right and wrong directly from you, which is invaluable in making the next book better than this one. And the one after that. And the twenty after that.

Website: gsjennsen.com
Wiki: gsj.space/wiki

Email: gs@gsjennsen.com   Goodreads: G.S. Jennsen
Twitter: @GSJennsen   Pinterest: gsjennsen
Facebook: gsjennsen.author   Instagram: gsjennsen

Find my books at a variety of retailers: gsjennsen.com/retailers

ACKNOWLEDGEMENTS

Many thanks to my beta readers, editors and artists, who made everything about this book better, and to my family, who continue to put up with an egregious level of obsessive focus on my part for months at a time.

I also want to add a personal note of thanks to everyone who has read my books, left a review at a retailer, Goodreads or other sites, sent me a personal email expressing how the books have impacted you, or posted on social media to share how much you enjoyed them. You make this all worthwhile, every day.

ABOUT THE AUTHOR

G. S. JENNSEN lives somewhere in the U.S., in a locale that may or may not be where she lived the last time she published a book (she's a gypsy at heart), with her husband and two dogs. She has become an internationally bestselling author since her first novel, *Starshine*, was published in 2014. She has chosen to continue writing under an independent publishing model to ensure the integrity of her stories and her ability to execute on the vision she has for their telling.

While she has been a lawyer, a software engineer and an editor, she's found the life of a full-time author preferable by several orders of magnitude. When she isn't writing, she's gaming or working out or getting lost in the mountains that loom large outside the windows in her home. Or she's dealing with a flooded basement, or standing in a line at Walmart reading the tabloid headlines and wondering who all of those people are. Or sitting on her back porch with a glass of wine, looking up at the stars, trying to figure out what could be up there.